RAISING ASSASSINS

RAISING ASSASSINS

THE COLLINS TWINS SERIES
BOOK 1

MICKEY HULL

Raising Assassins

Published by BooxAI
ISBN: 978-965-578-596-8

To my Fab V.

CHAPTER ONE

'What is her name, you fuck?' He asked in a gunslinger tone of calm rage.

Doyle, a dickhead pretty boy who played in a crap band and managed to fancy himself as a poor man's Bono, responded. 'Kelly.'

'Try again, motherfucker.' Jack smashed his face off the rear wheel of a car and asked. 'How does tire taste? I'll ask again, what is her name?' To Jack, this was just business that he managed with darkness. Jack firmly believed that bullies needed to be set straight. People that elect to mistreat women, that was another matter. Although Dante did not specifically define a layer of hell for these ass wipes, Jack had always trusted his moral compass. Jack thought as he administered justice: *You don't fight evil with tolerance and understanding. Hit a girl, my cousin and not expect a beating was a mistake.* 'Mother fuck, you bled on my Bobby Hull Blackhawks hockey jersey. I love this jersey. Wait, you are ok about the jersey. The golden jet would appreciate a little more blood. Gives it character. Where was I?'

'You asked me her name and it's Kelly.'

As Jack smirked and shook his dropped head, he thought: *The stupidity in people was nothing short of amazing.*

'It would appear we are at an impasse. As a gentleman, I am bound to smash your face against this car tire one last time and then I will curb you. Curbing is when I beat you hard and not gentle like before. Then, with tremendous regret, put your mouth on a curb, stomp on the back of your head and break most of your teeth. Got me? I suppose I should rephrase. The simple question I ask is: how much value do you place on hitting my cousin, whose only guilt was flushing your cocaine down the toilet? Is it worth waking me out of bed four hours before I depart for West Point? Are you regretting the decision? Kindly forgive my lack of patience due to a lack of sleep and a bit of anxiety, but make no mistake, I have made the time for this beating. What is her name?'

Kelly had called Jack from a locked bathroom after she was struck by Doyle. She ran away, hid and called Jack for help. Both Kelly and Jack had recently graduated from high school, shared the same birthday and were remarkably close. They lived four doors down from each other and both attended Catholic high school. Kelly graduated from the all-girl school and Jack graduated from the all-boy Jesuit school. Both schools were located on the Southside of Chicago. Kelly never missed one of Jack's basketball games. Jack never missed one of Kelly's calls.

Regretfully, all people speak the language of violence. Boy Bono finally responded. 'I don't know.'

'Well, was that so hard? Don't you feel better about yourself?' Jack asked with a mix of sarcasm and disgust.

'Yes.'

'Now that you are on the path to becoming a proper gentleman, when will you be seeing her again? Careful lad, be careful with your answer.'

'Never.'

'Is our little therapy session starting to take root? Are we experiencing a breakthrough? Your thoughts?' Iceman asked, anxious to end his session with Bono so he could return to bed.

'I agree.' Doyle mumbled and wheezed a sound, like a bit of a whistle, as he spoke through a broken nose, swollen and bloodied lips and a chipped tooth.

'Good man that you are, off you go, but if you approach her again, it would be a mistake. Got me?'

'Yes.'

Doyle started to walk away and Jack calmly warned. 'You might want to run before I change my mind.'

Jack turned his attention to his darling cousin Kelly as Bono sprinted away.

'What the fuck are you doing acting like shanty Irish white trash? Our ancestors did not work their asses off, immigrated to this country and got treated like shit. *Irish need not apply.* They survived the depression, two world wars and the Irish War of Independence, so you can be with a fuck like that. Our grandparents had our parents, aunts and uncles; ensured they were educated and knew the importance, and power, of the vote. Took our asses to mass and made a better life for future generations. In our family, we go to college and get advanced degrees. Every time we walk out our front door, we walk with and represent those before us. All this, so you can be a fuck? Seriously, you know I love you and believe in you, but knock this bullshit off. Please. I am leaving, so stop the drama, for fuck's sake. Be great, I believe in you.'

Kelly offered a half-ass response. 'I'll try.'

'We just wrapped up our family party as my sendoff. We had a blast. The food was great, two kegs, a bit of whiskey and old stories told an unknown number of times with no shortage of love. Now, if you shit the bed again, I will be forced to go AWOL to help you. Please stop. Don't try. Just do it.'

'Jackie, you got a party, what do I get? You are gone and I am stuck here. You are a star and I am a nobody. I am going to junior college and you are going to West Point. Jack, Jack, Jack is all I hear. Do not give me, *I am Jack and I worked brutally hard. So, if you work hard, you can do remarkable things too.* The gods touched you and they forgot about me. You did work hard, but you have so many gifts that the demanding work was worth it.' She started to cry.

'How would you know? How would you know who you are with hard work if you have never worked hard one day in your life? You waste the gifts these gods you refer to gave you. You whiny little girl. I am not going to apologize for being special and celebrated. You live your life, but rather than try to bring me down, you narcissistic fuck, why don't you try to rise up to close the gap between us? Our whole life, I have done nothing but believe in you. This is the first time I have doubt. In fact, I don't believe in you anymore. You act like a victim. From now on, good luck. You just lost the last person who believed in you. That only leaves you. You are the last person standing in the fight for self-esteem for Kelly.' Jack kissed her on the forehead and walked away, only to turn back. 'Fuck, I tried tough love. Look, I love you and believe in you.'

Kelly sprinted toward Jack, giving him a huge hug and Niagara Falls of tears flowed.

'I am going to miss you so much.' Kelly barely managed to utter between cries.

'You got this, but you must try. Don't be scared, just do the work. Fearless, be fearless.' Jack stated deliberately, turned and started his walk home.

During his short walk, he reflected on his life to date and his life going forward. Memories flooded his thoughts. Going to ball games, celebrating every excuse the family has to throw a party and playing sports. He thought about friends and realized he didn't really have any. Sure, he had buddies and was popular, but none he considered a true friend. Well, in fairness, he thought Kelly, while a mess, was as loyal as they came, but not a peer. Arriving home, he stopped at the front door, looked back at the neighborhood and nodded. As he walked inside, he glanced at all the pictures and trophies he and his brothers had won and exhaled. Jack saw a bottle of Jameson left over from the party on the dining room table and laughed. *Of course, there is a coaster under the bottle.* As he took two healthy swigs directly from the bottle, he thought aloud. *Maybe the difference between proper Irish and shanty Irish is merely a coaster. Maybe the coaster is a symbol of pride. Maybe, I should just shut the fuck up.*

He walked to the kitchen, looked for a snack and ordered an Uber. He did not say goodbye. He just grabbed his duffle bag from his bedroom, took care not to wake his younger brothers, jumped into the waiting car and headed to O'Hare Airport. He was not sure what the future held, but he did know his past. He waved to the house from the Uber and blew it a kiss. That was the moment Jack decided to leave the Southside of Chicago behind him and never return. West Point was his journey.

He thought about himself with closed eyes in the back of the Uber. West Point was getting Jack Collins, who grew up on the Southside of Chicago surrounded by aunts, uncles, cousins, parents and three younger brothers who built his foundation. Irish charm, laughter, beautiful blue eyes, light brown hair with more than a hint of red and a dangerous smile built the outside of the man-child he wanted the world to see. He pretended to be common and just one of the guys. A three-sport athlete, the competitor came out on the playground and in high school sports. The rage, ferociousness and fearlessness allowed his fists to fly. He loved every moment of competing. He could not stand the feeling of being so common that failure generated. If one did not try, they never failed, but could never be great. Standing 6 foot and 5 inches, weighing 185 pounds with a long, strong athletic build, the playground basketball court was his Cathedral. He hid his intelligence through disdain for teachers that he viewed as unnecessary and inferior. The rare teacher who offered insight and value, Jack treated with tremendous respect.

Colonel Sullivan found him and recruited him to West Point. He saw Jack's future even if Jack did not. *Why the fuck am I going to West Point and who is Sullivan? Why did I believe in him? Who is that guy?* With that thought, Jack fell asleep in the Uber.

'We are here, you ok, buddy?' The driver asked when they arrived at O'Hare.

'I am fine, always fine.'

CHAPTER TWO

'Mam, I am fine. I love you.' Sweet words spoken by an incredibly unique and special 17-year-old. He was 6'3 and built like a Greek god. Seamus had mesmerizing green eyes and a seldomly used easy smile. His father was black and a computer genius who moved from America to Ireland due to incentives offered by the Irish government. He brought to Ireland a vision in software design and Ireland rewarded him with a wealth of a young, educated workforce. His father built an innovative and successful software company. He fell in love with an Irish girl who was an Olympic swimmer. They married and had Seamus before his dad died in a car accident. Seamus was nine at the time of the accident. With his mother's strong and tender love, Seamus grew into an amazing young man. A star rugby player with his mother's gift of athleticism and first in his class care of his father, Shamus was a true scholar warrior.

'My little man is running off to the military.' His mother whispered in his ear as she gave him a hug.

'Mam, I am fine.'

Seamus was quiet and reserved. He never fit in with the small city where he was born and raised. He was Gulliver and the rest of the town of Ennis were the Lilliput people. Being so vastly different had a significant impact on Seamus. His father's tragic death had an even bigger impact. West Point represented a fresh start. He could play sports at full speed and not be concerned about killing an opponent. He would finally be challenged in the classroom. He could talk freely and not be restricted. Seamus craved freedom to grow and conquer challenges. He wanted to test his limits to find himself.

'I love you, my darling boy. I packed you three sandwiches and crisps.'

'Mam, you'll be ok.'

'I know, Seamus. I'll be fine being alone, but I will miss you. I am proud of the young man before me and I just wish your father were here to share this grand moment.'

Seamus' thoughts drifted towards his dad, but he quickly returned to his mother. Amazing does not begin to describe her. Strong, athletic and fiercely competitive was just the tip of an amazing iceberg. Warm, supportive, smart and loving, so very loving and caring. Not a soft love, but kind. The love was best described as firm and gentle. Like holding an egg, hold it too hard, it cracks, but hold it too soft, it slips and breaks.

He smiled and hugged her again, but this time a little tighter. 'Thanks for everything, mam.'

'My little boy is now a man and off to become a great man. Now, off you go. I really should drive you to the airport.'

Seamus walked over and gave her yet another hug. 'Mam, we went over this many times; I am taking the bus. I love you.'

As a dual citizen of Ireland and America, he headed for his Aer Lingus flight out of Shannon airport and on to West Point via JFK airport.

During the short bus ride, his thoughts returned to his father. His reflection, as he gazed out the window to the comforting landscape, focused on his father, always starting with why and how. *Why, my dad? A road he drove with the bend countless times. It just did not make sense. How could he have driven off? Yes, it was night and a soft day, so the roads were a little slick. Accepted, but it still did not explain how the devastation of losing his dad could be real.* He just shrugged and remembered kicking the ball around with his dad. He remembered the books his father handed to him and the discussions that followed. He smiled at the memory of the hours he spent with his dad working on his computer. He always ended his thoughts on the last hike that led to the last picnic lunch the small family enjoyed. The Saturday prior to his father's death was a magical day. He thought further about his dad and his amazing journey. He grew up black and poor in Atlanta. That had to be tough, but he never discussed it. After receiving a scholarship to Georgia Tech, he worked for a major technology company prior to starting his own company. He chose Ireland and met mam. Seamus wiped his moist eyes and drifted back to the present. He admitted to himself that he really did not understand how he was on a bus headed to the airport to attend West Point. He looked forward to the challenge, but was unsure of why West Point? He knew it was time to leave County Clare, but why West Point? He was leaving nothing behind except his mother. He had no friends and there was no girl he would need to write to. He dated, went to dances and, on occasion, hung out with the lads. Seamus just never felt the same as the others. The color of his skin may have been a factor, but Seamus never paid much attention to his skin color. He was just a man among boys. He took a deep breath and prayed to his father. *Dad, I am not sure why I am on this bus other than it feels like this is the start of my adult journey. Please continue to watch over me as you have in life and death.* Seamus didn't know what the future held, but he had himself. Seamus was enough and with the whispers from his mother and father guiding him, he was certain the journey would be memorable.

Colonel Sullivan, 3,000 miles away, silently agreed with Seamus.

Seamus' journey awaited him.

CHAPTER THREE

Three years earlier, in a remote basement office housed at the United States Military Academy at West Point, ColonelSullivan was introduced to Seamus and Jack. He kept a one-man office charged with leading Manpower and System Resources for the US Army. While his staff was based in Washington under the careful eye of Lt. Col. Black, Sullivan preferred to raise his daughter in the sanctity of West Point. His beautiful and lovely wife, Laura, felt West Point was better than Washington, D.C., to raise their only child, Molly, age nine. While the world believed Colonel Sullivan had chosen West Point as a safe place to raise a child, he made the decision to move without notice to perform his clandestine work as head of US recruitment for the Elders.

With the end of the Napoleonic Wars and the War of 1812, a group of nine men formed the Elders. Thomas Jefferson believed and promoted France as America's greatest ally and that held true throughout his presidency from 1801-1809. During the wars between England and France, the young US economy traded with both countries to build the foundation for the baby economy. England refused to allow the United States to trade with France during this time and set up blockades. The French did the same, although their Navy was not as powerful. France was near bankruptcy and faced a revolution. The Treaty of Ghent that ended the War of 1812 built the foundation for Great Britain and America to be powerful allies. The relationship has endured well-documented challenges. Nine of the greatest minds in business and academia from the United States and Great Britain, came together at the end of Jefferson's presidency in 1809 and the peaceful resolution of the War of 1812 to form the Elders. The Elders believed the future of the two countries was forged in the past. America was built on a British foundation, and while independent, the two countries needed to be aligned to support each other to prosper in the coming century. The nine elders were comprised of four great minds from America and four great minds from Great Britain. The ninth member was the Chief Elder, a position that was elected every ten years and alternated between countries. Like the Vatican, each Elder simply printed the name of their vote and the new Chief was elected once a consensus was achieved. The current Chief Elder reserved the right to elect his successor in the event of a deadlock. The founding Elders established a simple mission statement: to promote and protect British and American interests in the global theatre.

Although the amount is not known, every Elder contributed a significant sum of money to launch their enterprise. After two centuries, the investment requirement for a new Elder was $1 billion. The great academic minds were exempt from the investment. The Elders purchased an island 45 miles northwest of Barbados as their base. The Island was originally a naval base used to protect merchant ships from pirates that roamed the Caribbean. With the extinction of pirates, the base was abandoned and forgotten. The Elders silently purchased the Island from Great Britain. They are above all radar and government agencies, operating in complete secrecy. Presidents and Prime Ministers were aware of the rumors, but did not know if the Elders existed. Conspiracy theories persist as to a secret organization, within the global power structure, working behind the scenes, but the reality is that the Elders are simply just a rumor and a whisper as far as the world is concerned. The total assets of the Elders' fund are $900 billion. The contributions of new members over two centuries, coupled with exorbitant investment returns fuel an operation without a budget. The Elders' largest expense is research and development. Apple spends roughly $16 billion on research and development annually. The Elders invest $90 billion. Apple attempted to create products for the consumer and has multiple lines and multiple failures. The Elders conducted a sniper approach to R&D.

The Elders utilize four divisions led by four group leaders to achieve their mission statement. Research and Development (R&D), the first group, primary function is the development of algorithms and codes to stay ahead of all government and classified intelligence agencies. The hacking and interpreting of information through their software is paramount to the Elders' success. The Elders unite data through hacking. The NSA, Google, CIA, other international governments and private companies protect and rarely share their information. The Elders hack into their systems to create a complete global picture. Their software systems afford the Elders the ability to not only gather information deemed not accessible, but filter and interpret the overwhelming volume of data. America has agreed not to spy on its citizens and allies. The Elders have made no such promise. The relentless pursuit of information and the ability to interpret and respond to information is the driver for the Elders program. Analytics and Investments, the second group, interprets and acts on the information generated by R&D. The superior data access provides valuable insight for the investment team. Companies, institutions, technologies and commodities that clear the analytics department offer sound financial investments in the short and long term. The analytics team also gathers and interprets data for potential targets for the Black Ops team. Black Ops, the third team, is utilized when a threat is deemed too large, too sensitive, or too politically connected for national governments to address properly. The threat, after intense and exhaustive investigation, is voted on by the Elders to become a target. Once classified as a target, Black Ops is tasked with elimination.

Recruitment and Training, the fourth team, is a uniquely valuable department to the Elders. The ability to find the greatest minds of each generation is a challenge. Recruiting the identified candidates is a very delicate process. The recruiters are required to identify and close an exceptional teenager or young adult to an organization that does not exist and must ensure the Elders remain ghosts. The Elders is not Hogwarts. A magic wand cannot be waved to erase the candidate's memory. The recruiters sell the candidate a vision. The candidates are offered a full college scholarship opportunity to include a high-paying student job, paid summer internships and employment upon graduation. If the candidate is interested, a series of advanced tests begins the scholarship evaluation. The candidates are offered a series of tests to include IQ, language aptitude, behavior science aptitude, personality, morality, advanced mathematics and psychological. The hackers take the same test, but also take a test designed by the current hackers on the team. The Black Op candidates take the same series of tests with the addition of an eye exam, hearing test and complete physical to ensure they are medically fit with no heart conditions, weak joints, or other medical conditions that would prevent the candidate from being able to meet the demands of training or fieldwork. The Black Ops group also take a physical aptitude test to gauge reflexes, stamina, explosiveness, strength and the ability to improve in all areas. All the targeted candidates are offered no information about the Elders when they enter university but are assigned a required class list. The candidates who accept the scholarship sign a five-year commitment to work for the scholarship fund after graduation. The Foundation for a Better Tomorrow, the name of the scholarship fund, is the cover used by the Elders. No other company can boast working with the level of genius provided by the scholarship fund. They are not brought into the Black Ops side of their analytics during their five-year commitment. After five years the brightest candidates are awarded full-time positions as agents. Addicted to high pay, advanced technology and a brilliant work environment, most candidates accept. The agents are fully briefed and make a lifetime commitment to the Elders. The Black Op candidates are briefed immediately upon graduation. Training a recruit to become an agent of death cannot be hidden.

The task of finding these recruits fell into the hands of Dr. Grace Monroe and her team. She had Commander Henry Wilson of the Royal Navy recruiting in Great Britain and Colonel Thomas Sullivan of the US Army in America. Dr. Monroe was a Black Ops agent for ten years and, upon completion of her time as agent, she was chosen to pursue academia. Prior to Black Ops, she had graduated from Oxford, where she earned a master's in experimental psychology and took third in her class. She was a decorated soccer player, considered to be a terror on the pitch. After her tour as an agent, she attended Harvard University's Chan Department of Social and Behavior Sciences for her doctorate. Dr. Monroe worked with the analytics team to search and screen candidates. The hackers attacked targeted universities to include their athletic departments, specialized scholarship programs, specialty camps such as chess or mathematics, Olympic athletes, academic award winners, elite college scholarship recruitment; all to find the needle in the haystack. The tens of thousands of names were run through her initial profiling screening program and the haystack became significantly smaller. The list of candidates, now down to several thousand, was run through a second program. The second filter searched background information through school records, local media coverage, Facebook and other social media platforms, criminal records, family life and socioeconomic status to name a few. The haystack became manageable. The process began with candidates at 15 years of age and continued through age 20. The Foundation for a Better Tomorrow sent invitations to the applicants that comprised the remaining haystack. If the candidate was interested, they were invited to advanced testing. The results of the advanced testing further reduced the haystack. Once the intensive process was completed, Dr. Monroe personally entered the screening process. She reviewed the remaining candidates and after initial screening, immediately eliminated half of the candidates and the haystack was again reduced.

The hackers followed a different recruiting process. Dr. Monroe worked with the current hackers and not Commander Wilson or Colonel Sullivan. The hackers searched the dark web and started to initiate challenging hacks for prize money. The recruiting hackers hacked the hacker candidate and recruitment began. The hackers came from all levels of society; some were involved in criminal activities and some were even wanted by the FBI or MI5.

Dr. Monroe carefully examined candidates, including the hackers that remained. When her work was complete, names were turned over to the recruitment team led by either Commander Wilson or Colonel Sullivan. The teams were tasked with the recruitment and evaluation of the candidates and submitted their findings. Colonel Sullivan surprisingly received a candidate from Ireland. An incredibly unique candidate caught Dr. Monroe's attention, his name was Seamus Collins. She felt with the tragedy suffered by the death of his father at an early age, connecting with his roots in America would be healthy for Seamus. She encouraged Colonel Sullivan to personally handle his recruitment from start to finish to convince Seamus to attend West Point. At West Point, Sullivan could continue to be the mentor and father figure that Seamus craved. She set aside a second file for his attention and handling only. A true Mustang with unbridled talent that scored off the charts. He needed discipline, structure and a firm, but not dominant, hand. His name was Jack Collins.

* * *

While Colonel Sullivan studied the two files stamped priority, he was interrupted by a call from Dr. Monroe.

'Hello, Colonel. I imagine I piqued your interest about the two Collins candidates.'

'As a matter of fact, Grace, I am looking at them now.'

'Tom, if you are in the market for my insight, I am open for business.'

'Grace, you know I am always buying what you are selling.' The two of them chuckled.

'For Seamus, you will need to start by selling him on studying in America. I believe this will be an easy sell. The death of his father has left a hole in him. Coming to America will bring him closer to his father. Gently encourage him to take a free trip to America. Explain to him you will meet him in New York and then you will fly together to visit Stanford. After Stanford, fly back with him to New York to visit Princeton and then West Point. At first, he will balk at West Point. Sell him on how you went there, you live there with your family and it is the third most visited tourist attraction in New York. Explain the history and the lore of West Point. When he agrees to visit, travel in the order I mentioned. He will fall in love with Stanford. Get that out of the way and let his memory fade during the other visits. We do not want him to leave Stanford with loving thoughts going through his head on the long plane ride home. Princeton will give him some doubt about his decision as it too is a special place. Talk about Einstein, the history and the graduates of Princeton. He will be torn, we want him confused, but I expect he will still favor Stanford. Now, here is the important part, he craves a male role model, physical challenge and being a part of something. He lost his father at age nine; he is physically domi-nant, different and alone in Ennis. He cannot socialize with the *brain* crowd, because of his stature. He is isolated from the *jocks*, because he dominated them and his presence trivialized their stud persona. He is a physical specimen. The color of his skin also separated him from the mainstream high school pecking order. He just did not fit in. He is lonely. Talk about the camaraderie of the Core of Cadets. Talk about the physical challenges. Talk about the friends for life. Talk about the extremely competitive rugby team and, with him, West Point should win more national championships. Get him to ask, do not volunteer, why you went, why you liked attending West Point, why you look back on it so fondly and how it has helped you in life. Do you see where I am going with this?'

'I most certainly do and, as always, will use your pearls of wisdom. Thank you.'

'Tom, don't kid a kidder. We both know you are charming and quite clever.'

'Who me?' The Colonel responded innocently.

'Anyway, on to the next one, Jack. I am extremely interested to observe the two of you and the dynamic between you.'

'Why would you say that?' Sullivan asked genuinely intrigued.

'Tom, you know how much I respect you and recognize your amazing talent.'

'Thank you, Grace. Please, continue.' The Colonel requested, recognizing Grace's patronizing tone.

'This young man is a load. He will be a challenge even for you. He probes for weaknesses and is incredibly observant. He needs to be in control. Although I have never met him, even you have your hands full with Jack. His IQ is off the charts. He puts no effort in school and while his transcript, standard test scores and our advanced test results are impressive, he missed questions on purpose to hide his academic talent.'

'Why would you think that?'

'He got the wrong answers wrong. The questions he missed, he can easily solve. The most difficult of the questions he answered correctly. He cannot help himself when challenged to win. The mundane questions, by extension the mundane teacher and system, he has no respect or time for. Missing those questions was his way of playing a game, a form of revenge. He missed the questions deliberately to see if the teachers and recruiters were smart enough to discover what I discovered. He was toying with them, using riddles of right and wrong answers. He secretly told them to piss off.'

'Why?' Sullivan asked more interested than confused.

'Review his transcripts, he had two clear defining moments. In his early formable years, his grades were awful and his standardized test scores were worse. I am confident he was labeled stupid. While the teachers never said it, he would have been perceptive enough at that early age to notice it. Their tone, their eyes of pity, he would have noticed. The kids on the playground may not have been so subtle. Then at age 12 and carrying through his first two years of high school, he scored off the charts.'

'What changed?'

'Again, I have not met with him, but I am confident he had a learning disability, probably dyslexia. Dyslexia is common amongst active boys who struggle in school at that age.'

'Did he grow out of it? Was he medicated? What changed?'

'Maturing does have some impact, but not to this extreme.' Grace acknowledged and continued. 'He was never medicated and I am certain this went undiagnosed. During his young academic period, he would have been polite and quiet in the classroom. He would have been reserved and embarrassed, but most of all angry. In his heart, he knew he was smart. He felt anger with the system, the teachers and possibly his parents. The system was wrong and an angry hate grew with the passing of every year into rage. You can see it in the number of fights he engaged in and the destruction given to his opponents. The rage drove him to be an elite athlete. At 12 a light was switched.'

'What happened?'

'From my perspective, again not having met with him, he figured it out himself. Somehow at age 12, he managed his dyslexia on his own. When he solved dyslexia alone that was the end of authority figures for him.'

'Then why do you insist he is so special? Why do we want someone who will not listen to authority? He sounds like he cannot be trained.'

'You must not have heard me. He solved his dyslexia without any assistance. His power of observation exceeds both yours and mine. He will absorb training faster and better than any other candidate we have recruited. He will translate training into action better than any other candidate. I shared your concern until I read his essay for the scholarship fund. The essay asked the candidates to name five famous people who have shaped their lives. He wrote a publishable response that included Michael Collins, an obvious choice given his strong Irish family roots. George Washington, who he went into tremendous detail well beyond the cherry tree. Leonardo da Vinci, again way past the Mona Lisa. Charlie Chaplin, way past the little tramp. Malcolm X, to include his birth name Malcolm Little, right through to his final vision after making his pilgrimage to Mecca, that we can all live together. He even went as far as to name two Chicago black leaders as the assassins and documented his case. He added a sixth person and cited that while not famous, Coach Tishy was most certainly influential. Coach Tishy was his coach freshman year in football and basketball.'

'Interesting.'

'I thought so. Interesting enough for me to call four of his teachers and then Coach Tishy. I called two from his freshman and sophomore year. Both responded with overwhelming praise. Incredibly bright and gifted, he participated in class, was always on time, never had a bad day and never treated anyone poorly. Jack validated to himself that his self-taught program worked. He did not need the teachers. He did not need anyone. I then spoke to three teachers who taught him in either junior or senior year. Jack was still bright and gifted, but a change took place. The first two I spoke with clearly did not care for Jack. In fact, they went out of their way to ensure I knew he was not a suitable candidate for the scholarship. In all my years, I have never encountered that sort of hostile response. Jack found loopholes in the rules to avoid class, came late and left early. He never once participated in a class. His American literature teacher was confused about Jack. The teacher assigned various books for a two-week period during the semester. In that time, one book was taught, discussed and a report submitted. After a book was assigned, Jack consistently walked in the next day, mind you this is for every book, and turned in the report. The reports were amazing, so much so, that the teacher thought Jack had not read the book and could not have written that level of work with a day turnaround time. He was a junior in high school, so the teacher assumed he had cheated. He ran the report through a software system to detect cheating, but sure enough, Jack wrote it, he was clean. Still not convinced, he asked Jack if he would stay after class for a moment, he explained to Jack that he had something he needed to discuss with him. Jack declined and gave, in the teacher's words, *that look of his*. The teacher asked him again and conveyed the importance of the meeting. Jack gave him one minute. The class cleared and before the teacher opened his mouth, Jack challenged him. *I didn't cheat. I will do this only once, because I don't want to deal with it for the rest of the year. You have one minute to test me.* The teacher was still angry over the incident when I spoke with him. He peppered Jack with questions. Jack answered all with amazing speed and insight, but he never looked at the teacher. He only looked at the clock. When the minute was up, he simply turned, gave him *that look* again and walked out. Jack read a different book, one not included in the reading material, every day during class and never said a word. The teacher asked him to put the book down and participate in class. Jack said: *No. This is American literature, correct? I am reading American literature.* That was it. He gave the teacher *the look* that made him feel small and went back to his book. He got beyond an A in the class, but the teacher valued literary discussion, so class participation was important. The teacher warned Jack to participate, or he would be forced to knock down his grade. Jack just gave him *the look* and said he understood. The same was true with his physics teacher. He assigned homework and projects for two-week periods, because the homework and projects took time. Again, Jack turned in the homework and projects the next day. The first time Jack did it, the teacher said, *but we didn't cover that in class.* Jack responded, *I know, I read the book.'*

The Colonel commented. 'Jack conveyed he didn't need or want the teacher.'

'Tom, that is exactly it. The story goes one step further. The teacher graded his work as he had no other assignments to grade. He was so impressed, he asked Jack if he would present his work to the class. Jack said: *No, that's your job.* And smirked. Jack didn't give him *that look* of his, he just smirked.'

'Jack knew he was smarter than the teacher and could teach the class better. So again, what do I need you for?'

'Yes. Besides boredom, do you know why he reads in class?'

'To humiliate the teachers.'

The Colonel chuckled. 'I am beginning to see your point about him being a load.'

'Here is where things get interesting. I had not noticed until after my conversation with the physics teacher that Coach Tishy was also Mr. Tishy, Jack's history teacher.'

'This should be interesting.'

'It is. I asked first about the athlete. Tishy could not stop singing his praises. He said he wasn't sure he helped him all that much, he only had Jack as a freshman playing up on the sophomore team. Tishy immediately described Jack as a fierce, almost violent competitor. He quickly added that Jack was the easiest kid he had ever coached. Jack picked up everything he tried to convey on the first pass every time. Not just the X's and O's, but how the play sets up the next play. Jack made respectful recommendations. Without question the hardest worker he has ever coached. The smartest player he ever coached in both basketball and football. He just had a sixth sense. Jack was easily the best teammate he had ever coached. Nobody has ever treated the team managers, who are typically from the *dork squad* and just wanted to fit in, better than Jack. Never met a better or more natural leader. He ensured the team towed the line and his actions set an example. For instance, because of Jack, the team treated the managers with respect. If someone didn't, they answered to Jack.'

'Impressive, especially when you consider his teammates were all older than him. Now the classroom.'

'Tishy taught Jack as a junior, during his angry period, but the results did not surprise me. Tishy described him as pure energy. I asked about his book reading. He responded that he turned in all assignments, book reading and reports the next day. I clarified. *No, reading outside books during class.* He never did that. He was always engaged in the class. After Tishy read Jack's first report, he approached him the next day. He told Jack he obviously got an A+ and then proceeded to ask Jack, since he had time, if he would prepare a presentation on a battle for the class. The initial written report was to explain in detail the reasons for the Civil War. Jack said sure to the presentation and just call him up when Tishy was ready. Tishy was stunned. Tishy explained to Jack that if he needed time next week would be fine. Jack responded, *whatever works for you*. Now, Tishy was curious, so he asked: *Ok. How about tomorrow?* Jack responded: *Sure, works for me*. The next day Jack showed up ready to go. Jack had anticipated his presentation and the questions that followed would take up the whole period. Tishy, trying to manage expectations, explained to Jack not to expect too much participation from the class. Jack just half smiled and replied: *They will for me.'*

'Confident.'

'Very, but he was right. Tishy asked: *What battle are you going to present?* Jack responded: *Fort Donelson*. Jack explained that he figured at some point, Tishy had in his lesson plan battles like First Bull Run. Tishy acknowledged that was true. Jack continued: *I didn't want you to have to redo your lesson plans*. Jack was sure Tishy knew all about the battle, but the students would never hear about it even though it was one of the most important battles of the Civil War. Jack explained: *You know, Mr. Tishy.* Tishy made a point that Jack never called him coach in the classroom, which he appreciated. *Ulysses Grant got the nickname 'no surrender Grant' after the battle. He also got another nickname, 'drunk Grant.'* Jack laughed and told Tishy he had a couple of funny stories about the battle. One was when Lincoln heard his cabinet chastise Grant and his drinking and demanded he be relieved of command. Lincoln responded something to the effect: *Whatever he is drinking ship it to all my generals*. Jack continued: *The battle was Grant's first appearance on the national stage, he hit it out of the park and led him to eventually command the Union Army. The battle switched control of the western front with Tennessee and Kentucky falling to the Union. With the western border secure, the Confederates were trapped. The Confederates could not go west, the north was secure, the east was water and the south was water. The Union just needed to squeeze like a cobra wrapping its prey. The Union had a much stronger navy so the pressure from the sea was significant, especially the Mississippi River. Because of the battle, Union troops were transferred freely up and down the river applying more pressure from the west. The North was able to use the pressure, relentless pressure from all sides.* Jack asked Tishy if that was good enough and Tishy responded: *You covered the major points.'*

'Your picture of Jack is coming into focus.'

'The funny part of the story, Tishy admitted to me that he had to start the class ten minutes late. He told the class he needed to go to the dean's office and to work on their report until he returned. He did not go to the dean's office. Instead, he stepped out into the hall to google the battle quickly so as not to be embarrassed. He knew nothing about the battle.'

'That is funny. So, Jack can be smarter than the teacher and act like a complete gentleman.'

'If he respects you.'

'Right.'

'He is going to love you, Tom. You are a significant challenge to him. He will be very curious about you. He will then be curious about West Point. You and the dynamic the two of you create will land him on the Hudson. Keep him on the hook, do not reel him in. Little pieces of information, small bites at a time. He is like a sponge. He wants to absorb everything now. He will bait you into giving up information. Always have your guard up, he will be subtly relentless. Watch your body language, especially your eyes. The more curious he is the tighter he will bite on the hook.'

'I am not the child in your story, he is. This not my first rodeo Grace.' The Colonel was clearly getting agitated and a little insulted.

'We shall see and Colonel?'

'Yes, Grace.'

'It's your first rodeo with Jack.'

'You really think he is that special?'

'I do, but I read your candidate report too.'

'Have you now?' The Colonel asked, playing along with Grace.

'Yes, I did. Imagine my surprise to find there was a wonder boy before Jack.'

'Very funny, Grace.'

'Ok, wonder boy. Let's talk about school selection and visit strategy. Whatever you do, our recruitment dies before it starts if he visits Stanford. His belief in individual freedom will take flight and we will never hear from him again. He cannot visit Stanford. Use the stereotypes about California to your advantage. Flaky, self-centered, that is a big one, soft. Things like that will hit a nerve in Jack. Really pound, in a subtle way, self-centered. He will immediately choose Duke and there is nothing we can do, but work it to our advantage. Coach K, being from Chicago and the basketball program will be a huge draw for Jack. He doesn't need to be the star player. He already knows he is a star in life. He will be a star on Duke's team without starting. The players will look up to him and he will have led them to at least one national championship. Are you with me so far?'

'I am and Mike will do more to recruit Jack to West Point rather than Duke. Mike and I have a nice relationship. He loves Duke, but West Point has a special place in his heart. His time here as a cadet, player and coach are some of the fondest years of his life. He has often said: *There is no Duke basketball without West Point.* West Point was a critical piece in Mike's journey to greatness.'

Dr. Monroe jumped in. 'That is perfect. After meeting with Coach K, at the right time, bring up the concept, *do you want to be a copy of an original or an original?* He will eat that up.'

'I understand. Mike's players have not gone on to have much success in coaching compared to Mike because they are copies of the original. Always a little duller. Mike played for Bobby Knight at West Point. Bobby Knight was only a piece of Mike's adult journey. Mike's upbringing built his childhood foundation, but West Point built his adult foundation.'

'Perfect. After Duke, go to Boston College next. The Jesuit link to his high school and being in a major city like Boston will appeal to Jack. Do not spend the night. Visit, meet the coach and get out of there. The coach will spend the day with him and have a player walk him around. They will heavily recruit Jack and that is fine. Do not let him spend the night. He will fall in love with Boston and not the college. The huge Irish population, the pubs and the similarities to Chicago will be familiar to him. He will feel comfortable. Get him out of there and get him to Princeton. Take an early evening flight or drive the four-plus hours, stay in a hotel near Princeton and start in the morning. Have him spend the night and ensure that he spends the night in the dorms at Princeton after his meeting with the coach. He will be scheduled to pair with the best senior in a great apartment. Change the arrangements, so he spends the night with a younger player in the dorms. He will hate the people and the culture of Princeton. Early start in the morning for the drive to West Point.'

'I got it. I agree.'

'On the ride to West Point, pick at his curiosity, leak the challenge and tie it back to Coach K. *The challenge of West Point is overwhelming, but certainly manageable for a guy like him. If Jack wants to be an average cadet, Jack can coast through. However, to be great at West Point like Coach K was; well, that takes a special person giving a special effort.* He will love the use of special. Spend time with West Point's coach and prep him. Have him review as much of Jack's game film as possible. Sit with him and ensure he is prepared for Jack. Ignore his playing skills and tell the coach to do the same. His playing skills are a forgone conclusion. Say something to the effect, *Jack, we all know your skills on the court, but here is what stands out to me. What impressed me watching as much tape of you as I could get my hands on is your leadership.* Have the coach run a clip to demonstrate his point. Without a clip, Jack will dismiss the praise as a phony sentiment. The clip will show respect and commitment, think coach Tishy. *Jack, your poise*, show a clip. *Your competitiveness and toughness*, show a clip.'

'I love it.' Sullivan was making mental notes, embracing the challenge.

'*If you elect*, make sure he uses the word elect, *to come to West Point, those three characteristics will lead us to at least one conference championship and a trip to the NCAA tournament. Once in the NCAA tournament, it is a new season and anything can happen.*'

'Perfect.'

'One last thing, at the end of the trip, we are going to have to break prodigal. You will have to leak very subtly his true future. We must let him in a little too close. Whisper to him not everybody follows the path of the common. Special assignments are set aside for special people. He will look to have you open the curtain more. Simply explain, *I already told you more than I should have.*'

'Bravo. Grace, you have outdone yourself. This is your finest work.'

'It will be if you close him. Bring your *A-game* and land us our biggest fish and best pairing in our history together.'

'You got it.'

Colonel Sullivan most certainly did.

The Collins Twins were hatched.

CHAPTER FOUR

The United States Military Academy at West Point mission, *to educate, train and inspire the Corps of Cadets so that each graduate is a commissioned leader of character committed to the values of Duty, Honor, Country and prepared for a career of professional excellence and service to the Nation as an officer in the United States Army.* West Point is 50 miles north of New York City overlooking the Hudson River. Most of the campus's Norman-style buildings are constructed from gray and black granite. The academy was founded in 1802 by President Thomas Jefferson, it is the first American college to have an accredited civil engineering program. The technical curriculum became the model for engineering schools throughout the world. West Point's alumni include two U.S. Presidents, Eisenhower and Grant, presidents of the Confederate States of America, Nicaragua, the Philippines and Costa Rica, such famous names: MacArthur, Lee, Patton and Aldrin. The academy is America's top producer in Marshall and Rhode scholars and includes 76 Medal of Honor recipients. For admissions, candidates must apply directly to the academy and receive a nomination from a member of Congress, president, or vice president. Leadership is built with the development of four pillars of performance: academics, character, physical and military. The cadets compete in 15 varsity collegiate sports and those who do not compete in intramural year-round. The days are challenging and rigorous, and a special connection resides in, *The Long Grey Line.*

The cadet candidates arrived at West Point, sat with their families in the theatre housed in Eisenhower Hall and waited for entry into West Point. Jack and Seamus sat alone on opposite sides of the theatre. They both figured this was their journey and theirs alone; parents no need to attend. They said their goodbyes at home; Jack gave the Irish goodbye. He waved the back of his hand as he turned his back to walk out the door. Jack thought, *really, walking your kid to school? What is this kindergarten? The best and the brightest need their hands held and a hug. Ridiculous.* The cadet candidates said their goodbyes and filed out of Eisenhower Hall and assembled in Thayer Hall. Thayer Hall, originally designed as Riding Hall, was a grey, stoned, four-story Gothic Revival building that housed classrooms and offices. The candidates formed a single file line, that extended from the basement up the stairs and outside to be processed. Their authorized civilian gear was properly packed in the army way in a top-loading US Army-issued travel bag or duffle bag and placed into storage. The same big green bags are spotted in airports around the world. The candidates changed into PT gear. Shorts, T-shirt, but rather than athletic shoes, the candidates donned their authorized dress shoes and dress socks. The look had two purposes. The first was to embarrass and humble the candidate. A cocky recent high school graduate, stripped of their clothes, left in PT gear adorned with knee-high black socks and black dress shoes was not a fashionable look. The second purpose was to break into their dress shoes and learn proper care, including shining their low quarters. The candidates got measured for their uniforms and the males continued and got their hair cut tight. The candidates continued down the line to get their two identification pictures taken. One picture was for their ID card and the other was sent back home with a form letter documenting safe arrival. While the picture did document arrival, the scared look captured in most of the candidates' pictures caused parents concern about just how safe the arrival was. After the ID picture, the candidates were issued dog tags. The candidates were issued two tags on two linked chains worn around their necks. The first chain was a long chain used for identification. The second chain was much shorter and was linked to the longer chain. The candidates were initially confused by the two tags. The E-4, who issued the dog tags explained. *The reason for the two tags is simple. If you are killed in action, the little chain is ripped from the larger chain and inserted into your mouth, and eventually goes to records.* A message that did not provide comfort to the teenage candidates. The candidates continued down the assembly line to be issued their gear and ended with the Cadet in the Red Sash. The Cadet in the Red Sash directed the candidates to their assigned barracks and company. The upperclassmen were their superiors and they issued orders. Jack and Seamus reported to company A-1 and marched off to their barracks with the other A-1 candidates. Jack thought to himself: *This is pretty straightforward, no big deal. The Cadet in the Red Sash who assigned me to A-1 seemed uptight, but a decent enough guy. The experience was like the sorting hat in Harry Potter. Sash man bellowed, Candidate Collins you are, dunt, dunt, duh, A-1 and the crowd went wild.* In all fairness, the crowd of candidates were deathly silent, stricken with fear, but that's how Jack internally lived the story. While Jack was entertaining himself, Seamus was confused. He wasn't sure what was happening and he felt like he was walking in circles waiting in line. Hurry up and wait made no sense to him. The A-1 candidates walked into their barracks, through the entryway, up the stairs, into the hallway and in that moment their universe changed.

Prior to 2012, Beast Barracks was the cadet candidate's indoctrination to West Point. The intent of Beast Barracks and the entire plebe (freshmen) year was to create a highly stressful environment to weed out those who were not completely committed to being a soldier and a leader. West Point was a mighty challenge, because combat was a mighty challenge. In 2012, the commander started Cadet Basic Training (CBT), which was a modern approach to training. Candidates no longer faced the challenges of Beast Barracks. The candidates were addressed, if the need arose, in a firm, but respectful tone. Yelling was not permitted. Candidates no longer had table duties, because it was beneath them to serve their upperclassmen. The candidates were no longer required to ping, walking 120 steps per minute, to establish a sense of urgency and move with a purpose. To the alum that suffered Beast Barracks, the new generation strolled as if West Point was just another college campus. Many graduates saw the commandant's recent efforts to categorize the change to Cadet Basic Training as more professional, as nothing more than placating millennials. Beast Barracks was built to break arrogant teenagers and build them back up. Lazy teenagers were not supposed to break West Point. Colonel Sullivan most certainly saw it as tragic. He had trained and led soldiers of previous generations into battle. Finding, let alone recruiting a soldier in this generation was a mighty challenge. Millennials, in his view, were entitled, lazy and always the victim.

Using his title as Director of Systems and Manpower Analysis, Sullivan approached the commandant at the time, General Calderon, who did not support the changes made by his predecessor. General Calderon was more in line with Sullivan and most alumni who supported Beast Barracks. Sullivan proposed a study: he selected one company to conduct a full Beast Barracks to study that graduating class against the rest of the Core of Cadets in the same graduating class; then, he conducted a mini Beast Barracks for the upperclassmen of A-1 charged with conducting CBT; Sullivan filled the role of the upperclassmen and the upperclassmen played the candidates. After three days of training, the upperclassmen were more than ready.

Beast Barracks was a six-week test to ensure a cadet candidate was ready to make an enormous commitment to the rigors that awaited. Beast chewed the boys, who deep down wanted to go home and spit them out. The celebration back home, with all the congratulations and praise, quickly became a distant memory. Beast made quick work of those not ready for the challenge and moved on to boys who were prepared to be men. Men in the image of the statues candidates dare not look to for help. Statues of Patton, MacArthur, Eisenhower and Washington mock the candidates who accepted the challenge of joining their Core of Cadets. As the A-1 cadet candidates entered the hallway, they walked into a den of chaos. The upperclassmen, who were assigned to doctrine the boys into West Point men, stood ready to pounce. They took their job very seriously. The upperclassmen were waiting with an ambush of yelling, confusing, intense orders and constant evaluations. The swarm was intended to shock and awe the candidates to prepare them to focus on the mission when faced with chaos. The impact of the first day established command and control by the upperclassmen. The impact of the six weeks was relentless pressure that never let up or ended. A candidate must hold fast and function at a high level in an extremely difficult theatre. Overwhelmed, the candidates tried to stop the boulder of pressure screaming down a hill of accountability. The candidates needed to dig deep to stop the boulder's powerful momentum and then gradually push the boulder back up the hill to tip the struggle in their favor. Candidates had to face the heat of Beast Barracks with a big dose of humility and fear, but the sooner they stopped the upperclassmen's boulder rush, the shorter the push back up to the apex. The upperclassmen did not bully the candidates. Physical contact and abusive behavior were not tolerated. Any violations by the upperclassmen resulted in immediate dismissal from the Academy.

Beast barracks started with a roar and not a whisper. Rules, traditions and challenges were thrown at the candidates from all directions by the stampede of upperclassmen. They were in control. Where they saw a concert, the candidates saw chaos. Candidates were separated from the herd and in isolation, interrogated by the upperclassmen. Failure to answer questions that the candidates did not have answers to, resulted in pushups.

'How many days until the Army vs Navy game?' Thundered an upperclassman.

The stunned candidate stuttered. 'W,W,W,What?'

'What? Did you say what? Is *what* one of your authorized responses?'

'No, sir. Sorry.'

'Sorry? I should not be surprised. You are sorry. Is, *no sir, sorry,* one of your responses? Please don't answer and waste any more of my time. Tell my company commander you want to call home first chance you get. Please let your parents know you are not entering my Core of Cadets. Candidates far stronger than you have dropped and you will be joining them. Speaking of drop, drop and give me 25.'

The confused and scared candidate held back his tears as he struggled to knock out 25 pushups with his duffle bag secured to his back, said to himself: *I just need to get to my room and safety.*

* * *

'What's up, Junior?' Candidate Jack asked Candidate Seamus after both successfully navigated the first assault issued by Beast Barracks. As he entered their barracks room, they met for the first time and Jack did a brief sweep of the room with his eyes.

'Why are you calling me Junior?' Candidate Seamus asked.

'Wait, what kind of brother speaks with a Clare accent? And I am obviously Collins senior.'

'The kind of person from Clare and what do you know about Clare?' Candidate Seamus responded with disdain.

'My great grandfather was from Clare, much of my extended family lives in Clare and all around the west coast of Ireland. I visited a couple of times. While I never saw a brother there, the accent is unmistakable.' Candidate Jack responded with pride.

'Fine, but while we share the same last name, I will not be referred to as brother nor junior.'

'Fair enough didn't realize you were a rich kid, so Zeus how funny is this shit? This old-school gangster shit is being thrown at us. I've read about this and it's called Beast Barracks. Beast was supposed to stop in like 2012, but from what they described it must be back. Awesome.'

'Wait…' Candidate Seamus paused. 'Now I am Zeus?'

'Yes, motherfucker. Have you ever looked in the mirror? You are a genetic experiment that hit. I feel like Danny DeVito and you are Arnold Schwarzenegger in *Twins*.' Candidate Jack responded and continued. 'You play rugby. Cool.'

'Excuse me, you have provided several subjects in 15 seconds. What is so funny? How did you know I played rugby and how did you know I was a rich kid?' Zeus asked.

'Obviously, your grooming is first, like the expensive lotion that prevents ashing, which is when black people's skin goes dry. Second, your use of language, you are proper. The way you carry yourself screams rich kid. Then, there is a rugby ball under your bunk and what's going down outside this door is hilarious.' Jack responded as if all this was obvious.

'One moment, you noticed all that in 15 seconds.'

'Yep, now I am going to go play in the hallway, want to come?'

'Absolutely not, the upperclassmen are wreaking havoc and tormenting us.'

'Lad, I don't run from a fight, I sprint to it. Please, this isn't close to balling on the playground, hustling for money, let alone one of my family's backyard parties. These bitches be amateurs. Now suit up, be a man because our classmates are pissing in the sink in their rooms, because they are scared to go in the hallway to use the latrine. You are a monster, so they will not mess with you. I am fearless, so I don't give a shit. Where I come from, we don't bully, we don't get bullied and we assassinate bullies. Shit, this isn't even bullying, just a bunch of dumb questions and a couple of pushups. You ready? We'll see, I am going out there. The sink is behind me in case you need to take a bitch piss.'

Zeus was about to sit down, but decided to walk past the bitch sink and join his new crazy roommate's effort to draw fire to protect their classmates.

'You must be shitting me, what in the world are the Collins twins doing? Are you strolling down my hallway? No, no, hold hands like a date and move at 120 paces per minute as ordered.' The upperclassman shouted as his voice echoed through the hallways.

Candidate Jack responded. 'Yes, sir. No, sir. No excuse, sir. Sir, I do not understand.'

'What did you say to me, you Siamese pond scum?'

'Cadet Owens, sir. I am only allowed four responses, so I thought I would use them all and let you choose a response.' That did not go well, but some doors of scared classmates cracked open.

'You are mine, Candidate Collins.'

Zeus knew Collins was a party of two. He also knew Cadet Owens showed an instant dislike for Jack, so Owens was going to be a problem.

'Cadet Owens, no sir.' Candidate Jack said with firm resolve.

Zeus just closed his eyes for a second to calm down and opened them to find a swarm of upperclassmen gathering around the Collins twins as they were now known. The other candidates hiding in their rooms closed their cracked doors. The Collins twins were the only game to feed the upperclassmen's appetite for submission. The fact the Collins twins, well at least Jack, were arrogant, made the feast that much more special.

Cadet Owens set the table for the upperclassmen's feast. 'As you know,' the twins did not, 'you are required to know all the upperclassmen's names without looking at our name tags. If you miss, you owe me 10 pushups for each name. Let's get started. Collins twins turn your backs. Upperclassmen line up.'

As the upperclassmen lined up and the twins turned their backs, Jack stole a quick glance and smiled. He only needed a glance. Zeus was nervous and felt the exercise was unfair. *No candidate had set eyes on all the upperclassmen, yet they were required to already know their names, I guess that's where the no excuse response applies.* As the twins turned around, they found eight upperclassmen in a single file row with their hands over their name tags.

Without prompting Jack ran through the upperclassmen's names. 'Sir, Cadet Davis, Sir, Cadet Tomchec, Sir, Cadet Washington, Ma'am, Cadet Segerson, Sir, Cadet Fernando, Sir, Cadet Truax, Ma'am, Cadet Brown, Sir, Cadet Owens.'

Stunned, the group stared at Jack with blank faces and opened mouths. Jack interrupted the silence as he continued. 'You know Dasher, Dancer, Prancer, and Vixen, Comet, and Cupid, Donder and Blitzes…. but did you know the most…'

'Shut up and give me 50.' Upon Cadet Owens' order, the twins dropped and knocked out fifty pushups. Once completed, they continued to ping to the latrine with eyes front.

The twins had to fight the upperclassmen's next challenge on the way back to their room. The upperclassmen were not sure how

Jack managed to know their names, but tried a new tactic. Out of the corner of his eyes, Jack saw them lined up with their backs to the twins.

Cadet Owens smirked as he walked up slowly and close to Candidate Jack. 'Let's try this again. Turn and face the wall.'

The twins turned slowly to the wall. Just as Jack laughed to himself, they shuffled their order. He had remembered the cadets' names.

Cadet Owens ordered the twins to turn around with a smile on his face.

To Jack's surprise and disappointment, Zeus stole his thunder. 'Sir, Cadet Truax, Sir, Cadet Davis, Sir Cadet Tomchec, Sir, Cadet Owens, Ma'am, Cadet Brown, Sir, Cadet Fernando, Sir, Cadet Washington, Ma'am, Cadet Segerson.' Jack was not the only member of their room with a crazy memory.

After Zeus' display, the twins executed a right face and pinged to their rooms. The doors cracked again and the other plebes slowly began to use the latrine. The rest of the day and the next two were rough on the Collins twins, but the other candidates took refuge. The pissing in the sink stopped and the latrine was used full-time.

The Collins twins stood tall, held their ground, did their duty and excelled. They stood together to give and not take, showed respect and accepted all challenges thrown their way. Fair to say they fed off each other. Two vastly different people on the surface, but at the core they were kindred spirits. Their unbreakable bond established in hours gave the candidates of company A-1 confidence and frustrated upperclassmen who were lost in a new frontier.

The candidates of A-1 were confused and angry once they realized A-1 was the only company in Beast Barracks. No explanation was offered and the candidates had no choice, but to accept their fate. To regain control of the company, an officer joined the upperclassmen to reestablish authority. Captain Grainier joined the upperclassmen who had elected to call and assemble the troops. The mission statement was *to state what made each plebe special in high school.* The goal was to demonstrate power through grand high school memories. The candidates were forced to celebrate their importance in high school, but resign themselves to the fact their glory was gone. The former prom kings and football heroes belong to the upperclassmen now. The candidates were broken down and all the power was now held by the upperclassmen. The Collins twins were called on last. After hearing about all the class scholars, all state wrestlers, a guy that broke racial discrimination barrier from South Carolina in tennis, and on and on, Jack was stuck. He did not grow up in a small town like many of the others, but realized Chicago was a large pool and the accomplishments of the company, while extremely impressive, did not trivialize his. They hid in their rooms, while he and Zeus took the hit. The only response that resonated with him was Zeus'.

'Nothing.' Zeus responded. Zeus was a good man and not just a nice guy. Jack knew he would always do the right thing, as good men do, and not the popular thing, as favored by nice guys. Jack hated nice guys. If possible, Jack's respect for Zeus grew. The upperclassmen, intimidated by Zeus, quickly moved on to Jack.

'Candidate?' Captain Grainier asked Jack with cold eyes.

Jack responded. 'I read *The Far Side* comic for 63 days in a row and never missed a day.'

The candidates tried to hold it in, but exploded in brief and yet rewarding laughter.

The officer's eyes soften a bit, even he was entertained. He walked up to Jack's face real close and whispered. 'You and I got a problem?'

'No, sir.'

'What makes you so special?'

'Sir, as I explained, I read the far side comic 63 days in a row. Can you or anyone else in the room make the same claim? No? So, I am special by definition. Special per Webster's dictionary: *better, greater, or otherwise different from what is usual.* Your problem is not with me, but the question. You may want to consider in the future asking: *what is your proudest moment or greatest accomplishment that your parents celebrated?*'

Captain Grainier simply shook his head and walked away. Cadet Owen's immediately rushed Jack. 'Drop and give me 50.'

Jack slightly smiled from the right quarter of his mouth and thought to himself as he dropped down, *this has to be the easiest 50 pushups I have ever done.*

CHAPTER FIVE

Week two of Beast Barracks brought full room inspection to include all issued uniforms. The uniforms were stored in the cadet's room evenly spaced in a specific order. Footwear was shined and aligned under the bunk. As the twins prepared their room, Colonel Sullivan strolled in. The Colonel was checking in with his recruits. Unknown to Jack and Zeus, colonels did not recruit cadets. Both were surprised to see him.

'Well, haven't you two made quite the impression.' The twins just made eye contact with each other and shrugged. Colonel Sullivan continued. 'So, you two got company A-1. A-1, the toughest company historically at West Point. MacArthur's mother stayed at the Hotel Thayer in a corner room, while he attended. The corner room was significant so she could keep a watch on the greatest cadet in West Point history. She could see his room from hers. She checked to ensure he worked until lights out at midnight and awoke at 5:25 to verify he was ready for the day. Her husband was an accomplished decorated general and she spent the whole four years in the Hotel Thayer. MacArthur never received a demerit, so the legend tells us.'

Colonel Sullivan asked Jack to use the latrine so he could speak with Candidate Seamus. 'Apparently, you have no problem finding the latrine, and given the cadence of your strolls, we will have plenty of time to catch up.' The Colonel reminded Jack.

The Colonel asked Zeus upon Jack's departure. 'How is he?'

Zeus responded. 'I don't really know. He is a bit of a hurricane. However, while scary, he does not bring destruction, he makes everything better. I am not sure how he does what he does.'

Upon Jack's return, he asked Seamus to use the latrine so he could speak with Jack.

'Candidate Jack, your godmother is visiting this weekend. You will take her to mass, feed the ducks and brunch at the Hotel Thayer.'

'Sir, wait what? We can't even call home.' Jack asked genuinely confused.

'You heard me.'

'Ok, but not without Zeus.'

'Agreed.'

With that, the Colonel left, Zeus returned to the room and asked Jack. 'How do you know him?'

'He recruited me.'

Zeus nodded. 'Me too.'

Iceman paused and after brief consideration offered. 'You know, the Colonel reminds me of an American Pierce Brosnan.'

'I can see that. I am a huge fan of Brosnan. Did you know that back in the day he put his life on hold right at the beginning of fame to support his wife through cancer?'

Iceman, nodding his head, responded: 'I did. You know what's fucked up, he lost a daughter to the same ovarian cancer around the same age, like 40.'

'Fucked up. The Irish golfer Darren Clarke did the same thing.'

Iceman nodded. 'Right, I heard from a couple of caddies back in Chicago, he is the coolest golfer ever. I guess both were just being proper Irishmen.'

Zeus smiled. 'Absolutely.'

'I got it made. I have Irish DNA bred in America. Doesn't get better than that.'

'Or worse.'

'Roger that.'

The twins just looked at each other, nodded and returned to prepare their room for inspection.

* * *

Still baffled, the Collins twins followed orders and met with Jack's godmother. Jack was crazy about his godmother, who had fire red hair and whose temper and determination matched her hair. Zeus was immediately impressed with an imposingly strong lady who reminded him of his mother. The three attended mass at the Catholic Chapel, fed the ducks and walked to the Hotel Thayer for brunch. The stories started after the second mimosas flowed. While not a mimosa drinker, Jack was willing to consume, as the orange juice hid the alcohol not permitted to first year cadets. The waiter initially denied the order, but true to his godmother's resolve, they were served. A full brunch with prime rib, pasta station, shrimp and a full breakfast buffet was heaven to the Collins twins. As the family stories started to fly between Jack and his godmother, with truth not invading a better version of actual events, the only consumption larger than mimosas was laughter. Jack's aunt, godmother and idol raised five teenagers after her husband passed away far too early. Four of her children turned into fine adults with the usual bumps in the road. They worked hard at school, had jobs in high school and excelled in school, except for her baby. Her baby of the litter was Kelly. Kelly drove her mother crazy, but she always remembered Jack's efforts towards Kelly. Jack's godmother worked as a single parent, became a school principal and earned a doctorate in education.

The laughter induced by the mimosa, triggered by memories and stories of backyard family parties including, but not limited to: driveway basketball games, horseshoes, weddings, first communions, graduations and the juxtaposition of wakes and funerals, was hilarious. While Zeus was laughing, Jack saw a sadness in his eyes. Zeus' love for his mother was beyond strong, but they were a party of two and not a party of 66, like Jack's family. When Jack played in his high school basketball games, his cousins, including Kelly, were in the stands and a pizza party followed. Zeus walked home alone after rugby. As Jack looked over at his friend, he noticed for the first time the death stares coming from the upperclassmen. *Who are these candidates and who do they think they are? How can they be here? And are they drinking? No, that's not possible, or is it?* If the twins were not in the crosshairs prior to brunch, there was no denying they would now be on the post office wall under the most wanted candidate. Jack just smiled, finished his drink, looked to the waiter and ordered another round.

CHAPTER SIX

The candidates of company A-1 were not separated and conquered through the rigors of beast. They stood united. Company A-1 won every competition and met every challenge. They took the nickname Apache, because Apache translated is *your enemy* and started with an A.

'Very clever.' Zeus laughed at Jack when he thought of and implemented the nickname.

With four days remaining until completion of Beast Barracks, the upperclassmen marched the candidates 12 miles to Camp Buckner to train. For four days, the candidates trained and bunked at Camp Buckner while the other upperclassmen, not attached to Beast Barracks, returned from training at posts throughout the army and settled back into West Point life. The march on the fourth day was the last step of Beast Barracks. The candidates marched 12 miles in two columns, returned to West Point and anxiously awaited being welcomed by the entire Core of Cadets.

With a mile remaining on the march back, Jack called for A-1 to fall in. Zeus was the guidon bearer, carrying company A-1's flags with strength. Jack took the leadership position and ordered the assembled candidates to form a tight platoon: 'Right face, forward march. Left, left, left right left.' Jack yelled out to company A-1. 'Company, double time.'

With the order of double time, A-1 began to jog together while the other companies scrambled without success to follow A-1's lead. Jack's voice was so loud and deep that the cadence he sang was heard by the entire class.

Jack: 'C-130 rolling down the strip.'

A1: 'C-130 rolling down the strip.'

'Airborne Ranger gonna take a little trip.'

'Airborne Ranger gonna take a little trip.'

'We gonna stand up, hook up, shuffle to the door.'

'We gonna stand up, hook up, shuffle to the door.'

'We don't know if we're ever coming home.'

'We don't know if we're ever coming home.'

With a half mile until the parade ground where several parents, West Point leadership and the upperclassmen back from training waited the candidate's arrival, Jack turned up the volume of his cadence.

Jack: 'Because we are Airborne, Rangers.'

A1: 'Because we are Airborne, Rangers.'

'A is for Airborne.'

'A is for Airborne.'

'I is for In the air.'

'I is for In the air.'

'R is for Ranger.'

'R is for Ranger.'

'B is for Born to fly.'

'B is for Born to fly.'

'O is for On the go.'

'O is for On the go.'

'R is for Ranger.'

'R is for Ranger.'

Jack looked over at Cadet Owens and gave him a head nod towards the parade grounds. Owens noticed Jack's cue and he and the other upperclassmen ran ahead of the candidates to the parade ground. The candidates were reporting to the leadership team who raced to be in position.

'N is for Never quit.'

'N is for Never quit.'

'E is for Every day.'

'E is for Every day.

'A is for A-1.' The A-1 candidates smiled at Jacks insertion of A-1 rather than the script cadence Airborne.

'A is for A-1.'

With 100 yards remaining, Jack bellowed. 'A-1, quick time march.'

The A-1 candidates immediately resumed their marching pace.

With 50 yards remaining and now on parade ground, Jack barked, 'A-1, left turn march.'

A-1 performed a perfect left turn march and were now marching towards their upperclassmen, who were ready to receive them, led by Cadet Owens.

Jack: 'Left, left, left right left. A-1, halt. A-1, left face.' Again, A-1 moved in perfect synchronicity.

Jack studied the candidates, executed a perfect about face and snap salute. 'A-1 reporting as ordered, sir.'

Cadet Owens returned the salute and instructed Jack to return to formation. Before Jack could move, his order was interrupted by the Commandant of Cadet, General Calderon. The general addressed Jack. 'Where are your classmates?'

Jack immediately saluted the general, who returned Jack's salute. 'A-1 leads the way, sir.'

'It would appear so. I see them now.' With that the general saluted Cadet Owens. 'Carry on.'

As he marched back to formation and took his position as squad leader, Jack could not help, but look over at Zeus, who joined Jack with a smirk. The smirk, both knew, conveyed the sentiment without a word. *Did they really think they could break us?*

CHAPTER SEVEN

'What the fuck?' Jack exploded. 'I got 24 credit hours this semester. 24 hours, coupled with hoops and military, including formations, shining shoes, uniforms, room inspections, reading the New York Times prior to 0700 breakfast formation. When am I supposed to take the deuce? How many do you have Zeus?'

'What is the deuce? And I have the same.'

'The deuce is the two. How many do the others have?'

'18, what is the two?'

'A shit. Do I have school you on everything? Fuck, you'll be fine. You're a smart motherfucker, but I am screwed. You are a goddamn genius and I snuck in here due to hoops.' Jack continued his rant.

'Shut up.' Zeus responded clearly bored.

'Why? You have important appointments, hot date?'

'Everyone knows you are smart, so you can just stop.'

'No. I am clever, there is a difference. What the hell?! I got Spanish III. I suck at Spanish. I can barely speak English.' Cadet

Jack pushed back.

'I got Spanish III also and don't treat me like a fool. I don't like it. So, like I said, stop.'

'Whatever, what's your first period class?' Jack asked.

'Boxing.'

'Me too. Great… now I get to eat shit on a shingle and 15 minutes later get punched in the stomach. This is a bag of dicks. We get no free period, all this military shit, race to practice, attend after dinner formation and chow, and then, execute four hours of homework.' Jack was now venting.

'Yep, with one exception.'

'What's that?' Jack asked, obviously confused.

'You'll do one maybe two hours of homework tops, but nice try.' Zeus answered just shaking his head.

'And another thing, this old school shit needs to stop. Other plebes don't have to execute the announcing of the minutes until breakfast, lunch and dinner formation. *10, then 5, 3 then 1 minute until lunch formation.* What the fuck? Can't they tell time? Other plebes don't have to memorize the New York Times front page every day; other plebes don't have to ping every-where; other ple…'

With that, Zeus cut Jack off. 'Stop! Just stop. The only thing that is going to stop is you. They're not going to stop, so just shut the fuck up.'

'Roger that.'

CHAPTER EIGHT

The academic part of the day and the military responsibility were to be expected and manageable for the twins. The other cadets did not share in the twins' early success, they struggled to meet the overwhelming challenge of cadet life. Boxing and balling were different for the twins. Jack was a light heavy weight and Zeus was a heavy weight. Fortunately, they never had to box each other. Their classmates would disagree.

Zeus destroyed the field. They never had a chance. A six-week class that featured the other plebe varsity athletes must have felt like six months to them. The core squad, as varsity athletes were named, took first period PE so they could attend early afternoon practice and to protect the other plebes. Any plebe over 225 pounds, Zeus just ravaged. To the 225-to-275-pound heavy-weights, Zeus was like Mike Tyson against Michael Spinks. Zeus destroyed offensive and defensive lineman in football and all comers. The cadets wore headgear, but Zeus was so powerful his right hook rendered the headgear useless. He knocked one oppo-nent down with a straight right to the chest. Zeus unleashed his straight right, and his opponent was knock off his feet, flew three feet against the ropes and slumped to the canvas. The fight was immediately stopped. He won the plebe class I heavyweight championship, then won again in the spring when he fought the champions from classes II-IV. Plebes took and rotated through four PE classes: boxing, wrestling, gymnastics and drown proofing. Drown proofing was developed, because far too many soldiers died in World War II in amphibious landings. The landings often did not reach the shore and, the soldiers that tried to swim ashore in full gear, drowned. Drown proofing entailed letting all the air out of your body, sinking to the bottom, jumping out of the water towards the shore, taking a breath and repeat. Most importantly, run for cover when you make shallow water. The deployment boats, more than likely land on shore, but like horseshoes close must be good enough and a soldier needs to be prepared.

Jack had more trouble with boxing than Zeus. He was a light heavyweight and fought running backs, defensive backs and outside linebackers. His opponents were fast, strong and several had fought competitively. The first fights went well. Jack's advantage was years of landscaping had built extraordinarily strong hands. Basketball created fast hands and he could use both hands equally. Finally, 38-inch-long arms provided Jack with a tremendous reach advantage. During a fight, he switched left-handed and right-handed boxing stances, much like Marvelous Marvin Hagler. Jack broke his first three opponent's noses and had to escort them to the training room. The last two fights were very tricky. The semifinals matched Jack with Cadet Crossett, who won golden gloves in New York. The fight started as expected, with Crossett laying a beating on Jack. Jack weathered the storm with a left hook to the body and temple, a straight right to the nose, breaking another nose and another escort to the trainer. The championship fight made the beating he took by Crossett, which he barely survived, seem like walking the shores of Lake Michigan.

Cadet Martinez, his finals opponent, was from East Los Angeles, where he won the golden gloves. He was a combination of safety-linebacker, with quick feet and a devastating right hand.

The beating Jack took in his last fight, coupled with Martinez being significantly better, spooked Jack. Jack knew he was still hurting from his previous fight and was walking wounded to fight a badass.

* * *

The night before the fight, after lights out at midnight, Jack confessed to Zeus: 'Dude, he is going to kill me. This is a suck. I have no business being in the ring with him. Don't say shit, but I am scared.'

Zeus took a gentle breath and responded. 'You'll be fine.'

'Zeus, I am serious.'

'Shut up and go to sleep. You'll be fine. Go to sleep.'

Sleep was not an option as Jack replayed all of Martinez's fights in his head, probing for a weak spot. After obsessing over all of Martinez's sparring and fights, he discovered absolutely nothing. He knew he couldn't win and would just have to accept his beating.

He whispered to himself. *Just take it like a man. Just take your beating like a man.*

* * *

5:30 am: Wake up, a couple of hours to the beating.

7:00 am: Breakfast formation and breakfast, so 45 minutes until the beating. The moment could not come soon enough.

The man rings the bell and all the college athletes who took first-period boxing were watching. Martinez hit Jack as if he was Roberto Duran or Thomas 'Hitman' Hearns. Jack was hurt after one punch and the destruction began. Cut under his left eye with bruised ribs, Jack walked to his corner after the first round. The second round made the first round look like a picnic until the final 20 seconds.

Jack found Martinez's flaw with 20 seconds remaining in the second round. When he was ready to use his powerful righthand that did all the damage, Martinez dipped his right shoulder. While being overwhelmed by Martinez's talent and skill, Jack was determined to bring everything he had in those closing seconds. He was done with being Martinez's punching bag. Standing 6'5' as compared to Martinez, who stood 5'9', Jack used his 38' 38-inch arms to keep Martinez away from him and waited for his opening. He just had to hang in there for a few more seconds. Jack deflected or absorbed Martinez's left jabs and waited for that devastating right. Double jab to Jack's face, deflected again, and here it came the thunderbolt. Jack jumped the tell and his left hook punished Martinez's right cheekbone before Martinez could fire his missile. Jack lost the round, but won the last 20 seconds. The third round was going to be his.

In the corner waiting for the third round, Jack thought back to his first fight as a seven-year-old kid. The neighborhood bully, who was two years older than Jack, six inches taller and 30 pounds heavier, did what bullies do. At the end of the fight, the bully took the fallen Jack's head, turned it and rubbed his ear against the concrete. Jack walked home crying, embarrassed and ashamed, looking for comfort from his mother. He was greeted by his grandfather instead. His grandfather was a tough retired police officer who was raised by an even tougher father. Jack would find no sympathy here. His grandfather saw the fight from his window, across the street from Jack's home and immediately walked to greet Jack. Jack looked up at his grandfather, who wasted no time; he slapped Jack across the face. *No tears, Laddie. Go back out there and fight him like a man; fight him like a Collins.* Confused, Jack walked back and fought like a boy possessed. He took another beating, but the bully knew he was in a fight. He walked home with more bruises, but no tears, with his head held high. His grandfather simply said. *You won't be hearing from him again. Walk with me. Let's get you a soda pop.* His grandfather was right. The bully wanted nothing to do with Jack from that day forward. A smile crept over Jack's face. Jack deliberately and patiently waited until he was 12 to grow enough to return the punishment that he owed the bully. Vengeance was issued that day when Jack inflicted revenge on the bully. He returned to the moment with that memory and the sound of the bell. Jack stalked from the corner. Martinez knew he was in for a fight.

The third round started with Martinez on the attack. He immediately threw a big right that Jack slipped, moving smoothly to his left. After shaking off a couple of jabs that got through his defense, Martinez set to throw his big right. Jack saw the tell and threw a series of strong left jabs that rocked Martinez's right side. As Jack relentlessly pounded Martinez's exposed right side, Martinez moved his left and right hands to cover his face from the onslaught of jabs, inadvertently exposing his left jaw in the process. Jack anticipated the defensive counter and threw a mighty right hook of his own to the exposed jaw. Jack felt the punch connect and knew Martinez was hurt. Martinez went down. Jack knew he had really hurt Martinez's jaw with the right and did severe damage with the left jabs prior, so he was more than surprised when Martinez returned to the fight. The Chicago Irish Southside kid went at him with venom, smelling blood in the water, or was fear his motive? *What if Jack pissed off Martinez? What would Martinez do when angry?* Jack was not about to find out. 45 seconds later, Jack knocked him down again, spit out his mouth guard and screamed. 'Fuck you! Get up! I'm not done with you yet.' Jack stood over Martinez, just as Ali stood over Liston, waving his right hand in the 'get-up' motion. The fight was stopped. Jack won the light heavyweight division class I.

Martinez stayed on the canvas and needed time to visit the trainer. An injured cadet must walk with an escort to the trainer, so Zeus jumped in to walk with Jack. 'I told you all was fine.'

'If this is fine, I have no clue what miserable is.' With that, Jack nodded his head to his friend.

Because Jack was so beat up, he could not wait for Martinez, and another cadet had to walk Martinez to the training room. He caught up with Jack and asked. 'Why didn't you go down? I beat you bad.'

Jack responded. 'I don't know. You are a hell of a fighter, clearly better than me and I wish I had gone down. I just couldn't.'

'Jack, you know you won.'

'Lad, just stop. You are better. I just hung in there, and besides, nobody wins a fight. You still look gorgeous, and if possible, I am uglier.'

Zeus introduced himself. 'Nice fight, Martinez. I was pretty excited when you were putting a beat down on Jack. I was hoping you would break his jaw, so it needed to be wired shut. I could use a few weeks of peace and quiet.'

Martinez smiled. 'Trust me, I did my best.'

Jack shook his head, still trying to make the ringing sound in his head stop. 'Zeus, you are a funny guy. Zapata here tried to kill me and all you can manage is canned material. With my life on the line, you should have the decency to be funny, you big fuck.'

Martinez taken back. 'Zapata? You mean me?'

Jack looked at Zeus and then around the training room, 'Do you see another badass Mexican in the room? Zapata was the Mexican version of Michael Collins.'

'I know who Zapata was, you fucking idiot. Who the hell is Michael Collins?'

'Now, I am the fucking idiot?' Jack smiled. 'Michael Collins was the Irish version of Zapata.'

'Jack, you are an odd motherfucker.' Zapata shook his head at Zeus, who simply nodded his consent.

'Misunderstood, lad… misunderstood. My genius struggles to find an audience.' With that, Jack waved his hand in a dismissive gesture. The wave hurt Jack because his whole body hurt.

'Dude, stop making me laugh. It hurts my ribs.' Zapata shook off the bonding moment and laughed again despite the pain.

'You can't be serious. Yo, you put a beat down on me. Fuck you.' Jack got up slowly and went to Zapata to go again. Zapata, who also got up slowly, prepared for another fight.

As Zeus pinned Jack back, he glared at Zapata. 'If you want this wanker off the leash, go ahead and serve it up. Trust me, he won't be gentle like before in the ring.'

Jack, struggling to breathe given Zeus' agonizing grip, just laughed.

Zapata was shocked. 'I didn't say anything.'

Zeus laughed. 'I know. We were just fucking with you.'

Zapata, Zeus and Jack became good friends from that moment on.

After winning class I, Jack went on to destroy class II-IV champions in the spring. None of the fights saw the third round and all fights ended with broken noses. Jack set the cadet record for broken noses issued.

Zapata, not eligible for plebe open due to his loss to Jack, offered his violence to the brigade open. Rather than beating up plebes, Zapata unleashed his sweet science on the upperclassmen. He elected to continue to box and play football.

Jack and Zeus happily retired from boxing.

CHAPTER NINE

'Huddle up, let's begin with the starting five and run through the offense.' Coach Durham bellowed to start the first practice of the season.

Jack took the court and was immediately confused. Cadet William McDowell was a high school all-state player from Virginia and a three-year starter at West Point. Jack found himself standing in William's position, realizing there were now six players on the court, not five.

'Country, you are in my position.' Jack walked up to William slowly and too close.

'Rookie, get off the court.' Responded William with disgust.

'I said, you bitch motherfucker, get off my court.' Collins stared down William.

Coach Durham screamed. 'COLLINS, GET OFF THE COURT!'

'Yes, coach.' he acknowledged coach and returned to William. 'Best be knowing, I am coming for you.' As he walked off, he held his glare at William McDowell. 'You might want to work in another position, know what I am saying?!'

The practice proceeded for 15 minutes while the coaches ran through the offensive sets with the starting five. Unable to reign himself, Jack was done and started to walk to the locker room while he dropped his practice jersey on the hardwood floor.

'Collins, just where do you think you are going?' Coach Durham snapped at him.

'The ticket office. If I am going to watch and not play, I feel like I should pay admission to this comedy, or should I say tragic comedy?'

'If you walk into that locker room, there is no coming back.' Head Coach Durham exploded.

'Got it. Bye.'

As Jack walked to the locker room, Assistant Coach Phillips picked up his barely used practice jersey, walked into the locker room and asked Jack, 'What did you expect?'

'A chance. If he or the other four players on the court are better than me, I can accept that, but I expect respect. *Acta non verba* - actions, not words. The court is pure and true. Handing someone a job, let alone a starting job, is the reason this team sucks.'

Phillips responded. 'What do you want? What do you suggest?'

'I don't suggest anything. Coach, give me any other four and let's ball and find out who can play.'

'Let me see what I can do, but coach is going to be upset.'

'If having a losing record doesn't piss him off more, I don't give a flying fuck.' Jack responded, regretting his choice of language.

Phillips heard the passion and intensity in Jack's message and responded, 'Give me five minutes and here is your practice jersey 44.'

Four minutes later, Phillips returned and talked to Jack in a calm tone.

'Jack, you get your game, but coach wanted you to know this cannot be a habit. Agreed?'

'Yes, I appreciate his willingness to change his bad habits. Very cool.'

'Jack, he was referring to you.'

'Fair, but I will be heard. I will hold my thoughts, talk in private to you and coach, and not in public anymore. I get it, but I will be heard.'

Coach Phillips accepted.

The game was seven on the black team against seven on gold. The best seven wore black and had two substitutions to rotate the starting five. The players that were on Jack's team wore gold and were comprised of the 9th through 14th rated players on the depth chart. Coach Durham was sending a clear message to Jack: *Be careful what you ask for because you might just get it.* The matchup was tremendously lopsided to the team in black. Jack was excited to meet the challenge.

'Lads, we are overmatched, but I have a plan.' Jack rallied the gold team. 'Beat them up with physicality and overwhelming effort. Give me the ball and leave Sir William to me. He is all mine.'

'You are a nobody.' William spouted off as the scrimmage started.

'True that, but while I agree with you that I am a nobody, what are you after I bust you up? You are about to catch embarrassment. A nobody throws you a cup of reality, whoops your ass, busts you all up. You are an arrogant fuck and I am about to slap the shit out of you. And that's Mr. Nobody to you.'

The game was on. The gold team fought hard and played with passion. Jack and William had several confrontations.

Jack made a quick shoulder fake, followed by a jab step, exploded past William and scored. 'Where were you? I had the ball, you were guarding me and then I don't know what happened. I was going to buy milk just to see if your picture was on the missing person side of the carton. I left you so easy I thought something happened to you. I was concerned.' Jack mocked William as they ran down the court.

'Fuck you, Jack.'

'Can't help you with that, lad. I be doing all the fucking out here. I be fucking you up all over this court. I'll leave the money on the nightstand. I am using you like a whore.'

With gold in the lead and tempers rising, Coach Durham called a time-out.

As the two teams broke for water, Jack cut William off in line. 'What kind of brother calls himself William? William McDowell. Wait a minute… McDowell? You be a *Coming to America* motherfucker. Hey, golden arcs, where is your Soul Glo?' Jack was referring to the movie *Coming to America* starring Eddie Murphy. McDowell's family business was a rip-off version of McDonalds that the cute girl's father owned in Queens, NY. Her boyfriend's father owned Soul Glo, which was a business that manufactured and sold hair care products.

Jack was relentless and just would not stop his verbal assault on the court. 'Hey William, supersize my meal and throw some extra fries in the bottom of the bag. Beating your ass all up and down this man's court, my court, is hard work and a man such as myself has earned an appetite. Wait, does McDowell use supersize, or is it like jumbo for trademark reasons? You know what?' Jack needed to pause to get through a screen; once clear, he continued his verbal assault. 'My game is like McDonald's and yours be all McDowell's. You are a generic, trademark-violating motherfucker, who should be watching and not playing.'

Collins' outburst was enough for Coach Durham. He immediately canceled the rest of the practice. He could see his best player, William, had enough of Jack and neither was going to back down. 'Tomorrow, you toddlers are mine. Any child can have a temper tantrum, but how did we get better today?'

Walking off the court and to the showers, Jack approached William. 'You are a nice player. I'll make us better, but we obviously need you. We cool, Willie Mac?'

'Willie Mac, I like that, Iceman.' Willie quickly responded.

'What?'

'You're a cool ass whiteboy, Iceman.'

Stunned, Jack responded. 'Other than watching Paul Newman in *Butch Cassidy and the Sundance Kid*, this is the only other time in my life I wished I were gay.'

They laughed their asses off and became friends for life.

* * *

'What's up, Zeus?' Jack asked as he walked into the room after dinner.

'Nothing, but I gather you had quit the eventful day.'

'Nope, just went to class. I won some writing award, so I get to sleep in that class until dethroned. Pretty cool of the professor to offer that and then went to hoops.' Jack responded.

'Wait, you won a writing award?'

'Yes. I wanted to sleep in class, so I remembered my James Joyce, wrote and won. Grabbed a nap. Isn't that what you were talking about?'

'No, moron. I was talking about you and William.'

'Willie Mac and I are cool; he is a good dude.'

'Wait, what? Who is Willie Mac?'

'Willie Mac was in my spot on the court and we worked it out. Ain't nothing, but a chicken wing on a string. What's up with you?'

'I got asked to join the football club.' Zeus mumbled.

'First, it is the football team and not club, and second, you could be like that guy on the All Blacks who played for New Zealand. The Dallas Cowboys wanted to sign him… sorry, an NFL team.'

'I know who the Cowboys are. I grew up in Ireland, not Mars.' Zeus continued to wonder why they were good friends.

'Anyway, before being rudely interrupted, I was saying you would be great.'

Zeus now remembered why they are great friends. 'Thanks, but I passed. I like rugby.'

'Cool, Zeus. That's cool. What are you up to in the fall? Like, play intramural with the sink pissers? You'll kill them.'

'No, while the rugby season is in the spring, we have fall ball. In the winter, we focus on lifting and conditioning, and then, we give our best effort in the spring.'

'Quick question: does anybody in the US rugby world know about you?'

'No.'

'Well, shit, I am not missing a home game.' Jack answered with genuine excitement.

'Jack, I won't miss your games either.'

'You are a good man, Charlie Brown.'

Confused, Zeus asked, 'Who is Charlie Brown?'

'I was told you didn't grow up on Mars. Never mind, it was a compliment.'

'Whatever you say, Iceman.' Zeus said with a smile. 'My room-mate, the cool ass whiteboy.' He laughed and continued. 'That Snoopy cracks me up.'

Iceman smiled. 'Funny guy knew all about practice and *the Peanuts*. Aren't you the clever one?'

CHAPTER TEN

Unable to control his intense competitive rage, Iceman started to hyperventilate before his first game. Army faced St. John's at home. St John's was nationally ranked and Iceman was determined to ensure this season was not going to be like the previous season when Army only won nine games. Prior to the game, the trainer and team doctor tried to calm Iceman down through meditation and visualization. He missed the pregame speech, but took to the court in time for warmups. True to his word, Iceman accepted not being in the starting lineup, but was given the chance. While he disagreed with the coach's decision, he respected his right to make it.

Six minutes into the game, Army was down 14-2. Iceman started screaming in constant cadence, 'Put me in, put me in, put me in, put me in, put me in.'

Coach Phillips whispered into Coach Durham's ear. 'You might want to put Collins in.'

Coach Durham snapped and dictated. 'Collins, you are in for Willie Mac.' As he ran to the scorer's table to check in, Jack noticed even the coaches were using Willie Mac rather than William. Jack thought as he waited to be buzzed in: *Willie Mac is just a ball player's name. Willie Mays. Willie Stargell, Joe "Willie" Namath, for fuck's sake, were all ball players.* Back in character, Collins passed Coach Durham and barked. 'I will never come off this court again.'

After being buzzed in, Collins sprinted onto the court; Zeus, Zapata and Colonel Sullivan cheered hard in the background. He continued to think: *Willie Randolph, Wilma Rudolph is the girl version of Willie. Ok, stop! Game time, enough about Willie.*

'Bush, you out.' Iceman yelled.

Cadet Bush was by far the weakest link in the starting five. A small, slow point guard who couldn't shoot and could not keep up with division I athletes. If that was not enough, his defining characteristic was arrogance. Bush couldn't be more white. Iceman hated him. As Bush trotted off the court, Iceman approached Willie Mac.

'My brother by another mother, how you been? In all fairness, I'll answer, you be a broken bitch. I was supposed to pull you. Fuck that shit. We need to get longer and more athletic. Remember when I said learn another position? Today is that day. You're on the bounce, playing point guard and I am taking your spot. We cool?'

'Yes. Thanks, Iceman.'

'Bitches, huddle up; this shit ends. We are five, a fist and a force of nature. We be coming and the beating stops; our turn, our time. Let's go hurt some feelings. I don't care if we win or lose, but when they walk out the gym, they know they were in a fight.' He then turned his attention to St. John's and smirked.

Coach Durham went to call a time-out to control Iceman and his decision to pull Bush, but changed his mind when Coach Phillips held his arm and whispered: 'Give him a chance. We are down 14-2 and I need this job.' Coach Durham nodded.

Collins hit his first two shots on the first two possessions. His second shot was a 3-pointer and Willie Mac followed when he destroyed a dunk on a breakaway. The Army defense held the line and fought. Collins deliberately and aggressively knocked down the best player on St. John's and was called for a foul.

Iceman's only reaction was to stand over his prey as he shook his head. 'Common. You're just common.'

The game was on. St. John's hit one of two free throws that brought the score to 15-7.

The game continued, as did Army's confidence level, and by halftime, Army was down 38-33.

During halftime, Iceman approached the two coaches in private as promised and asked, 'Will you add Johannsson to the lineup, please?'

'No, we need the size.' Coach Durham responded.

'Sir, with respect, I am right. Our five best athletes are between 6'5 and 6'8. We can switch on every screen and pressure the ball. More importantly, we play in transition, take 3's and chase down the long rebounds in the event of a miss. Our big and strong line-up is a problem. St. John's is bigger and faster than our big men. We have no chance. Go small and make them chase us. Johannsson is good, a fast 6'7 and jumps through the gym. He and Willie Mac can run with these guys, and I'll do whatever it is I do. We are playing with house money being this close at half, please.'

'Agreed.' Coach Durham consented after making eye contact with the approving Philips.

With that message, Iceman walked over to Johansson's locker. 'Lad, I got you in the starting line-up for the second half.' A fellow plebe, he was from some small county in North Carolina. Johannsson was getting the same chance Iceman had fought for.

'Dude, I believe in you. Do you believe in yourself?'

'Yes.'

'Right, but here is the thing. Your Tupperware or candle party attitude you bring to practice ends. We are assassins. Am I clear? There is another gear in you, no pussy bullshit, suit up.'

'You got it.' Johannsson replied with a smile.

Iceman stared at him with a dark, evil stare. It took tremendous effort to not slap that stupid grin off his face. 'Nope, try again, you weak ass motherfucker.'

'I said I got it.' Johansson said angrily.

'All right then.'

The cadets took the court with five that were ready to compete as one. Iceman simply said. 'Take the fight to them. We are Army strong. Unleash violence. They are athletic and talented, but we are Army strong.'

The half began and Army brought immense intensity and St. John's, to their credit, held their ground. This game was going to be a battle. Iceman, who scored 8 points in the first half in limited playing time, caught fire in the second half. Halfway through the second half, with 10 minutes remaining, Army was down 54-50; Iceman had 19 points. While St. John's was on the free throw line, he casually walked over to St. John's coach and in a condescending tone, suggested. 'You better get somebody out here that can guard me.'

Overhearing the exchange, Zeus, Zapata and Colonel Sullivan just shook their heads.

Colonel Sullivan asked Zeus, 'How do you live with him?'

'Prayer.'

As St. John brought the ball up the court, the cadets sprung a two-man trap that took St. John's by surprise. The cadets stole the ball and the outlet pass was thrown to Iceman, who raced down the court and attacked the rim. He was challenged by the best player in St. John's, whom he had knocked down earlier. Feeling he was coming for Iceman to repay the knock-down, Iceman went up to dunk and *announced his presence with authority* (a quote from the movie *Bull Durham)*. At the last moment, he flicked the ball behind his ear in an arcing fashion and forced the charging threat to pause as he followed the ball. Johannsson was sprinting down the court ahead of the pack in an effort to catch Iceman. Iceman saw him out of the corner of his eye and threw the arcing alley pop pass to Johannsson, who gratefully accepted the gift with a thunderous dunk. While running back on defense, Iceman thought: *Damn, I was right. That Norwegian fucker got hops. He threw that down like Thor and the ball was his hammer. Thor, I like that. Shit, get back to the game, stupid.*

The game raged on. Physical and tough, both teams played hard. The inner-city kids from NY were met with the soldiers from Army. Pushing, shoving and hard screening were the themes of the second half. Johansson, now named Thor in Iceman's world, played hard, having a big impact on the boards and in transition. In the end, the superior talent level won out and St. John's earned a well-deserved 68-66 victory. While there were no moral victories, the message was sent that Army was a date you didn't want on your schedule.

Before showers and press interviews, Iceman walked over to Johansson and, with a cup handshake and a butt-out hug, said, 'Thor, that's the good shit right there.'

'Thor?'

'Yeah, Thor, with your blond hair and biceps that you work so hard on. Ha, I said hard on. Anyway, wait, you know biceps don't help you in basketball; work on a jab step.'

Thor looked at Iceman, confused.

Iceman pushed on. 'If we are not going to suck, we need what you brought in the second half. Got me?'

'Yes.'

'Yeah, but here's the thing. You've got to bring it every day at practice. You have to bring it when nobody is watching. Like Mohamed Ali, you have good looks and talent. Unlike Mohamed Ali, you don't work. One of my favorite quotes from him is: *The fight is won or lost away from the witnesses – behind the lines, in the gym, and out there on the road, long before those lights.'*

'I get it.'

Walking to the shower, Iceman patted Thor on the shoulder. 'We'll see. I hope so. But trust me, while it's your journey, I'll be in your ear.'

Thor and Iceman became great friends from that moment forward.

* * *

After a shower and press interviews, Iceman walked out of the locker room. Colonel Sullivan, Zeus and Zapata had waited for him.

'Great game.' Colonel Sullivan complemented.

'Lad, you were great.' Zeus added.

Zapata jumped in. 'You are a bad man.'

Iceman responded. 'We lost.'

Zeus jumped in to pick up his buddy. 'You led the team in scoring, assists and rebounds.'

'Nope, I led the team to a loss.'

Colonel Sullivan carefully studied the phenom of Iceman and Zeus as he handed Iceman a box. 'Here is your dinner.'

'I don't want it.' Iceman's eyes were a million miles away.

Colonel Sullivan nodded. 'How about a ride to the barracks?'

'No, sir. I am going to walk. Please drive these two.'

'You are after hours, missed the bus and will get in trouble without my escort.' Colonel Sullivan reminded him.

Iceman's eyes immediately shot up; his look was atomic as he coldly eyed the Colonel. 'Sir, do I look like I care? Trust me, no one is going to approach me.'

Zeus, while knowing it was futile, asked. 'Want company?'

'Fuck no.' as Iceman started the two-mile walk to the barracks, he doubled back. 'Zeus, you're a good man, sorry. Thanks, that's on me.'

'It's cool, I get it.'

Iceman walked back to his barracks only to find Zeus had placed the box dinner on Ice's desk. After the 30-minute brisk walk, Iceman had calmed down.

'Thanks, Zeus. I'm starving.'

'No problem.'

* * *

The next morning, the upperclassmen showed Cadet Jack a new level of respect. Company A-1 specifically, but the entire Core of Cadets gave compliments and head nods. Jack felt uncomfortable with the attention and just kept quiet with his head down until lunch.

'What's up, money?' Reese fist-bumped him.

'My man.' Ty backed up Reese.

Reese and Ty really liked Iceman as he has always showed them respect when most cadets ignored them. They were minimum-wage employees who delivered family-style meals to the cadets. The waitstaff was responsible for serving the entire Core of Cadets in one 25-minute seating for breakfast, lunch and dinner. Iceman, on every shift they worked, shook their hands, asked how they and their family were doing and said thank you. Showing respect was free and he never understood why people were condescending based on job description.

'First game and you fucked them up.' Reese celebrated.

Ty commented. 'That's the good shit I am talking about right there. I shake the hand of a superstar.'

'Thanks, guys, but we lost. That's it.'

'We heard all that, but you brought back energy and hope. Shit, it is one loss. Did you think you were going to be the 1976 Indiana Hoosiers and go undefeated?' Reese came back.

Ty jumped in and added. 'Man, I wish I were there.'

'Hold up, you guys need tickets?' Iceman asked.

'We can't afford no tickets.' Ty dismissively responded.

'I didn't ask you that. Want tickets?'

'Shit, yeah, Iceman. We know you smooth and all, but how are you going to do that?' Ty asked.

'A little-known fact: players get two complimentary tickets to each home game. Most of the tickets are used on beautiful babies to hook up with. While I do not want to hook up with you two, I am prepared to acknowledge you are beautiful.'

'You said four, not to be greedy.' Reese casually mentioned, looking down at his shoes.

Iceman thought, *I didn't offer four, but no matter.* 'No, it's cool, have you seen my teammates? Ain't no beautiful babies comin'.'

They laughed. 'I got a friend on the team,' Iceman was referring to Thor, 'that owes me a favor. Go to will call and show your ID and you're hooked up.'

'Thanks, my brother, and we have a little something for you. The cook made a stop being a bitch meal to cheer you up.' Ty smiled.

'Did you make Zeus a plate?'

'Shit, how do you think we knew you being a bitch?'

'Fair, thanks.'

'No, thank you, Iceman. You are good people. Willie Mac nailed it. Iceman, cool as what did that guy on ESPN used to say?

Iceman answered. 'Stuart Scott.'

'Right, right. I had that shit. *Cool as the other side of the pillow.*'

While the Core of Cadets chowed on mystery Mexican shredded chicken based on a dare, Zeus and Iceman dined on chicken fried steak, mashed potatoes, creamed corn and a biscuit. Zeus told Reese and Ty about Iceman at breakfast and told them this was one of his favorite meals. Reese and Ty did Iceman a solid and he really appreciated it. After lunch, Iceman walked into the kitchen, thanked the cook with compliments, took off his dress grey jacket and helped Reese and Ty with the dishes.

'Don't you have class?'

'I am not doing all the dishes, but respect. Where I come from, when somebody cooks for you, then you help with the dishes. I got a little time. Besides, so what if I am late. Fuck it, I am a superstar, remember?' Iceman said with a smile.

The kitchen exploded in laughter.

Reese and Ty became Iceman's good friends.

* * *

After his last class of the day in Differential Equations, Iceman changed in the barracks into PE gear and ran to the arena. All the other players in all other sports took the bus. Jack arrived 35 minutes earlier than the others and had the gym to himself. The facility manager, Marcus Johnson, approached him. 'Great game.'

'Thanks, but we lost. We will continue to get better.'

'Iceman, why do you run to the stadium when all the football, hockey, basketball and lacrosse players take the bus?'

'Why does a gazelle run from the lion?' Iceman responded.

'But it is two miles up hill, then practice, then two miles downhill.'

'Does the gazelle stop running after distance or when the lion quits?'

'Got it.'

'Respect, Marcus. Talk to you soon. Thanks for your hard work.'

'Can I ask you a question?'

'You just did. What's up?'

'My kid Marcus II was at the game and I was wondering if you would sign an autograph for him? It sure would mean a lot.'

'No, I am a nobody. Does he play ball?'

'Yes, but he is not that good and I thought the autograph would give him, you know, a bit of a pick me up.'

'I am on a team that hasn't won a game, so I am not that good either. Your boy alright? How old?'

'12 and he's good, just being 12, I guess.'

'Right. Give me a minute.' With that, Iceman's thoughts were focused on himself as a 12-year-old. 'Ok, I'll make you a deal. I have on post privileges on Sundays from 0900 to 1400 hours during the season. On post privileges translate to walking within the post, one mile outside post, but not beyond that area. During the other hours of the week, us plebes are restricted to assigned posts. We don't have practice on Sunday until 1500. The arena is closed until practice, but you have the key. Bring your boy here at 1000, open the gym and have him here with his hoop gear. He can rebound for me during my shooting drills.'

'That's great.'

'I am not finished with my terms. I will coach him up after my workout, give him a tour of the locker room and talk with him about things.'

'Iceman, thank you.'

'Now about the fee. I will require a program in my locker today, a pizza on Sunday with orange pop and whatever your son likes, because pizza and pop can open a boy up. I'll also need a media cart and the movie *White Men Can't Jump.* Do you accept my terms?'

'Yes, but Iceman, you can jump.'

'Not the point of the movie. Anyway, I am almost finished. I have two guys from the mess hall that have been a solid, so I hooked them up with season tickets. Can you greet them at the next home game, issue them some bullshit VIP badge and direct them to a concession stand? Take care of them the best you can; I am sure nobody counts popcorn. Anything you can't cover, bill me.'

'Iceman, how about this: hotdog, pretzel, popcorn and a drink for $10 a game?'

'$10 for all four, you sure?'

'Iceman, you know what? You are going to fill the arena. We all good.'

'No, I take no charity. $10 is fair and I'm not arguing with you about it.'

'Deal, Marcus II and I will see you on Sunday.'

'Bet, I'll see you then.'

Iceman used the program to have every member of the team, including coaches, write a note next to their picture to Marcus II. The team is bigger than him and no one is bigger than the tribe.

Marcus, Marcus II and Iceman became friends for life. Iceman never received a bill from Marcus.

CHAPTER ELEVEN

After three road wins, Army played Yale at home. Army won, bumping their record to 4-1. Army played well and were starting to gel as a team.

The next morning, Iceman exited breakfast formation and headed to the Cadet Mess with the other members of the Core of Cadets. The Cadet Mess, located in Washington Hall, featured a statue of Washington on horseback in front and the Cadet Chapel high above as a backdrop. The Cadet Mess was adorned with military and historical artifacts, stained glass windows, and murals. The most famous mural, located in the southwest wing, depicted the history of weapons in warfare used in the 20 most important battles in history. At the time of completion, the mural's surface of 2,450 square feet was one of the largest interior paintings in the world.

At breakfast, Ty and Reese approached Iceman. 'My man, that was the jump.' Ty said, smiling.

'My kid actually got up for school like I am gonna rock this school shit.' Added Reese.

Ty jumped back in. 'You know we got VIP badges, a hot dog, hot pretzel, popcorn, and an orange drink?'

Iceman responded, 'That's the good shit right there. Much deserved.'

Reese jumped the conversation. 'We heard from Marvin Gaye and his grapevine that you dig a Philly cheese steak.'

'This is not a wedding,' Iceman turned the Marvin Gaye reference, 'but I do. What about…'

'Shut up, we got Zeus. Your lunch will be waiting.'

'Thanks. Can I be a dick? Wait, I am already a dick. Can I be a bigger dick? Wait, my dick is already big. I guess what I am trying to ask, and it is totally cool to say no, is if you could add Willie Mac, Zapata and Thor to my man crush list?' Iceman asked with a bit of regret. 'If you can't, can you make it a rotation?'

The Core of Cadets ate by their assigned company in the mess hall, A-1 ate with A-1. The core squad athletes, better known in college as varsity athletes, ate in a separate wing with their teammates. The core squad athletes were served one and a half portions and, in some cases, two times the portions. Eating with their teammates afforded the serving of special meals without attention or concern.

'Brother, we can hook you up.'

Ty walked closer and whispered. 'And we got another hook-up for you after lunch, 4-1 record this party needs to get jumping.'

'I'll see you after lunch. I won't forget this favor.'

'Bet.'

'Peace.'

After lunch, Zeus, Thor, Zapata, Willie Mac, and Iceman walked into the kitchen, took off their grey uniform jackets and helped with the dishes. As they walked in, they all gave a butt-out hug and whispered respect. Reese and Ty walked up to Iceman and asked for a moment.

'What's up, watcha need?' Iceman asked with his curiosity peeked.

'No, nothing like that.' Reese countered. 'We got you a gift.'

'Fuck that shit, you don't owe me nothing.'

'Shut up and take it.'

'Alright, thank you. To be honest, I did not expect lotion. You two are mummy-looking fucks.'

Ty shook his head. 'It's special lotion.'

'Like Alvera?'

'First, it's aloe vera lotion and I dig on coconut body lotion myself.' Ty scolded Iceman.

'Right, something other than the knockoff cologne you fancy smelled funky.' Iceman laughed as he examined the bottle.

Willie Mac excused himself and walked to class. As a firstie, the cadet term for a senior, Willie Mac had invested too much and had earned freedom in his last year at West Point. He did not want to be anywhere near any talk of suspect plans.

Zeus was done listening to Iceman and nervous about class. His next class was computer programming, and even though he should have been teaching and not taking it, he had enough. 'Ice, just open it.'

As Iceman acknowledged Zeus' command, he turned the top off the lotion, 'The blind man said I see. I know this smell.'

'We know you Irish like your whiskey, and we know it is contraband, so we invented this whiskey in a lotion bottle.' Reese smiled, proud of his gift.

'I believe that might have been a song by *the Police,* but never had no coconut lotion flavored whiskey. While I appreciate your effort, the reality is it is based on bigotry. All Irish enjoy Irish whiskey? I do not and I am insulted.'

'Iceman, we are…'

'I am fucking with you. This is the greatest gift I have ever received. I assume you'll be getting Zapata tequila and Thor moonshine next time, you two racist great gift-givers.'

They all laughed except Zeus. 'No.'

Before exiting Washington Hall, Zeus repeated. 'No.'

Iceman innocently looked at Zeus. 'What? I didn't say anything.'

Zeus knew that look in Iceman's eyes. He knew. 'No.'

'Zeus, I hear what you are saying and you are right. The idea of bringing water to the desert is ridiculous.'

'Jack, seriously. Just stop.'

Iceman paused with Zeus' use of his proper name. 'Zeus, you are right. When you are right, you are right.'

'Thank you.'

Thor asked. 'What are you two talking about?'

Iceman innocently responded. 'Nothing, really. Well… never mind, it's dumb and reckless. Right, Zeus?'

'Yes.'

'What?' Zapata asked.

Iceman responded. 'Nothing. I am not even sure I have an idea, let alone a good idea. The whiskey in the bottle sounds a bit brilliant, but how do we hook up right thinking cadets who are thirsty? That is the question and if we profit from the fulfillment of said need, where is the harm?'

Zeus immediately responded. 'We get kicked out of school.'

Iceman nodded. 'True, there is that, but that makes a couple of large assumptions. You assume if we get caught, which we won't, we get kicked out rather than just get into trouble. Further, and this is most important, you assume we care about being kicked out.'

The group went to ask questions all at the same time, but Iceman calmly raised his right hand and explained. 'Let's shelve the discussion until I have had a chance to think. We gotta get to class and I need three days to think. We will meet in Zeus's and my room after dinner in three days. We will crack open the lotion and I will discuss my plan.'

With that, Zeus and Iceman pinged off to class; Thor and Zapata walked. Iceman pinged with a look of mischief and a smile, Zeus with a look of concern, Zapata and Thor walked with a look of confusion.

Iceman addressed Zeus with his eyes front after ensuring he was safe to talk. 'I understand, but just maybe… never mind, you wouldn't be interested in working with Reese and Ty to provide more lotion and distribute said lotion to select plebes. My only concern is Reese and Ty and their families. I am a giver like that. If you can help society, then you have a moral obligation to do so, but that's just me. I understand the concept of just looking out for yourself and not the financial windfall afforded to them and, by extension, us. We help a couple of friends, get a little something for the effort and we provide the service that gives select plebes a false and temporary sense of self-esteem.'

'Iceman, you are a wanker.' Zeus just shook his head.

'Yep. I need three days to map this out with no risk. Profit will be secondary to risk, but if I figure it out, by my initial calculations, it will be fun and we can each make $250 a month. Reese and Ty pull down around $1500 a month now. We could add a nice bump in pay with straight cash.' Iceman smirked and continued. 'Like I said, Zeus, there is a moral obligation to help a man provide for his family, legally, by the way.'

'It's not legal. Our customers are underage.'

'Details, drinking in college is pretty much legal. Close enough. Great, so we both agree. Perfect. Give me three days.'

That night, Iceman waved over his shoulder at Zeus as he left the room and headed to the Hudson River. He walked in the shadows of the river, because the Hudson was a grey area in terms of restriction. Plebes were required to be in authorized areas. The library was authorized and close to the river. The Hudson, while not technically an academic zone, Iceman figured was close enough. After a brisk 30-minute walk, Iceman had the core of the plan. Over the next two days, he focused on risk assessment. The lads could not get caught, and while Iceman was confident in his plan, he had to attack it from all angles to eliminate risk and, if not, at least minimize it.

Three days later, the four met in the twins' room under the guise of a study group. Books were opened, and Iceman walked under the sink and removed the lotion by Jameson courtesy of Reese and Ty.

'Fellas, we've got to kill this in short order. The less time it is in the open, the less chance we have of getting caught. The fact that we kill this quickly to generate a quicker buzz is a bonus.' With those comments, Iceman took a healthy hit. He passed the bottle around, and after the third pass, the bottle was gone. Iceman rinsed out the bottle with soap and water. He then swirled in some mouthwash and rinsed. Finally, he added a couple of ounces of lotion and shook the bottle. To the unknowing inspector, the bottle was an empty lotion bottle thrown out in the latrine.

'Alrighty then, let's talk a little treason. As you saw, the lotion bottle was not an effective delivery nor storage device. If discovered during inspection, the lotion fails, because the bottle was stored in the room and the beverage of choice does not smell like lotion. If the room was inspected closely, the lotion bottle would not stand up to the challenge. A better delivery and storage method is a cleaning bottle. Because the cleaning bottle smells like alcohol, it is a better cover than lotion. More importantly, the cleaning bottles will be stored in the cleaning closet next to the service elevator on each floor. The bottle will be hidden in the back and will go unnoticed. In the event of an intense room inspection, the room is clean. Wearing our white parade gloves when handling the bottle will eliminate figure prints. Each cleaning closet will be assigned two bottles. One bottle is for storage, and one is for exchange. The bottles will have a designated hidden delivery location for pickup and delivery to the cleaning closet. Just like the milkman, you exchange empty for filled. Got me?' Heads nodded as Iceman paused to await their reaction.

Thor responded. 'The industrial sink cleaner from Home Depot, that what costs a buck, is genius. I love hiding it in the back of the common area that each floor has. Love it. You are a sick motherfucker.'

'Thor, I am a highly functional sociopath. Huge difference.'

Zapata added, 'Isn't the use of our white parade gloves a little excessive?'

Iceman smiled and answered. 'Yeah, no chance. I am wearing gloves, but you got to admit it was cool, added a dramatic effect.'

Zeus was silent. The rest laughed and were excited about the plan.

Iceman continued. 'I am not finished. We include other right-minded plebes, but we can never be tied to the operation if someone gets busted. We use the library. We will have 10 captains, and each will be assigned a book. The book will be in the stacks across from Patton's statue that faces the library. Do you guys know why Patton's statue is located there? Have you noticed he is holding binoculars and did you know it took him five years to graduate? When he was asked as a cadet, *where is the library?* He responded with no clue. With some help and time, he eventually found it. He only needed to die to have a statue built to include binoculars to find it. Who says the military doesn't have a sense of humor? Maybe not; they probably did it by accident. Are we going to help cadets find the library, good men that we are? The order and cash are placed in the assigned book. The order is collected by one of us, and a pick-up date and location are left in the book. We rotate our visits to the library and the days we collect. We leave no pattern, and we raise no flags. The orders are delivered to Ty and Reese. Ty and Reese refilled the empty bottles and delivered them to the designated location. No one gets dirty or exposed. We will make $30 a bottle net of expenses. Ty and Reese get half and we get half. Zeus and I got more than you two, because that is just the way it is. Anybody steals from us, Zapata and I will handle the beating and after one, it will never happen again. That's the plan. All in?'

Zapata and Thor immediately and enthusiastically jumped in with two feet. With that, they collected their books and returned to their barracks.

After they left, Zeus looked at Iceman. Zeus whispered in quite rage to Iceman. 'We can't do this.'

'Zeus, we are doing it. This place is boring as fuck. We handle our shit and if we can continue to help kid cadets to stop pissing in the sink, we are doing this. Think of the children. Seriously, what is the worst that can happen? You go to Harvard and I go to Fordham or Boston College. Fuck it, let's be proper gangsters.'

'All right.'

'My man.'

* * *

With a mission to become proper gangsters, Iceman approached Ty and Reese. 'What's up, fellas?'

Ty responded. 'Nothing, how about you? What are you doing for Thanksgiving?'

'We have a basketball tournament in New Mexico. Given it is too far for Zeus to go home, and they don't give a shit about Thanksgiving in Ireland, I got him named team tutor, so he is jumping in with us. We have a Thanksgiving banquet with the other teams, but I am sure we will sneak off a couple of times and see what Albuquerque has to offer. The weather will be nice.'

Reese nodded. 'That's cool.'

'Hey, I got something to run past you two and you are going to like it.' With that, Iceman explained his plan. 'What do you think? It's cool if you need time to think about it.'

Ty and Reese looked at each other and agreed. 'We are in.'

With that, Iceman handed them $50 to buy industrial cleaning bottles and $500 to build inventory for the orders.

'I need eight right away for the crew and here are the details for the locations to stash the first order for the usual suspects.'

Ty and Reese nodded.

'Thanks guys, see you tomorrow. This will be fun. One more thing: cut the bottles with water for the other cadets and buy cheap liquor. They won't know the difference. If we are going to be bootleggers, might as well be proper bootleggers.' Iceman cupped his hands and shoulder bumped them and was off.

After the goodbye, Reese turned to Ty and asked. 'What do you really think? He is a crazy motherfucker.'

Ty responded. 'True, but he is a smart motherfucker. This is so crazy that it will work. Look, man, I hate this job and it don't pay shit. The only reason I took it and stayed is for the medical benefits. The cadets treat us like shit and Iceman and his crew are the only ones that treat us right. Because of them, coming to work doesn't suck, I mean, sucky suck. Shit, other people from cadets to supervisors need to be treating us better.'

Reese nodded. 'That's true.'

Ty continued. 'The medical benefits are much needed as we both got growing families, but we can get the same thing at the hospital. My cousin told me they are hiring up there. I do need the money and the benefits, but I figure they got way more to lose than us. Besides, ain't nobody going to give us no never mind anyway. I figure we got nothing to lose.'

Ty always has good points. Reese thought. But those thoughts brought back other conversations they had in the past. Reese took pride in being a good father and husband, just like Ty did. They both stood tall, having avoided the life of easy money that many of their friends and family had chosen. In their households, money was tight despite both parents working hard. So, Reese couldn't shake off the realization: *Goddamn Air Jordans be expensive, even bought off the truck. $500, maybe $1000 cash, earned without doing anything wrong... that could make a real difference. Take my baby to a nice meal once in a while, to a nice date and even a little cash for myself to throw a couple back with the crew. Yeah... that would be nice. But I'd have to be honest with her about the source, so she won't be concerned with easy money.*

'Agreed.'

The business model worked and word spread quickly in a tight circle. The crew no longer had custom lunches to avoid attention. However, Ty's wife cooked well, really well. With the delivery of the cleaning supplies came secret homemade meals for the twins. The food bill was deducted from the gross revenue of the business. In addition, the servers wore the same shoes as the basketball team. Iceman furnished slightly used 12s for Reese and 13s for Ty. Iceman continued to turn a frown upside down, and they all smiled at the latest basketball shoes on Reece's and Ty's feet. Whenever Iceman walked into the mess hall and looked down at the shoes, he would just laugh and shake his head. He laughed at the stupidity and sadness because Reese and Ty were truly invisible to the West Point community. Nobody noticed their shoes. Pathetic.

CHAPTER TWELVE

After formation, the twins braved the cold December wind from the Hudson River, followed their usual routine, walked into lunch and said hi to Reese and Ty.

Reese asked. 'How was the Army Navy game?'

The Army vs Navy Football game was the big annual event, even bigger than graduation weekend. Throughout the post, Go Army beat Navy was displayed to include the entire roof of the main academic building. During the week leading to the game, the cadets were buzzed by flyovers courtesy of Navy during lunch formation. The attack jets roared up the Hudson River in attack formation to remind Army that the Navy was coming. Army implored the same mental tactics on Navy with attack helicopters and tanks. The game was nationally televised and was quite a spectacle. The armed forces were on display and celebrated throughout the world. The celebration extended to the midshipmen and cadets, who blew off steam in a Mardi gras fashion after the game.

Iceman responded. 'I don't know. I wasn't there. We had two games in Buffalo. We beat Niagara on Thursday night and Sienna on Saturday night. I did find the Anchor Bar and destroyed wings and beer. You know buffalo wings were invented at the Anchor Bar in Buffalo, hence the name.'

Ty laughed. 'How you know all this crazy shit?'

'This time, I read the back of the menu. Zeus made the trip.'

Reese asked. 'Well, how was it, Zeus?'

'Embarrassing. Both sides were like amateurs at a frat party. From what I heard, after the game, both sides just acted the part of drunk fools. I lost interest and just chilled in the room. The game was fun even though we lost, but I lost interest after a couple of hours of postgame antics.'

'Zeus, tell them about your teammate and sick call. Tell them what the nurse said.' Iceman was baiting Zeus. He had told Iceman his teammate visited sick call, because it burned when he pissed. To make the embarrassing moment worse was the female doctor who reported. *We have visitors.* 'No, I don't think so.'

'Come on, you got to tell it.'

Zeus glared at Iceman. 'I said no.'

'Ok, cool, man.'

In an effort to change the subject, Ty asked. 'What are you two doing for Christmas?'

Zeus calmed down and answered. 'Heading back to Ireland to see my mam.'

'And your boys, right?'

Zeus dropped his head slightly. 'Sure, them too.'

Iceman jumped in, knowing Zeus didn't really have a crew. 'I think I am going to Key West. I only get three nights because of hoops, so I thought I would check it out.'

Reese was surprised. 'Who are you going with and you aren't headed home for the holidays? What about your family and friends?'

'I am going alone. Going to check out what all the fuss Hemingway made of the place. I have been to a lot of Christmases at home, but never been to Key West.' Iceman answered and made it clear the subject was closed.

* * *

Later in their room, to let it go, Zeus asked. 'Are you seriously not going home for Christmas?'

'Nope. Everybody gets to leave, but we still have two practices and a game at Manhattan. I am checking in at the Trump after the game, ordering room service while I take a bath, eat, hit a couple of bars and catch the first flight out of JFK to Miami International Airport the next morning. After a two-hour layover, I am in Key West for three nights. Fly back in time for 1900 hours practice.'

'Ice, you gotta go home.'

'Nope.'

'Iceman, please listen. What about…'

'I said no.' As Iceman interrupted Zeus, he held an intimidating stare.

Zeus understood the conversation was over, but did not understand Iceman's decision.

CHAPTER THIRTEEN

Iceman walked through JFK in a good mood. He hung 27 points on Manhattan in a win, enjoyed the nightlife afforded by the city that never sleeps, headed to JFK and cougar town. Iceman created the term cougar town for his tactics to score free food and drinks. He identified older, attractive women business travelers on an expense account and flirted to dine for free. He entered the bar outside his gate, found a cougar and Iceman did what he does. After three Guinness, a shot of Jameson and a turkey sandwich, care of the cougar, Iceman found his first-class seat. He ordered his first-class meal, and when the traveler next to him passed, Iceman asked if he could have it. With his 100-watt smile on display, he received the meal, but more importantly, he received a 100-watt smile back from the flight attendant. Iceman was warming up his Irish charm as his excitement built for his Key West adventure. He took advantage of the complimentary alcoholic drinks and had three Budweiser while reading Papa Hemmingway in Key West.

The third person off the plane in Miami, Iceman walked towards his connecting gate and found a nice spot at the bar, but not a cougar to be found. He shrugged it off, had a beer and finished his book. He ordered another beer and a turkey sandwich when he heard a voice.

'He doesn't want a turkey sandwich.'

Iceman turned his head the wrong way to identify the voice and had to turn back to find her. A cougar to his rescue.

'Sweetie, you are in Miami. You want Cuban food, come with me. Johnny, we will be right back; please save our stools.' She turned her attention back to Iceman.

'Jack.'

'Right, please watch Jack's stuff while we grab food. Can I get you anything?'

'No, thank you and no problem, I'll keep an eye on your spot.' The bartender, Johnny, held a knowing smile.

Jack asked. 'Where are we going?'

'Heaven, or as close to heaven as you are going to find in Miami Dade.'

As they walked up to two oversized concession carts like those found in baseball parks, Jack was a little surprised. While they waited in line at Sergio's, Jack studied the menu. Everything looked good and he was struggling to decide. When the time came to order, Jack's concerns were put to rest by the cougar.

'We'll have two Cuban sandwiches, please.'

'Excuse me, can you add an order of rice, black beans and a bowl of the split pea soup with potatoes?' Jack's menu study identified other items for his Cuban fest.

'Coming right up.'

Jack turned and realized he did not know her name. 'What's your…'

'Heidi, to answer your next question, it's an elegant sandwich with a combination of pork, ham, Swiss cheese, pickle, mustard and Cuban bread.'

'What is Cuban bread?'

'The key to the sandwich.'

'Ok, didn't answer my question, but sounds good. I'm in.' Jack gave her his smile.

'Oh my, what a dangerous smile.'

The cashier called out that their order was ready and the cougar paid.

'Thank you, Heidi. You didn't have to do that. It smells good.'

Heidi smiled at Jack. 'Consider it an investment. I have a couple of hours to kill, my flight is running late. You are my entertainment.'

'I see. I have a couple of hours to kill also.'

'I know, we are on the same flight. We are both going to Key West.'

'How did you know that?'

'Your book on Hemmingway. Where else would you be going from Miami?'

'Good point.' Jack conceded.

'I am excited to witness you enjoy a Cuban sandwich for the first time.'

'That good, huh?'

'That good.'

Johnny came over to get their drink orders and waited for Jack to finish his first bite.

With Johnny and Heidi watching, Jack took his first bite and announced. 'That's a damn good sandwich.'

Johnny asked. 'What would you two like to wash it down with?'

Jack went to order a beer, but was cut off.

'Two mojitos, please.'

'When in Rome, right?' Jack smiled with mustard at the corner of his mouth.

'Right. Have you ever had a mojito?'

'No.'

Heidi offered a smile. 'Your first Cuban and your first mojito.'

Johnny yelled across the bar. 'Did I hear you say first mojito?'

Heidi answered. 'Yes.'

'Well then, I'll have to make it special.'

Jack yelled back to Johnny. 'Is special code for strong?' Johnny just looked at him. Jack shrugged. 'I'll take that as a yes.'

Finishing her first bite, Heidi asked Jack. 'So, is the Cuban your favorite sandwich?'

'Second. No, third best. There is a deli on the near Southside of Chicago named Manny's. Best corned beef sandwich in the world. That is my favorite sandwich. My second favorite sandwich is the combo. There is a beef stand on Taylor St. in Chicago named Al's. The sandwich is a combination of Italian beef and spicy Italian sausage with giardiniera on a soft French roll dipped in spicy au jus. I've got to stay true to my roots and represent Southside Chicago strong. This is the third. Then, the meatball sandwich at Rosebuds, also near Southside down the street from Al's on Taylor St. Rounding out my top five is the McRib.'

'The McRib? From McDonald's? That's gross.' Heidi shook her head in disgust.

'Absolutely.'

Heidi looked over at Jack. 'I see you liked the mojito. Johnny, can you get Jack another, please.'

Heidi took a sip of her mojito, a couple of bites of her sandwich and looked over at Jack. He was wiping his mouth. All the food was gone, as for the second mojito.

'Holy shit. You ate all that and downed another mojito?! I am only halfway done with my sandwich and mojito. What did you have? Sandwich, bowl of soup, rice and beans? You are like a circus act.'

'It's been said before.'

'Amazing.'

Changing the subject, Jack observed. 'You obviously travel a lot; you know the bartender's name, not a great mystery.'

'I do, international law.'

'Impressive.'

Heidi waved her hand dismissively. 'Boring, let's get back to Key West. My girlfriend and I meet in Key West every year for Christmas. Our way of shaking off the holiday nonsense. We stay at the Casa Marina.'

'Me too.'

'Your first visit to Key West?'

'Yep.'

'First Cuban, first mojito and first trip to Key West. Well, aren't you too much fun? Bar plan?'

'First stop is Captain Tony's. I want to visit the wall that Hemmingway ripped the urinal out of. He took it, because he felt he had spent enough money at the bar that he owned it. Now the urinal sits on the lawn outside his historic home and the six-toed cats that roam his house drink from it.'

'Look at you. Most people go to Sloppy Joe's, because that was the name of Captain Tony's when Hemmingway drank there. Sloppy Joe's moved in 1938, because the landlord raised the rent by $1 a month. The patrons took everything and moved to Duval St. There are other great bars. There is…'

'I know. I researched it.'

'Ok, Mr. Google Man, did you come across the bar with no name?'

Jack, puzzled, reached for his phone. 'Bar With No Name?'

'Put the phone away, stupid. It is not a name; it is a bar with no name.'

'I see, interesting. How do I find it?'

'I'll point you in the general direction from Captain Tony's, but it's simple. Walk to the marina and turn right from Duval St. Walk past Conch Republic Seafood Company and listen for the noise and music. Follow your ears and thirst and you can't miss it. The bar is completely outdoors with no walls, old sails for shade and a dump with great music.'

'Perfect.'

Heidi called Johnny over and paid the bill. 'Drink up, we are boarding.'

'Right, I'll be right behind you.' Jack got up, headed straight for Sergio's and ordered another Cuban Sandwich for the flight.

Jack boarded the plane and walked to his seat to find Heidi sitting next to him. 'Coincidence?'

'A little. We are both in first class, so I asked the flight attendant your seat assignment and this nice gentleman switched seats with me. We have more Key West planning to do.'

The flight attendant approached and took their order. 'No food for me. I'll have a mimosa and he'll have a beer.'

'I'll take her food, so please bring me both options. Thank you.'

'You can't be serious, more food?' Heidi simply shook her head, accepted the mimosa and passed Jack his beer.

The emptied mimosa glass brought take off and sleep for Heidi. Jack started Hemmingway's Key West and thought, *I can't get trapped with Heidi. Shut up, Jack, just walk the earth and if she is a part of your journey, when you bump into her, just flow.*

As they started their descent, Heidi woke up, ordered a mimosa and beer for Jack.

'You can't be serious.' Heidi declared. 'Enormous early lunch, two first-class meals, and what is that, is that another Cuban?'

'I told you I liked it.'

Shaking her head again in disgust, she said, 'When we land, we will share a ride to Casa Marina.'

Jack went with the flow. 'Sounds good. I have my bags, so while you hit baggage claim, I will hail us a cab.'

'Honey, do I look like the sort of person that hails cabs?! I do well for myself, but I skinned my ex-Wall St. cheating ass tycoon. I nailed him to the wall. I have transportation taken care of.'

While driving to Casa Marina in the hired Escalade, Heidi gave Jack more instructions. 'You'll beat us to Captain Tony's, because my friend and I will get a massage, lay by the pool for a couple of hours, then we'll head out to visit Tony. At the bar, you will meet up with Lars. I texted him while I was waiting for my baggage and he is heading over there now. You'll spot him; he's a Viking of sorts and you are hard to miss. I found you easy enough.'

* * *

While Jack was checking into the Casa Marina, Seamus was kissing his mam goodnight. He walked upstairs to his old room and started to read Clear and Present Danger. He finished Hunt for Red October on the flight from New York. Iceman recommended Tom Clancy's series featuring Jack Ryan. Seamus enjoyed the first book and identified with Ryan. As he sat up in bed, looking around the room, he thought, what am I doing here? I love my mam and I love seeing her, but what am I doing here? There is nothing in this room, this house, or this town for me except my mam. He had no interest in seeing his high school classmates or accepting invitations to play in the men's rugby league. He only left the house to go for his seven-mile runs. Tomorrow brought Christmas Eve and then Christmas with his mam, so he should be happy. I am happy, he thought. Seamus picked up Clear and Present Danger and started to read.

* * *

Jack found his room, paused at the shower, but dismissed the idea. I am going to a dive bar; showering would be pointless. He didn't bother to unpack. He simply rifled through his duffle bag, found a pair of shorts and flip-flops, and was out the door off to Captain Tony's. As he walked down Duval St., he took notice of the businesses he recognized from Yelp and some he did not.

He walked into Captain Tony's, ordered a Bud and a shot of rum. Captain Tony's was truly a dump. The smell and the condition of the bar were awful. Captain Tony's was much worse than Yelp described. Captain Tony's was perfect. It was too hot for whiskey, so again, when in Rome. If rum was good enough for

90

Hemmingway, it is good enough for me. Jack drew the line at daiquiris, Hemmingway's favorite drink.

Jack made quick work of the first round, and after he ordered a second, he heard a voice coming from four bar stools down to his left.

'I got those, Rob.'

'Thanks, Lars, I am assuming.' Heidi was correct. Lars was a Viking of sorts. Jack laughed to himself; Thor would be jealous. Lars had surfer boy blond hair that touched his shoulders, a deep tan and salt water-punished body and clothes.

'Jack, you are correct, sir.'

Jack shook his hand. 'Nice to meet you. That Heidi is a piece of work.' Jack took his shot and Lars joined him. No cheers or toasts amongst deliberate men.

'God broke the mold, that's for sure.'

Jack nodded. 'Heidi didn't say anything about you.'

Lars shrugged. 'Do you really give a shit?'

'Nope.'

Lars laughed. 'We'll get along just fine.'

Sunday brought NFL football. The Chicago Bears were playing the New York Jets in the late game. 'Where is a good place to watch the game tonight?'

'Most people will say Jack Flats, but I like the Sandbar. Want company?'

'Sure, it will be fun watching a Long Island Jets fan cry in his beer.'

'Funny guy. You know Long Island?' Lars asked.

'No, a bunch of lacrosse guys I go to school with are from Long Island. The accent is distinct. Hoping to get out there some summer.'

'Long Island is nice and fun, but I'm happy to be here.'

Lars and Jack sat at the bar for a couple of hours; several locals joined them and the group just hung out.

Lars asked Jack. 'Are you hungry? I haven't eaten all day.'

'I could eat.'

Lars announced to a couple of guys at the bar. 'Guys, I'm grabbing Jack and we are heading over to DJ's. Save our seats, we won't be long.'

'What's a DJ's? Jack asked.

'A clam shack.'

'Cool.'

DJ's was close and Lars ordered three fried clam boats for the two of them.

After his first clam, Jack nodded his approval. 'Clams are tasty.'

'Is this your first-time eating clams?'

'Yep.'

Lars ate a few clams, took a couple of sips of beer, and looked over at Jack, who was on the third order to be shared.

'Holy shit. Hey, remember half of those are mine!'

'Of course. I am going up for more. Want anything?'

Lars shook his head, so Jack came back with two orders of clams and two beers.

'I said I was good.'

Jack nodded while swallowing a mouth full of clams. 'I know, they are for me, but I figured you wanted another beer.'

Minutes later, they were walking back to Captain Tony's and passed a pizza joint.

'Hey, I am going to grab a slice. Want one?' Jack asked.

'Sure, Pepperoni.' Lars answered.

Jack walked out and handed Lars his slice. Jack took his two slices of pizza and folded the slices over so the crust was on the top and bottom.

'You didn't eat today?'

'No, I ate.' Jack mumbled with his mouth full.

'What are you some kind of freak eater?'

'And drinker.'

Lars laughed. 'Apparently, you must have the metabolism of a hummingbird.'

'It's been said.'

Jack finished as they walked back into the bar and reclaimed their stools. A little under an hour later, Heidi and her friend showed up.

Heidi threw up her arms in the air and announced to the bar. 'Heidi and Claire are here; now the real fun can start.'

The bar erupted with cheers. She approached the group with Jack and Lars. 'Hello, boys.' She turned to Rob as she drank Lars' beer. 'Two of your special daiquiris.'

Jack thought, there it is again; special means strong.

After an hour of laughter, dirty jokes and naughty stories, Lars got off the bar stool and grabbed Jack to head to the Sandbar to watch the game.

Heidi yelled across the bar. 'Just where do you two think you are going?'

'The Sandbar.' Lars replied.

'Fine. Rude, but fine. We will meet you there a little later.'

'Sounds good.'

Back on Duval St., Jack turned to Lars. 'Heidi is hot, but what the fuck is Claire? She is fucking crazy smokin' hot.'

'Right.'

They watched the first half with the Chicago Bears up 14-3. A little after halftime, the ladies showed up.

Heidi walked over and took a drink from Jack's beer. 'Miss us?'

Lars smiled. 'Of course, we are only human.'

Claire kissed him. 'So yummy.'

As the game wore on, with the Bears clearly in control, Lars lost interest in the game and found interest in Claire. Jack figured this was not Lars' and Claire's first engagement. Heidi talked less to Claire and focused on Jack. Midway through the fourth quarter, the decision was made to go back to Captain Tony's. Seated at the bar, Claire and Lars broke all outside contact and were clearly on the runway to carefree sex. Heidi zeroed in on Jack. Jack sat and had a couple of beers while Heidi was all over him. Jack stood up to use the restroom. He entered the facility, walked past Hemmingway's urinal hole and laughed at it again. Never gets old. When he exited the restroom, he walked to the other side of the bar, away from Heidi and company, giving the Irish goodbye. Not saying a word to anyone, he headed to the exit with his back to the bar and waved goodbye.

'Lars, did Jack just give me the Irish goodbye?' Heidi asked, genuinely confused.

'Appears so.'

'Nobody has ever given me the Irish goodbye before.'

Claire smiled and handed her a shot of rum. 'First time for everything.'

Jack started his walk back to the hotel, but not done with the evening, stopped at Smokin' Tuna. He ordered a Bud, a double order of spicy wings, more clams and fried jumbo shrimp. He ate in silence as he listened to the live music. When he finished, he got up, accomplished his walk to Casa Marina, took a shower and went to bed.

The next morning, he woke at 0700, brushed his teeth, skipped the shower, dressed and headed to the bar with no name. From his walk yesterday, he remembered passing a breakfast and lunch café. He walked in, ordered four breakfast sandwiches, two apple juices, milk and a bottle of water all to go. While he waited for the breakfast sandwiches, he drank the juices and milk. He grabbed the sack of sandwiches, finished them on the walk and chased them down with the water. He took the right as instructed, passed Conch Republic Seafood Company, and sure enough, just followed the noise. The Bar with no name lived up to the hype. As Jack enjoyed the music, Lars sat down next to him in the same clothes from the previous night.

'Morning.'

Lars grunted. 'It will be. Two shots of rum and two Buds, Alex. Jack, do you want anything?'

'I'll have the same, but skip the rum.' Jack had decided rum had too much sugar and shots, in general, was a bad pairing for the trip. The days were too long and hot not to stick to beer, for the most part.

'I can only have another round the same way to chase off the cobwebs. I am taking you and the girls out today on my boat.'

'Really? Nobody told me.'

'Yeah, I am a boat captain and own my own charter company. That's how I met Heidi and Claire; they charter my boat every time they are in town. My first mate is loading the cooler and I am meeting him in an hour to get it set up. I'll see you in two hours.'

'Lars, I don't know.' Jack offered, then took a pull from his beer.

'Alex, another round the same way and cash me out. Jack, shut the fuck up. I'll see you in two hours.'

'Sounds good. I got these.'

* * *

Coming up on two hours, Jack made the short walk to the marina and Lar's boat. Heidi and Claire were already on board and, when Jack joined them, Lars set out for sea.

Lars looked back at Jack. 'Do you get seasick?'

'Don't know. This is the first time I have been on the ocean.'

'You're kidding.'

'Nope.'

Lars was still amazed. 'You are going to make up for that starting now. You met Scottie, my first mate. He will watch the boat and us while I take you snorkeling and spearfishing.'

'Cool.'

'I'll make you a deep-sea fisherman out of you.'

'Sounds great, thanks.' Jack replied, anxious for the new adventure.

For half a day, the group took advantage of the water.

Lars taught Jack how to properly equip himself for snorkeling. He then handed Jack the spear gun to get a feel for it. Once Jack was all set, they jumped into the warm, calm ocean with their feet scissored. As they treaded water, Lars continued to teach. 'Jack, use the tip of the shiny spear as a lure. The fish are attracted to the shiny tip. Stay as still as you can while you are submerged and let the fish swim to you. Wait for the fish to turn its head so you only see one eye. When you see one eye, let her rip.'

Lars watched Jack practice snorkeling for a few minutes, and once Jack was ready, Lars went in search of a target-rich environment. Jack waited for Lars to surface, not sure where he had gone off to. He was amazed and concerned, waiting for Lars to surface; he was gone for several minutes.

He finally surfaced about five yards from Jack. 'I found a school of white fish about 30 yards that way.' Lars announced, pointing over his shoulder.

Jack responded. 'What are you, fucking Aquaman? I can't do that. I can't stay underwater like that.'

'You don't have to; that's my job. You just do what I told you and you'll be fine.'

'Roger that.'

Jack followed Lars instructions and held his breath the best he could. He was still, taunting the fish with the shiny tip and waiting for the curious fish to approach. Fighting his desire for air, the approaching fish finally turned its head. Jack let her rip and success, a direct hit. After several more dives resulted in more hits than misses, Jack was immediately hooked. After a successful spearfishing campaign, Jack switched to snorkeling the reefs. He was amazed by the texture of the reefs and the vibrant colors of the fish. The experience was magical. He never felt such peace; it was just him and his fish. The outside world was gone. Jack never felt tranquility and the underwater experience stayed with Jack.

He returned to the boat and Lars asked. 'Well?' Jack just smiled. Lars continued. 'Knew it.'

The group turned their attention to deep-sea fishing. Lars clearly knew his way around these waters. He found a school of tuna and he set up the poles for his passengers. Heidi, Claire and Jack took turns battling the tuna, struggling to reel them in. The day was a success. Jack started to wonder, as they motored to the marina, What would Lars do with all the fish we caught? He looked up and noticed the group was not returning to the marina; they were headed toward a tiny island.

Jack asked. 'What's that?'

Lars wiped some sweat off his face. 'You'll see.'

As they drew closer, Jack saw a bar alone on an amazing beach. The smell of the grills was mouthwatering. Lars grounded the boat and they walked to the bar over the warm, soft sand. As they approached, Jack laughed to himself. Of course, another bar with no name on an island with no name. Lars asked Jack for help carrying the cooler packed with fish to the bar. The cook immediately went to work preparing the catch. Jack watched with amazement the speed and precision of the cook as he worked on the fish, some still moving. He returned to the bar to relax and drink his beer. The ladies went for a short walk along the beach, while Lars came over and handed Jack another beer and a shot.

After a head nod and shot, Jack said, 'Good day.'

Lars asked Jack. 'Now that we are alone, I got to ask you: why didn't you get it on with Heidi?'

'Not my thing.'

'Her age?'

'No.'

'Cheap, meaningless sex without consequences, explanations, or commitment?'

'That.'

'You're a curious dude, Jack. I think I am glad I don't know you any better.'

'Roger that.'

The ladies returned just as the tuna platters were presented. The cook, called Chef, saw Jack was confused, so he explained. 'Smoked, pan-fried, steak cut, taco prepped and ceviche. Which one is your favorite?'

Lars, Heidi and Claire said in unison. 'First time.'

The group burst out in laughter. Jack had never tried fish before and was blown away by all the platters prepared by Chef. On Fridays during lent, Jack would diet on cheese pizza, grilled cheese and peanut butter and jelly sandwiches. Whatever fish his mother made, that forced Jack and his brothers to eat in the basement of their home because of the smell, was not this.

Returning to the marina, the exhausted group said goodbye and headed to a well-deserved nap. On the way to Casa Marina, Jack stopped at Captain Tony's for a couple of beers and some alone time before going down for his nap. A couple of minutes later, Lars walked in with a small cooler and handed it to Rob behind the bar. Rob traded Lars another round for the cooler.

Jack asked. 'I was wondering what you did with all that fish, but they don't serve food here?'

'After we ate, I kept half and Chef kept half of the leftover fish. He prepped all the leftovers while we ate. Restaurants and bars can't serve this. The fish has to be caught by a licensed commercial fisherman. The fish I gave Rob was for him and the staff. They get the absolute best seafood and I get to drink for free, unless I am with a client, because in that case, I stick them with the check at full price. Don't worry, you are with me. I drink for free off the Heidi's of the world and Rob, Chef and company clean up on tips.'

'A full-service operation and I do mean full service.' Jack was obviously referring to Claire. After a pause, Jack shook his head. 'Sinner.'

They laughed and Lars asked. 'Do you want to go out tomorrow?'

'Yep, but no chicks, if that's cool. I am happy to pay. I just have had enough of them; you know what I am saying?'

'I thought so. I won't charge you for the charter; just fill up my tanks with gas.'

'Lars, I don't want you to do…'

'Just gas and the cost of beer, rum and sandwiches.'

'I think I would rather pay the charter price.'

'The way you eat and drink, you are probably right.'

Jack said his goodbye to Lars and Rob, then headed to the Casa Marina for his nap. He stripped, finally showered and laid on his bed naked. As he enjoyed the cool air in his room and began to fall asleep, he said to himself: You made the right call leaving the Southside behind you. There is a big world out there.

* * *

Seamus and his mam had a pleasant Christmas Eve and Christmas Day. By tradition, they ate several seafood courses on Christmas Eve and a beef tenderloin with all the trimmings on Christmas Day.

On January 30th, Mrs. Collins decided Seamus needed a night out. 'Seamus, let's celebrate New Year's early before the amateurs come out tomorrow night.'

'I don't think so, mam. You know I love your cooking.' Seamus felt uncomfortable with his mam's offer. He thought she was taking pity on him.

'I know, my sweet boy, but mam could use a night off. I know, let's go to Brannock's; you love their fish and chips.'

'I do. Alright, sounds like fun.' Seamus thought, *I do like those fish and chips; dinner will be nice.*

'Lovely, I'll ring us a fare for 8:30.'

'A taxi?'

'Seamus, I am of drinking age and it is New Year's Eve. Of course, I will hire a taxi.'

They arrived at Brannock's, a casual restaurant with lively music and décor, and were seated. Drinks were ordered and appetizers served. Mary, Seamus's mam, waited patiently for the conversation to move past idle chitchat. After dinner wore on, Seamus slowly started to open up.

'Please tell me about West Point. Not your classes or the brochure material, but you at West Point.'

They talked in general about Seamus' friends. His mam already knew Jack was a little off and different, but he gave her a little more insight into him. She knew about the boxing championship, but he talked about a couple of the fights. He explained that he and Jack were called the Collins twins and she found that amusing. She also liked his nickname, Zeus. As Seamus ordered a third serving of fish and chips, he continued to leak details, including Colonel Sullivan, whom his mother had not met, but remembered. He skimmed over bootlegging and Mrs. Collins added it to the list of subjects she would dive into deeper. Topping the list was this Iceman, Jack. He avoided explaining the nickname. She was very curious about him. He had a significant impact on Seamus. Mrs. Collins was so relieved that Seamus was coming out of his shell. She had always worried that

Seamus never really found his way socially. As a boy, he was forced to play sports with boys who were three to four years older than him, because of his size and freakish athletic skills, so he never really connected with his classmates. After his father's tragic death, Seamus just shut down and never showed or shared his feelings or emotions. Even at his father's funeral, he didn't cry, not one tear. Mrs. Collins had never heard him laugh hard. He was just so reserved, guarded, in control that she sometimes wondered if he was at all happy.

The two enjoyed each other's company during the two-hour dinner. At 10:30, Mrs. Collins paid and they exited. Seamus went to find a taxi when his mam spoke up, 'What are you doing?'

'Getting us a taxi to get home.'

'But it is only 10:30. New Year is a bit away. I thought we would go to Nora Culligan's to ring in the New Year. I like it there.'

'Mam, Nora Culligan's, the pub?'

'Yes, Seamus. I am neither old nor dead.'

Seamus, embarrassed, stuttered. 'Ahh right, sure… I mean, yeah, right, sounds good.'

Seamus found a taxi and they took the short ride to the pub.

To his mam's surprise, Seamus marched into the crowded bar with such confidence that people made room for him to pass. As a boy, he hated crowds. Now, as a man, he controlled them. He protected her as he found a table in the center of the pub, not the edges as she had expected. He immediately got the waitress' attention. A cute redhead flirted with Seamus; he flirted right back and was warmly received.

'Mam?'

'An Irish coffee for me. Thank you.'

'And I'll have a Guinness and a shot of Jameson.'

A shot of Jameson? She was a little surprised when Seamus ordered a Guinness with dinner after she ordered white wine. She had never seen him drink before. Now a Guinness AND a shot of Jameson? She was looking forward to seeing how the night was going to develop. The drinks arrived promptly with a side of waitress smile and hair flip.

Seamus raised his glass. 'A toast. Happy New Year, mam. To us.'

As they clinked glasses, she again was surprised. A toast? Seamus took a gulp of his Guinness and chased it with the Jameson. That went down easy.

As they enjoyed their first round, they picked up where they left off. Seamus continued to provide the overview of his journey, taking care to avoid too much detail. Mary was a sponge. She managed to wait patiently to pry more details from him. She had plenty of practice; his father was the same way.

Seamus asked. 'Do you want another?'

'Not right now, but later.'

Seamus had no trouble finding the waitress. As soon as he looked around, she found him.

'I'll have another of both, thanks.' He turned his attention to his mam. The waitress looked disappointed that Seamus had not flirted with her.

Mary found her opening and Mrs. Collins did not waste time. Before the disheartened waitress turned to leave the table, Mary asked. 'Hello, I am Mary and this is my son Seamus. And who might you be?'

'Bridget, nice to meet the both of you.'

Seamus turned on the charm, a charm his mam didn't know he possessed. 'The pleasure is ours.'

Bridget left to get the drinks. 'Pretty girl.' Mary noted.

'Mam.' Seamus gently scolded his mother.

'Well, she is.'

Bridget hurried back with Seamus' order. Seamus and his mam both noticed it was a double.

Bridget, with an angelic look, simply said, 'Whoops.' As she walked away, she looked over at Seamus and winked.

Seamus took the double with one motion and chased it with a gulp of Guinness. The double started to take effect and Seamus started to really open up.

'You should have seen Zapata in boxing, he blah blah…' And told the whole story.

'Who is Zapata?'

'Martinez.'

'Right. He's Mexican. Ok, got it.'

'You should have seen Thor, sorry Johannsson, when we were in New Mexico. You know that trip I went on during Thanksgiving break with the basketball team?! I was the tutor… anyway, we are in a bar in Albuquerque and he blah blah blah. It was so funny.'

'Oh, and then Iceman, you know Iceman?! These Vassar girls approached him after the game and we blah, blah blah. It was too funny.'

As the clock approached midnight and the pub started to thin out with closing time looming, Mrs. Collins waved to Bridget. 'We would like two chilled flutes and a half bottle Krug vintage champagne.'

'What are you two celebrating, if you don't mind me asking?' Bridget asked, wanting to engage in conversation with Seamus.

Seamus responded as his mam just laughed to herself. My boy, the flirt. 'We don't mind. We are celebrating New Year's a day before the amateurs.'

'What a fun idea. I better hurry then.' Bridget hurried back with three flutes and a bottle of champagne. 'I hope I am not being too forward; it just sounded like so much fun. I thought a full bottle was in order.'

Seamus smiled. 'We don't mind at all. To Mam, me and new friends, Happy New Year.'

They clinked their glasses and Zeus gave his mam a kiss on the cheek. Mrs. Collins gave Bridget a kiss on the cheek and Bridget slapped a lip kiss on Seamus. With that, she was off and started to help with closing time.

Seamus and his mam left the pub and hailed a taxi. Seamus opened the door for his mam and went to follow behind her.

'Just where do you think you are going?' Mary asked in a statement tone.

Seamus, confused, answered with a question. 'Home with you?'

'I don't think so. You stay out and have some fun.'

'Mam, I am coming home with you.'

'I know Seamus wants to come home with me. Does Zeus?'

Zeus smiled. 'No.'

'Good night.' And with that, mam was off and Zeus went to find Bridget.

'Seamus, you're back. What do you want to do?' Bridget smiled and gave him a hug.

'You can call me Zeus; all my friends at university call me Zeus.'

CHAPTER FOURTEEN

The Elders met twice a year on their island retreat compound 45 miles outside Barbados. The director, Bill Zera, joined the Elders on the Island and provided secure video briefings from his leadership team during their retreats. The dates were fluid to accommodate the Elders' busy schedules. In preparation for her briefing, Colonel Sullivan provided a detailed evaluation to Dr. Monroe on all his trainees, including the Collins twins. A week after the brief was sent, Dr. Monroe and Colonel Sullivan discussed his report. The discussion added color and clarity, as required by Dr. Monroe. The Elders were a tough, brilliant audience and Dr. Monroe knew being over-prepared was impossible. If there was a hole in her evaluations, the Elders found it.

Dr. Monroe started. 'Tom, another fine report, incredibly detailed. I know the recruits better, thank you. We are short on time and we have much to discuss. I would like to discuss the Collins twins first. As you know, I have a special interest in these recruits. This being their first report, I want to ensure we dedicate sufficient time analyzing their progress with proper thought given to potential problems.'

'Understood.' Sullivan had plenty of experience with Grace and empathized with the pressure she was under.

'Great. How confident are you in the bug you placed in their room? As you know, I was concerned about Jack.'

'Excuse me, Grace, as the report indicated, we refer to them as the twins: Iceman and Zeus.'

'Yes, quite correct. I was concerned Iceman would notice the bug somehow. A casual slip of your tongue with information you should not have, he detected the slip, and we lost him forever. My question is, was the bug worth the risk? Should we remove it and take our gains, or is it still worth the risk?'

'From a profiling perspective, I believe the bug has served its purpose. Both twins individually have exceeded our expectations. Their results in the classroom speak for themselves. Their leadership skills, while different in style, scare the upperclassmen and officers. The twins can motivate a group to achieve their personal mission. If they agree with the mission assigned by the upperclassmen and officers, they are a tremendous asset, but if they disagree, they are a tremendous threat to their superiors. The twins, not the chain of command, controlled the A-1 plebes. A good example is their bootlegging mob, which is detailed in my report. The twins thought the rule was stupid, so they made their own plan. The chain of command has no idea about bootlegging, but they are certainly aware the twins are intimidating. A force that they do not have control over. As I said in the report and earlier, they have exploited the helplessness the chain of command feels about them. We know from the bug that they work as one. Zeus is extremely risk-averse; he would rather not challenge his abilities to the fullest; he would settle to be great with no risk rather than a once-in-a-generation talent. Iceman is clearly comfortable with calculated risk. The important word there is calculated. We knew he was not afraid of risk, even an elevated level of risk. He has demonstrated that his tolerance for risk is extremely well-calculated, because the risk is so well accounted for, Zeus reluctantly agrees to Iceman's plans. Iceman has moved Zeus to be a once-in-a-generation talent by taking calculated risks designed by Iceman. Zeus, in turn, cannot stop Iceman from executing his plans once Iceman has committed, but he does have the ability to regulate the frequency of the plans. Iceman has more plans in what he refers to as his laboratory and was prepared to launch. Zeus managed to slow Iceman down, never stopping him, just slowing him down. After the bootlegging was a success, Iceman was ready to launch another brilliant laboratory-generated plan involving a van and the waiters in the mess hall. Zeus agreed with Iceman's new idea, but suggested to Iceman to give the bootlegging a little more time. He again celebrated the new plan and the bootlegging plan, but got Jack to buy into the concept of time. He explained to Iceman the last variable in the bootlegging plan was time. Everything worked exactly as Iceman forecasted, but will it stand up to the test of time? Because Iceman has tremendous respect for Zeus, he agreed to wait.'

'I agree with you and what an encouraging development. At the time of recruitment, we concluded their relationship, as we have now witnessed, was a very real possibility, but never did I imagine it would be this strong, and never, in my wildest dreams, this soon. Do you think it will last?'

'Yes.'

'That's it? Nothing you care to elaborate on?'

'No, they will never turn on each other. In each other, they found something they have been desperately searching for: a peer, an equal, a trusted friend. They both accept and protect that friendship; they will never let it go.'

'I read in your report the bug was still valuable to protect them. Can you expand on that in a little more detail or an example?'

'Sure, Grace. Let's stay with bootlegging. If the chain of command is closing in on them, I can protect them. I would rather have them caught drinking than caught for bootlegging. Drinking is a recoverable offense. Bootlegging is not. If they got caught bootlegging, they would be dismissed from West Point, heading off together to Stanford or some other university and be happy. I am confident they would stay together, but I am not confident they would stay with us. If I do not have the bug, I'll never know their next plan. If I don't know, I cannot protect them.'

'Thank you for clarifying that point, Tom. I agree with you. The bug stays for now. But, Tom, be incredibly careful around Iceman. Not just your words, but your body language, especially your eyes. He tracks eye movement like a hawk.'

'Understood.'

'Any sign, no matter how slight, if you think he is on to you or even the smallest of suspicions, we pull the bug.'

'Agreed.'

'Very well. Let us move on to the individual assessments. Tell me how Zeus is without Iceman?'

'Iceman has tapped into Zeus' inner confidence. Since he has arrived at West Point, Zeus is definitely more confident in himself. He is more vocal and willing to challenge himself as well as others. As identified in the report and earlier, he is taking a calculated risk. When Iceman is around, he defers, but less now than a few months ago. Rather than being a spectator in the conversations Iceman engages in, he is now a participant. I expect he will grow into an active participant by the next report.'

'That soon?'

'Yes.'

'What happens in the next months?'

'Rugby season. I have reports of him and his actions in the prac-tice field; he is a force of nature. We are in basketball season now, so Iceman is the star. In the spring, Zeus will be the talk of the post. He will share the same star status as Iceman.'

'Interesting, I am making a note to follow his rugby season more closely and the subsequent off-the-field impact.' Grace paused to make her note, then asked, 'How is Iceman without Zeus?'

'As I discussed, Zeus' impact on Iceman is not felt daily. Day to day, Zeus has no impact on Iceman. Zeus' impact is measured over the course of a semester or a year. His impact on Iceman is long term.'

'I made the diagnosis without meeting with him. Iceman had an elevated risk of having bipolar symptoms. My diagnosis of early childhood learning disabilities, coupled with his transcripts and his performance on the personality and psychology testing administered during recruitment, led me to that potential conclusion. Has his behavior manifested any of the systems I described to you?'

'Yes, most certainly. If you hadn't explained the signs and the impact of the mental health issue, I would have missed it. He certainly has it, but he hides it well. His condition is more extreme than you prepared me for. He does have meteoric explosions of energy that allow him to conquer the world. What makes his comet express different from what you told me to look for is time. You spoke in terms of days, his last for weeks. He sustains an impossible pace for months. A pace you or I could manage for a day or two. Conversely, his periods of depression are not for a day or two as described in the report. His depressed state lasts weeks and is hard to watch, something I cannot imagine living through. When he is in a depressed state, he relentlessly beats himself up physically and mentally. He is loaded with doubt and fear of failure. He finds every fault in himself, but a fault to him is being above average. When he is in a depressed state, he kills himself physically. He does not eat, sleep, read outside books, or do his homework or study. His whiskey consumption spikes dramatically. He focuses his overwhelming energy and brain power and turns it on himself. However, somehow, and this might sound impossible, I believe he controls the condition, not the other way around. He knows he has it. He figured it out. He refers to his meteoric rides when he uses phrases in conversation, such as: I'm coming. Hold on, it's going to be quite the ride. When he is feeling depressed, he uses phrases, like: I am just going dark for a minute, or just working in the laboratory. I know it does not make sense, but…'

Dr. Monroe interrupted. 'Tom, everything you said makes perfect sense. You are correct. The longevity of the mood cycle is extremely rare. He drinks to access for two reasons: one, the alcohol assists him with beating himself up; second, he is self-medicating. The alcohol slows down his brain. His brain, during the extreme highs and the extreme lows, is on fire. He feels as if he is on the verge of insanity. During the dark periods, again, without seeing him, he is searching for failure. During going dark, he is beating the world to discover his failures before the world finds them. Once he successfully navigates the failure minefield, he explodes with his cosmic flight. Courtesy of your bug, his thoughts and phrases, such as: Who were they to doubt me? We'll see who is left standing. I'll make you famous. His dark period comes back to his core, which he discovered on his own at age 12. So, you think I am not good enough? We'll see. Anger and rage fuel his comet. With time, he has learned to mask it and control it with humor and charm. He will be at his most vulnerable when the comet is the brightest at the end of the high cycle. He feels euphoric, unstoppable, because he has conquered his fear of failure. At the end of the high, he is susceptible to mistakes. Use the wire to listen for, I can't fail. Listen for changes in his planning process. Ask yourself, is he taking calculated risks or careless risks? Most importantly, monitor his tone and dialogue with Zeus. Is he pushing or ignoring Zeus to push up a timetable or implement a plan against his console? Is he condescending to Zeus? Talking down to him? He Is dangerous when his comet is the brightest. Do you understand?'

'Yes, but what should I do?' Sullivan asked with concern.

'You are also at risk here, because he will be at his absolute best. His power of observation will be heightened. You must approach him very carefully. When the comet is the brightest, you may want to use your protection plan and get him into a little trouble to trigger the dark period. Save him from himself.'

'Understood.'

'I would like to go back to the beginning. Can you give me an example of why you think he has control over his condition?' Grace asked.

Colonel Sullivan did not hesitate. 'Iceman's preseason to the basketball season, he burst on the scene and expectations were high. I regularly observed practices and as the preseason carried on, I witnessed him shut down or, as he put it, go dark. He lost weight, did not shoot unless wide open. He was quiet in the locker room and on the court. Played well, but with no swagger. The coaches were planning to put him in the starting line-up after the first week of practice, but he regressed. Prior to the first game, he hyperventilated, missed all pregame and barely made warmups. The coaches were both concerned and confused. The ball went up in the air for the jump ball to start their first game and a light switched. He exploded to life and he constantly roared: put me in, put me in. The coaches yielded to his demands and he mushroomed on the scene. He has not slowed down since that jump ball.'

Grace responded. 'I see your point. Good example. As we wrap up the twins, and before we move on to other candidates, I would like to discuss what I believe is the most telling moment or defining moment to date.'

'Please do.'

'You described in your report that the twins were in their room, just after lights out, when Iceman told Zeus he feared his boxing match with Martinez the following morning; Zeus told him he was fine and to go to sleep. I also read that Iceman was beaten up pretty badly in the fight, but won. He showed his fearlessness, toughness, resiliency, intelligence and…'

Colonel Sullivan interrupted her. 'Excuse me, Grace. Yes, the fight showed a lot about Iceman, but that is not the point. Iceman was scared and he never shows his fear. The fact that he would admit he was scared and told Zeus, speaks volumes about their relationship. The way Zeus handled the vulnerable confession, and the way Iceman accepted it, clearly illustrated the power of their relationship. Again, developed in such a brief time.'

'I told you so.'

'Grace, did you really say, I told you so? Are we on the playground?'

Over the laughter the two enjoyed, Grace managed, 'Well, I did.'

CHAPTER FIFTEEN

Bootlegging was going well, as was school and basketball. Army improved to 16-9 and could invert the 9-17 record from the prior year with a win. The last regular season game was against Navy. With a win, Army would be 17-9 compared to 9-17 for the final regular season record. The game was in Annapolis, Navy's home court and the Army team took a bus to the airport. On the bus, Coach Durham asked his coaching staff. 'Who is watching Collins?'

Iceman tended to disappear in airports, visit cougar town, flirt for free drinks using his uniform, and board the flight at the last second. The coaching staff were quiet as they did not want the challenge nor the responsibility of the mission impossible. Coach Durham decided to assign the detail to Coach Phillips. 'He is all yours.'

As soon as they got off the bus, Coach Phillips was prepared to lay down the law when he asked, 'Where is Collins?'

Collins was already a fart in the wind. He had checked his bag with the skycap, given him a fiver, dashed for a different terminal, cleared security and headed to the pub. Because Coach Durham was anxious for the big game against their rival, the team arrived two hours ahead of boarding. Iceman had plenty of time to implement plan cougar and have a craic. He arrived at his secret spot in a remote corner of the airport in the American Airlines terminal as the team flew United. As he approached, the bartender laughed. 'Hello, a Guinness and Jameson coming up.'

'Thanks, lad.'

'Well, aren't you the cutest man ever?! Love a man in uniform.' A lady business traveler on an expense account asked, impressed with Iceman in his Dress Grey uniform.

'I get that a lot.'

'I bet you do. Not just cute, but sassy and charming. Daryl, put those on my check.'

Iceman went into humble mode. 'You really don't need to do that.' He said with a boyish smile.

'My pleasure.' She responded.

'You are too kind. Do you have any Irish in you?' Iceman asked over his pint of Guinness with a devilish grin.

'No, I am Greek Italian.' She responded. 'Why do you ask?'

'Do you want some Irish in you? That was a reference to my wiener.' They both laughed. 'Old joke, but it's all I got to thank you for the snacks.'

'What is your name and why are you here?'

'I am catching a flight for a basketball game.' He intentionally omitted his name.

'Are you going to be famous?' The cougar asked.

'I am shooting for infamous.'

The coaches were on a manhunt while Iceman enjoyed the free conversation, turkey sandwich, Guinness and a Jameson. When his time was up, Iceman slowly walked to the next terminal and wandered into the boarding line. Upon his casual arrival, Coach Phillips immediately exploded, 'Where were you?'

'Coach, where were you? I was lost and everybody left me. My feelings were hurt.' Iceman said with a smile that clearly celebrated the moment of fun he felt he deserved.

Upon landing at their destination, the team managers took the team's bags to the hotel in one bus along with the support crew, which included press and army officer representatives. Colonel Sullivan had made the trip. The hoop team headed for the Naval Academy with their carry-on bags that contained their practice gear. After the 90-minute flight, power nap and bus ride, Iceman was ready for practice. After breaking a sweat and losing the last of the booze, Iceman was back in form. After practice, he called the team together in the visiting team locker room and began. 'Fuck Navy, I took a shit in the toilet and didn't flush.' The problem was that the Navy had a tremendous player and were ranked nationally in the top 20. Army was ranked in the top 75. Army really had no chance. 'Fellas, we are outgunned, but that doesn't mean we can't fight. Whatever happens early in the game, just keep the fight. Remember your General MacArthur: *On the fields of friendly strife are sown the seeds that on other days, on other fields, will bear the fruits of victory.* While our strife will never be friendly, the message still applies. What we do against Navy defines us.' In his heart, he believed they could win both on the court and possibly the scoreboard. 'If we stay together and fight, we win the court. If we score more points than those bitches, we win the scoreboard. I am going to fuck them up, anyone else?'

The locker room exploded in the player's only meeting. Willie Mac ignited the chant. 'Who, Navy? Who, Navy?'

Back at the hotel after dinner, Iceman approached the coaches in private and made a request. 'I want Kong to start.'

'He hasn't played a minute all season.' Durham responded, baffled by Iceman's request.

'So, he is rested. We all know why he is here. He is 7 feet, 300 pounds, guilty of collecting money for the NY mob and the judge offered him jail or the military, because his father was some bigshot on Wall St. He enlisted, and while brutally violent, is also incredibly bright. He tested off the charts and West Point found him. Trust me, if we surround him with our best four, Kong will overpower Mr. Wonderful and even take the soul of Mr. Freak, the 6'9' concert pianist. I can see it in his eyes; he wants none of a man like Kong. King Kong will expose him as the soft man that he is.'

Both coaches immediately replied. 'No.'

'Then Thor and I have injuries and Willie Mac is working through a high ankle sprain. I apologize for my decency, but it was not an ask.'

Both coaches looked at each other in resignation and Coach Durham spouted. 'You are a fucking pain in the ass, but fine. I'll think about it.'

'Coach, that is the first time I ever heard you curse, so maybe this team is no longer a bag of bitches. I agree that I am a pain in the ass, but have I ever been wrong? If not for me, you both would have been canned like tuna after this season, so let's stop the circle jerk. I am better at this than you will ever be at anything in your life. Rather than getting fired, the two of you will get a three-year extension and a new shoe contract that will double in value, because we don't suck. You will do what I say, because I am right and you are in the last year of your contract. You wanna dance? I'll dance! It's your call, but I'll make you famous. I am saving you from yourself and a job selling life insurance. Good talk.'

Iceman stormed away; not finished, he turned back and screamed at the coaches, 'How many did you lose to Navy by last year?

22? Fuck off if you think I am ever losing by 22. We will never have this conversation again.'

Iceman stalked to find Kong. When Ice caught up to him, he punched Kong in the chest. 'Kong, if you shit the bed, I will beat you.'

'Iceman, what?' Kong was genuinely confused as he dressed without urgency for the game.

'I got you in the starting lineup. You better do everything I say, or I am going to look like a clown for believing in you. You suck at basketball, but you are a bad man.'

'Ok?'

'You got to beat the shit out of the talent. He is a nice man. You, well, you are close to evil without crossing the line. On every screen, remember he is a lefty punch him in his left bicep, not obvious, just enough to wear him down. Relentless pressure will be the key. Do not worry about a rebound, never turn your back on him, always your eyes on his eyes and keep him away. We need to make this four-on-four and not five-against-five. I believe you can make him cry. Everything came easy to this fuck. Good looking, smart as shit, great son, amazing athlete, musical, fucker can probably paint impressionist art, but I know he has never been in a fight. That ends today. Got me? On every shot that goes up, jab him in the kidneys or the bicep. The refs are idiots; they'll watch the ball and not the beating.'

Iceman was riding the end of his comic flight, he felt invincible and answered to no one. The tone he took with his coaches, the supreme confidence he felt attacking Navy and his near-violent confrontation with Kong served as examples of his manic episode.

On the jump ball, Navy, as expected, got possession. Iceman ran over and jabbed the talent in the kidney with his powerful left and winked at Kong. 'This be on!' he yelled. 'Fuck the prom king. Prom King is going down. We got King Kong.' Game on.

Army fought the good fight. Kong took talent's pride and Iceman was on fire. The battle faded with 10 minutes left in the game. With 10 minutes remaining, the game was tied at 48, but Kong fouled out. Without Kong, Army held strong, but the talent was well, the talent. He was simply amazing and Army lost by five. After the game, the teams went to shake hands. The first Navy player in line was from Chicago, who had played against Iceman in high school. The midshipman was a senior and Iceman was a freshman. He started a chant of 10 years, 10 years, as Navy had beaten Army for 10 consecutive years. Unfortunately, Iceman took exception and knocked him to the ground with a left hook. He proceeded to stand over the dazed Midshipman and spat out, 'We will never lose to you fucks again on my watch.' While Iceman was dropping a bad habit, the Army team assembled for a fight behind him. Navy, not prepared for the confrontation, was confused. Iceman erupted. 'Fuck them, let's go. You go, we go.' An expression taught him from the Chicago Fire Department and the movie Backdraft. He took one step towards Navy with Kong on his heels and a phalanx behind him. They lost the game, but disrespect demanded a beating.

A commander from Navy and Colonel Sullivan intervened, ordering, 'Stand down.' Colonel Sullivan looked at the fire in Iceman's eyes and asked him to stand down. 'Please, Jack, stop.'

'Yes, sir. Sorry.' With that, he looked at Navy with, I'll remember this disrespect forever, eyes. Iceman smirked at his fellow Chicagoan. 'Next play, tell your boys they're mine. Enjoy it, and while you will be gone, tell them the man be coming.' He turned to his teammates with his eyes still on Navy, 'Stand down, lads.'

After a shower and the press, Iceman walked out and bumped into the talent. 'Good game, money. You are really good.' Iceman shook the man's hand.

He responded. 'So are you, Jack. We cool?'

'Of course, that was just the mission. You bring what you've got; your team has talent, we don't, but doesn't mean you can't test a man's will. How you think we won these many games? We suck, but we fight. I am incredibly impressed with your finish to the game. I thought you would quit, but you fought back. Well done.'

'You are a hell of a leader, Jack.'

'I don't know about all that, but what I do know is Nick, the captain of the Navy rugby team, well, his dad and my dad made the flight from Chicago. They are hosting a little something, something at the Hyatt. Nick is bringing a few rugby players. Be cool if you and a few of your lads popped over for food and a beer. Wait, one condition: you got to bring my homeboy from the Southside over.'

'You sure?'

Iceman answered. 'Yes, we fought a good fight and Navy won for the last time on my watch, but we are brothers in arms. Right?'

'Right.'

'Goddamn, you and my roommate are the most proper brothers I have ever met in my life. Peace.' With that, they hand gripped and butt out hugged.

* * *

'Dad, I have a request and I understand if you need to say no. I invited five of the Navy hoop players to join the few Rugby players we discussed. I already committed to the hoop players and space will be tight. Would you book the suite next door with adjourning doors?'

'Sure, Jackie, no problem, but I think the suite may be booked. The hotel is busy.' Jack's father and his childhood friend were excited to spend time with their sons.

'I'll handle that, but I wanted to check with you first.'

'Very well. I'll make sure there is enough food, but you will explain the large credit card bill to your mother.' He said with a smile.

'No need for more food. I will order pizza and pay cash. I just can't book the suite under NCAA regulations.'

'I see. Are you sure you are permitted to host this engagement?' His father cross-examined Jack.

'Yeah, all good, and dad, mommy likes me more than you, so no trouble on your allowance.' They actually giggled, both loving the same classy lady that they never crossed. A beautiful smile backed by warm Irish charm masked a tough lady they both respected, and while neither would admit it, they were both a little afraid of.

'Thanks, Dad.' With that, Iceman walked to the front desk. 'Hello, how have you been?' He said to the concierge.

'Well, and you?'

'I am in a bit of a pickle and was looking for a little help. My father would like to book the suite next door to us tonight, because we just played Navy in hoops and want to chill. My pops and his buddy have rooms, Army has 26 rooms and my dad already rented a suite to allow us to relax. The thing is, a handful of Navy rugby and basketball players are coming over. We need the space next door.'

'I am sorry, there is nothing I can do; it is booked.'

'How do you want to handle this? The easy or hard way?' Iceman asked, not surprised, but amazed at the concierge's elitist ignorance.

'I do not understand?' Replied the concierge.

'I understand and that's what matters. We can be gentlemen. You will offer a better suite to the current occupants at the same price, period. They are happy and we are happy.' Iceman was cut off.

'I cannot do this.'

'What I do know is you will allow me to finish, that I do know. I am prepared to trash a good portion of the Army rooms and force you to face public scrutiny for disrespecting Army and Navy. Good luck working through the Pentagon for collection on damages and complaints.' The concierge went to speak. 'Shut up! I am speaking to you; you are a rude little man. I represent a uniform and you dress up for a costume party. Again, we get the suite, you rent another suite and we act like gentlemen, but if you want to fuck over the people that provide the blanket of freedom that allows you to continue to act like an arrogant fuck in some knock-off designer suit, that's your call. You have a choice, much like I do when I can, by right, take a fork and shove it in my own eye. My right, but does that make it a good idea?' Iceman stared at the concierge. Dangled his fingers at his side like a gunfighter, leaned in much too close and whispered. 'Take peace and the extra revenue, or I will walk away from the destroyed rooms, find you, and well, it won't be pleasant. Got me?'

'I'll see what I can do.' The concierge responded with fear, but not conviction.

Iceman grabbed him by the tie and not gentle like before. 'That's fine and I will start letting the lads off the leash. Please keep me informed, as I will not need to keep you informed. You will most certainly know by the noise that will carry all the way to your little perch. Get more people on the phones, because there will be complaints and plenty of them. I thank you in advance for the upgrade in suites for our neighbors and the bottle of champagne I was prepared to buy them. You will obviously now deliver the champagne compliments of the house. Good talk, you have one hour.' The stupidity of man continued to stun Iceman.

Two hours later, the food provided by Jack's father, whom he loved and respected, was redirected to appetizers. The main course arrived later in the form of 12 pizzas funded by Jack. The Army basketball and Navy rugby players all met and began to warm up to each other. Jack interrupted the laughter. 'Lads, I invited a few additional guests and remember we are brothers in arms.' With that, he opened the other suite and the Navy ballers walked in. 'Bitches be bitches, let's get our jump on. However, I promised the douche at the front desk we would be respectful to our neighbors. Cool?' Heads nodded around the room.

The gathering was electric and all had fun. The group had the feel of a family reunion. Even having just met, they were a family built on similar experiences, frustrations and commit-ments. The Midshipmen and Cadets laughed, but did not party. Beer, pizza, cards, coupled with great appetizers, fueled a great night. Jack walked over to his dad and said simply, 'Thanks.'

His dad replied, 'No, Jack, this is really something. Thank you. I have no idea how you pull these things off, but you just make it better. I am so proud of you.' Jack's dad did the totally unex-pected and hugged him. Jack was never told by his father that he was proud of him, let alone receive a hug. Both the hug and the compliment stunned Jack into a moment of vulnerability that forced him to drop his head, lean in, tear up and mumble. 'Thanks, dad. You are such a good man. I will be too.'

'You already are son.'

Jack wished Zeus were able to get off post to rock the night. Zeus missing bothered him. With that thought in his head, Jack found Nick as he exited the door. 'Nick, wait up. Good luck this rugby season.'

'Thanks, Jack. This was fun.'

'Yeah, yeah, yeah. I mean, good luck this season. You're fucked.'

Jack's comment caught Nick by surprise. 'Jack, we beat Army last year.'

'You haven't met Zeus.'

CHAPTER SIXTEEN

With the basketball season over, Iceman turned his attention to training, because he knew he had to get stronger for his second season. He hung tough in his first season, but he was a child playing with men. He vowed to be ready for his second season. He would no longer hold the line; he would establish it. He was determined to add 15 pounds of muscle to his 185lbs frame. He awoke every morning at 4:45, worked his core and stretched while the other cadets slept. When they woke, he joined the normal routine. Ice played in limited scrimmages and chose to bury himself in the weight room. He drank and took supplements to gain weight and get healthier. He asked Reese to provide two sandwiches after every meal to take to the barracks. He ate to the point that it became a chore. He estimated his calorie intake at 10,000 a day. He lifted until his legs made the run back to the barracks almost unmanageable and his arms could not be raised above his shoulders. Wiping himself after using the restroom was difficult. He was obsessed with being ready for the next season.

Iceman's commitment to the offseason was in the shadows of the new star. The season was spring and spring brought rugby season, the season of Zeus.

Iceman set off on a mission to make Zeus' season amazing. Zeus was incredibly great to Iceman; the time had come to repay all the generosity. Iceman was determined to build a circus to make Zeus' rugby season memorable. He set off on one of his infamous walks and an idea he had been brewing began to finalize.

Three days later, Iceman called the usual suspects for room cleaning, which was code for whiskey party. 'Ok, let's chat. I got the plan for rugby season. I'll buy a $4000 cargo van and title it in Reese's or Ty's name; they're already in. Reese and Ty will stock the van, park it in the hills and rotate parking lots using different parking passes. Marcus, from the sports complex, is hooking me up with several parking passes. I'll tell Reese and Ty when this is over, they can keep the van, or the business going and consider it profit-sharing. I will have 10 additional keys made for the van. Four for us and an additional six will comprise the Members of the Key. Members of the Key are required to sign a receipt for the key. If they feel the need to rat, we hold the document as leverage. They did the crime, they alone do the time. Members of the Key must always maintain possession of their key and may escort up to three guests to the van during their assigned usage times. A member, I say again, must always be present. Any violation of the rules will be met with membership immediately revoked and a beat down. We will keep our distance from the ownership of the plan and no direct connection will be linked to us. Reese and Ty will issue the keys and assign a color. They will hold the color directory to identify each member. The members will not know the identity of the other members. An assigned book in the stacks in the library will house the master calendar. Each member or color will have their own book. The key members provide for their guests; that is not our problem. The 300% markup generates profit. The members will push the product and take the risk. The van is used to recruit increased sales in the industrial cleaning business. No prepayment, no booze. Reese and Ty will fill the van and cut the alcohol when transferring it to the spray bottle. We have already started to water down the spray bottles in the barracks, thus boosting our returns. We also buy cheap whiskey and call it top shelf. These practices obviously do not apply to us and we continue to roll with only top shelf. The business will grow exponentially from the spray bottles purchased and brought back to the barracks by the guests. This is a safer and more profitable delivery system, and more fun too. Hanging in the woods on a nice night, say, before a rugby game, will be fun. Obviously, none of the rules apply to me.'

Thor jumped in. 'Especially when the ladies start meeting us up there.'

Iceman smiled. 'Roger that.'

Thor continued his line of questioning. 'What do I get out of it?'

Iceman dismissed him. 'A key.'

'None of the profit?'

'Roger that.'

* * *

Iceman grabbed Zapata, Thor, Ty and Reese to discuss the first home rugby match. 'Ok, here is the deal: Zeus has his first Rugby game and I don't know fuck about rugby either, but I do know Zeus, so you bitches are going to represent in a big way. We will tailgate, get tuned up and support Zeus. It is non-negotiable, nor am I. Ty and Reese bring some brothers to support a brother. I also expect you two to provide the spicy chicken wings. Zapata, Thor and I will rally the cadets. Got it! That was not a question.'

Heads nodded.

Iceman continued. 'Usually, 40 people show up to these games. We will bring 200 motherfuckers to every home game. Period. Each of you is required to bring your share to the game. Be

127

extremely careful with your limited and carefully screened invitations to the tailgate. Meet most of your guests at the game. Be sure of the guests you invite to the tailgate, because if you are sure about them, you better be sure. I don't want to get jammed up with dickheads exposed at a large tailgate. All about risk, got me?'

All agreed.

* * *

As the Army team took the field, a community of fans fresh off a bootlegger tailgate erupted and almost started to yell, 'Fuck 'em up, Zeus.'

Iceman, at the last second, halted the enthusiasm, 'Officers present, PG language only.' With those words of wisdom, the chant was modified to Zeus, Zeus, Zeus.'

Iceman walked behind the visiting team's bench and bellowed. 'Go home and save yourself the embarrassment. I hope your parents and girlfriends aren't here. You should have stayed home. Just go home.' The chant of Zeus continued to echo through the crowd.

Zeus was only described as Hershel Walker at Georgia, or Bo Jackson at Auburn. Watching Zeus, the 200 fans shared the same sentiment of what was that? He was amazing and simply different. He was everywhere. When he got the football in the open field, the defenders parted like the Red Sea. The other team was terrified of him. Standing 6'3', weighing 235 with a 4.45 speed, he was just too much for the opponent. He was not only physically overwhelming, but he was also smarter. Zeus started playing the game at seven and was well-coached. While the other players were raised on pee wee football and little league baseball, Zeus played rugby. On defense, he knew where the next pass was going before the opponent pitched it. Zeus didn't really play a position, he played Zeus. He was everywhere. His tackles were violent; some were made with such force that the crowd was made uncomfortable. On the rugby field, Zeus was transformed into a Zulu warrior. The guy Iceman knew was not the rugby player he was watching. He never let up and was a man possessed. After Army had immediately destroyed Harvard, Zeus was pulled halfway through the match.

Ty laughed. 'Fuck that shit. We'll be bringing more to watch. I didn't know a brother be wrecking rugby. This shit is tight.'

Reese responded. 'Right, true that. Zeus brought the heat.'

Ty asked Iceman. 'Why didn't you tell us about this shit, it's tight?'

'What the fuck, because I am white, I know about rugby? You're black and you don't know shit about hoops, motherfucker.' Iceman looked ready to throw down. The group laughed hard, coming down from their buzz. 'Shit, it's a dumb-looking football, but Zeus is a beast, know what I am saying?!'

Heads nodded all around and Zapata chimed in. 'Dude, he is a load. Fuck, this is awesome.'

Iceman just nodded, proud of his guy. 'Love the fact they took Harvard's soul from the jump. I hate Ivy League schools.'

After the match and handshake, Zeus walked over to his crew. The Zeus from the barracks was back and the Zulu warrior was put away until the next match.

Iceman greeted his lad with a look of, wow. The rest just shook their heads in awe.

Iceman broke his silent amazement and asked. 'Zeus, you weren't like that in boxing. You won, of course, but you were a man on fire out there. Where did that rage come from?'

'I don't like boxing. I love rugby.'

Iceman nodded and responded. 'Sure, sure, I can see that; it makes sense.'

The celebration of Zeus was interrupted by the three senior officers in attendance. They wanted to shake Zeus' hand and be close to greatness. Colonel Sullivan carefully watched from a distance and absorbed the display. Word quickly spread about Zeus and the remaining home matches had to be moved to the football stadium. Most of Michie Stadium remained sealed as capacity was 40,000, but two sections remained open to accommodate the 500-1,000 new rugby fans in attendance. A concession stand was even opened and restrooms were needed. Zeus became a can't miss cheering. He never disappointed. In fairness, and Zeus brought this to Ice's attention, his teammates were well-conditioned and good in their own right. When Zeus was pulled, the opponents never cut into the lead. The other members of the Army team were smart, disciplined and fierce.

Army went on to win the national championship with ease, with Zeus awarded the most outstanding player in the country.

CHAPTER SEVENTEEN

'Zeus, I got summer school, although I didn't fail anything. Wait, I was on the honor roll. I was also assigned to Airborne school and a pathfinding school. I get five days off! What the fuck is this summer assignment all about?'

'Me too. Don't know.' Zeus shrugged.

'All the others who didn't fail a class go to Camp Buckner after getting six weeks off and easy shit. What the fuck?'

'Don't know.'

'What are you doing with your five days?' Iceman asked, resigned to accept his summer fate.

'Going home to see my mam.'

'Can I come?' Iceman did not want to return to the Southside of Chicago, so he asked to join Zeus to feed his desire to travel whenever time allowed.

'Yes.' Zeus answered and was excited to have the company.

'Can I chill at your mom's place?'

'Of course.'

'Am I going to meet that chick? That girl you met over Christmas break. Does she have hot friends?'

'No, remember she moved to Australia.'

'Right, thanks, man, for the invite.'

* * *

Zeus and Ice took two classes called military counterterrorism and military countermeasures. There were only six cadets in the class. They left Thayer Hall after the first day of summer school classes.

Iceman asked Zeus. 'What the fuck was that?'

'Don't know.'

'Why are we being forced to take those two classes?'

'Don't know.'

'The classes don't fit with being a second lieutenant, right?'

'Don't know.'

'For a smart motherfucker, you don't know much.'

'For a dumb motherfucker, you sure do talk a lot.'

'Really?' Iceman feigned offense to Zeus' insult.

'Iceman, I'm sor...'

'Lad, it was funny, so it's free. I was just joking too.'

'Cool, just is what it is.' Zeus summarized the twins' situation.

'Roger that, but after one last thought. Why are we being treated differently? Not just this summer bullshit, but everything, the loaded class schedule, the special...'

Zeus interrupted. 'Don't know. Now shut up, 20 questions is over.'

'Roger that, but you didn't say please, so kind of rude.' Iceman and Zeus smiled and continued their walk to the barracks.

* * *

With their successful completion of their summer courses, Iceman and Zeus immediately headed to JFK. They were late, so Ice could not introduce Zeus to cougar town. The twins made up for it on the six-hour international flight that included complimentary drinks. The flight attendants were only too willing to overserve the twins.

Seamus's mam met them at Shannon airport. Jack fell back as Seamus rushed to his mam and gave her a giant hug. After they hugged, she pulled back, leaving her outstretched arms resting on Seamus' mighty shoulders and observed. 'You look good, filled out some more.'

Seamus smiled and Jack thought. Filled out some? How could she notice? He was a monster when I met him.

Mrs. Collins could not resist. 'Give your mam another hug.'

As they parted, their eyes remained fixed on each other as they walked away towards the car.

Jack felt awkward and wished he had not come, but reluctantly broke their trance. 'Excuse me, sorry, very sorry. I need to visit baggage claim to retrieve my bag.'

Seamus and Mrs. Collins turned to each other and laughed. 'I am so embarrassed. How very rude of me.'

'I understand, Mrs. Collins.' Jack never felt more like a third wheel in his life.

* * *

The ride from the airport was not long, but very pleasant. Mrs. Collins ensured Jack was a part of the conversation.

'Jack, Seamus told me you have family in Ireland.'

'Yes, Mrs. Collins, I have second cousins, aunts and uncles, mostly spread along the west coast.'

'Some close to us?'

'Yes, ma'am. Very.'

'Jack, please don't call me ma'am. I am not old enough yet.'

'Yes, ma… Mrs. Collins.'

'Have you ever visited?' She asked.

'Yes, twice when I was young.'

'You are still young.' Mrs. Collins joked.

'Fair enough when I was six and eleven.' Jack answered.

As they turned into the house, Jack was immediately impressed. A gorgeous rehabbed five-bedroom home on a small lake decorated with a warm feel. Mrs. Collins instructed Seamus to show Jack to his room and come down for sandwiches.

Jack enjoyed the sandwiches. 'Mrs. Collins, thank you for the meal and you have a lovely home.'

'Thank you. Mr. Collins and I loved working with the contractors together. We did the interior design together and Mr. Collins guided the architects. A true labor of love.'

'It certainly shows. The house has great natural light, amazing views and a powerful warmth.'

'Well, aren't you sweet for saying so?! Seamus, why don't you take your car and show Jack around?'

Jack had the addresses, provided by his godmother, to a couple family members near Ennis.

'Seamus, before we hit the pub, would you mind doing a drive-by just to see my family's houses?' Jack asked.

'Sure, no problem.' After Iceman gave Zeus the addresses, 'I know where they are, not far at all.'

The twins drove past two modest, well-maintained homes, saw a few sights and returned the car. They had decided to walk the mile, to allow freedom of intake, to the local pub named O'Hagan's.

They bellied up to the bar and ordered the usual.

The bartender brought the drinks and asked Seamus. 'You're the kid rugby player, right? I never got your name; we just called you Wonder Boy. Where have you gone to?

'My name is Seamus Collins, nice to meet you. Went off to America to university.'

'Dillion,' and they shook hands, 'and your lad?'

'My name is Jack.'

'An American. You met at university?'

Jack nodded. 'Roommates.'

'Where do you share a room?'

Seamus answered. 'West Point.'

'Military men. Seamus, how did you get mixed up in all this?' Dillion asked as he cleaned used pint glasses.

'Dual citizenship. My dad was from America.'

'I see. Jack, your roommate was a terror in rugby. He practiced with the men's club team to get competition. Even at an early age, he was the best man as a boy on the pitch. We expected him to play on the national team. Do you still play in America?'

Jack interrupted. 'He still plays. I'm confident that you were a far better match for him than anything he faced in America. He destroyed last season. Was MVP in all the land.'

'I'll buy a round to that and join you in the short one.'

The twins walked home to find Mrs. Collins had left lamb stew on the stove for them. Seamus grabbed the ladle and scooped several for them to enjoy. He handed Jack half a loaf of brown bread he had broken off and half a stick of butter to go with the stew. Hearing the noise, Mrs. Collins walked down to say good-night. She found the boys eating quickly and quietly. She brought them Guinness to wash the stew down.

'Mrs. Collins, I love lamb stew and this is the best I have ever had. Thank you.'

'Jack, you are quick with the lovely compliments. I am glad you are enjoying it, or should I say enjoyed it?! Would you care for more? There is plenty.' She looked again and laughed. 'There was plenty, but there is still enough left.'

'Thank you.' Jack was not shy about his lamb stew.

After she served Jack, she kissed Seamus good night. 'Just leave the dishes in the sink. I am off to bed, so I'll get to them in the morning.'

Jack went to protest, but Seamus cut him off. 'Good night, mam. Thanks, I love you.'

'You are welcome. Good night, Jack, sleep well.'

Still confused, Jack followed along. 'Good night.' He turned to Seamus. 'We're not letting her do the dishes. You know my policy.'

'Of course not, but if we protested, she would have stayed awake and insisted she cleaned them herself. Let her go to bed, grab us another beer and we will do the dishes.'

'Got it. Say, Zeus, I was thinking of popping over to my cousins on Saturday. Do you want to come?'

'Sure.'

'Cool, do you think your mom will want to go?'

'Yes. What time is the party?' Seamus asked.

'Not sure, I haven't spoken with them.'

'Aren't you going to ring first? Are you sure there is a gathering, and if so, are you confident my mam and I can come?' Seamus struggled to understand Jack's ability to extend invitations without a scheduled engagement.

'No need. Family. Everything will be fine.'

* * *

The three began their pilgrimage on Saturday afternoon by visiting the first house on Jack's list. The house was empty.

'You should have called.' Seamus lectured Jack.

'We're fine. Just go to the other house.'

When they arrived at the second house, both Clare families were present, along with other family members who lived in the general area. In all, 25 family members gathered to welcome Jack. Introductions were made and the fun started. Seamus was amazed; they acted like they had just seen each other last week-end. There was nothing uncomfortable about the visit. Seamus and his mam just slid right into the mix and were treated like old friends.

'Mrs. Collins, what a pleasure it is to meet you.' Looking over at Seamus, Jack's aunt continued. 'And what a gorgeous young man.'

'Thank you and please call me Mary.'

The party raged on and the fun extended into the evening. During cleanup, Jack's cousins Pat, Tim and Matt asked the twins to join them at the pub. The twins didn't hesitate. Goodbyes were shared and Mrs. Collins drove home. The five enjoyed each other's company and Seamus remained in awe at the chemistry shared by cousins who barely knew each other and had not seen each other in almost 10 years.

Waiting for the taxi, Seamus turned to Jack. 'What a family, but I just don't understand it. You all acted so familiar.'

'Fruit from the same tree. We are family.' Jack simply answered.

'It was like they knew you were coming.'

'They did, my godmother set it up.'

Zeus laughed at the response. 'I can only imagine what the Chicago family parties are like.'

'No, you can't.'

* * *

The next day, the twins were treated to a full Irish breakfast courtesy of Mrs. Collins. After the giant breakfast, Jack lay on the couch in a food coma.

Seamus asked. 'Fishing is a big thing out here. Do you want to go?' Ice looked at him like he was stupid. 'Didn't think so.'

Zeus put on a football match and Ice said, 'Perfect.'

'I thought you hated soccer.'

'I do. The game is so boring it will put me to sleep. I am taking a nap.'

After a three-hour nap, Seamus asked Jack. 'Do you want to go to O'Hagan's for food and watch the rugby match?'

'Sounds good.'

They walked down to the pub and took a seat at the bar. They said hello to Dillion, ordered food and revisited stories from the visit to Jack's family. Jack was interrupted in the middle of a story by Seamus' head turn.

Iceman asked. 'What's up? What's wrong?'

'Nothing.' Zeus responded as he tried to make his massive frame small.

Iceman turned around and saw five guys roughly their age gathering around a table. 'You know them?'

'High school.'

Iceman looked again and made eye contact with one in the group. 'Dicks?'

'Yes.'

'The guy in the rugby, well… they're all wearing rugby shirts. The guy in the tweed hat, is he the biggest prick?' Iceman asked, referring to the guy he had made eye contact with.

'Yes.'

'Thought so.'

'Iceman, don't, seriously don't.' Iceman just turned and looked at Zeus.

Dillion came over to talk to the twins to prevent trouble and Iceman just looked at him. Startled, Dillion slowly walked back without saying a word. He poured the twins a Guinness and, while it settled, went to get their whiskey. He paused and questioned the value of whiskey as tempers were escalating. He noticed everyone's temper was up, but Jack's. He was uncomfortably calm. He served the round and proceeded to walk around the bar and approached Rory, the guy in the hat. 'They are minding their own business, let them be. There are five of you and two of them. Let it be.'

Rory nodded while Iceman begged to himself: *Please, give me a reason.* At the same time, Zeus begged to himself: *Please, don't give him a reason.*

Rory rose, followed by his crew. Zeus stood to block their path to Iceman.

Over Zeus, Rory asked, 'So, Seamus, who's your friend? Hey friend, are you a rich kid too? A kid that got everything he ever wanted.'

Without bothering to turn and face him, Iceman simply responded with eyes front. 'Nope.'

'Just an American joining his pampered friend to see how the other half lives?'

'And visiting family.' Iceman coolly responded, enjoying his pint.

Ignoring Ice's comment, Rory followed his usual script. 'Seamus, what brings you back to mingle with the common folk? How do you know your friend?'

'He's my roommate.'

'I'm sorry, roommates?' Rory laughed. Ice looked up at Dillion behind the bar, who shook his head to convey that it was not his fault. Iceman nodded as Rory continued. 'So, Seamus, did America turn you into a fairy? Are you two fairies? I bet you like to suck cock.'

Without turning around, Iceman smiled. 'All I can get.' He used a quote from one of his idols, Paul Newman, in the movie Slapshot to embarrass and taunt Rory. Ice was close to getting his reason.

'What are you a wiseass?' Rory asked in a threatening tone, trying to regain control of the situation.

Ice smiled again with his eyes front. 'No, it only appears that way to you, because you are a dumbass.' Behind the bar, Dillion held back his laugh.

Rory took exception to Dillion's response and screamed. 'What are you fucking laughing at?'

Iceman removed his wristwatch, put it in his pocket and replied. 'You.'

Zeus saw the wristwatch come off, the equivalent of a samurai warrior drawing his sword. There must be blood. 'Iceman, let it go.'

'I'm good, Zeus.'

Rory laughed. 'Did you hear that? The fairies have pet names.' The crew's laughter added more gang confidence and encouragement to Rory. 'You know what? Turn around when I am talking to you.' He started to walk towards Iceman. Zeus shook his head. Big mistake. Rory grabbed Iceman's right shoulder and attempted to spin him around. Iceman did not move. Rory went to reload, pushing Iceman's shoulder forward to gain momentum in a second effort to spin Iceman around to face him. Rory miscalculated. Iceman used the forward momentum against Rory. Iceman, in a flash, swung his left arm, grabbed Rory's right wrist and pulled him hard. Rory rocketed forward and smashed his head against the bar. Iceman refused to release his vice grip. He slid his right hand into Rory's secured hand. Ice interlocked thumbs with Rory and snapped his wrist. Rory had to turn his body to follow the violent twist. If he had remained standing, his wrist would have broken. So, he chose to roll to the floor. Iceman released his grip and took a step back to join Zeus. Rory jumped up, still lightheaded from kissing the bar in a rage, ready to attack Iceman, but he paused. The crew was confused by their leader's concern. Rory thought: The American should be scared; five of us and two of them. Rory's rage had quickly turned to fear. He made eye contact with Iceman and received no emotion, only a chilling stare. Ice looked right through him, like he was not even there. Rory felt he had ceased to exist. Rory had never felt so small.

Dillion bailed Rory out of big trouble. 'Rory, grab your things, your mates and go home. You had a long day and it is closing time.'

'What about those two? We are your regulars. We will be here long after they are gone. We have been good customers. You owe us.'

'I owe you 'thanks' and 'I look forward to seeing you again soon.' Now, go home.'

Dillion smartly responded. 'Fuck you.'

Rory yelled as he headed for the door and turned back. 'And fuck the both of you too.'

'Rory, I am in town for a couple more days, I won't be seeing you again. Got me?' Iceman served notice as he put on his watch and returned his attention to his Guinness.

After Rory made his exit a little production, Dillion apologized to Seamus and Jack. 'Buy you another round? I'll join you. I'll clean up in the morning. It'll give Rory a chance to cool off and head home.'

Jack shook his head. 'He's not going home. He knows where Seamus lives and the route home for us. He'll make another go at us.'

After a second round with Dillion, the boys said their goodbyes. The walk home was peaceful, to Iceman's disappointment and Zeus's relief. Iceman thought to himself, *Rory has a bit of sense.* Although they only had five days to spend in Ireland, the twins enjoyed the trip.

CHAPTER EIGHTEEN

'Six minutes, six minutes shuffle to the door.'

As the twins hooked up, Iceman whispered to Zeus, because he was not taking on the jump master. 'Why are we jumping out of a perfectly good airplane?'

'Shut up.'

'You know, in the Battle Of The Bulge, the paratroopers were critical to holding the line while the…'

'I said shut up.'

'You're scared. Big bad Zeus is scared of heights. Got it.'

Zeus did not whisper. 'I said shut up.'

The Master Sergeant, a tower of male dominance, marched down the aisle and screamed. 'Are the twins deliberately trying to fuck up my perfectly planned jump? Are you intentionally insulting me?'

The twins yelled back over the roar of the engines and the open door. 'No, Master Sergeant.'

'Then shut the fuck up.'

'Yes, Master Sergeant.'

Waiting for the Master Sergeant to return to his post as Jump Master, Iceman whispered to Zeus. 'Cool man, just your time of the month. We'll be fine. Just breathe.'

'Shut up.'

To distract Zeus from falling, rather than jumping off an airplane, Ice continued his antics. 'Roger that. Did I tell you about my prom disaster in high school? So, it started poorly and…'

'Dude.'

'Wait, it's our turn. Let's go.'

With that, the twins shuffled to the exit, jumped and rolled upon contact with the ground to avoid ankle injuries.

Airborne school passed quickly and revealed the twins' mutual disdain for heights. The three short weeks, as it was referred to, were not a summer vacation for the twins. At the end of three short weeks, the twins finished first and second in their class. Ice beat Zeus, but never said a word in celebration. He shut up and held his slight victory silently. However, Iceman found it interesting that a star basketball player would be exposed to ankle injury well ahead of other cadets.

Upon completion of Airborne training, the twins were taken to Pathfinder School.

'Zeus, shoot an azimuth? What are we doing? Are we going to use a plumb bob next?'

'Shut up.'

'I don't know if you realize this shut up thing is a reoccurring theme.'

'I realize it. Do you?'

'Do you think we need couples therapy? I feel like I am the only one committed to this relationship.' Iceman's boredom continued to fuel his banter with Zeus.

'Shut up.'

The twins finish first and second in their class again. Again, Ice beat out Zeus. He couldn't remain a gentleman in his second victory of the summer. 'Sorry, you lost again, but do you want to hold my medal?' The medal was a metaphor. There was no medal.

'Shut up.'

'Maybe, in a safe place, you can hold my medal, like when we go to couples therapy.'

'Dude.'

'Can I buy the best loser in the class a pint?' Iceman asked, knowing he had pushed Zeus to his limit.

'Yes.'

Iceman could not resist the need to push the conversation too far when he continued. 'Thanks. While I would not put, I got my ass kicked not once, but twice by Iceman. On your Christmas card, hold your head high.'

'Shut up.'

'Roger that, but one last thing. Thanks, we kick some serious ass.'

Head nods followed. Both knew they pushed each other to be the absolute best.

Iceman mumbled. 'My man.'

Zeus simply replied. 'Always.'

'Mr. Always, let's get drunk. I have an airport scam that works every time and with you, it will be a turkey shoot. Did you know

Benjamin Franklin thought the wild turkey and not the eagle should be the symbol of…'

'Shut up.'

'Roger that. Just that's the origin of turkey shoot was not addressed to wild turkeys, who are, in fact, very smart and difficult to hunt. The origin of the turkey shoot cliché is…'

'Your hustle better work, because I cannot hang with you sober much longer.'

'Imagine being me 24/7. You get a break from me, I don't.' Iceman said without regret, but acceptance.

'Sorry, Ice.'

'It's cool.'

'What now?'

'I gotta take a piss and find a cougar on an expense account.'

Both missions were accomplished. Iceman took his piss and found a cougar.

'Well, aren't you the cutest thing ever?' The cougar asked.

Iceman responded, 'Thank you.'

'I wasn't talking to you.'

Ice nodded and mumbled. 'Of course.' But he did enjoy his turkey sandwich and beers. Jack had to work to attract cougars; Seamus just had to walk in the room. Whatever. Jack thought. I got snacks.

* * *

The transition from summer back to West Point triggered an unscheduled meeting between Dr. Monroe and Colonel Sullivan.

'Good morning, Tom. Let's get started with the twins.' Dr. Monroe began. 'How was their summer?'

'Good morning, Grace. Productive, very productive. They both excelled in all areas of training.'

'Thank you for the overview, Tom. Let us dig a little deeper. I see Iceman was first and Zeus second in both schools they attended this summer. What is your takeaway?'

'The twins are exceptional. More important, they make each other better. The twins do not compete with others; they compete against each other. The gap between the twins and the field is enormous. The gap between the twins and the other candidates in our program is significant. Individually, the twins are better than the others, but together, they push each other to new heights. To beat their twin takes performance at the highest level I have ever seen in a candidate. My other takeaway is equally important. The twins love the intense competition they share with each other. While fierce, the competition is enjoyed and conducted with mutual respect. They thrive and celebrate the elevated level of accomplishment created by battling a formidable foe.'

'Why did Iceman win both times?'

'Timing. When Iceman's mental condition is in the high to exceedingly high, he is unbeatable. He draws on reserves of explosive energy that maintain the highest levels of performance for sustained periods of time. Iceman can only operate at that level for three to four months at a time. As we have discussed, when Iceman goes dark, Zeus is better. When Iceman is ramping up his high and escaping his low, the twins are even.'

'During our second meeting, Iceman was finishing his basketball season. We identified his condition as a bright comet, the hottest he runs. We were extremely interested in the probable dark period that we anticipated. Your report referred to his spring as a dark period. You commented that you were correct when you diagnosed Iceman as able to manage his condition. Please elaborate on the management process.'

Colonel Sullivan took a sip of water and cleared his throat. 'Iceman ended his basketball season at an emotional high. His meteoric rise produced endless energy and he felt a feeling of euphoria. His game against Navy brought witness to a man possessed. He returned to West Point after the trip to Annapolis with no fear or respect for failure. He was ready to launch several plans as an offshoot of bootlegging. Zeus listened to Ice's ideas and plans with a patient clinical assessment. Zeus challenged Iceman. He found the holes in Ice's plans and, because he respects Zeus, he listened. You instructed me during our last review to watch for Iceman to argue or become angry with Zeus during the extreme high. Iceman, to my relief and delight, respected Zeus enough to act on the observations. He calmed down and drifted into the dark phase without self-destruction. Iceman withdrew from the world for three weeks. His drinking increased. His coaches grew concerned he was going to transfer after a successful first season. NBA scouts contacted the coaching staff and asked for a video, and rumors spread that he was transferring to Duke. All rumors about his future were inaccurate. Concerns about his behavior were valid. He ran to the basketball facility and lifted weights alone. His teammates rode the bus and arrived 45 minutes after Iceman. When they used the weight room, Iceman used the gym alone. When his teammates scrimmaged in the gym, he returned to the weight room alone. During meals, he ate in silence. In the room, he rarely spoke to Zeus and took long walks. At the end of the three weeks, Iceman approached Zeus with a well-thought-out plan to use a cargo van as a food and alcohol truck. Not multiple high-risk plans, just one simple plan with little to no risk. The beginning of a new comet cycle began with Zeus's first rugby game. He soared through the summer and is currently riding his comet. I expect he will go dark and begin to ride the high in October. He will go dark, anticipating the basketball season and unleash the comet in the first practice.'

'Thanks, Tom. Your review highlighted just how valuable Zeus is to the team. We focus much of our attention on Iceman, but Zeus is obviously as important to the team as Iceman. To stay in Iceman's world for a moment, the twins are much like Michael Jordan and Scottie Pippen: they both need each other to play at their best.'

'Grace, I didn't realize you were a basketball historian, or are you showing our age? I agree with your assessment of Zeus.'

CHAPTER NINETEEN

Upon returning to West Point for their second or yearling year, Iceman picked up right where he left off in year one when he complained. 'Same crap. Same bullshit class list. Same practice schedule. Same food. Same uniforms. Same shit.'

Zeus shook his head in wonder, *How am I going to put up with this guy?* 'Come on Ice, it's different. We don't have to ping, announce minutes and all that plebe shit. We have one PE class, not four and no boxing.'

'Roger that.'

'Get on board.'

'Right, you are right. Now that we are upperclassmen, are we going to haze the plebes, light 'em up?' Iceman asked as he returned his focus.

'No, they are like everyone else. Our plebe year was a case study, a onetime thing.'

'That's a shame.' Iceman commented with true regret.

'Agreed. Let's go. We have to meet our plebes next door.'

'Why?'

'Do you read anything they give us in our orders? Or listen to any of the briefings? Never mind a rhetorical question. They report to us.'

'Right, let's go.' Iceman joined Zeus as they exited their room.

After two knocks, the plebe room responded, enter. The twins walked into the room and were greeted by their three plebes locked in attention.

'Cadets, identify yourself.' The three spoke their names and Iceman shook his head. 'Wrong, it's I don't give a shit. That is your name to us.'

'Where are you from?' Iceman continued and the three responded. 'Wrong, it's I don't give a shit. Handle your shit and be the best in the company. Shit the bed and we will pay you a visit.' Iceman locked eyes with the three plebes, who were beyond scared and intimidated. The twins left the room.

'Your trip down the shit river was a little harsh.' Zeus laughed back in their room.

'We'll take care of them, but they need to know we don't fuck around. *Nobody will fuck with our plebes; only we can fuck with our plebes.* A reference to what movie?'

'Don't know.'

'*Animal House.* I thought you weren't from Mars.'

* * *

The first semester was smooth sailing for the twins. They established a reputation as the pinnacle of cadet success. Cadets were judged and rated in academics, athletics and military. Zeus and Iceman scored at the top in each category. The rankings in each category were totaled to create a cadet score. Zeus ranked first and Iceman eleventh in their class. Iceman's refusal to be in the top 5% academically to avoid wearing a star on his uniform caused him to drop. His dismissive attitude towards senior cadet leaders and officers did not help his military score.

The Army team got off to a good start to the basketball season. Thor had worked on his game in the off-season and developed a jump shot to complement his athleticism. Because of the success enjoyed last season, two prized recruits joined the ranks led by Iceman and Thor to form a young, talented roster.

With a good start to the season and Christmas on the horizon, Iceman was in a good place.

'What are you doing for Christmas break?' Zeus asked Iceman.

'Running it back in Key West. You heading home again?'

'That's what I wanted to talk to you about…'

Iceman put down his book, which was not school-related, intrigued and he gave Zeus his full attention. 'What's up?'

'Well…'

'Shitty water comes out of well. Just tell me.'

'We thought mam would come here over break. We started a tradition last year of celebrating New Year's Eve on the 30th.'

'I remember that cool tradition avoiding the amateurs.'

'Thanks. So instead of me going to Ireland, we thought mam would come here and celebrate in New York. We will spend a week together over the New Year.'

Iceman knew where this was headed, but decided to entertain himself and play dumb. 'What are you going to do for Christmas?'

'Right, that's the thing. So, right, umm, she wants to see shows and stay in the city. She also wants to see West Point and watch you play. You have a game on the 28th, so that works.'

'You are still talking New Year. I was talking about Christmas.'

Zeus was uncomfortable and knew the conversation was not going well. He had rehearsed his request several times, but found himself thinking aloud to Iceman. 'I was wondering, and it's totally cool to say no, because I know you like to be alone sometimes and well, I was wondering if I could jump in with you and go to Key West with you.'

'Of course. Duh.'

* * *

The twins followed their usual routine at JFK. Bar, cougar, food, first-class flight, food, drinks; all the boxes were checked. They arrived in Miami on time and headed to the bar. Jack laughed when he saw Johnny, the bartender.

'Hey Johnny, long time no see. You probably don't remember me, but I was here last year on this date and…'

'First time, of course, I remember you. Mojito?'

'No, but later, we'll start with a couple of Buds and Jameson.'

'Coming right up.'

Zeus laughed. 'You must have made quite the impression.'

'This time, it wasn't my fault; it was more Heidi than me. You remember Heidi from last year. I told you about her.'

'Sure, I remember Heidi.'

'Oh Jack, you flatter me so; you remembered.'

Jack turned around. 'Hello, Heidi. I had a feeling I might run into you.'

'You do not need psychic powers for that. Same date, same time, same flight. I mean Jack, please. Who is your gorgeous friend?' She asked as Johnny served drinks. Iceman and Zeus took their shot and Jack answered.

'Heidi, Johnny meet Seamus.'

'Well, hello, Seamus. My aren't you gorgeous?!'

'We got it the first time. You don't have to celebrate it.' Jack pouted as he took a big gulp of beer.

'Sensitive.' Heidi playfully chastised Jack. 'I know your game, mister; you had your chance. You are just a tease.'

'Who me?' Jack asked, playing along with Heidi.

'That dangerous smile of yours will not work on me this time.' Heidi declared with a flippant tone.

'If ever a man was misunderstood.'

'Ok, you can stop with that smile. It still works and I find it rude.' Heidi announced.

Jack appreciated Heidi's expertise in flirting as he finished his beer. 'I saved you a seat next to me; that must count for something. The bar is full and I had to fight them off.'

'You saved me a seat so I can pay the bill.'

'Never.' Jack loved his banter with Heidi. She was a pro and Jack enjoyed the challenge.

'Never mind that move over. You are sitting in my seat; you saved that seat for yourself. I am sitting between my two young bucks.' Heidi settled into her seat and noticed Jack's drink selection. 'What happened to the mojitos? I thought I cultured you.'

'You did. I was waiting for you and the food.'

Heidi dismissed Jack. 'Johnny, I'll wait on the mojito. Get my boys another round and I'll have a special Bloody Mary.' She did not need to add, put it on my check.

Jack laughed to himself. There's that use of special for strong.

'Seamus, what made you come join all the fun?'

'Jack told me all about the trip and I wanted in.' Seamus answered, caught up in Heidi's energy.

Heidi put her hand on his thigh. 'I'm very glad you did.'

The energy suddenly turned from fun to scary. Seamus drank his shot, gulped his beer and headed for the restroom.

'Did I offend him?' Heidi asked with genuine concern. She wanted a playdate with Seamus on her trip.

Jack knew it was wrong, but just could not resist. 'No, not at all. He just got nervous. He is a little shy in the beginning, but he warms up. He took a little fancy to you.' Jack knew he was going to hell for unleashing Heidi on Seamus, but it was just too much fun.

Heidi set her drink down. 'You're just teasing me. You are such a flirt and tease.'

'Nope. He is just reserved in the beginning. With a little persistence, you'll see.'

'Yes, maybe I will.' She thought for a moment and let her mind drift to bedding Seamus. 'If it doesn't work out and you are full of shit, which I am certain you are, I have backups.'

'I would be highly disappointed if you didn't.'

Heidi called out. 'Johnny...'

'I know, I got it. I'll watch your stuff and save your seats. Yes, I will take something: I would like a Cuban sandwich and I'll have the mojitos ready.'

'You're such a doll.' With that, Heidi blew him a kiss.

The three drank, enjoyed Sergio's, Heidi was again disgusted with the amount of food digested by the twins and they boarded. The first night was a replay of Jack's previous visit. Jack introduced Seamus to Lars at Captain Tony's; the three relaxed, took in Duval St and were met by Heidi and Claire. Seamus loved almost everything about his first night. Heidi was very persistent in her pursuit of Seamus. Jack ate it up.

The next morning, after boating with the girls and visiting the island with no name to sample their catch, the twins and Lars sat in Captain Tony's. Lars mapped out the next day for the guys. Lars liked Seamus from the jump and after Lars laid out the next day's plan, Seamus was excited.

The twins left Captain Tony's and headed back to Casa Marina with two stops for food and drink.

'Iceman, that was the day of days.' Zeus relived the day with Iceman over spicy wings. 'Spearfishing was the shit. All of it was the shit. Obviously, I am used to fresh seafood, but that was crazy good. The best I ever had.'

'It's because you caught it.'

'Yeah, there's that, but Chef and that bar was crazy awesome.'

* * *

Early the next morning, Iceman took Zeus to the café to get breakfast sandwiches and an eight-pack of Gatorade. Their meal took a little longer to prepare, because the twins ordered nine breakfast sandwiches.

As they entered the bar with no name, they took the last bite of sandwich and spotted Lars.

'What's up?' Lars asked, greeting the twins.

'Nothing, Lars. We brought you a couple Gatorades and a sandwich.' Seamus did not mention the twins' order.

They sat around the bar and enjoyed the music. They talked easily with each other and the other people at and around the bar.

Seamus shook his head and laughed. 'Happy hour from 7 am to 9 am is hilarious. Look around you, it's 8 am and this place is packed. Surreal.'

Jack jumped Seamus. 'Surreal? Really, surreal? Did you really drop a surreal on us? Look around you. Do you really need to reach into your ACT bag and pull out surreal? Lars, what do you think?'

'I'd call it fucked up.'

Jack held out his arms, exasperated. 'That's all I'm saying.'

'Alright, what's the story with you two?' Lars asked the twins.

Jack took a gulp of beer. 'I thought you didn't give a shit?'

'I do now. Do you guys play ball? You look like it. Jack hoops? Seamus football?'

'I play rugby and Jack plays basketball.'

'Where?

Jack answered. 'A school in New York.'

'Really? I pitched for a SUNY school. What school in New York?'

Seamus replied. 'West Point.'

Lars spit his beer out. 'Get the fuck out of here. You two go to West Point? Seriously?'

The twins laughed. 'Yep.'

'Fucking A, that is cool. Thank you for your service.'

Jack shrugged. 'We haven't done shit yet except waste taxpayers' money.'

Lars laughed. 'Are you two ready for shark fishing?'

It was the twin's turn to spray beer out their mouth. 'Who said anything about shark fishing?'

'I just did. That's the second part of the plan. I lied last night about the plan for the day. I figured you'd chicken out. The real plan is we get tuned up all morning and into the afternoon. Get a good bar crawl in and take a long nap. I'll crash on the boat. Meet me at 11:00 tonight and we'll shove off. A warning: the ride is long and bumpy. Get Dramamine and take it right when you wake up from your nap. I am not joking. Take it. Casa Marina has it in the gift shop.'

'Roger that.'

* * *

The twins ate on the way back to the room and grabbed two pizzas for later. They took their long nap, woke up around 2100 hours, ate at Smokin Tuna and walked down to Captain Tony's.

'Fuck, we forgot to take the Dramamine.' Zeus realized.

The twins walked back to the hotel, took the Dramamine, and on the walk back to Captain Tony's, Zeus asked. 'What do you think about this shark idea?'

'Not a huge fan. Always thought it was a good policy in life not to mess with sharks. You?'

'Agreed. Why are we going again?'

'We don't want to look like pussies in front of Lars.' Iceman answered honestly.

'Right. That's it.'

* * *

The twins arrived right at 2300 hours and Lars was all set to go. Jack reached into the cooler, cracked open a beer and drank it with enthusiasm.

Lars heard the distinct crack and turned to Jack. 'You might want to go slow until we get out there. The water is a little rough.'

Halfway out, Zeus decided that shark fishing was a bad idea even before they were near a shark. 'You call this a little rough.'

'I may have misled you a little. The sea is rough. I didn't want to scare you and have you weasel out.'

'No chance. We would never chicken out. Bring the sea, my friend. Bring it rough. I like it rough.' Lars laughed at Jack and turned back to watch the sea. Once Lars' back was turned, Jack whispered to Zeus. 'I would have absolutely chickened out.'

'I would have been ahead of and not right behind you.'

After another 30 minutes of rough sea, Lars killed the engine and the sea was much calmer. He immediately went to work and explained his process for shark fishing. He described his recipe for chum in great detail. The twins did not know what chum was, let alone that a recipe was required. The bait, the location, the reels, the rods and everything that went into shark fishing was explained in considerable detail.

Seamus asked. 'Are we really going to catch a shark and reel it in onto the boat? I mean, am I going to be standing next to a live shark if we catch one?'

'Oh, we will catch one maybe two. No, we don't bring the shark aboard; they stink up the boat. Sharks piss out of their skin. It's nasty.'

'Yeah, that's what I was concerned about, the shark piss. Not the razor-sharp teeth that could shred me. I was worried about hygiene.'

'Good one, Zeus.'

'Thanks, Iceman.'

'Wait, what was that? Zeus? Iceman?'

Iceman answered for the twins. 'Our nicknames at school.'

'Ok, Zeus I get. Pretty obvious.' Jack rolled his eyes. Every fucking time. 'Why do they call you Iceman?'

Zeus fielded this question. 'The guys on the football and basketball team gave it to him. There goes Iceman, once cool as whiteboy.'

Iceman corrected Zeus. 'In fairness, it was Willie Mac that gave me the nickname. The football team made it stick.'

Lars nodded his head. 'Iceman, I like it. Now that you've explained it, the nickname is as obvious as Zeus. Iceman, you are a cool ass motherfucker, white or black.'

Jack was stunned as he thought. Aquaman just called me a cool ass motherfucker. That is some serious street cred.

The captain and his timid crew waited. Then they waited and to change it up, they waited some more. As the hours passed, Iceman's fear of the sea faded as the Buds went down smooth. Bored, Iceman thought it would be fun to get Zeus seasick on the ride home.

'Zeus, cannonball coming.' He threw Zeus a Bud and then another and another for hours.

'Sorry, guys. I thought we'd have a lot more action by now.'

'It's cool, Lars. Just being able to say we went shark fishing is tight.' Iceman was sincere with his sentiment and relieved not to face a shark.

'No, we'll get you a shark.' Lars was determined to repay all the laughter the twins provided with one hell of a memory.

Another hour passed with still no action. The twins were feeling the effects of the Bud and fought to stay awake.

Zeus spoke up. 'Lars, it's cool. We can head back; it's getting kind of early.'

'Just a little longer, I am sure we…' Lars was interrupted. One of the reels jumped to life.

'I did my job and now it's up to you two. Take turns; this is going to be a fight that drags on.'

Zeus asked. 'Is it a shark?'

'Yeah, buddy.'

Iceman started to reel in the shark while Lars screamed instructions. Iceman battled for 20 minutes, then Zeus jumped in.

'Zeus let her run; give her some line.'

'What the hell does that mean?' Zeus asked, now more nervous about letting down Lars than the shark.

Lars showed him. While it seemed counterintuitive to give up line and let the shark run, only to reel in the ground already conquered, Zeus just shut up and followed Lars' lead.

'Good Zeus. Pull up strong, and on the way down, reel like hell. That's it.'

Iceman, drenched in sweat, cracked open his second beer since battling the shark. 'Nice work, Zeus, but in all fairness, I did all the heavy lifting. I wore her out and left the cleanup for you.'

As Zeus was lowering the rod and prepared to reel fast and strong, he managed a, 'Fuck you, Iceman.'

Lars laughed at the ribbing between the twins and announced. 'Get ready, Iceman. You are almost up.'

Iceman chanted, 'Six minutes, six minutes, yes. I'm gonna shuffle to the door.' He thought of his Airborne chant.

'Sit the fuck down.' Zeus managed with gritted teeth. 'And you're a fucking dick feeding me those beers.'

'What? You looked thirsty. I think you meant to say thank you. Fuck that, Zeus, you had your turn. Not my problem you couldn't close the deal. *Put the coffee down. Coffee is for closers only.* Great quote. What movie, Zeus?'

Lars answered immediately. 'Glengarry Glenn Ross.'

'I asked Zeus. Seriously, dude, I'm up. Put the rod down. The rod is for closer only.'

Zeus did not speak; he didn't need to. He just turned and glared at Iceman.

'Roger that. *You see this watch? That watch costs more than your car.* Love that movie. Alec Baldwin's…'

'Big rip, Zeus, and reel like a motherfucker. I think I can almost hook her. Reel buddy, reel and… got her!'

Zeus, exhausted and out of breath, sweat pouring down his body, was greeted by Iceman. 'We don't have coffee, so you'll have to settle for Bud, you closer, you.'

* * *

As the twins walked back to the room studying the pictures of the captured shark on their phones, Zeus told Iceman, 'Thanks a lot, man, this is fucking great. I really appreciate you letting me tag along.'

'Don't be stupid. You did not tag along.'

'You know what I mean.'

'I do and it's stupid.'

'I'm glad you thought of buying those pizzas yesterday and leaving them in the room. I'm starving and nothing is open.'

As the twins destroyed their pizza, Zeus asked Iceman, 'We are coming up on commitment day.'

Commitment day was the date the cadets, after their second year, committed to graduating from West Point and fulfilling a five-year commitment as an officer in the Army. Iceman shook his head and finished his bite of pizza. 'I know. I am not sure what I am going to do. I haven't really thought about it much.'

'Bullshit, you think about everything too much.'

'Why did you ask?'

'Ice, it's no secret you could transfer, and if you transferred, you have a real shot at the NBA. If you stay at West Point and honor the commitment, your window is closed.'

'I don't think I can play in the league, but I could play in Europe for sure.'

'Ok. Play ball in Greece, or sit in the desert on patrol and get shot at?' Zeus' concern about Iceman's likely departure had been building. He felt shark fishing and pizza presented the best opportunity to address his concerns.

'Go on patrol with sand in my ears, eyes, nose and butt crack. I get it, but I don't like Greece; terrorists and they don't go to work.'

'Ok, take Greece out of it, a place you do like. Back to the NBA, you are listed in the power rating for future NBA prospects to watch. Wouldn't you regret not knowing?'

'Yes, if I had the slimmest of chances to get a chance. Do you know what I mean? If I get an invitation from an NBA team, I will make that team. The issue is, will I get the invite? Right now, I firmly believe I am a good college player, but not enough for the league. Then what if I make the team? I am the 12th man and sit way down on the bench. How much fun do you think I will have sitting on the bench watching 82 games? I think I can live with it; maybe I could have made the team and build my life with that wonder, because riding the bench is not worth the answer.'

'I see what you mean. What about the army? Are you going to be happy for five years?'

'I don't think so. If we are in peacetime and I am not deployed, then I have to listen to the sink pissers be all full of themselves. You know, the hard-core fucks that are all hoorah and two hockey seasons ago were pissing in their sink. I'll get kicked out of the army for smashing a sink pisser's face off my knee. Then if we go to combat, I would be active, but it would suck. I have zero interest in killing someone who has done nothing to me. Some 19-year-old I got no problem with, who just happens to be wearing another uniform, I have to kill? I am supposed to be fighting for my country. Ok, I am cool with that, but what am I fighting for? The revolution and independence, cool. World War II, freedom and democracy, I'm in. What are we fighting for now? The war on terror? Ok, I am good with that, but all I see the armed services doing is being recruiters for the terrorists. Men on the ground are protecting what? Tribes? Central governments that have no rule? The only damage I see getting done on our end is in intelligence. Freeze a bank account or track down the face card leaders and send in Delta. The only way I can see myself functioning is to be in an elite unit. I can't play with the sink pissers. You, on the other hand, will get pulled immediately and find a most wanted terrorist cell with your mad skills in computers and analytics.'

'Your analytics are way off the charts; they'll find you too.'

'No, I am viewed as a blunt instrument. When they think of you, they think: genius. When they look at me, they see: dumb basketball player.'

'Not true.'

'Doesn't matter. I can't sit and look at a computer screen all day like you can.'

'True. So, you really have already made your decision.'

'Nope. If you had told me in my junior year in high school that I was going to pick West Point, I would have thought you were crazy. But when the time came, it felt right. I made the right choice; I am cool with the rest of my time at West Point. I think my development has been amazing. I recognize that. I would not have grown into such a badass anywhere else.'

'Me too, but Duke and total freedom of choice must be tempting.'

'Coach K has never recruited me and he never will. He likes me too much. He knows West Point is better for me than Duke.'

'Ok, another school.'

'Maybe. Let's shelve this. Are you tired?'

'No, not after that afternoon nap. I still have the adrenaline flowing from shark hunting.'

'Me too.' Ice offered. 'I am jumping a shower and heading to the no name bar. You in?'

'Yes.' Zeus popped up and headed to the shower first. While he showered, he thought about Iceman and West Point. What would West Point be without Iceman? Fine, but not like now, not great. Iceman is right. I will get pulled to be part of a team that tracks the bad guys. That could be cool. But no Ice, that's tough.

While Zeus was in the shower, Ice finished his pizza in thought: *I really don't want to be just another soldier and I definitely can't function in a think tank. Special Ops is my only choice. I'll have to talk to Colonel Sullivan about it before commitment day. If I go, leaving Zeus, that's tough. Maybe he can transfer with me? Maybe pick a school together? That's not fair to Zeus. He'll do it, because I talked him into it, then two years later, what does he have? I can't put that on Zeus. He chose West Point, likes it and will like the Army. Don't do that to him. Fuck it, let's get drunk.*

CHAPTER TWENTY

'February sucks here.'

'You say that about every month.'

'True, but this time I mean it. The sky is grey, the uniforms are grey, the buildings are grey and shit, my pasty skin is grey. When was the last time we saw the sun?' Iceman asked.

'10 days ago.'

'Exactly, January. One month. February sucks.'

'You love it here. You love balling. You love outsmarting the hard-core cadets and the officers that search for a reason to bust you. You are a star and love it and they hate you for it. Everyone knows you are up to something, but they have no clue. You love every second of it. You would be bored at a normal college. The alcohol flows at normal college, no need for a super gangster bootlegger.'

'Speaking of masterplans, I have a great one brewing in the laboratory.'

Zeus interrupted Iceman before he could get started. 'We agreed with no masterplans during basketball season. You kill yourself during the season and you just don't have enough gas in the tank to take on a new project.'

'I know. I was just thinking about spring.'

'Don't. You and I both know if you like the plan and get excited about the plan, you won't wait. You have to stop thinking about it. I'm serious.'

'Agreed. It's just… I was trying to take my mind off the big game coming up on Thursday.'

'You play Fairfield. I mean, I know they are good, but why is this game a big deal to you? You've played against better.'

'The guy I am going against is filthy, but that's not it. Fairfield is a popular choice for kids from my high school. The Jesuit all-boys school and the Dominican all-girls school feed into the Jesuit catholic college. The college counselors push product towards catholic universities. 11 people from my class go to Fairfield, add the other years and a lot of people know me. I anticipate a crowd of Southsiders will represent and support one of their own. They will most certainly report back to the Southside.'

'I thought you left the Southside behind you.'

'I didn't leave my family. I represent my family in all my actions.'

'I understand.' Zeus admitted to himself. He understood the words, but not the powerful feelings or emotions. The over-whelming feeling of responsibility and duty to family name was foreign to Zeus. He was envious. 'Iceman, do you remember the night before the Zapata fight?'

'Yes.'

'I'll say again, you're fine. The only difference is this time, I believe it.'

Iceman, laughing hard, responded, 'Fuck you, Zeus.'

* * *

Fairfield's basketball team was led by Jim O'Malley. Under his leadership, Fairfield emerged as a strong mid-major program. O'Malley was a hot prospect for upcoming coaching vacancies at major programs. Good-looking, smart, charismatic and a tireless, successful recruiter, O'Malley was everything major college programs were looking for in a head basketball coach. O'Malley brought Ty Bell, a 6'5' senior, off guard who was a serious NBA prospect. The two best players on the court, Iceman and Bell, were set to face off. If Iceman didn't match Bell's performance, Army had no chance. Bell was a special talent and Iceman was forced to accept he could be embarrassed by Bell in front of several Southsiders. He knew he could not shit the bed and embarrass his family. Big game.

For the first time since his debut, Iceman missed pregame. His mind was racing as he visualized the game and, specifically, Bell's tendencies. He lost his breathing rhythm and had to force himself to calm down. He made it in time for warmups and was more than ready. Prior to tip-off, Iceman walked across halfcourt onto Fairfield's side, a gross breach of etiquette. He stalked Bell and, in front of the watchful Fairfield team and crowd, said simply, 'Game on.' Bell was surprised, but that feeling changed to concern when he investigated Iceman's cold stare. Bell felt chills throughout his body as he attempted to regain his composure. He was warned about Iceman in the scouting report, but reading it and living it were vastly different. After an uncomfortable moment, Bell managed to offer in a weak and muffled voice, 'Game on.'

Army got the ball and Iceman was immediately upset. Bell was not guarding him. Some 6'7' muscle-packed bench player drew the assignment. Iceman immediately knew O'Malley's game plan: goon up Iceman, beat him up and wear him down. He quickly looked over at Fairfield's bench. He saw two other bench players with their warmups off. Short shifts to keep the defenders rested. Three defenders, each with five fouls to give, allowed them the freedom to punish Iceman. Iceman changed his offensive game plan. He attacked the defenders and drew fouls to go to the free-throw line, where he shot 90%. He continually changed from an attacking style to misdirection, allowing Iceman to use their over-aggressiveness to his advantage. He sold running out to the three-point line and as the defenders over pursued, Iceman went backdoor to cut behind the defender's back to the basket. He used screens as a magician used misdirection. He kept the defenders guessing, and because of their over-aggressive play, when fooled, the defenders were fooled badly and Ice was left wide open. He wasn't upset that O'Malley put goons on him. He respected O'Malley's decision and would have tried the same thing. In Iceman's mind, he took it as a compliment. O'Malley was protecting Bell from Ice. He was angry, because he wanted a showdown with Bell on both ends of the floor. Let's see who the better player is. Bell got to rest on defense. Iceman had to work hard on defense to guard Bell. Iceman thought, O'Malley knows who the more dangerous player is, me.

Iceman's strategy worked. Army was up 38 to 32 at half. Iceman outscored Bell 21 points to 7. Jack went 8 for 8 from the free-throw line. The Southside of Chicago was well represented and they cheered loudly for one of their own. During halftime, Iceman did his best to hydrate. He was covered in ice bags, which dulled the pain and postponed swelling. Bruises had already started to appear. The team and coaches knew Iceman took punishment, but didn't appreciate just how bad it was until they saw his condition. Iceman blocked out the room and the pain, focused on replaying the first half and Bell's performance. He zeroed in on what adjustments he would make if he were O'Malley.

Coach Phillips pulled Coach Durham to the side. 'We have to protect him. Look at him.'

'I know. He took more punishment than I realized.'

'I think we should put Kong in.' Philips offered.

'How can he protect Iceman?'

'He can't, but he can punish Bell and we can send a message to O'Malley: We can beat up your star too. O'Malley has used their center to set physical and illegal screens on Iceman to wear him down to free Bell. Put Kong on their center and when Bell comes off the screen, Kong is there to greet him in Kong fashion. He'll punish Bell. Bell is not programmed like Iceman and he won't accept the punishment long.' Phillips offered.

Durham did not take long to decide. 'Get Kong ready.'

The teams took the court for the second half and Kong was primed and ready. Iceman's adrenalin and blood flow faded during halftime; fatigue and pain settled in. Iceman laughed as he thought of Alfred's question to Bruce Wayne in Batman Begins: *What is the point of all those pushups if you can't lift a bloody log?* He then thought to himself, This is why you ran to practice; this is why you ate until you were sick; this is why you lifted weights to the point of immobility. Your body is built to take the punishment. You added the 15 pounds of muscle; the body is ready, is the mind? I am mentally tough enough to go again! Mentally tough. I am a badass motherfucker. Unleash hell on the whistle.

Iceman gave Bell a physical lockdown performance on defense in the first half. He was ready for the goons on offense and Bell on defense in the second half. Fairfield had the ball to start the second half. Fairfield ran their base set and Bell came off the screen, set illegally, and Iceman lost a half a step due to the force of the screen. He lost Bell for a moment. Where did he go? Iceman found him on the floor; Kong had knocked Bell down hard. Bell attempted to get up, but his legs and head betrayed him. The gym was spinning and his legs felt like cooked spaghetti. The trainer ran out and escorted Bell to the bench. Kong was called for the foul and headed to the bench. Mission accomplished.

The goons, upset with Bell's treatment, intensified their efforts on Iceman, who could not be happier. Bell was Konged. Iceman took great satisfaction that he never went down. Not in boxing, not in hoops, always the last man standing. He knew Bell would return, but there was no changing the fact that he went down. Fairfield fought hard and, in some ways, were better in the brief time Bell was out. Filled with emotion that energized a talented roster without Bell, Fairfield held Army's lead to three. Bell got up to report to the scores table and Kong immediately jumped to his feet to join him. Bell was terrified of Kong. As they entered the game together, Kong barked. 'Mine, all mine.' Bell was lost for the game. He drifted around the perimeter and never entered Kong's area.

With 2.1 seconds remaining in the game, Fairfield was forced to foul Iceman to stop the clock. Iceman, at the top in the NCAA in free throw shooting, took the line with 37 points and Army winning 71-70. He calmly made the first free throw, as expected, to bring his total to 38 and the Army lead to 72-70. He stepped up for the second free throw, took his three warm-up dribbles with confidence and released a pure shot he knew was in. The unthinkable happened: the ball rattled around the rim three times and finally rolled out. Iceman was stunned and, for a split second, forgot his defensive assignment. He sprinted to his left to guard the area around half-court. He recognized Bell and zeroed in as he caught the ball. Bell took one dribble and, as he was about to shoot, Iceman exploded in the air with his arms fully extended. Bell released the shot and Iceman fully expected to block it. The release was confident, but Iceman just missed blocking the shot. Ice saw the release and immediately knew that the ball had a chance. He started to walk to his bench with his back to the shot. The crowd noise said it all; Bell made the game-winning 3-point prayer from 46 feet. Army lost 73-72.

As Bell walked off the court in a sea of celebration, Ice approached him. 'Good game, Ty.'

Ty broke away from the crowd and escorted Iceman to a quiet spot. 'Jack, we both know you took it to me tonight. The video and scouting reports don't do you justice. You need to get out of West Point, because if you go to a real program, I'll see you in the league.'

'Thanks, Ty. I had my moments, but you hit the game-winner. The only shot that counts and the only shot people will remember.' They grabbed hands and pulled in for a shoulder bump.

Iceman ignored the coach's post-game talk, blew off the media and walked out to say hi to the Southsiders, who were kind enough to wait. He was greeted with applause, high-fives and hugs.

'Thanks. Thanks, everyone, but we lost.' The group did not care. Jack wanted to be anywhere but with the crowd. The group was so kind and sincere. He knew he had to stay. He didn't want to be rude, appear aloof, or alienate himself from the group. Word would get back to the Southside, Jack was a dick. The family would be beyond angry. A group of people make the effort to celebrate you and you shit all over them? *Yeah.* Jack thought. *That would be bad. Every compliment served as a reminder of that split second.* No one saw his split-second pause; no one knew Iceman's mistake; only Iceman knew he had lost the game. Any effort to explain the split second would be pointless. Jack knew, and he never forgot the feeling, nor did he forgive himself.

Antwan, a high school teammate, approached Jack. 'Great game. You were nasty in high school, but you got better. Look at you; you're all swollen with muscles now. You grew a little and your handles are sick. I mean, you had hops in high school, but you got mad hops now. How'd you do it?'

Jack thought, *Seriously?* 'Practice hard work.'

'We'll it sure paid off.'

'Thanks.'

'Jack!' Kathleen, a girl who fancied Jack in high school, gave him a big hug. She was proudly wearing an Army basketball sweatshirt and was what could be described as cute and fun. She was not tall, but wore her auburn bob hairstyle in a messy celebration. She had a nice body and smile; the type of girl you brought home to meet your parents. 'Jack, you were great.'

Jack remembered he always liked Kathleen; she was cool. 'Sorry, Kathleen. I haven't showered yet. Thank you, but we lost and it was my fault.' Jack's thoughts raced to get the hell out of there. He paused before he started to leave, considering the Colonel's offer and Kathleen's. He dismissed it. As he went to say goodbye, Thor walked out of the locker room, freshly showered, ready to join the group to make a memory.

'Hi, everybody.' Thor announced as he scanned the group and assessed the talent level of the girls present.

'Everybody, this is Thor. Thor, this is everybody.'

Jack again went to fade away from the group, but Kathleen's eyes never left him. 'You're coming with us, right? You're just going to shower and come back out, right?'

Before Jack could answer, an incredibly hot chic added. 'Jack, Kathleen has spoken about you a lot leading up to the game. I have been looking forward to getting to know you. I'm Sloane.'

'Nice to meet you, Sloane. I am afraid I am beat. I need some treatment tonight and probably an IV. I have to pass.'

Antwan overheard the conversation. 'Fuck that. You are 100% coming. Come on, man, we'll never see you. You never go home.'

Thor looked at Iceman and knew his friend was checked out. 'Please come. I need this.'

Jack carried on to the locker room, ignoring their pleas. 'I am sitting this one out. Kathleen and Antwan take care of my good friend. Thor, you're in good hands.'

Kathleen and Antwan nodded. Thor tried again. 'Come on, you know you make it better.'

Iceman turned and walked to the locker room.

Sloane was the first to comment. 'That was rude.'

Kathleen added while Antwan just shook his head. 'I don't get it. What happened to him? That's not Jack at all.'

Thor came immediately to Iceman's defense. 'That's totally him. I don't know how well you think you know him, but that is him.'

Antwan took exception to Thor's comments. 'I do know Jack, well, real, well. He always went out after the game and was a terror of fun.'

'After a win, yes. How was he after a loss?'

Antwan thought a moment. 'We didn't lose much, so I don't remember. Wait, I do remember after our last game. We lost in the state playoffs to the number one team in the state and the number four team in the country. Simeon was heavily favored, but Jack swore we would win. Nobody believed him, but he was insistent. We lost by six, Jack blamed himself. We didn't see him for a week.'

Thor took Antwan's story further. 'That's him. He blames himself for every loss and takes no credit for a win. He doesn't celebrate a win; he expects it. He destroys himself after a loss. When people say they hate to lose, they have no idea how much he hates to lose. He replays the game over and over in his head, finds one or two mistakes he made and uses those to destroy himself. He just needs a minute, one of his favorite expressions and he'll be the guy you think you know. He'll come out. Guaranteed, and when he does, hang on. For some reason, he took this loss especially hard, even by his standards.'

Iceman sat in front of his locker and replayed the game again. He came to the point of obsession with his fraction-of-a-second failure. *How could I be so pathetic and miss my assignment?*

Coach Phillips walked into the locker room. 'The bus is leaving, time to go.'

Iceman just looked at the coach the stare said enough. Phillips went to speak to him; he did not want to leave Iceman alone. Colonel Sullivan saw the exchange from the doorway and walked over to Phillips. He put a hand on his shoulder and gave him a look to convey he had it. Coach Phillips exited and Sullivan sat down next to Iceman.

'Iceman, take all the time you need. I spoke with Coach Durham and he agreed. You have friends here who are excited to see you. As I offered you before the game, get a little taste of home.'

'I'm good.'

'I don't think you understand, I am giving you a free pass. Go have some fun. No bed check. We'll see you at breakfast.'

'Thanks, you know I appreciate it. I'll think about it.'

'Good man, you do that.' Sullivan left confident that once Iceman cooled down, he would join the reunion.

Iceman was incredibly grateful to have Colonel Sullivan in his life. The Colonel just understood him. Iceman had the upmost respect for him.

After he showered and changed, Iceman headed for the exit. As he walked down the corridor, he saw O'Malley walking towards him. The two were alone in the hallway.

'Jack, what a game, what a game; that's why we lace 'em up, right? For games like that. You were tremendous. You are a hell of a player and no matter what your future holds, it was a pleasure to watch you compete.'

Iceman responded with a firm push that launched O'Malley into the wall. O'Malley hit the wall hard.

'What the fuck Jack?'

'You push me, I push back.'

'Point taken.' O'Malley yelled out to Iceman, who had resumed his walk to the exit.

* * *

After a two-mile walk, Iceman sat in his hotel room, freshly showered and found ESPN on the television. He opened his boxed lunch with disgust and turned up the volume; Sports Center was about to begin. After the famous DaDaDa DaDaDa, the broadcaster promoted the show with quick highlights of great plays to draw in the audience. We have spectacular finishes. To Iceman's horror, the lead was Bell's shot, with Ice entering the picture front and center. The announcer continued after the 2.1-second clip ended with the swish and yelled, yes. If the 2.1-second clip that kicked off Sports Center wasn't bad enough, ESPN played the clip three more times in rapid succession. All three times, the shot still went in and the announcer screamed: Yes! Yes! Yes! Iceman threw his box lunch at the television, got up, and said, 'Unreal. Un-fucking unreal. My first time on ESPN and they lead with me as the clown. Fuck it, I am going out.'

He walked towards the strip of college bars. As he got close, he realized he had no idea where the group had gone. He figured there were not that many bars, so he looked for Thor. Iceman listened for the loud bars and popped his head to look for his 6'7' friend. He spotted The Levee; he knew he would find them inside. Sure enough, as soon as he walked in, he spotted Thor. As he was close to joining the group, they went silent. He wondered if they were upset with him.

The group erupted. 'DaDaDa DaDaDa.'

Thor grabbed Iceman from the crowd and laughed. 'Thanks, we really needed you here.'

'You set this up? You knew I was coming?' Iceman laughed and grabbed his good friend, who was a bit nervous. 'It was brilliant.'

Thor grabbed him again. 'Come on, superstar, let's get you hammered.'

'Roger that.'

As Thor and Iceman walked to the bar, Kathleen watched Iceman's walk and turned to Sloane. 'Hang on, we are in for quite a ride.'

Antwan joined them at the bar. After a shot of Jameson and a couple of Bud chasers, Jack asked for two waters. He knew he was still dehydrated and had to protect himself from himself. He reached for one of the waters with his right arm and winced in pain. The Jameson should kick in and help with that.

Antwan turned to Thor. 'So, you know this guy pretty well?'

'I do believe I am in store for a history lesson, Iceman, the early years. Serve it up.'

'Did you know this crazy motherfucker somehow got looped in to playing on one of the biggest drug dealer's basketball team? They played for big money and the players got a taste.'

Iceman jumped in. 'Erroneous, that would be a violation of NCAA regulations.'

Thor shook his head. 'That's how you have all that money.'

'Erroneous, my money was made landscaping.'

Both Antwan and Thor just laughed at him.

'Anyway, the way I heard it, the kingpin loved Jack and provided him protection. Something about him being a wizard with numbers and putting money to work.'

'Erroneous. Everybody knows the playground is a safe harbor.'

Antwan laughed. 'Yeah, but is the walk home safe harbor with a wad of cash in your pocket?'

Iceman was silent.

'That's what I thought.' Antwan laughed and continued. 'Another thing I heard was, no matter how much Jack fucked them up, his team still got the odds. The brothers never could accept they could be beaten by a whiteboy.'

'True.' Iceman raised his beer in consent.

'Why do they call you Thor?' Antwan asked.

Iceman answered. 'He is from Norse descent. Did you see his two dunks, dunks of thunder?'

'Got it. Why do they call you Iceman?'

'I'll tell you later. I am going to thank Kathleen.'

Thor jumped at the chance to talk to Sloane. 'We'll come with you.'

'Hello, Kathleen. I understand you rallied the troops. Thank you, that was very kind.' Jack dropped his smile on her.

Sloane looked at Kathleen, then back at Jack. 'Now I see what all the fuss was about. You are someone to know.'

'Who me?' Jack asked humbly.

'I haven't had the pleasure, I'm Jack.' He turned to the new girl.

'Yes, I know who you are. I'm Beth.'

Jack took her hand. 'Nice to meet you.'

Antwan jumped in. 'Ok, now explain why they call you Iceman.'

Thor answered. 'The coolest whiteboy on the planet. Iceman.'

Sloane laughed. 'I knew you were someone to know.'

Jack liked Sloane instantly, and his first impression was correct, she was sizzling. She was tall with silky long onyx hair, olive complexion and stunning green eyes. Jack had her pegged as a mix of Greek and Irish. Jack returned his attention to Kathleen. 'You look great. Fairfield agrees with you.'

'Yeah, I like it.'

'Got great friends from what I can tell.'

'Thanks. Sloane is from…'

'Manhattan. I am thinking a place in the Hamptons too.' Jack interrupted.

Sloane, puzzled, replied. 'Yes.'

Kathleen, equally surprised, continued. 'Ok. Beth is from…'

'Give me a minute.' Jack studied her for a moment. 'New England? I am thinking New Hampshire.'

Beth asked. 'How did you do that?'

'A carnie never reveals his secrets.' Iceman laughed to himself. How obvious could they be with their accents?! Sloane was obviously from Manhattan and serious money. The place in the Hamptons was an educated guess, but she had certainly been there and I could have spun it. Beth's accent was even more obvious.

'Ok, Zoltar, tell us a high school story.' Sloane challenged Iceman.

'Nice reference to the movie *Big*, starring Tom Hanks and directed by Penny Marshall. Sorry, I don't live in glory days.'

Thor primed the pump. 'Ask him a direct question about an event or rumor. He hates direct questions.'

'Why?' Kathleen asked.

'I have trouble not answering them honestly.' Iceman replied.

'Well, this is fun.' Sloan smiled. 'Kathleen, what have you got for us?'

'I am ready. Tell us about the fight you and your basketball friends got into with guys from the other Catholic high school in the area.'

'Nothing much to tell.' Iceman knew the rumor Katie was referring to. The true story was better than the rumor. Iceman withheld the true story and teased the crowd about the rumor.

Sloane was quick to respond. 'What a gyp. That's bullshit.'

'More specific.' Kathleen was not to be denied. 'I heard you and three of your public-school basketball friends went to a party and a fight broke out. The four of you beat up 19 guys from a different high school, and please, provide a detailed report on the incident in question. I know and withheld some details, so come clean.'

Iceman turned to Thor. 'Public school friend is code for black inner-city friends.'

Thor nodded. 'Got it.'

'Nothing big, really. We met some girls and got along. They had invited us to the party, so we met them there. My friends from Simeon, that I balled with on the playground, were black and not gentle. Very cool and polite, but you don't want to fuck with them. The high school fuck stains didn't care for us talking to their girls and drinking their beer. They approached us. Words were exchanged and one of them hit Angry Mike over the back with a wooden chair. Apparently, being black was an invitation to the racial slurs that followed. Angry Mike shook off the now-broken chair and went to work. We couldn't leave Mike hanging, so we cleared the room, took the keg, a bunch of girls and headed to the beach. We killed the keg, left the barrel and kept the tapper. Nothing really to tell.'

Sloane asked. 'How many?'

'Don't know and didn't count. In fairness, several ran away. The legend is bigger than the actual event.' Iceman knew the legend was close to the truth. The quick destruction of the mob was impressive and legendary.

Kathleen smirked. 'If you say so.'

The night carried on and Thor's interest in Sloane became obvious. Jack really liked Sloane, but could not act on it in respect to Kathleen, who he really liked too.

'Thor, give me a minute.' Ice pulled Thor aside. 'Pump your breaks on Sloane; focus on Beth. She's cute, cool and funny.' Beth was, in fact, a very appealing target. She was attractive with her sandy blonde hair and she gave off a kind energy.

'Are you saying Sloane is out of my league?'

'Yes. Stay in your lane and you have something in Beth. She is into you, I can tell.'

'Alright, I'll take your word for it. Thanks, you somehow know these things.' Thor replaced his disappointment about Sloane with excitement about his prospects with Beth.

Sloane noticed the exchange, saw Thor's behavior change and made a note of the event. She wondered if Iceman was clearing the deck to be with her, which didn't make sense, because he really seemed interested in Kathleen. The night got interesting.

The night carried on and Kathleen was focused on Jack. Last call was announced and Kathleen had a plan.

'Iceman, do you and Thor want to come back to our place? The night is young and we usually keep going after last call. We live in a rental on the beach and you two are more than welcome.'

So now it's Iceman, Jack noticed. 'Sure, that would be great.' He thought back to Colonel Sullivan. That guy knows what time it is. He knows his shit.

* * *

On the walk home, Sloane pulled Iceman aside. 'I saw your little act with Thor.'

'What are you talking about?'

'Don't insult me. You know exactly what I am talking about. What am I not good enough for your precious Thor?'

'You're too good.'

'What?' Sloane did not expect that answer. She scrambled to regain her composure. 'Say, you're right. What about me? You clearly like me, but you are into Kathleen.'

'Right.'

'Thor is a hell of a lot better than anything at Fairfield.'

'True.'

'So, what about me? This sucks.'

'Do you like rugby?

'What?'

'You will.' Iceman left Sloane confused and speechless. She was not familiar with either.

They arrived at the house and were loud and silly. The fourth roommate came down soon after they arrived. Iceman noticed she had obviously just got out of bed, but quickly took the time to make herself up. She looked good.

Sloane saw an opportunity. 'Mr. Zoltar, let's see you do your thing to our roommate Gina.' Iceman spit out his beer and thought, Impossible. This is shaping up to be too perfect. 'What's a matter? Don't got it?'

'Let's make it interesting. If I am right, I take Kathleen to the kitchen and we make out for one minute.'

'What if your wrong?'

Before Iceman could answer, Kathleen jumped in. 'He spends the night in my bed with boxers and a t-shirt on at all times.'

Iceman was not fazed as he wandered around the house to build suspense. 'Let's change the bet. When I am right, I get both. The reward for being wrong should not exceed being right. That's too much to ask. Let's up the bet. If Zoltar dazzles you, I get both.' Iceman walked over to his greatcoat and pulled out a bottle of Jameson.

Beth asked. 'Where did that come from?'

'The bar, I grifted it.'

'How?'

Thor shook his head. 'Don't ask.'

Iceman took a couple hits from the bottle, replaced the top, returned the bottle to his great coat and began. 'I grant you this is a tough one. Gina, you say. Gina from Brooklyn.'

Sloane conceded. 'You got it. Fucker.'

'Yes, but I have not dazzled you yet. Here we go. Gina, short for Regina. Regina from Brooklyn has an Italian father and a mother from Mexico. Regina is a name accepted in both cultures, but your father calls you Gina to celebrate the Italian side. You might, or make that, have a brother named something like Antonio, but everybody calls him Tony.'

'Fuck that, who told him?' Gina demanded.

The room was silent and everyone just shook their heads. Iceman laughed again to himself, while wandering the house, the mighty Zoltar saw Gina's family Christmas card proudly displayed on the refrigerator, names included.

Gina refused to believe Iceman nailed it on his own. She was right, but could not unravel the mystery of Zoltar's powers.

Thor put his hands behind his head, flexed his prized biceps for Beth's benefit and broke the silence. 'Told you so.'

Gina started to come around, looking at Beth and Sloane, she asked. 'He did it to you two also?'

Beth answered. 'Yes, it's crazy.'

Before anyone else could speak, Iceman took Kathleen's hand, gave her his charming smile and led her to the kitchen. They did not return. They moved upstairs, where they kissed, did a little exploring and cuddled in bed. Iceman never removed his boxers or t-shirt per the terms of the bet, despite Kathleen's efforts to at least remove the t-shirt.

Iceman and Thor woke up at 0600 and were careful not to wake the girls.

On the walk back to the hotel, Thor asked. 'How much trouble do you think we are in?'

Iceman handed Thor what was left of the whiskey. 'None, the Colonel gave us a free pass.'

After taking a healthy swallow to chase the demons, Thor handed the bottle back to Iceman. 'Why didn't you tell me?'

'And ruin all the danger?'

'Right.' Thor acknowledged and changed the subject. 'Why did you spit out your beer when you heard Gina's name?'

'I was just thinking about rugby season.'

* * *

Iceman returned to West Point and walked into the room to find Zeus with two pizzas, a six-pack of coke and a cleaning bottle.

'A little early for spring cleaning. What's the occasion?'

'I heard about the game and thought you could use a slice and a little pick me up.' Zeus reached over and handed him the bottle.

Iceman took a healthy pull. 'I think you meant to say saw what happened, DaDaDa DaDaDa. Are you trying to use pizza and the bottle to open me up and explore my innermost feelings?'

'Just being a friend. What did you do this time to lose the game?'

'I shit the bed. I missed the free throw and then compounded the mistake. I should have blocked Bell's shot. I was late getting over.'

'You obviously know you're being stupid.'

'If you say so, let's enjoy the pizza and clean the room.'

'Hang on, that was too easy; what happened out there?' Zeus knew his friend was taking the loss and subsequent ESPN embarrassment in stride. He never did that. Zeus wondered where the dark cloud that followed defeat was.

'Nothing, eat up.' Iceman had no interest in further exploration.

'No. something happened. You are taking this too well.' Zeus set his slice down and watched Ice eat. 'How were the Southsiders? Did you meet up with that girl you thought was cool?'

'The Southsiders came and represented strong. It was cool.'

'And the girl, was she cool?'

'Kathleen, yeah, she was cool. She set the whole thing up.'

The answers were presenting themselves, Zeus continued. 'Because she likes you. Did you two have a connection?'

'Yes.'

'Great, what's the plan?' Zeus was happy for his friend and impressed with Kathleen's positive impact on Iceman.

'Zeus, are you testing me? No plans until after the season. You know that.'

'Fair. Will your spring masterplan need to be changed to accommodate her?'

'Yes.'

'Alright, so what are your thoughts? You like her?'

'After the season, right now I am eating pizza and cleaning the room.' He took a bite of pizza and washed it down.

'You're learning.'

'I have a good teacher.'

* * *

Iceman called Kathleen five days later from the sports complex. 'Hi, it's me.'

'Fred? The dorky accounting major? Look, Fred, last night was a mistake…'

'Funny girl.'

'How are you, stranger?'

Iceman responded defensively. 'I was clear. I was going to finish the season and come back. I only have a minute, but I wanted to let you know I was thinking of you.'

'Jack, it is just an expression. I totally understand. Before I ask what I want to ask, I totally understand your terms. I would like to take the short ride from Fairfield and watch one of your last games at West Point.'

'Sorry, I am booked with Vassar girls.'

'Funny guy. So?'

'Nope.'

Dejected, not by the answer, but by the curt tone. 'I understand.'

'I have to go.'

'Bye.'

'Hang on, I wasn't finished.' Jack had softened his tone and continued. 'I get two leaves a semester and save them up for after basketball season. I am awarded a third leave for forfeiting Christmas break, because of hoops. During leave, we get Friday at 3:00 to Sunday night at 6:00 off. I have also planned a weekend on post to watch a rugby game. We'll make a master plan after the season. I like it when you call me Jack and not Iceman.'

Kathleen teased. 'Jack, are you asking me to be your girlfriend? What about Fred and my many other suitors?'

'Remember your Crash Davis from Bull Durham. *I'm not interested in a woman who is interested in that boy.* Good night.'

'Jack, I was just kidding, I wasn't… Did he just hang up on me?'

* * *

With one week left in the season, the buzz throughout the Core of Cadets was spring break. As plebes, Zeus and Iceman were not eligible, but as yearlings, spring break was fair game.

'Iceman, spring break is coming up and you haven't told me about your master plan for us.'

'I have hoops.'

Zeus knew that Army would have to win their conference to earn the automatic bid to the NCAA tournament that took place during spring break. Zeus had all the confidence in the world in Iceman, but the rest of the team wasn't enough. The star recruits were fine, but were not as advertised, and Thor, while improved, was a good player, but not great. Army finished third in the conference, all due to Iceman. The first two teams were ranked and already secured a bid to the NCAA. The gap between Army and the co-champions of the conference was vast. Army had no chance to beat both teams in the tournament.

'Ice, I'm just saying, you know, what if…'

'I have hoops.'

* * *

Army walked through the first two games of the tournament due to Iceman's efforts. He scored 41 and 39 points, respectively, and was at the peak of his game. Iceman generated national buzz and the semi-final game was televised on ESPNU. He did not disappoint. He had a career-high 49 points and led Army to a shocking upset. The hype that followed Iceman's performance continued to grow and the championship game was televised on ESPN. The Army coaches were ecstatic about the national attention, but were privately worried.

In the Coach Durham's office, he asked Coach Phillips. 'You know him better than me. Is he gone?'

'Yes. I don't think he is going to sign the commitment letter. I think he will follow O'Malley wherever he lands. O'Malley is going to a major university after the season. Iceman likes O'Malley and O'Malley has made no secret in the press about his admiration for Iceman. He has clearly been recruiting Iceman through the media. He is now on every NBA team's radar. O'Malley can offer a college experience, a bigger stage, a campus that will adore and celebrate him, not harass him like some officers and senior cadets have. They follow him around, looking to make a name for themselves by being the guy that busted Iceman. The biggest thing is that Iceman saw what O'Malley did for Bell. We both know he is better than Bell. Iceman knew it that night at Fairfield. He's gone.'

Coach Durham dropped his head. 'It was fun while it lasted, we got new contracts like he said.'

'Contracts that exceeded any expectations we had and the shoe contract is amazing. A five-year deal with Nike all because they wanted him wearing their shoes in the Army uniform, a marketing dream. Coach, have you been contacted about other coaching jobs?'

'Yes, but we are in the first year of a five-year deal. We have to wait it out. I know it's a long shot, but if he stays two more years, our ticket is punched. We will get a significantly bigger deal and the next job will buy us out of our contract with only two years remaining on the Army contract. We just need a little luck.'

'Like winning the lottery luck.'

* * *

The conference championship and Jack's future brought the media in mass. Reporters were not interested in the game; they were interested in Jack's future. Jack was short with reporters. Jack's only response was, I play for Army. Next question, the same question was asked differently, I play for Army. Some in the media took out their frustrations on Jack. The media was sitting on a story and Jack was giving them nothing. High-profile coaches, many of which wanted Jack in their uniform, came to his defense. The coaches praised his focus on the task at hand and his commitment to his team. Whatever Jack decided about his future, no one could question the contributions he made to Army. No coach was louder than O'Malley.

The game started and Bucknell appeared to win the tap, but Jack stole it, took two dribbles and launched a 25-foot three-pointer before the defense could set. The swish ignited the announcers.

'Collins has picked up right where he left off. Bucknell is still favored, but our friends in Vegas have this as a closer game than when the tournament started. Bucknell better have an answer for Collins.'

Bucknell did. They changed their defense to a box-in-one. One player was assigned to Iceman and covered him from baseline to baseline. The other four players played zone and focused on Iceman. Anytime Iceman made a move to the basket, he was immediately doubled teamed. Bucknell was determined to have anybody beat them, but Iceman. He had not faced a box in one in college, but had in high school. The only way to beat a box in one was to use the double team against the opponent and, if left open with the slightest daylight, take the shot. Iceman's best looks were in transition before the defense could set up, exemplified by the jump ball. Any look inside 30 feet, he took. There were few good looks. Iceman used the double team to draw fouls and create good looks for his teammates. He knew his teammates' limitations, so he attacked offensive rebounds created by his teammates' misses.

'We are seeing a new side of Collins. The facilitator, the rebounder, Collins has dug into his bag of tricks to beat the double team.' The announcer celebrated the versatility of Collins' game.

Four games in four days did not wear Iceman down. He grew stronger as the game went on and the other players faded. Iceman repeated to himself: This is a war of attrition. They didn't run the hills and work like you. Keep coming. Relentless, you are relentless. Take their will. The game ended and the battle was lost. Iceman did not score in the 40s; he had 31 points, 14 rebounds and 10 assists. He had triple-double and did all he could to contribute to a win. Iceman hated the loss, but allowed himself to accept he didn't lose the game. He played the best game of his career and could not find a mistake. He was proud of his teammates, who played their best. The better team beat Army's best effort. For the first time in a loss, he walked off the court in peace.

* * *

Back in his room, Zeus delicately mentioned. 'You know we have time to plan a spring break.'

'The season is not over.'

Zeus knew not to state the obvious and remind Iceman the season was over for him. 'So, what are you going to do? Everybody is leaving except the plebes.'

'Stay here.'

'Iceman, you can't, we have to leave.'

'Nope.'

'Maybe go to Fairfield and see Kathleen, if not the whole time, at least a couple of days?'

'Nope. I'll be fine.'

Zeus shook his head. 'I am going back to Ireland then. Do you want to come?'

'Nope.'

* * *

Iceman sat in his room and mapped out his day.

0530: 5-mile run.

0700: Breakfast – Iceman sat alone, occasionally joined by Reese or Ty at the other end of the mess hall, next to the kitchen and away from the plebes. He enjoyed a special menu made by his favorite cook. Sandwiches to go.

0830: Run to the basketball facility, stretch, ball handling drills, lift upper body.

1030: Run back to the barracks.

1045: Shower, eat sandwiches, walk the Hudson to reflect on his master plan, read.

1200: Lunch, again custom, with sandwiches to go.

1330: Run to basketball facility, sprint steep ¼ mile steep hill behind the basketball complex 20 times, shooting drills, plyometrics.

1530: Run back to the barracks.

1545: Shower, eat sandwiches, walk the Hudson to work on master plan and read.

1900: Dinner, again custom and sandwiches to go.

1930: Walk to basketball facility, shoot while visualizing games from last season.

2000: Lift legs.

2100: Jump a ride to Newburg with Reese and Ty to the Ground Round. Watch a ball game, enjoy bar conversation while throwing back only Bud and no Jameson.

2359: Uber, return to room, eat sandwiches, a couple of nightcaps, lights out.

Repeat. Remember to hydrate.

While enjoying a quiet and relaxing spring break in Ireland, Zeus' thoughts often turned to Iceman. He knew spring break marked the beginning of Iceman's dark period. Zeus understood Iceman wanted to be alone, but was concerned for his friend.

CHAPTER TWENTY-ONE

Zeus returned from Ireland, set his bags in the twins' room; Iceman was not present. Dinner formation was at 1900 hours, he figured he'd see Iceman then. He was interested in Ice's week and hoped he had stayed out of trouble. Zeus left concerned that a master plan had taken Iceman on a reckless journey. Ice was dark with the end of the season and commitment day weighing on his mind. After he squared away the room, Zeus headed to dinner formation, but there was no Iceman. Zeus did not know that Iceman had an excused absence. Several officers saw Iceman as he ran all over post at all hours. The officers approached Colonel Sullivan and asked, 'Why did Collins lose spring break privileges?' The officers who disliked Iceman were excited about the prospect of him finally getting caught crossing the line. To the disappointment of some and the surprise of other officers, Sullivan explained, 'He is training for next season.' All the officers, including the cynics, were impressed. A new level of respect was given to Iceman. Colonel Sullivan issued a special pass for the last day of spring break that allowed Iceman to return by lights out. The consensus was he was authentic. He was a machine. The Core of Cadets saw him missing from formation and immediately assumed he had transferred. They could not blame him; playing at a major university with the prospects of the NBA was impossible to pass up. Even though it was not logical or fair, they felt betrayed. Zeus knew he had not left. Granted, Iceman could have left his clothes and everything behind, that was in his personality. No matter what, Zeus was confident that Iceman would have called him. As Zeus was ready to turn off the lights for the night, he grew more worried about his friend. Zeus hit the lights, and before he reached his bed, Iceman turned them back on.

'Iceman!'

Surprised, Ice asked. 'Who were you expecting?'

'Where were you?'

'The Ground Round.'

'You missed dinner formation. You were AWOL.'

'No, I wasn't. I had a pass.'

'You should have left a note.'

'What? Are we married? Good night.'

* * *

Iceman was dark for the next three weeks and spoke little. He honored his promise to Kathleen and took a weekend pass. They met in Manhattan, stayed at the Trump across from Central Park and had a nice weekend. Ice's detachment from the Core of Cadets confirmed the rumors he was leaving West Point. The cynics returned to their pursuit of Iceman with renewed justified vigor. The cynics had their proof that he was a fraud. Iceman was never deeply committed to West Point. Through the drama, Iceman remained quiet, doing what he does. The week before the first rugby match, Iceman came alive. He coordinated a visit for a rugby game with Kathleen and her housemates. He recommended that each girl get their own hotel room. Hotel Thayer was not an option; the cadets were not on leave and it was too public. The West Point Motel, while not fancy, was just outside walking privileges so the guys could sneak out. Iceman told Kathleen to use the code name Reese and he assured her the front desk would understand.

Hours before Saturday's rugby match, the girls arrived at West Point and had to be cleared at the front gate by the MPs. They were able to skip the line for the public and use the line reserved for authorized guests. Iceman got their information from Kathleen and submitted the information to be approved as his guests. They asked for directions to the basketball complex and arrived to see Iceman, Thor and Zapata waiting. Introductions were made and they took the mile walk to the concession van. The tailgate began with food courtesy of Ty's wife. As the tailgate got humming, Sloane's temper began to rise. She pulled Iceman aside.

'Is this a fucking joke? Three guys? Do you enjoy fucking with me? First you, that I understand and respect, then Thor, now this shit.'

'Relax, you know I like you. I take care of the people I like. There aren't many. Are you excited for the rugby game?'

'Are you serious? Look at them; Thor and Zapata have potential. I get the rugby gorilla?'

'Give it a minute and then judge.'

'He better be some kind of superhero.'

'He's not, he's a god.'

'What?'

'Trust me.'

They arrived at their seats surrounded by the usual suspects. Energy started to build.

Sloane impatiently asked. 'Where is he?'

'In the locker room. Don't worry, I won't have to point him out.'

With five minutes on the scoreboard that marked the start of the match, Navy took the field. After Navy settled into warmups, Iceman started the chant. 'Zeus, Zeus, Zeus.' The thousand in attendance chanted as if ten thousand. Army took the field.

Sloane awed. 'Oh-my-God.'

'No, oh my Zeus.' Jack laughed.

Zeus was his usual self, and although Navy was ranked third in the country, it made no difference.

Kathleen turned to Sloane and Jack. 'He's amazing.' She was referring to his play.

Sloane smiled. 'He sure is. He's gorgeous.' She was not referring to his play. 'Thank you, Jack. I should never have doubted you.'

'He's more gorgeous on the inside.'

'Seriously.'

'Dead.'

* * *

On the march back to the concession van, Sloane pulled Jack over. 'You know she really likes you.'

'I like her too.'

'Don't break her heart.' Sloane demanded with a look of stern concern.

Jack stopped cold and looked into Sloane's eyes; she was notice-ably uncomfortable. 'I will.'

After a brief post-game celebration, the boys hustled back to their barracks. As they were not on leave, they could not join the girls on Saturday night at the motel. The girls left the cadets and went to check-in.

'Hi, I'm Kathleen. You have four rooms under my name.' The front clerk paused. 'Sorry, Reese sent us.'

'I see your reservation for six rooms. Here are your keys.'

Confused, Kathleen explained. 'There must be a mistake. Don't you need my credit card and ID and we only reserved four rooms, not six?'

'No mistake, enjoy your stay.'

Still confused, she handed out the keys and the girls went to their rooms. Kathleen checked her first room and it looked normal, so she sat down her overnight bag. She walked back out and checked her next room. The room was full of food and drink on ice. Kathleen picked up a board game and realized it was Twister. Only Jack. The room adjourned to her third room, where beer pong and other drinking games were set up. Only Jack. Early Sunday morning and the start of walking privileges, the cadets dressed in their exercise gear and ran to the motel. The eight had a fun time eating, playing drinking games and enjoying full-contact Twister. The boys had to be back by 1900 hours. The party and games were cut short so that the girls could give the boys a personal tour of their rooms.

Underwear and T-shirts were optional.

CHAPTER TWENTY-TWO

Colonel Sullivan reviewed his notes and glanced at his blank computer screen as he waited for Dr. Monroe to join him on their secure video call. The Colonel was not scheduled to meet Dr. Monroe, but his short report set off concern. The call and the actions taken, because of his report served as a career-defining moment for the Coronel. Both he and Dr. Monroe had reported to the Elders that the twins were the best pair of candidates in the Colonel's and Dr. Monroe's time with the Elders. The Elders eventually agreed after several detailed reports.

'Hello, Tom, thank you for being available for this emergency meeting.' Grace began the call.

'Never a problem. I assume you read my report?'

'It did not take long. *We have a serious problem with the twins.* You got my attention with the eight-word report. I assume you have a full report ready when we conclude our conversation.'

'I have a draft and I will amend it after our conversation today. The situation requires your assistance and the report will reflect what we agree upon today.'

Grace quickly noticed the nervous tone in Tom's voice, a reaction she had never experienced with him. 'I accept that, please begin.'

Sullivan regretfully began his report. 'Iceman is gone. When he is asked to sign the commitment letter, he will resign.'

'Did you get this information from your bug in their room?'

'No, I am just certain he is leaving. Since the end of basketball season, he has just shut down. He is too quiet. He doesn't talk about commitment day. When asked, he uses the same reply to the media and classmates: I am at Army. I had the hackers snoop around his computer and all his electric equipment, but they produced nothing. I tapped the phones at the basketball facility and he only made calls to his girl of interest. He is gone, and if he goes, Zeus most certainly will follow.'

'Your report was accurate; we do have a serious problem and an emergency on our hands. We have the best two candidates by our own accord and now we lost them. Not good, not good at all. The Elders will not be pleased. What do you recommend?'

'I have to brief them in.' Sullivan knew he was asking for a mighty concession.

'Not a chance.' Grace responded automatically without thinking.

'Then we lost them. If I do not…'

'Wait, I was too quick to respond; I did so reflexively. I see your point, but you are asking a lot.' Grace took a moment to gather her thoughts. 'Iceman will leave, but if you brief him in, the lure of the impossible mission could return our little sheep to the flock. The two immediate questions come to mind if I am even going to consider your proposal. First, are they worth it? I can answer that question for both of us, yes. The second question is, are they ready? We must move the timeframe up two years, which is not good. Worse, they go back to the same environment after the briefing. We keep Black Ops candidates in the dark for four years for two reasons: training and security. We use the training to mature the candidates, allowing them to grow to accept the awesome responsibility of being a Black Ops agent. While the candidates mature at an accelerated level, we protect the Elders' existence. After graduation, the Black Ops candidates are isolated from the world for three years to allow the message to be fully absorbed. Are they ready for the awesome responsibility?'

After investing a considerable amount of time asking himself the same question, Sullivan did not hesitate to respond. 'Yes. I am more than confident that they are. Their performance exceeds our lofty expectations, not solely due to their natural talents. The twins have a maturity level and mental toughness that drive their talents to unprecedented levels.'

'You been given this a little bit of thought, haven't you?' Grace joked to break the tension.

'Just a little.'

Returning to business, Grace asked. 'What if they say no? They decide Black Ops is not for them, then what?'

'They leave West Point and do not return to the training environment. They will maintain silence. On that, I have no doubt.'

'I agree with you. We have no choice. Send me the report.'

'I'm not finished; we have a second problem.' Sullivan knew he was asking too much of Grace.

'Tom, you are certainly full of good news.'

'Grace, we are not at fault. We did our job too well. Found ideal candidates, they trained to exceed even our tall projections. They know how good they are and being a second lieutenant in the army based at Ft. Bragg holds no interest to them.'

'Thank you, Tom. Please get to your second point.'

'If you're not crazy about the first point, you won't like the second.'

'If the Elders say no to the first point, everything else is irrelevant.'

CHAPTER TWENTY-THREE

Decision day was five days away. Iceman remained quiet about his thoughts and gave no hint. He did not have to, because all of West Point had already decided for him. He was gone. He wanted to make an informed decision and had one stop to make. Time to meet the Colonel.

Iceman stated in a cool and harsh voice. 'Colonel, I have and shown tremendous respect to you. I am leaving the Military Academy as is my right after my second year. I will not serve in the army and I will not speak to you again. I am leaving for Europe to play basketball professionally. I will put my name in the NBA draft in two years. I hate school and have no interest in college. Getting paid to play the game I love, play against the best competition outside the NBA and tour Europe for two years or more, if the NBA passes, is good with me. I am going to ask Zeus to join me and pick a university he would like to attend and I will play ball in that country. He, of course, can say no, but I want to give him the choice. I am certain he will be intrigued by the idea of returning to Europe. Kindly pass on my best to your bride and daughter, as they have been exceedingly kind to me.'

The Colonel responded. 'Iceman, I have no idea what you are talking about. You will not speak to me again?' The Colonel was blindsided by Europe. He had planned to talk Iceman out of going to another school. Playing basketball in Europe was genius, a perfect master plan. He had to give Iceman credit; he played his hand masterfully. He was amazed that Iceman had kept his entire thought process hidden from him. Iceman did not offer a hint, not the slightest tell, as to his master plan.

'You don't need to. Goodbye and thank you again.' Iceman walked to the door, determined to begin his next journey.

The Colonel was slightly intimidated by Iceman's calm control of the conversation. Sullivan lost a little composure. 'Wait, what do you want?' He meekly asked.

'Not to be treated as a fool, but with respect.' Iceman responded with calm intensity.

'I have respected you.'

'No, you have not. I am a good man, a loyal man and I will never be disrespected. I have talked to almost every cadet over the last two years, and other than Zeus, none were recruited by you. All the others worked hard for a Congressional nomination; we just got ours in the mail.'

'Let me explain.'

'Don't bother and do not interrupt. I am not finished. My godmother came and stayed at the Hotel Thayer during our special Beast Barracks at a time when the Academy only sends a picture home for proof of life. A visit she made when my class-mates in A-1 were not permitted contact with the outside world, including the phone. We went to mass with her, ordered to feed the ducks with her and went to brunch, including mimosas. I know A-1, because Zeus and I had Beast Barracks.'

'I understand, let me explain.'

'Sir, I was clear. Do not interrupt me. Head of Manpower and Use of Human Resources based at West Point? Your team is in the Pentagon. You work in the basement in an obscure corner of the post with no staff under the pretense of quality of life for your family. Fascinating, you say you commute to D.C. to the Pentagon, yet you have only visited a handful of times in the last two years. You disappear, but where? What is more interesting is that you are the senior officer for the basketball and rugby teams, traveling with both teams. Wait, what do those two teams have in common: me and Zeus? When you picked me and Zeus up to have dinner at your home, which was lovely, at the beginning of the plebe year, your Toyota Camry had 27, 345 miles. You have two cars, you walk to work, you have taken few flights in two years, yet you have 57,643 miles the last time you picked us up. You are so full of shit and Europe is calling me. I just wanted you to know I don't get played. Ever. I am sorry it ends like this, but I am more pissed off that you wasted two years of my life.' Iceman did not believe the last part of his speech. He was grateful for his time at West Point, he added it for drama.

'How do you know my flight history?'

'Seriously? Is that rhetorical? We both know Zeus hacked the information. You know what? Show me your frequent flyer miles. I'll wait. How did you put so many miles on your car? Where do you go? While we are talking conspiracy theories, I think you bugged our room. On a few too many occasions, you knew the answer before we told you. Your eyes betrayed recognition of information that could only be gathered in our room.'

'Are you finished?'

'Most certainly, goodbye.' Iceman stated with finality.

'Wait.'

'No.'

'Please.'

'Alright, only because I do like you. What do you want? And you better tell me the truth.'

'Agreed.'

'You are lying.'

'Wait, wait, wait. Hear me out.' Sullivan had promised Grace to hold back as many of the disclosures as possible. He knew he had to press the limits agreed upon with Grace and the Elders.

'Fuck off, as I have resigned, I can tell you to fuck off with my right to free speech.'

'Correct, but do you mean these resignation papers?'

'Incredible, just proves my point. You pulled my resignation papers.'

'Just give me 20 minutes, please.' The Colonel requested.

'You are lucky or unfortunate that I really do like you.'

'Ok, let's get started.'

Iceman candidly responded. 'No chance, not without Zeus.'

'Agreed.'

* * *

'Cadet Collins reported as ordered, sir.'

'At ease, Zeus.'

Confused, Zeus took a seat. He was sweating out of nerves, confusion and the long, fast run to the remote office occupied by the Colonel.

'I cannot tell you everything. I can give you an overview of some of the mission plans on the condition you are sworn to secrecy. Iceman, sit down.'

'Sir, I am out of here.'

'I said, sit down. You are acting like a child; if you demand respect, then you must give it. Sit.' The Colonel desperately tried to regain control. If Iceman left, the Colonel knew he did not have a second chance. The Colonel's door might have well been a portal to Europe.

'Yes, sir. No excuse, sir.' Iceman responded with true regret for disrespecting the Colonel.

'Again, as I was saying. I cannot and will not give you all the details, but I will bring into focus our vision for you two.' The Colonel felt the pressure of his window to retain the twins closing quickly.

'Why didn't we get to choose our majors after completing the core curriculum after two years? Why were we assigned three majors rather than two? Why did we take 24 credit hours a semester rather than 18, play ball and attend summer school? After summer school, we attended Airborne and Pathfinder school last year?' Iceman interrupted to keep the Colonel off balance and maintain control of the conversation. 'Now, this summer, we are assigned summer school again, Air Assault and Combat Medic School. Just stop.'

'Does he always talk this much?' The Colonel asked Zeus to draw his focus away from Iceman.

'Yes.' Zeus answered, uncomfortable with the tension in the room.

'Stop talking, I will continue.' the Colonel stated firmly to Iceman. 'Back to the program.' The Colonel, in broad strokes, laid out the Elder's mission statement and the twins' role in it.

'We have been training to be James Bond based on the life of Ian Fleming. Zeus, you probably don't know this, but the James Bond series was President Kennedy's favorite book series. He was Irish Catholic like us. Maybe don't read *Live or Let Die*, though; it is racist against black people, not Irish Catholics. Colonel, would you kindly finish your story? I have a plane to catch.' Iceman responded. He never took his eyes off the Colonel. He was intensely probing for subtle tells.

'Iceman, I know what you are doing.'

'What?' Iceman responded innocently.

'You are dissecting me.'

'What do you mean? I don't follow?' Again, the aw shucks, I am just an idiot look, Iceman loved to use it.

'Just stop. Have you ever lost in cards?'

'Yes, once on the five of clubs in a gin game. Shit, with the files you kept on me, you probably already know that.'

'How many cards were played?'

'43.'

'The probability?'

'If I held the five of clubs, I would have won, and if I threw it 92.4% chance, I would lose.'

'Why did you throw it?' The Colonel asked, confused why Iceman lost on purpose.

'I was up $25 and lost $5 on that game. I could double the bet after my opponent's masterful win. If I had won, he would have quit. So, I lost $5 to win the next $125, because our bet doubled; he won two other players and thought they had a chance. I cracked them and walked with $500 in my pocket.'

As he told the story, the aw-shucks look was replaced with a cold stare. The angry competitor was not caged.

'How old were you?'

'16.'

Sullivan continued his probe. 'Who were your opponents? Older, I would guess.'

Iceman, remembering the card games fondly, replied. 'Sometimes, I would go with my dad to work on Saturdays. If he was busy with a trial, he would go to his law firm on Saturdays to keep up with the workload. Some of the other partners in the firm would pretend to go to the office to work, but they really went to play cards, usually gin. The morning games were friendly, and I played in those. The later games were high stakes, too rich for my blood, and I went home with my dad anyway, so those games were not an option. I was banned from all the card games after I snuck into my first match in the high-stakes game.'

'What happened?'

'I cleaned out my dad's partners. He was really pissed.'

'Are you certain you are not dissecting me?'

'No, sir. I am.' Iceman smiled with pride.

'Now stop, shut up and listen.'

'Ok, on one condition, you tell everything to Zeus and me and not what you are selling.'

'Agreed.' The Colonel responded. He could report to Monroe that he did his best, but Iceman blew through their first level of protection for the Elders.

'You sure? Because if you're sure, you are sure.' Iceman asked, giving the Colonel fair warning that this was his last chance.

'Alright. I can take you through the plan, vision and choice in detail on graduation day. I must reserve full disclosure and your complete commitment until graduation day. Is that fair?'

Iceman turned to Zeus and explained. 'He is not lying. If you are in, I am into listening and might be buying what he is selling. I would just sunburn outside the gym in Greece anyway.'

Zeus nodded.

'Again, as I was saying, we started a program well…'

'Well, it is shitty water just details, please.' Iceman refused to give up the room.

'You two were identified as unique at age 15. Compare it to being recruited to Duke Basketball or that book series my daughter fancies, Harry Potter. There are others of you right now in other universities, but you two were identified as unique.'

'We are the two candidates you have selected for a unique program after West Point.' Iceman stated and did not ask.

'Yes, as of now, but the final decision is confirmed two years from now. A lot can happen in two years. Again, I must stress complete secrecy. Speaking of this would be a life-changing mistake for you.'

Iceman responded while Zeus digested the information and asked. 'Understood. We have the right to say no?'

'Yes, you would enter the Army as Airborne, Air Assault, rangers with your choice of station to execute your five-year commitment.' The Colonel finished. 'That is all I can comment on at this time.'

'If we say no, can our five-year commitment include special forces, dark Ops?'

'Asked and answered Jack.'

'Yes, sir.' Iceman got it, definitely dark Ops. He also noted the use of his proper name.

Zeus asked. 'Anything else we should know?'

The Colonel nodded. 'Your unique journey is deadly.'

* * *

On the long road back to the barracks, Iceman asked Zeus. 'What do you think?'

'Don't know. You?'

Iceman just looked at Zeus.

Zeus stopped and looked back at Iceman. 'We are committed.'

Iceman replied. 'Right, I was there.'

A few minutes later, Zeus worked through the true impact of the commitment. 'We started the bootlegging business, because we could just walk away. We can't just walk away anymore.' Zeus continued, 'We must shut down the business. Where are you going?'

'A detour, I need to walk the Hudson. You make a good point.' Iceman answered.

30 minutes later, Iceman returned to the barracks and started. 'I figured it out, but like most of my ideas that have all worked, you may be hesitant. I need the business to keep my sanity. I am staying in the business, and I would like you to stay, so I will meet you halfway. We stay in for our cow year, then leave the business to Reese and Ty. We are done and will never use or be involved in any way during our last year here. We have enough leave this year to keep us busy, and with bootlegging, I can make it through the year. During our firstie year, we have our freedom, so there is no need for the business. We are untouchable now, you heard Colonel. If we get caught, they can't kick us out; they need us. We will receive a mild reprimand and shut the business down. Fair?'

Zeus thought a moment. 'Fair.'

'Let's get ready to chase and avoid death.'

CHAPTER TWENTY-FOUR

Another season of suck was highlighted by summer school, Air Assault school and Combat Medic Specialist School. The twins were scheduled to take the 16-week medic training in six weeks. They were scheduled to attend a special camp in Nevada, three hours from Las Vegas, to accommodate the six-week schedule. Their schedule was so packed that they did not receive the five days of leave enjoyed the previous year.

'Are you ready to kick off another exciting summer school experience? I'm pumped; let's light this candle. I know you are pumped, Zeus; I can feel it.' Iceman celebrated in a tone dripped in sarcasm.

'Summer school is fine and this year we have freedom after classes. Let's make the most of it.'

'I'm your guy for that. Astronomy and Spanish in Conversation? Seriously? How is that useful?'

'Astronomy is helpful when we get lost at sea or on land. We study the stars and the stars guide us home. Last year we graduated from Pathfinder school and Astronomy was helpful when we fuck that up. We are fluent in book Spanish, but we both know people don't speak by the book. Conversations flow with slang and common language. Both classes make complete sense.'

'Check out the big brain on Zeus. We have two hours of astronomy and two hours of Spanish in the morning before lunch. After lunch, we have two more hours of Spanish. I need four hours to workout, then dinner. After dinner, we hit the Ground Round.'

Zeus liked the schedule and asked. 'Do you want a workout partner?'

'Nope.'

'Didn't think so.'

In the third week of class, Iceman walked alone after lunch from the mess hall to class. Zeus walked ahead, because Iceman dragged his bullshit session with Reese and Ty too long.

During his walk, he heard a distinct voice with a unique accent. 'Iceman, Iceman, do you have a moment?'

'Hey, Prince. How have you been?' Iceman liked the Prince from Cameroon. West Point had a handful of foreign dignitaries studying in the Core of Cadets.

'I am in need of your assistance.' Prince requested.

'Sure, what can I do for you?'

'My country is playing in the World Cup final tournament and I am extremely excited. It is the first time in many, many years we have qualified.'

'Nice. Kind of funny, my country is an expression, but for you, it's a reality.'

Prince, too nervous to understand Iceman's joke, continued. 'I am in need of your assistance to get a group of people to cheer with me and a place to go.'

'I can make that happen, when is it?' Iceman was always excited for any reason to throw a party.

'Tomorrow at 1600 hours. Maybe we can get there early.'

'Absolutely.'

'Would you mind terribly riding with me? I do not wish to arrive alone.'

'Of course, but two things. First, Zeus needs to ride along. Second, should we take an Uber, because of the drinking?'

'I do not drink alcoholic beverages.'

'Perfect, I'll drink for the both of us. Prince, you and I were destined to watch the World Cup together.'

* * *

Zeus asked Iceman. 'Where are we supposed to meet Yannick to walk to the parking lot?'

'Yannick? You mean Prince? Down the hill in five minutes. We aren't walking up that mountain to the lot, he insisted on picking us up.'

Zeus shook his head in disgust and asked. 'Are you serious? You talk to him all the time and you didn't know his name is Yannick?'

'Prince works just fine.'

Prince Yannick pulled up in a BMW 750li.

Zeus and Iceman looked at each other and nodded approval. Zeus jumped in the front seat, excited to talk football. Ireland had also qualified for the final championship. Iceman jumped in the back.

As they pulled away, Iceman asked. 'What is the World Cup? Sailing?'

Prince and Zeus looked at each other, mortified and both started screaming at Iceman.

Iceman was immediately placed on the defensive. 'Take it easy, take it easy. So, this is some big football, soccer thing, got it? Like the Super Bowl.'

Zeus shook his head. 'The Super Bowl is not even close; it is a national game. The World Cup is global. You don't cheer for one team that, in all probability, isn't your favorite team, because they didn't make it. You cheer for the team you gambled on, or you like to watch the commercials. The World Cup, you cheer for your country. Not close, stupid comment.'

'My mistake, but it's still just soccer.'

'Shut up.' Zeus was done with Iceman's silly ignorance.

'Roger that.'

* * *

The 750li rolled up to the Ground Round, greeted with stares. The luxury sedan stood out in the working-class parking lot. As they walked up to the bar, Iceman looked around to spot their group, but they were the first to arrive. Walking up to the bar, Iceman ordered. 'Two Buds and two double Jameson, Prince, what do you want? I got the first round.'

'No, no, I insist.'

'Ok, I'll get the next round.'

'Iceman, I am your host. I must pay for everything.'

Zeus disagreed. 'Prince, really, that's not necessary.'

'But it is. I'll have a juice.'

'Cranberry?' Zeus asked.

'Hang on a second, this is a big game. You need to get tuned up. You don't drink, so let's throw some caffeine down your throat. How about a coke?' Iceman offered.

'A coke would be nice.'

'Alright, a coke it is.' Iceman turned to the bartender. 'Throw in a coke with the order and start this man a tab. I'm starving. It's 25-cent wing happy hour. Prince, you got the drinks, so Zeus and I will get the food. I'll order us 40 wings to start. We like spicy. Is that cool with you, Prince, or can I get some mild if you want?'

'Iceman, please understand, you and the others you invited are all my guests. I am your host. I am fine with spicy like you two.'

'I feel kind of uncomfortable. We are not here for free drinks and food. We are here to hang with you and watch the boats.'

'Very funny, Iceman. I invited you, because I knew you were not the type of person to take advantage of my obligation.'

'You're a good man, Charlie Brown.'

'Who is Charlie Brown?'

'Ask Zeus… never mind that; it's not important. Just remember the good man part.' Zeus smiled and looked over at Iceman, who laughed at him. 'He's not from Mars either.'

Two carloads of Iceman's hand-selected cadets rolled in and introductions were made. Most were excited for the big match. Rounds were ordered, countless wings were delivered, fries and onion rings were added and the group settled in.

Cal, the fullback on the football team, walked over to Iceman and company, joining them to make a fourth at their tall boy table. Cal was from Collinwood, a poor black neighborhood in Cleveland. He did not receive the best education growing up, so academic demands were tough on Cal. Iceman could relate to Cal, because of his playground experiences on the basketball court. Many of the playgrounds were in Englewood, one of the poorest, most violent neighborhoods in Chicago. Iceman tutored Cal in all his subjects. They came up short in Physics and Cal had to retake the course. Cal was not permitted off post, nor were several of the other guests in attendance. Required summer school due to academic deficiencies brought lockdown. Iceman handpicked right-thinking cadets, so the infraction was safe. The trustworthy rogue cadets used escape maneuvers designed by Iceman to free themselves from post. 'Iceman, you know anything about this World Cup shit? My car about pissed themselves in excitement on the way over.'

'Something about boats.'

'Boats? Why is there soccer on?' Cal asked.

Zeus finished his wing and wiped his face. 'Stop with the boat thing. You sound stupid. Cal, it's football, not soccer.'

Yannick added. 'My country has advanced to the final's championship tournament. We take great pride in our team's accomplishments.'

Cal went to ask. 'So, it's like the Super…'

Iceman slammed down his beer and interrupted. 'Don't do it. I already got my head knocked off for that. Prince, do you know Cal?'

'Only to watch him when I attended football games.'

'Cal, this is Prince and Prince, this is Cal.'

Zeus added. 'His name is Yannick.'

Cal laughed. 'Who the fuck would want to be called Yannick when his title is Prince? Riddle me that, Seamus.'

Iceman and Prince joined Cal in the big laugh at Zeus' expense. Prince quickly turned to the match and Iceman quieted the room.

Cameroon took the field. The match started and waged on for nine minutes without a score.

Iceman mumbled to Cal. 'As boring as I thought. Look at those two; they are on the edge of their seats. For what? Nothing is happening, you know what I am saying?'

'Yep, but we got beer, wings and buddies.'

'Roger that.'

The game continued in silence. The only voices heard were orders of wings and beer, and those were usually hand gestures. Iceman couldn't take anymore and got up to take a piss.

* * *

'Did I miss anything?' Iceman said jokingly as he returned from the men's room.

Prince shook his head. Zeus explained to Iceman. 'Prince is nervous, because England has dominated the time of possession. The action has been on Cameroon's end, so they need to clear their end and keep possession on England's end. England is putting too much pressure on the Cameroon defense.'

'Got it.' Cal, listening in, nodded.

At the 21:35 minute mark, England scored. Zeus and Prince were defeated.

'What's up? What did I miss? It's only one goal and there is a ton of time left?' Iceman was baffled.

Zeus explained. 'One goal is like 10 points in basketball or two touchdowns in football. To make matters worse, England is great at defense and ball control. Cameroon really needed to score first to pull England out of their conservative style. Cameroon is the underdog; they really needed to score first.'

'Fuck, but great comebacks by underdogs is why sports are great. Come on, Prince, let's get you another Coke. All is not lost. The next 24 minutes suggested otherwise. England dominated possession and should have scored one, maybe two more goals if not for the brilliant play of Cameroon's goalkeeper. The crowd jumped and twisted with every attempt and roared when the goalkeeper made a miraculous save. Even Cal and Iceman were swept up in the tension.

To start the second half, Cameroon took the kickoff and established possession in England's end. At the 51:32 mark, Cameroon launched a deliberate shot on goal.

Iceman jumped off his seat with his mighty vertical leaped 36 inches in the air in excitement. 'Go to your home, motherfucker.' England's goalkeeper, with tremendous effort, managed to deflect the missile. Prince and Zeus dropped their heads. Iceman got pissed. He yelled at the funeral. He found his inner John Belushi while the play was stopped. *Over? Did you say over? Nothing is over until we decide it is. Was it over when the Germans bombed Pearl Harbor? Hell no!* He was interrupted by the placement of the corner kick. He started to chant. Who? Who? Cameroon: Who? Who? Cameroon. The cadets jumped in on the chant as the corner kick was off at the 51:36 mark.

GOOOOOOOOOOOOOOOOOOAL, GOOOOOOOOOOOOOOOOOAL, GOOOOOOOOOOAL.

Prince started to cry, hugs were everywhere, high fives were slapped and more beer was ordered. England had a fight on their hands. The momentum turned and Cameroon, ignited with renewed energy, was ready to keep the pressure on England. The game raged on, as did the Cameroon fans at the Ground Round. *Who? Who? Cameroon,* the cheer was so loud patrons of the restaurant side came into the bar area to jump in the excitement.

Cal, during a short break in the action while the others drank greedily, exclaimed. 'This shit is intense, tight as shit.'

A brief delay in response as Zeus finished his gulp of beer. 'Told you.'

Iceman acknowledged. 'You were right. Now, shut up, game on.'

It happened at the 74:48-minute mark. After the tension and cheering, the moment came.

GOOOOOOOOOOOAL, GOOOOOOOOOOOOOOOAL,GOOOOOOOOOOOOOOOAL.

Cameron 2, England 1.

If Cameroon could just hang in there and hold the lead for the next 15 minutes and change, Iceman thought, Prince would lose his shit. Shit, I might lose my shit.

The next 15 minutes felt like 15 hours, with every shot taken by England a pressure cooker for the crowd at the Ground Round.

Iceman felt the tension, so close, just two more minutes, but he refused to say anything. He didn't want to jinx Cameroon. One minute, they got it. The ball is in their end and England is putting on the pressure, but they got this. 30 seconds... then 10 seconds... 90:00... They did it.

Iceman shot out of chair along with Cal. 'They fucking did it.'

The crowd yelled shut up. Iceman looked around and then at the television. *Why are they still playing?* 'Zeus, why are they still playing?'

'Shut up. Stoppage time.'

What the fuck is stoppage time? How long is stoppage time? Why is the time clock wrong? I was right. This is a stupid game. Iceman was snapped out of his trance with the roar of the bar. *Who, who, Cameroon.* He looked at Prince, who was hysterically crying and hugging everybody. Game over. Still don't understand stoppage time, but Zeus and Prince were right: this shit is off the chain.

As Iceman drank his celebratory beer, Prince approached him. 'Thank you, Iceman. This is one of the happiest days of my life. You made me feel like I was watching the game with countrymen. I told my father of your kindness and he is grateful to you.' He turned to the twins. 'Will you watch the next match with me again?'

Iceman jumped the invitation. 'Fuck yes. Right, Zeus?!'

'Great time, great match and a great host. Of course. When is it?'

'Next week, Monday, so just five days.'

The twins looked at each other and back at Prince. Zeus spoke for the two of them. 'Sorry, Prince. We ship out on Saturday. We report to Air Assault School on Sunday. I'm really sorry.'

'I don't understand. The summer school will not be over.'

'It will be for us; we are the only two people in our classes and our schedule was cut short so we could attend other schools. I'm sorry, man. But you got Cal, right Cal?'

'I got you, Prince.'

'Cal, can you bring more cadets?'

'Maybe just a few more, Prince. More isn't always better.' Cal advised.

Prince still choked up. 'Thanks, guys. I've got a crew.'

The three monsters pushed Prince in a playful fashion and Iceman yelled. 'Barkeep, another round and kindly supersize my friend's coke. He deserves it.'

* * *

After being dropped off at the bottom of the hill, the twins walked back to the barracks.

Iceman turned to Zeus and asked. 'Did you hear my Bill Murray moment from the movie Caddyshack? The King of Cameroon is grateful to me, *so I got that goin for me, which is nice.*'

Sabalauski Air Assault School, located at Ft. Campbell, KY, was the next stop for the twins.

* * *

During their trip to Kentucky, Iceman commented. 'Zeus, I googled Air Assault School. Check this out.'

'Iceman, we got all that and more in our briefing packet. Why don't you just read them?'

Iceman tuned Zeus out. 'We are trained in insertion, evacuation and Pathfinder missions, whatever that is. The Pathfinder shit should be easy since we already did it. We focus on mastery of rappelling techniques and sling load procedures. What the fuck is a sling load procedure?'

'Don't know, hence training.'

Iceman continued to ignore him. 'At the end, all we have to do is a timed 12-mile rucksack march. Only 10 days long, pretty easy.'

'We'll see. Did you read the part that Air Assault School is called the 10 toughest days in the army? 15% of the class drop out the first day and only 45% graduate?'

Iceman, still not impressed with the challenge, asked. 'What's your point?'

* * *

The Air Assault cadets loaded the aircraft and when settled, Iceman asked. 'Where are the seat belts and why are the doors open?'

'Centrifugal force.' Replied the Master Sergeant.

'What?' Unlike Airborne school, where Iceman did not want to jump out of a perfectly good airplane, he was more than ready to jump out of a centrifugal death trap called a helicopter. 'Zeus, did you hear him? Centrifugal force, what the fuck kind of answer is that?'

'Please, shut up.' Zeus pleaded.

'Right, big bad Zeus is scared of heights. I forgot.'

'No, you didn't.'

'Now, I know how you feel. Come to think of it, I am embarrassed. I shouldn't be surprised. All the war movies with helicopters show the doors opened and I never did see a seat belt.' Iceman used his stories to annoy Zeus and draw his fear of heights to Iceman and his rambles. This time was different: Iceman told the stories to distract both Zeus and him. 'What is your favorite war movie? Patton is great, but I have to go Apocalypse Now. *I love the smell of napalm in the morning. You know, one time, we had a hill bombed for 12 hours. When it was over, I woke up. We didn't find one of 'em, not one stinkin' dink body. The smell, you know that gasoline smell?! The whole hill. Smelled like victory. Someday, this war is gonna end.* Damn good Duval impersonation, don't you think? How good was Duval in…'

'For the love of God, please shut up.'

'Roger that. Hey, we are up.'

The twins came in first and second again in Air Assault school. Iceman's enthusiasm to get out of a helicopter mistaken for motivation won out. Next stop for the twins was Combat Medic Specialist Training Program.

* * *

'Why the fuck are we here?' Iceman asked Zeus.

'I'm not sure.'

'Is this why they told us to wear civilian clothes?'

'I'm not sure.'

'Good talk.'

A car that looked military-issued, but did not have government plates, picked up the waiting twins at McCarren's Airport in Las Vegas. The twins knew there were several military installations outside of Vegas, but what they were looking at, when the car stopped, was not military. The compound looked like a massive training facility. The driver dropped them off, never exited the car and drove away.

'I'm guessing that big black guy walking towards us has all our answers.' Iceman suggested.

'So, the wonder twins report for training. Let's get started. I'll walk you to your barracks. Your gear is stowed in your foot-locker at the end of your bunk. Change into PT gear and meet me out front. I'll be your instructor for the next six weeks. The course is designed for 16 weeks, so we have work to do and we ain't cutting no corners. Colonel Sullivan informed me the fearsome Zeus and Iceman can handle the challenge. I'll decide if he was correct.'

The twins quickly changed and reported as ordered.

'Well, well, well, we got Gary Grant. Gary, are we unable to meet your fashion demands?'

Iceman confused, paused and replied with complete innocence and stupidity. 'Sir, it's Cary Grant.'

'Boy, did you just call me sir? Do I have a look of me that suggested to you that I do not work for a living? My name is Master Sergeant Iownyourass, but you will never speak it. I knew Cary Grant. He was good, elegant people. That is why I named you Gary. Think of it. Hold up, don't bother thinking; nobody gave you permission to think. Accept it like the dog. No, a dog is too high a compliment. I like dogs. Think of it as a rat that invaded your home… hold up, you ain't got no home, just my home. So, I got to take you into my home, a home where you are not welcome. A rat that I am forced to live with, so I am forced to give it a name. So, Gary, I ask you, do you accept you are the rat I am forced to live with, or should I call an exterminator? I have no need to hear you speak; this is the last time you will be asked to imagine. Me and my people be doing the imagining for you. Just shut up in my line that is only but a part of my world and knock out 50 push-ups.'

As Iceman dropped and followed orders, he strangely noticed. *That sergeant, while spitting in my face, had remarkably fresh breath.*

* * *

After three days of intense training, Master Sergeant Iownyourass became civilized to the twins and allowed them to speak.

Zeus took advantage of his earned privilege and asked. 'What is this place called?'

'Fort None of Your Business.'

'What is your name?'

'I already told you, Master Sergeant Iownyourass. We are not friends. I will continue to train and evaluate you in the three fields: Emergency Field Technician, to include Basic Life Support, Field Craft with an emphasis on Tactical Combat Casualty Care and general emergency care, including biological and chemical warfare. You will finish with Field Training exercises to model real combat missions. Your training has been modified

226

for noncombat medical emergencies to include using available resources. In the field, you may not have a full medical bag, but you will be trained in quick patch-ups with available resources. On every mission, you will bring duct tape; it is second in value only to your weapons. Off you go.'

The twins hustled to their next lesson, Iceman commented. 'He seemed nice, a real conversationalist. It was good to get to know him better.'

The twins completed the 16-week program in six. Iownyourass trained them hard, but provided no compliment or feedback regarding their performance. He simply dismissed the twin at the conclusion of their training. Iownyourass did report to Colonel Sullivan. 'They were as advertised. Zeus edged out Iceman for top man.' After his brief report, Iownyourass ended the call.

The twins departed Fort None of Your Business, sat at the airport bar and waited for their flight to JFK. Zeus toasted. 'Here's to us.'

'Roger that. What a boring summer.'

CHAPTER TWENTY-FIVE

With four weeks until the start of Iceman's third basketball season, just prior to him going dark, he invited the Fairfield housemates to a weekend at West Point. Cows, third-year cadets, were entitled to four weekend leaves a semester and Iceman was granted an additional leave for forfeiting his Christmas break for basketball. Iceman used three of his nine leaves prior to the visit to spend time with Kathleen. They spent two of the weekends in Manhattan together and the third was a group visit to Fairfield. Kathleen was excited to visit West Point again and to see Jack in the black gold scrimmage prior to the football game, because it was a football weekend, hotels were booked years in advance. The West Point Motel desk made some questionable cancellations to accommodate Iceman. Ice did not want to be greedy, so he accepted only four rooms. The hotel manager insisted on six, but Iceman refused. Jack explained to Kathleen, who explained to her housemates the boys could not leave post on Friday or Saturday, but could on Sunday. He explained only amateurs got stupid and broke the rules on football weekends. The officers and hardcore cadets were on vigilant watch for drunk cadets or cadets not on post. No one watched Sunday morning; the event was over. Therefore, girlfriends and families headed home.

Iceman outlined the plan. They meet at the basketball complex at 1800 after basketball practice on Friday. Saturday morning, the girls attend the cadet parade, followed by Zeus escorting the girls to the basketball facility to watch the black and gold basketball scrimmage. After the scrimmage, the group walks across the street to watch Zapata play football.

The girls arrived at the basketball facility on Friday as planned. Thor escorted them to the basketball conference room. Iceman was taking off the aluminum foil from the platters of food served courtesy of Ty's wife. Marcus, the complex director, helped her and set up the hidden adult beverages in his office.

Iceman toasted the group. 'This is a tailgate. In an hour, we walk across the street and watch Zapata's roommate play 150lbs. football.'

150lbs. football was a fast, fun game to watch. The players weighed in at 159lbs. or less the Wednesday before the game. The players cut weight early in the week and gained weight late in the week, much like wrestlers. By kick-off, the average playing weight was 165lbs. The linemen, running backs, linemen in all positions were roughly the same weight. Army was extremely talented, with several former high school stars who were too small for major college football. Army dominated the first half, so the group walked and got ice cream after a brief stop at the concession van.

'I thought drinking like this on a football weekend was danger-ous.' Kathleen asked Jack.

'We have 45 minutes until the assholes raise their antennas. Ice cream is always safe.'

The game and walk were fun, they all enjoyed themselves. The group heckled Iceman's ice cream consumption rate, which he turned into a celebration of being impervious to brain freeze. The group became close, and relationships continued to grow. After ice cream, the girls returned to the motel and the boys walked back to the barracks. The next morning, the girls were surprised to find breakfast to include mimosas and bloody Mary's delivered as room service. The motel obviously did not provide room service. Ty and Reese had surprised them. After breakfast, they arrived at the basketball complex. Iceman reserved them a parking space in the coaches' lot between the basketball arena and the football stadium. The tailgate, sponsored by a restauranteur from Manhattan, had already begun to set up. Kathleen saw Jack from a distance, almost sprinting towards her.

'Hi, you. Sorry, I can't make out with you in public. PDA is frowned upon.'

'Hi, PDA?' Kathleen asked with a flirty, pouty face.

'Public display of affection.' Jack explained.

'Silly.'

'Very.'

'Where is every one else?' Kathleen asked about the other members of the team. 'Where's Thor?'

'Taking the bus later, they will be here in 45 minutes.'

'Why don't you take the bus?'

'Long story.' Jack's eyes drifted towards the other girls. 'Hey, they are waving at us; you better get going. I'll see you soon. Do you know where you are going?'

'Not really.'

'Follow them.' Jack pointed to the massive herd walking down from the parking lots in the mountains, past the athletic facilities, to the parade ground.

'What is the story with this parade? Why is it such a big deal?' Kathleen asked just as Jack was running off.

'I've never done it or seen it. We always have practice, but I understand it is packed with thousands of people and it's pretty cool. The parade is not a parade, it is a cadet review. The Core of Cadets march in full dress uniform past the senior officers for inspection. The review takes place on the plain, surrounded by famous statues. You'll have a little time to wander after the review. Zeus has to change out of his full-dress uniform into dress grey. Make sure you walk around the plain and find Patton's statue facing the library. You and I both need to go. Wait, hang on a second. Tell Sloane Zeus is in the very front of the review.' With that, Jack was off and Kathleen joined the group.

Iceman finished his morning workout and returned to the locker room to get ready for the black-gold scrimmage. While in the locker room, the players fueled up and hydrated. The black and gold scrimmage was usually the starting five against the bench players. Iceman insisted that he play with the bench players who worked hard to push the starters to get better in every practice. While the team was in the locker room, fans were waiting for the football game. After the cadet review, they walked in to watch. Several hundred people at any given time watched the scrimmage. Zeus escorted the girls to their seats. The team took the court and the scrimmage started.

Beth asked Zeus. 'Why is Thor playing against Iceman? I thought he told me the starters play against the rest of the team?'

'Usually, that's true, but Iceman likes to beat up on the starters as a thank you to the practice players and to push the starters. You'll hear him talk the whole time. The coaches tell him repeatedly to watch his language.'

Sloane laughed. 'None of that comes as a surprise.'

Zeus said simply. 'Enjoy your laugh now, it gets pretty uncomfortable.'

Kathleen, concerned with the warning, asked. 'How so?'

'He is ruthless.'

Coach Durham threw the ball to black. 'Black ball coming down.' Then it started.

'Where that superstar rookie at, the one playing in my spot, he's all mine. Come on, rookie, enjoy this moment in front of fans. Once the season starts, you'll never play in front of fans again. I never come off my court. Get superstar the ball, big-time recruit. Come on, big time, get open. Someone set him a screen, some help; he's dying over here.'

Thor made a post-move and scored.

Iceman turned to his teammate in gold. 'Not a problem. You made him work, but he can't do that all game. I'll get three back right here on Superstar. Give me the ball.' Holding the ball, Iceman told Superstar. 'Ok, big time.' Superstar reached for the ball and Iceman told him. 'Don't reach. You reach, I teach.' He reached again only to find his face hit Iceman's somewhat legally thrown elbow. 'That had to hurt, told you not to reach. I am going to drop a three right here.' Iceman pointed to the floor where he stood, gave up the ball, faked going to the basket and shot back out to the spot he had pointed. Before the superstar could recover, Iceman got the ball back and the shot was off in a flash. As soon as the ball left his hands, Ice called out. 'Three, big time, get that out of the net.' Iceman was at half-court when the ball went in.

Kathleen turned to Zeus. 'This is uncomfortable. Why does he do it?'

Before Zeus could answer, Sloane interrupted. 'I love it.'

'He is making them better. He gets them to play harder than they thought possible.'

The game wore on and Iceman switched players to guard a different starter.

'Why is he switching players?' Kathleen asked.

'He guards all of them during the scrimmage. He knows he would break a player if he stayed on him too long.'

Beth spoke up. 'I noticed he hasn't guarded Thor.'

'He saves him for last and it is nasty.' Zeus paused. 'After a few minutes of Iceman on Thor, the coaches usually call the practice. Thor gets extremely heated and Iceman is relentless on him.'

'But Thor is bigger.' Kathleen asked.

'The Jack you know is not Iceman.' He turned to Gina. 'Zapata is an unbelievable boxer and punished Iceman.'

Gina responded. 'So, Iceman is not the toughest. My man beat him.'

'I didn't say that. I said he punished him; I didn't say he won.' Zeus explained.

'You were awesome at rugby; you weren't like this.' Kathleen noted.

'We are different guys on the field, ring, or court than off it. Here we go, Iceman and Thor.'

'Bring that weak ass shit, Thor, bring that tired ass weak ass shit of yours. Same tired game since I met you.' Thor got the ball and with his strong, quick hands, Iceman ripped it out of his hands and sprinted down the court. Thor chased in hot pursuit. Iceman raced down the left side of the court and moved slightly to his right to throw down a monster two-handed dunk at the front of the rim. Thor almost caught him, but it was too late. Iceman crushed the dunk, but Thor's momentum crashed into Iceman, who went down hard. The crowd sucked in a deep breath. Iceman popped up. 'You can't even knock me down hard.' And the crowd exhaled.

Sloane turned to Kathleen. 'He's crazy.'

Zeus overheard. 'Sometimes, well, maybe all the time, but it is always controlled. He knows what he is doing. Watch him after the scrimmage.'

A couple of possessions later, Iceman had to leave Thor to help a teammate on defense. Iceman deflected the shot, but it landed right into Thor's hands. Thor smiled as he wound up to dunk on Iceman, who was clearly beat. Iceman jumped anyway, to Thor's surprise and delight. Thor's dunk was going to embarrass Iceman. He never should have challenged him. Thor was right; Ice knew he was beaten. In midair, he kicked his right leg into Thor's groin. Thor bent over and dropped the ball.

'You thought you were going to dunk on me? You must be crazy.' Thor got up angry and started to approach Iceman. 'Now I know you're crazy. Check yourself, Thor, don't walk up on me. You knocked me down; I got you back. Don't make it worse by catching a beating.'

Coach Durham roared. 'Practice is over. Go to the locker room now.'

'You alright?' Iceman asked Thor.

'Fucker, I knew you were coming for me, but that was offsides, even for you.'

'Valid point, let's go say hi to our chicks.' Jack acknowledged and with that, Iceman was gone.

As Thor and Jack walked over to say hi to the group, their pleasantries were interrupted by Coach Durham. 'I said the locker room now.' Thor and Jack nodded to the group and headed to the locker room.

Zeus escorted the group out of the basketball facility and offered an explanation. 'I am sure the coach is pissed at Iceman for taking over the scrimmage. They'll be out soon enough. Iceman told me this might happen, so we have time to kill. I thought we could walk around the tailgate lot and find a friendly group. We still have plenty of time. We will join them in 45 minutes for their tailgate.'

Sloane asked. 'A friendly tailgate?'

Zeus responded. 'Right-thinking Americans love to feed cadets. More important, the good ones know how to slip us drinks. All free.'

'Iceman?'

'Yes, Sloane, Iceman taught us the clever method to get picked up.'

Sloane laughed. 'Like prostitutes and johns.'

'Something like that.' Zeus acknowledged.

After Coach Durham destroyed the team and the quality of the scrimmage, Iceman and Thor were pulled to the side while the other players quickly showered and changed. The tailgate outside the gym doors was starting soon and the other players did not want to miss a minute.

'Just what in the hell was that? Iceman, that was absurd even for you.' Coach Durham paced and gritted his teeth as he delivered the message.

Iceman just shook his head and, before he walked away, he muttered. 'I disagree.'

With that, the conversation was over. Thor and Iceman returned to the locker room, showered and changed. As they began to get dressed, the locker room cleared out. Iceman reached into his locker and handed Thor a water bottle filled with whiskey courtesy of Marcus.

'Here, take some of this for your nut sack.'

Thor drank greedily and returned the bottle to Iceman. 'A nice gesture, but not even close to making up for your assault on my family jewels.'

'Have some more. After we put a serious dent in this bottle, I am certain all will be forgiven.' Iceman laughed as he handed Thor the water bottle again.

Thor and Iceman walked out of the gym to join the tailgate just as Zeus and company returned. Kathleen, Sloane and Zeus immediately found Iceman, who had already started on his first plate. Kathleen went to express her concern about the scrimmage, but he was all smiles. Kathleen paused, captured by Jack's smile; she knew Iceman was gone.

'You guys hurry up and get some lamb chops; they go fast.' Jack spoke with his mouthful. 'Give me a second and I'll go with you.' Jack finished his plate and escorted them to the buffet table. After they ate, said hello to the host and his guests with proper introductions and small talk, Jack pulled Kathleen to the side and began to escort her back to the basketball arena.

Coach Phillips approached them. 'Where do you think you two are going?'

'Inside, Kathleen needs to use the lady's room and I am giving her a quick tour.'

Despite Phillips' sour look, Jack walked Kathleen into the locker room and grabbed what was left of the water bottle from his locker.

'Bottoms up.'

Kathleen smiled and cautiously drank from the water bottle. 'Gross, I don't know how you drink this stuff.'

'Have another, I want your vision impaired, so I look good when I kiss you.'

They spent 10 minutes together and enjoyed the water bottle between kisses before heading back out. When they returned, Thor and Beth took their place.

Sloane was not too pleased with the turn of events. 'What about us?'

Gina jumped in. 'Yeah? What about me? Just because my guy is playing football, I get shut out?'

Jack smiled. 'Have a coke and a smile.' He and Kathleen brought out Coke cans with half soda and half whiskey.

The game was about to start, the tailgate broke up and they all headed to the stands. Zapata played well on special teams and made several tackles as a strong safety on running plays. Army won and the group waited for Zapata. Once the group was assembled, they snuck into the basketball complex and settled into the meeting room. Ty again brought his wife's cooking, more water bottles and Coke. The group ate, laughed, and when finished, cleaned up. Marcus asked that they bag everything and lock the garbage in his office. He disposed of it safely the next day. After post-game dining, the group headed to Eisenhower Hall, and for the second night, enjoyed ice cream. They ate the ice cream as they walked the boys back to the barracks. When they arrived at the barracks, the boys said their goodbyes. Sure enough, later that night, just before bed check, several cadets were caught and punished for drinking on post, just as Iceman had expected. Iceman and Zeus just laughed and enjoyed the anonymity provided by returning hours earlier. The twins' real fun started first thing Sunday morning at the West Point Motel.

CHAPTER TWENTY-SIX

Spring again brought the end of basketball season and the start of rugby season. Iceman had another memorable season, was named conference MVP and the team excelled. Army still didn't make the NCAA tournament that year, but they're favored for next season to win the conference and the automatic bid. Zeus was still Zeus in rugby. Zeus and Iceman used their passes, sometimes together and sometimes apart, to spend time with Kathleen and Sloane. Everything flowed smoothly. The bootlegging, classes, relationships, athletics and the military all rolled along nicely.

Iceman reflected on the year and smiled. He turned to Zeus and asked. 'What do you think they have in store for us this summer and what do you think the Colonel has to say?'

Zeus pondered and offered no answers.

As the year was ending, the Colonel asked the twins to lunch at the Hotel Thayer. He had just finished briefing Dr. Monroe about the twins' year and his commitment to dramatically amend their training schedule. The second phase of his plan was reluctantly approved. Colonel Sullivan knew all the responsibility was clearly on his shoulders. He went out on a limb for a plan that he strongly believed in and the only option was to retain the service of the twins.

The twins exited their room, concerned about the surprise invitation to meet the Colonel immediately for a special lunch. They walked down the hill and headed for the Hotel Thayer in silence. Both were lost in thought. 'What are you thinking about this mystery invite?' Zeus finally broke the silence.

Iceman shrugged. 'Don't know.'

'Ok, cool.' Zeus accepted.

'You still have stuff on your collar, young lady.' Iceman could not resist; Zeus was again a star man for his academic excellence and displayed the star on the collar of his uniform.

'Shut up.' Zeus hated the attention of being a star man.

'I know something is up, because we usually have our orders for the summer by now and everyone else has got theirs. What do you think?' Iceman asked again, thinking out loud.

'Don't know, but the Colonel did tell us he would talk to us after year three about our choice.' Zeus pointed out.

Iceman dropped his head. 'Something is off, Zeus. The discussion and decision were supposed to be after year four and graduation. This is fuck sandwich. Something is definitely rotten in the state of Denmark.'

'What is it?' Zeus knew Ice's head was spinning.

'Don't know and it is driving me crazy, but he is going to drop a bomb on us.'

Iceman hated the unknown.

* * *

'Cadet Collins and Collins reporting as ordered, sir.'

'Come with me.' Colonel Sullivan jabbed.

The Colonel escorted the twins into a private dining room. Iceman had dinned in the same room with a Supreme Court Justice and the Chairman of the Joint Chief of Staff, with Zeus, of course.

The menu was preordered by the Colonel. Iceman looked at Zeus, then the Colonel. 'What is this?'

'A seafood tower.' Sullivan replied.

'A tower of shrimp, lobster, oysters and salmon?' Iceman asked as the salmon brought back memories of Key West.

'Yes.'

Iceman mouthed to Zeus, not good.

They destroyed the tower, Caesar salad, steak and dessert; add in the beers, dessert whiskey and the penny was about to drop.

'Sir, as the great John Belushi was told: *Fat, drunk and stupid is no way to go through life, son.* I feel like that now. Serve it up.' Iceman was ready to battle.

The Colonel had diligently prepared the second part of his plan. Grace and the Elders had required the Colonel's unprecedented plan to be perfect.

'You need to sign these NDAs, nondisclosure agreements, or walk out the door. Fair warning: you will be incarcerated in the event of a leak. Your choice. Stay and listen with the option of acceptance or rejection, but either way, confidentiality is your only choice other than prison without any rights, you disappear.' The Colonel glared at the twins with a face they had never seen before. 'I am profoundly serious. You will be wiped off the map.'

Iceman looked back into his gunslinger's eyes. 'Yes.'

'Yes, to what?' Sullivan asked.

'Yes, I am in.' Iceman committed to Sullivan's and Zeus' surprise. 'I will listen while you explain to Zeus whatever the plan is, but I am all in.'

'Congratulations, Iceman, you just graduated from West Point in three years. Your specialized training and additional class hours enabled me to offer you early graduation. Zeus, where do you stand? Do you need more information to make an informed decision?'

Zeus paused and looked down, then back at the Colonel, then settled his eyes on Iceman. He stayed focused on Iceman and replied. 'I'm in.'

'Zeus, are you sure?' the Colonel asked with true concern. 'I knew Iceman was in, although I had expected more discussion, but I am concerned about you.'

'I said yes.' Zeus stated firmly.

'Very good. We need you two to train three more years in Black Ops, then engage in the field to make the world a better place.'

'Wait, who is we?' Iceman asked. 'You didn't say your country, nation, or government; you said we.'

The Colonel paused; he was upset with the slip. Grace warned him to be careful. 'I can't go into that.'

'Sir, you promised. Say what you mean and mean what you say. Honor your promises, because if you don't, I assure you I will go to prison. You think the NY Times will love this? Please be straight with me and I will be with you.'

The Colonel and Iceman eyeballed each other. The Colonel responded. 'The world is not what you think or were taught. Allow me to explain.' Zeus zeroed in. 'Ok, here we go. As I explained last year, you two were identified by PSAT scores coupled with an algorithm that compiled intelligence, athleticism, compatibility, psych profiles, and in some cases, criminal records.' He looked at Iceman.

'How? That's impossible, no one knew and I was never charged.'

The Colonel shook his head. 'We knew and an investigation was launched.' He continued. 'In addition, medical records were part of the evaluation process.' He intensified his attention on Iceman. He wanted Iceman to be on the defensive, not on the attack. 'What was it like to be stabbed in the upper abdomen after hustling for money in basketball on the Westside of Chicago, walking to your car to grab a tire iron, violently assaulting your opponent, then drive yourself to the ER?'

'Zeus, I think he is talking to you.' Iceman mumbled.

'Shut up.' Zeus responded.

The Colonel ignored Iceman's misdirection. 'Why did you go to Cook County Hospital, a center for those who do not have insurance, rather than Loyola Medical Center?'

'I didn't want anyone to find out, but apparently you did.'

'Why did you do it?' The Colonel asked.

Iceman answered. 'He owed me money that I earned honestly. He was wrong. The code on the playground is a safe harbor from the violence that surrounds it. He broke the code by stabbing me in addition to not paying me. Because I was white, he assumed I would shrink up and run away. His assumptions about my skills in basketball and violence were wrong. He paid the price of justice.'

The Colonel responded. 'The ability to stand the line, coupled with your sense of loyalty and duty, along with your surprising intelligence enhanced with cleverness, are rare. You have a moral compass that fits with our organization.'

'Thanks, I think.' Iceman was not accustomed to his IQ being complimented.

'Zeus, your IQ is only surpassed by Iceman, and your computer and data skills are very mission-critical. Obviously, your physical gifts are extraordinary. You two have a unique chemistry and a rare ability to complement and support each other.' The Colonel explained.

'Sir, are you celebrating your badass self?' Iceman joked. 'So, it was all your work and Zeus and I were a forgone conclusion? While I have the dance floor, did you say I was smarter than Zeus?'

'One could say that.' The Colonel responded with a smile.

'Sir, one just did and it was you.' Iceman tried to hold back his laugh, but failed. They all exploded with laughter.

'Check, please; we have an appointment. Let's go.' The Colonel stated. 'You two are off to training now.'

Zeus asked. 'What about our personal effects?'

'There are no personal effects; we took the liberty of disposing of them. All pictures and memories are wiped. Zeus, we set up a method for you to stay in contact with your mother, but everything else is gone. Iceman?'

'I don't give a shit. Burn it all, next play, but unless you are prepared to drive me naked, we need some cash and clothes.'

Colonel calmly responded. 'Here are your ill-gotten gains from your various business ventures. We, again, took the liberty of securing your secret stash of cash. We will make a brief stop for clothes and here is $10,000 cash in addition to your secret fund.' The twins walked away with almost $18,000 each and tried to breathe.

Iceman processed the news and grew concerned. 'We have a phone call to make.'

The Colonel shook him off. 'No, you don't.'

'Colonel, we can't just leave those girls. They have been good to us, and they deserve a goodbye. Granted, a shitty goodbye, but at least something.'

'No.' The Colonel looked at Iceman, knew this was going to be an issue and relented. 'One call each. Iceman, you are being transferred to the Pentagon after extensive back surgery. The back surgery is your cover for the media to address missing your senior year in basketball. You can tell Kathleen that back story. Zeus, you are going back to Europe to finish training, so you can let Sloane in on your back story.'

Iceman was upset with Sullivan's response and asked. 'How did you know their names? You were never introduced.'

'I saw them plenty at your games.' Sullivan retreated in his response.

'Sure, but how did you know their names? You were never introduced.'

'Somebody must have told me.'

'Was he named Mr. Bug? You bugged our room. I knew it. That's how you knew where to find our bootlegging money. You don't need to answer. I knew it.'

'You knew and didn't tell me? Never mind.' Zeus felt stupid as he looked at Ice.

'Back to the clothes, don't worry about fashion, you won't need it.' Sullivan said with a smile as he changed the subject.

While changing in the bathroom of Walmart, after the painful phone calls to Kathleen and Sloane, Zeus asked Iceman. 'What is…'

Iceman jumped him. 'Stop. I have no idea either, but it's like two elephants fucking. Something big, loud, and important is happening, but it's over my head. I have no clue, but I am in.'

'You want to fuck an elephant?' Zeus cracked himself up.

'While I could satisfy said female elephant, it is not germane to the story. Some cool shit is going down and I am sure I want in. I am not listening to some stupid military sink pisser fuck give me orders only to then walk away frustrated and join the bitches on Wall Street. You do what you want, but I know there is more to my life than that cliché. I will make a difference. Put on your Walmart crap.' Iceman said, changing into his shit bird clothes.

As they departed Walmart for the two-hour ride in Colonel Sullivan's Camry, Iceman immediately started again. 'Who is 'we'? You never answered. When you were grilling me about getting stabbed, you said our organization.'

'The best interests of America and Great Britain.' The Colonel responded.

'Hold on. So, all of the interests? What does that entail?' Iceman continued to pound away at the Colonel.

'Whatever you are ordered to do.'

'Hang on.'

'Enough for today. I promise to visit and keep you informed.' The Colonel closed the conversation.

Iceman nodded at the Colonel. 'Close, you almost had us. You need to give us more.'

The Colonel knew the relief he felt was too good to be true. He knew Iceman would not be satisfied. The we slip up was costly, but the *our organization* was worse.

'All right, but I mean it, whatever I am about to tell you, is it. I am not playing. Are we there yet?'

'Iceman, I am not going to be badgered by you for the entire ride. Do you understand and do you agree?'

'Yes.'

'No bullshit, no clever game or twist? This is it until I decide otherwise. Agreed?'

'No bullshit.' Iceman agreed.

Sullivan took a deep breath. 'Welcome to Black Ops. Black Ops is a group of 3-man teams trained to execute the kill order. All eliminations are to appear of natural events. A plane crash, car crash, heart attack, allergic reaction, or death by a rival are some of the techniques employed by Black Ops. Anyone can kill. The Elders want headlines to read 'Shocking,' 'Surprising,' 'Tragic,' not 'Killed in Cold Blood,' or 'Assassinated.' The agents, the title given to the life-takers, are a part of a team. After individualized training is completed, the agent is put in the field for ten years with a partner agent.' He stopped and looked back and forth at Zeus and Iceman. 'The two agents train and remain together for the ten-year tour unless killed in action. The two agents are led by a senior agent. The senior agent conducts and supervises the training program and stays with the assigned agents in the field if the team survives intact. An agent is promoted to senior agent if he or she is not eliminated.'

When the Colonel was finished, they rode in silence. As the countryside passed his eyes, Iceman drifted off and thought of Sloane's concern. Don't break her heart. I will. At least I was honest. That's a pretty lame rationalization. Is what it is. Next play.

After an hour drive, the twins arrived at an isolated farm in Sullivan, NY. The 300-acre farm greeted the twins as they parked in front of a massive barn and were met by a very, very deliberate man.

CHAPTER TWENTY-SEVEN

'Sir, reporting for duty.' Zeus introduced himself as the Colonel drove away.

The senior agent walked up to Zeus real close and spoke softly. 'You have not earned the right to speak to me. Everything came easy to you; I get it. Go to the fucking barn. I will be in the house and I will contact you when I want to be addressed by you pussy soft motherfuckers.'

Zeus dropped his head and Iceman raced to fight the senior agent, only to quickly realize he was severely overmatched. The senior agent saw Iceman charge, and as he wound up to throw an overhead right, the senior agent moved quicker than a mongoose, deflected the assault with his left hand, swept his right arm under Iceman's exposed right, caught his neck with his outstretched hand and easily slammed Iceman to the ground. Before Iceman could pop back up, the senior stomped his chest. Iceman gave out a painful grunt, quickly rolled to his left, avoiding the second stomp and jumped to his feet. Iceman approached his foe with caution and faked a left jab. The senior agent moved slightly to avoid the anticipated punch and opened a small window for Ice to throw a right hook. Iceman seized the opportunity and launched the hook. He missed the senior's chin, but hit his right hand. By hitting his right hand, Iceman further exposed the senior agent's right side. Both Zeus and the senior agent paused, surprised that Iceman had missed. But he had not missed; he returned the thrown punch with a punishing elbow to the handler's exposed right temple. The senior agent was knocked dizzy and Iceman followed the elbow with a left hook to the same temple. The senior almost went down. Iceman attacked with a kick to the groin, but the senior agent was too quick. He managed to slide and absorb the blow in his inner thigh. The senior agent, well trained in hand-to-hand combat, recovered with Brazilian jiu-jitsu, threw and hurt Iceman again. As the senior agent used the Brazilian technique to take Iceman down to the ground in a joint lock, Zeus jumped in. He sprinted to Iceman's rescue and went to tackle the senior agent. The senior agent released his grip on Iceman to confront Zeus. He rolled onto his back and lifted a knee into the flying chest of Zeus. Zeus brutally absorbed the knee and rolled painfully to the ground. The senior agent immediately rolled over and delivered a smashing elbow into Zeus' upper abdomen. Zeus felt his life expelled from his mouth and begged for air to return.

The two attackers lay on the ground and the senior agent stood over them. 'Here's the end of the lesson. The barn, with beans and rice, is over that way. There are also two MREs in there in case your seafood tower was not enough. Report in the A.M. before me.'

Iceman asked. 'What time?'

'Did I say you did or did not have the right to speak to me?' The handler dismissively responded as he stared down at Iceman.

'Do not.'

'Yet, he speaks again. You will report before me and show proper respect. You have already wasted too much of my time.'

Iceman turned to Zeus as they walked to the barn with nothing more than the Walmart clothes on their backs. 'Can you find me a sink; I have to take a piss.'

* * *

'Zeus, get up.' Laughing, Iceman erupted. 'What did you sleep in? You got grease and dirt all over your face.'

Zeus looked at his hands, which were filthy. He must have used his dirty hands to wipe his face while he slept. 'Shut up.'

'Whatever, it is the first time I have been better looking than you.'

Zeus, after cleaning his hands, wiped the sand from his eyes. 'Regretfully for you, that is not true. I am still… anyway, what time is it?'

'0330, this fuck is not taking us. Come on, we are going for a run.' The twins went for a quick 40-minute run and returned to find their handler waiting near the barn.

'I said report before me not leave without me. Can we not follow orders?'

'In all fairness, fuck you. We reported before you. You didn't say wait for you.' With that, Iceman charged him again and, as expected, got his ass kicked. He popped up again, walked close and simply stated. 'We understand we need to be trained, but you need to understand we will be respected. Got me?'

'No.'

'I am sorry for my ambiguity, but Zeus and I will fight you together next time and we will win.'

'You won't win.'

'Fair, but you'll have to kill me. I will never stop coming. Now, show us respect, teach us, work us, whatever, but we deserve respect.'

'Umm.' The senior agent paused to consider the request.

With that, Iceman charged him again and Zeus jumped in. While the handler continued to deliver punishment, the twins kept coming at him. After the fifth beating, the twins got up to go again.

'Wait. Just wait. The reports are correct. You two are the real thing. Iceman, where did you learn combat hand-to-hand fighting? Yesterday, your fake right hook that you deliberately missed to set up the elbow to my temple caught me by surprise. An impressive move.'

'I don't know, we just called it street-fighting.'

The handler nodded with respect. 'You two come into the house and grab a bunk.'

Iceman asked simply. 'Can we get proper gear to train in? While Walmart is lovely, built for orange slices and weekend kid soccer games, we need proper gear.'

'Move into the house where you will find your bunks and gear stored in your trunk.'

Zeus asked, walking into the house. 'We have nothing to move. What do we call you if not sir?'

'Conjar. I am yours for the next 13 years.'

'Roger that, Conjar. Nice to meet you. In all fairness, I thought you would be tougher.' Iceman offered.

Conjar stared back at Iceman, paused and laughed. 'Like I said, you are everything as advertised.'

Conjar took the twins for a five-mile run, then watched them swim three miles in the lake across from the farmhouse. The run was easy for the twins, but the swim proved to be a serious challenge. Neither had trained in the water, so their strokes were inefficient. After the swim, they sat around the dining room table for breakfast. The house was one of four located on a large property. The lake was 400 yards long, which made a nice distance for swimming laps for the daily three-mile swim. During the run, the twins noticed an outdoor gun range, two other barns and a small apartment building. On the run, Conjar did not take the time to provide them with an explanation of what they were seeing.

'Alright, today and for the rest of your stay, we will follow the same basic schedule, PT, followed by three months of basic training. I will teach you the fundamentals to build a foundation so you are prepared for the specialized camps located off-site. Any questions?'

Zeus asked. 'Can you tell us what the other houses and barns are for?'

'Sure, the houses are for other teams. We are the only ones here now, but typically, another team or two would be here. Each team bunks together and has the house to themselves. At the other end of the property is a married couple that takes care of the place. They pay the bills, stock the fridge and stuff like that. The barn, where you two slept, is for storage; the other two are for training. The apartment and office complex are also used for training. You'll see both later today. We train from 0600 until dinner at 1800 hours. After you shower, you have a couple of hours of homework to do. Some weeks, the material is military, like a field manual, but it is educational. Later in the year, you have training sessions in the classroom, but let's not get ahead of ourselves.'

Iceman nodded. 'Great, thanks.'

* * *

The twins ate breakfast, returned to their trunks and changed into their training gear. They reported as ordered and Conjar followed up. 'The gear alright, got everything you need?'

Iceman nodded. 'Since we eat at 1800 hours, is their sandwich meat or something we can make ourselves after dinner?'

'Shoot, I should have mentioned that; thanks for reminding me. The kitchen is stocked and everything is self-serve. We take turns making the meals and all pitch in to keep the place clean. On the hanging clipboard, there is the grocery order sheet. We order twice a week, so we can fill it out together and plan our meals. In addition to food, include toilet paper and shit like that so the couple that takes care of the place knows what we need.'

Zeus looked around and approved. 'Thanks, sounds good.'

'Can either of you cook?' Conjar asked.

Iceman raised his hand. 'I can. How about you, Zeus?'

'A little.'

Conjar slapped Zeus on the back as he handed him a dirty dish. 'Maybe you can't cook, but I know you can clean.'

* * *

Conjar walked the twins to the first barn and unlocked the door. The twins walked into the barn that housed a full gym with a large, matted area surrounded by workout equipment. Conjar turned on the lights and pushed open a couple of windows to recycle the air. The barn had a massive exhaust fan that generated air movement in the stuffy barn.

After that, he escorted the twins over to the mat and said, 'Take a minute or two to warm up, then we'll get started.'

Zeus offered after 10 minutes of warm-up. 'All set. What are we doing?'

'I am going to get you started on hand-to-hand combat. We'll work on this every morning after breakfast for a couple of hours. We are going to start with the Wing Chun principles.'

Iceman asked. 'What is a Wing Chun?'

Conjar replied. 'You begin your training with the basics. Wing Chun is a kung fu style of defense that builds the foundation for more advanced techniques. Like you were in boxing, you both should be able to naturally adapt to Wing Chun. In boxing, you both displayed fast hands and a strong lower body and both are vital to Wing Chun.'

Conjar trained the two of them hard and the twins were surprised how fatigued they were after the two-hour session.

'Zeus, thank God he did so much teaching and talking. That shit is tough.' Iceman moaned.

Zeus concurred. 'I thought boxing was tough, but when we were sparring, I was spent. I am positive I am going to discover muscles tonight that I didn't know existed.'

Conjar walked behind Zeus and overheard the end of the conversation. 'Speaking of hidden muscles, let's hit the mat again; we have an hour of yoga.'

'Yoga? Seriously? That's not very assassin-like.' Iceman observed.

Conjar took his place on the mat. 'How many assassins do you know?'

'I get it, none. So how would I know?! Just get my ass on the mat.'

After an hour of yoga, the twins started laughing as they grabbed some water.

'Zeus, I don't know what Conjar is doing to us, but I am beat.'

'I know and it's just after 1100 hours, I came here in badass shape. The two runs were fine, swimming was tough and this mat crap is a killer.' Zeus continued the thought process. 'Dude, I'm telling you, it's this new muscle shit.'

'It's wreaking havoc on my body and shit, my mind too. Let's grab lunch and chill for a couple of hours. I am going to rinse off after lunch and take a quick nap, I think.'

'We only have two hours.'

'I know. I'll take a short ranger nap.'

After lunch and Iceman's nap, Conjar took the twins to the other barn used for training. They walked in to find an indoor target range with eight shooting lanes.

'This is just like all the cop shows with the paper targets that run forward and back. Sweet.' Zeus was impressed.

Iceman just kept walking with Conjar and Zeus had to catch up. Conjar stopped at the door at the end of the barn and slid it to the side to reveal a large steel door.

'Conjar, that's some bank vault you got there.' Iceman pointed out.

As Conjar opened the vault door, he replied to Iceman. 'When you see what's inside, you'll understand.'

Zeus was shocked and observed. 'That is not a vault, it's an armory.'

Conjar laughed. 'This is nothing. This is light weapons training. You visit a camp for heavy weapons, the big daddies. We can't blow up trees out here. You need more land to blow up for that. I'll get you started with this room; you may never use the big stuff anyway. Your hands, knife and pistol are all the hardware you're probably ever going to need. The most important weapon is your brain. You'll win more fights with that than everything in this safe combined.'

* * *

After dinner, the team did the dishes, ordered the groceries for the next few days and picked their meal assignments to prepare for their stay. Conjar loved to cook breakfast and Zeus was useless, so Iceman took dinner. Zeus had lunch and a protein shake detail.

Conjar figured. 'Pretty hard to fuck up a sandwich and a blender. I think you can manage, Zeus.'

After the day was over, the twins walked into the family room to see what game was worth watching.

From his room, Conjar yelled, 'DON'T FORGET YOUR NIGHTTIME STUDIES!'

Iceman looked at Zeus and admitted. 'I did forget, fuck. Let's knock it out real quick and come down for a snack and ESPN. If we don't have time to watch a game, we might as well watch highlights.'

The books were not military handbooks; instead, they were textbooks for finance. The twins were not pleased to do homework so soon after graduating from West Point.

* * *

The days became weeks and the weeks became months. The time passed quickly and the routine was broken by a visit by Colonel Sullivan. The twins exited the lake after they completed their morning swim to find Conjar greeting Sullivan as he exited his Camry. Iceman smiled to himself. I wonder how many miles are on his odometer. Conjar and Sullivan spoke briefly.

Conjar yelled over to the twins. 'Come on over here. We are headed for the kitchen; the Colonel has something to discuss with you.'

The twins jogged over and took a seat at the table. Pleasantries were exchanged and the Colonel got straight to business.

'Conjar has kept me informed about your progress. He has reported good things, you two are more than holding your own. I promised you more information, so here I am.'

'Nice to see you, sir. Thank you for the compliment. We look forward to what you have to say.' Zeus responded while he washed his hands in the sink.

'Nice to be seen. In the Black Op…'

'Hang on, Colonel. Let's go back to the *we*, then you can talk about job descriptions. Who is we?' Iceman did not forget and held on to his question after the seafood tower.

Conjar looked over at Sullivan with a look of concern. Conjar knew that question would not be addressed for another three years once Black Ops' basic training was completed. Sullivan knew Conjar was worried and had not briefed him in detail just how much the twins knew and expected to know. He turned to Conjar with a look of resignation. The Colonel was determined not to speak of the Elders in detail. The twins were not ready, so he settled on their cover story.

The Colonel started. 'You are employed by OWL.'

'What is OWL?'

'Iceman, if you would kindly keep quiet, I can get through my briefing.' After a pause and consent, the Colonel continued. 'Let's review. The three of you are an execution team. As I have already told you, all eliminations are to appear of natural events. The agents, the title given to the life-takers, are a part of a team. After Black Ops training is completed, the agent is put in the field for ten years with a partner agent. The two agents train and remain together for the ten-year tour unless killed in action. The two agents are led by a senior agent. The senior agent conducts and supervises the training program and stays with the assigned agents in the field if the team survives intact. An agent is promoted to senior agent if he or she is not eliminated.' The Colonel paused for confirmation.

Zeus responded for the twins. 'We got it.'

Iceman just stared at the Colonel.

The lecture continued. 'If death occurs within a team, the team is disbanded. The surviving agent or senior agent is pulled from the field and reassigned within the organization. The Ronin agents, as they are called, are named after the samurai warrior who lost his master, can be paired with another Ronin. The two Ronin agents pair with a Ronin senior agent to form a Ronin team. The Ronin team train together for one year to develop a sixth sense within the team dynamic. All senior agents are responsible for executing the mission provided by the architect. The architect, Jasper Cooper, works with the Black Ops' senior agent, Conjar, to design the assassination plan. His code name is a play on his nickname, Jazz, which is short for Jasper. Duke, his codename in tribute to the famous jazz artist Duke Ellington, is the bridge between analytics and operations. He turns the theoretical from analytics to reality with input from the senior agents. Physically not imposing, Duke was successful as an agent and senior agent due to his amazing tactical skills. Duke attended Sandhurst prior to joining Black Ops. After tours as agent and senior agent are completed, the senior agent is promoted to rank of statesmen. The statesmen are routed to another position within the organization. Duke is a statesman. Typically, the statesmen select a position at one of the offsite advanced training camps, but some elect a different, more passive position. With me?'

Zeus again answered for the twins. 'Yes. We are looking forward to meeting and working with Duke.'

Iceman again remained silent.

'Iceman, anything?' Sullivan asked cautiously.

Iceman was angry with being jerked around with the we. He gave himself brief relief from his simmering temper and asked. 'What happened to you? How do you fit in with Duke and Conjar?'

'Good question. I stay with you through the first mission and then transition out once you prepare for your second mission.'

Iceman smiled deliberately. 'You are going to tell us about the *we* before you step foot in that Camry.'

On the surface, the Colonel ignored Iceman's threat, but internally, he was preparing for the showdown. 'The couple that manages this facility are statesmen. The Elders is a lifetime commitment. The statesmen train twice a year for one month at one of the training camps. Rust proofing, as it is referred to, includes a physical fitness test and continued training evaluation. The statesmen are called upon to go hot in emergency situations. William Taylor is head of the statesmen program. Interestingly, he was recruited by both MI6 and the Elders while attending Ludgrove School for secondary education. He attended Sandhurst after Eton and, prior to becoming head of the statesmen, he was a legendary agent and senior agent. As a senior agent, he led his team to what was considered an impossible assignment. A Russian oligarch, buried behind tight security in his mansion located in the closed cottage village named Florence, was the target. His team somehow evaded the security measures of the fortified mansion and eliminated the Russian. The assassination, amazingly, was ruled an accident. Death by slipping in the shower, alcohol involved was the headline. He speaks six languages, has an eidetic memory and loves to gamble. The joke about him is, give him a box of cigars, a bottle of whiskey, a card game and you'll know where to find him at 0300. His code name is a cliché. He was viewed as if he were created straight from Churchill's vision of counterintelligence or Ian Fleming's famous character. William's codename is Bond. Bond is the classic British spy and assassin.'

Conjar asked the twins. 'Did you get all that? Any questions?'

Zeus nodded. 'No, I got it. Nice to know the structure and plan. I am sure there is plenty more, but I am up to speed at this point.'

Iceman wasn't satisfied. 'I still have heard the *we*. Who is the *we* that we are fighting for? What and who are The Elders?'

Colonel pressed on with the briefing. 'I'll continue. OWL is your cover story. All Black Ops personnel are employed by OWL. Black Ops are forensic accountants who document and justify their travel all over the globe. The agents and senior agents in Black Ops are on the grid with their given names. The agents and senior agents are classified and treated as OWL employees. They receive their salary, health benefits, 401k and documented income through OWL. OWL manages all financial transactions related to salary. Bills are paid, investments are made and taxes are filed. The money that is paid off the books is handled by a dedicated group outside of OWL. The dedicated group ensures no transactions made by an agent in their black account draws unwanted attention. The salary is $125,000 a year for agents and $250,000 a year for senior agents.'

Conjar checked. 'Are you with us so far? Never mind, forget I asked. Colonel, how about the backstory of OWL? When challenged, do the twins have a credible backstory? Just the high-level discussion, I'll fill in the details and grey areas.'

'Right. OWL. We see in the dark. OWL is a legitimate private financial company that follows all government laws and restrictions. OWL has offices in San Francisco, New York and London. The employees of OWL own the company. The employee fund is comprised of current and retired employees. The size of ownership interest is tied to the pay level and performance bonuses. The CEO and President of the company is Paul Stephan. Paul spent his first five years with OWL, getting his master's in accounting and finance from the University of Chicago, Booth School. He is a CPA, certified public accountant, and CFA, certified financial analyst. He drives and manages the work product through three divisions. Private equity is the investment division. Private equity raises capital from wealthy investors, pools the investor contributions, invests the pool and generates a rate of return. The private equity group generates fees and a percentage of the gains or losses generated by the fund. The minimum investment for a client is $50 million. The fund is held at $10 billion to stay small enough to avoid attention. Analytics and investment, the second group, uses software to gather and interpret data on targeted investment opportunities. Forensic accounting, the third group, investigates companies to ensure there is no financial misconduct. Cybersecurity, a large team within forensic accounting, offers consulting and cybersecurity software and systems. Both teams sell their services to government, public and private institutions. The forensic accounting and cybersecurity teams work together to perform deep dives into the financial, compliance and overall health of a targeted entity. The forensic accounting team and cybersecurity team investigate and monitor the investments made by the fund.'

Conjar interrupted. 'I know this is a lot to take in, but we have time in your training to go into more detail. This is just a briefing for the two of you to see the big picture. I'll continue to discuss the details during training.'

Zeus took notes in his head. 'I see the point of the finance textbooks. We'll need the required skill set to protect our identity in the field. We will also use the skills as cover, so we must be actual forensic accountants and cybersecurity experts. I already have the cyber skills and we will be trained as proper consultants.'

'Well said. I'll continue. For example, in a transaction, OWL used proprietary software to search for anomalies in the market, and those anomalies were routed to the analytics group. The software provided the analytics group with an interesting anomaly: a solar energy company. The analyst assigned to the investigation went to work. The solar company was on the brink of developing revolutionary technology, but was extremely over budget and years behind schedule. The private equity group that funded the company had grown tired of, almost, and we are close. The solar company faced certain bankruptcy. The analyst performed a deep dig into the solar company and their private equity firm. After her investigation, she was still interested in the solar company and turned the file over to forensic accounting and cybersecurity. Cybersecurity not only defends systems, but can attack systems to execute a deep dig. The team easily invaded both the solar company and their private equity company and ensured the analyst had all the data she required. Ms. Roman, the analyst, took the data and information generated and made several interesting discoveries. While the solar company had several setbacks and burned through cash, they had made considerable progress. She was obviously not an expert in the field of solar energy, but she did identify the tone between company management and the vice president of the private equity firm had changed. For the first four years, the tone of the emails, courtesy of cybersecurity, was positive; everything was going great and would be great, full steam ahead. In the following three years, the tone of the emails was clearly negative. Frustration and fear led to ultimatums and threats by the private equity firm. However, the most recent six months showed the tone had moved to guarded optimism. The optimism was crushed by the private equity firm's board of directors. The board had enough and the request for additional investment was unanimously rejected. A $500 million investment had swollen to $750 million and an additional $250 million was required for development and another $250 for manufacturing and sales. $1.25 billion in total. In addition, the private equity firm's new capital raise to fuel future business had stalled, according to information discovered by cybersecurity. The firm invested in several companies with huge upside and only needed a couple to hit for the firm to generate exceptional returns. The problem they faced was only one investment hit; the rest missed and missed bad. The solar company was not the only company facing bankruptcy in the firm's portfolio. The private equity firm went for the home run and struck out. She also turned the private equity firm over to the forensic accounting group to verify their troubled status. Before final approval, she researched the solar product and enlisted expert consultants in the field of solar energy to verify the reasons for optimism. The consultants were blind to the company name and potential investment. All agreed that the innovative technology was revolutionary and the solar company was close to production. The ability to efficiently process and store solar energy was a generational change. The technology, coupled with governments around the world, push to become less dependent on fossil fuels and the Middle East to stem the funding of terrorism, made for a perfect storm. Significant government incentives and legislation were anticipated over the next five years. The forecasted demand would only grow over the next ten years and exponentially thereafter.'

'The group offered $200 million for the $750 million investment. The private equity firm had no other choice, but to accept the offer. The group then approached management and offered the $500 million required in new investment capital in exchange for ownership of all patents. Management paused, but reluctantly agreed. They had no choice. The investment group committed $700 million for a $1.2 billion project with seven years of development. The investment group offered management an incentive. If the product was ready for production in one year, management would receive 10% ownership in the solar company. The solar company started production nine months later, and the product was, in fact, revolutionary.

'OWL held their interest in the solar company. The solar company was extremely profitable, with sales and revenue growing at 225%. Margins on sales exceeded the forecast. The solar company had more orders than manufacturing could fill. OWL is preparing to exit and placed a value on the $700 million investment in the solar company at $2.5 billion five years later. A tremendous investment, wouldn't you agree?'

Zeus was excited with the briefing. 'Absolutely, interesting stuff. I look forward to the details and our studies.'

Iceman did not share Zeus' enthusiasm. 'Still haven't heard about the *we*.'

The Colonel took a deep breath, held it and exhaled. 'I already told you too much. I will return to continue the briefing at a later date. Iceman, we work for the good guys. That is all I can say at this point.' The Colonel packed up his presentation and said his goodbyes. He left briefing packets with Conjar.

After he left, Iceman turned to Conjar. Conjar stopped him. 'Don't bother, you have to wait. He is going out on a tremendous limb confining in you two this much information this early in training.'

Iceman was silent, but Zeus spoke for the twins. 'We understand.'

Conjar studied Iceman and decided to continue his briefing. 'Iceman, you must take a chance and trust us. You know the Colonel well; he is taking tremendous risks to meet you beyond halfway. Let's sit down to eat and I'll give you some grey area insight.'

Iceman agreed, the three sat down to eat and Conjar started. 'Here is the deal: you will die before 30.'

Conjar attempted to continue, but Iceman jumped in, shaking off his doubt with humor. 'Can we get a double 0 number? James Bond got the same warning; I believe it was Goldfinger. Wait, no, Casino Royale and got it again in the remake of Casino Royale, which was loosely based on the original. Judy Dench, who is awesome and brilliant, plays M in the latest version. So here is what happens to 007…'

With a mouthful of pancakes, Zeus interrupted. 'Shut up.'

'Roger that. I fancy Sean Connery, but got to tell you that Daniel Craig was good in that movie, but the others not so much.'

Iceman continued to tell tales to distract and throw Conjar off guard to analyze him.

Conjar was briefed about Iceman's techniques. Unlike Colonel Sullivan, Conjar could care less about Iceman's games. He was tasked to build the perfect assassin. 'Again, the reports were true, but Zeus, does he really always talk this much?'

'You already know the answer.'

'Iceman, if I wanted to hear from an asshole, I would have farted. Do not interrupt me. In the field, no one is coming for you. All we got is our team and the probability is, you will not see 30.' Conjar looked as if he was attending their wake. 'You are dedicated to one mission a year. You train and prepare for that one mission. The missions are not difficult. The CIA and military handle difficult.'

'I can see that. So, we are more Ethan Hunt. Our missions are impossible. Speaking of Mission Impossible, I had reservations about Tom Cruise, but I got to tell you…'

Zeus and Conjar in cadence, 'Shut up.'

Conjar responded to Iceman. 'The missions are not like the movies. There is no nuclear-ticking bomb that James Bond must deactivate with seconds remaining.'

Iceman interrupted. 'Goldfinger. Zeus, Conjar is referring to the James Bond classic.'

Zeus ignored the comment and Conjar continued. 'The missions are well planned, the targets are dangerous, but there is no spectacular finish, just a dead bad guy.'

'Roger that.' Iceman understood Conjar's message, then changed gears. 'Quick question, in the year off, where do we live?'

Conjar carried on with his briefing. 'As the Colonel stated, after 10 years in the field, you are promoted from agent to senior agent.'

Iceman smiled that gunslinging smile of his. 'If you make it to a senior agent, I have no concerns. But then what? We give 25 years of our life on death missions, then statesmen, and in all probability, die for a cause that, in fairness, I have no clue about?'

'Iceman, shut up. You get $500k a year off the books in an account invested and controlled by a dedicated group. They pay that much, because your missions deliver billions in return benefits and provide security for our way of life. As a senior agent, you get a million dollars a year, and after 20 years, you get $10 million; let's call it a profit-sharing plan. After 25 years, you have the choice of several fewer active roles. You will be statesmen and can be called up to provide service at moment's notice. I wouldn't worry about 25 years from now. I would be concerned about making it through today.'

Iceman shrugged his shoulders twice. 'You are right. I may not see 30, but fun and not a gun will kill me with that kind of bank. Bring it, as Doc Holiday said: *I'm your huckleberry.*'

The next day, Iceman woke at 3:35, used the latrine and went for an hour walk to process. The fear of failure he constantly ran from caught up to him. He said to himself: A super spy? An assassin? What am I thinking? I am not going to see 30! Fuck, calm rage lad. Commit and all in. This is your calling. Not the money, but the mission, roger that. I believe in you. With his internal voice verifying that which he believed in, he ran off the fear of failure. Dying before 30 meant he failed. Dying didn't concern him. Failure did. If he died before 30, he failed the mission. Patton ran through his mind. No dumb bastard ever won a war by dying for his country. He won it by making some other poor bastard die for his country. Five miles later, a 27-minute run, he yelled from the kitchen. 'WHAT THE FUCK? Are we going to be assassins or jean models?'

* * *

Training settled into a routine. Conjar worked with them on hand-to-hand combat and added Jeet Kune Do to the Wing Chun technique. Jeet Kune Do was a hybrid martial art developed by Bruce Lee. The twins were exposed to various handguns and rifles, but trained with the Heckler and Koch USP 45 combat tactical pistol with silencer and the HK MP7 assault rifle with silencer as their weapons of choice. Both weapons with proper ammunition pierced body armor. As Conjar explained, all the weapons in training were exceptional, but he preferred the HKs. The unit used the same equipment, so ammunition and weapons were interchangeable and could be exchanged in a firefight. The HKs also had the benefit of being quite common; nothing about the weapons could be linked back to the Elders. The latest and greatest weapons or customized weapons were the equivalent of leaving fingerprints.

The routine was dramatically broken during the final three weeks of basic training with Conjar. Conjar tried his best to break the twins with a regiment that exceeded SEAL Hell Week. The specialized training the twins had received in pathfinding, medical, Airborne and Air Assault provided a good foundation. The twins became experts with the LAR V Draeger Rebreather, designated as MK 25. The MK 25 underwater breathing gear was pure oxygen that recycled air to prevent expelled air bubbles. The MK 25 was chosen for the twins, because of its small size and front-worn configuration, which is suitable for shallow water over shorter distances. The twins wore the MK 25 to include the oxygen tanks on their morning five-mile run and three-mile swim. A special torture to start the twins' day. After a MRE breakfast, Conjar escalated the intensity, duration and violence in martial arts training. With only the 0330 MRE in the twins' belly, the afternoon began with a one-mile run in their MK 25 chest high in water. The twins followed the torturous run with a second three-mile swim underwater that concluded with the placement of sniper targets across the lake. The twins returned from the torture to train on the targets with their Mawhinney's

M40 sniper rifle. The twins were sniper-qualified on the M40, but exhaustion added a merciless challenge. After a dinner of insects, the twins abandoned their usual studies to end their day of torture. The twins concluded training at 2359 hours after treading water in their MK 25 with their hands above their heads for hours. The twins slept in the woods, smelling of vomit, only to wake up at 0330 to repeat the process. Hell Week for SEALs lasted five days and the twins survived 21.

CHAPTER TWENTY-EIGHT

As the twins sat at the all too familiar bar in JFK airport, Iceman asked Zeus. 'I always wanted to visit Las Vegas, but not like this.'

'I know what you mean. Living in a shithole motel off the strip in northeast Las Vegas and working as a dishwasher for some Mexican restaurant is not my ideal vacation.'

'Lindo Michoacan.'

'What?'

Iceman explained. 'The restaurant is Lindo Michoacan.'

'Right.'

'I googled it. Food looks good. A cool story, the family immigrated from Mexico and started the restaurant. We are working in their first restaurant that is in a crap neighborhood, but the place did so well that they have other locations throughout Vegas. Pretty cool story.'

'I was thinking there may be better ways to learn conversational Spanish than being a dishwasher. Want another round?' Zeus asked and continued. 'The food better be good. I lost a shit ton of weight during that last phase of hell training.'

'Conjar sure broke our bodies down. We'll recover with plenty of refried beans for protein. Besides, I don't know, we made a good team washing dishes at West Point.'

Zeus sat his beer down and laughed. 'You are looking forward to this.'

When Conjar laid out the next five months of training for the twins, Iceman was initially taken back by the dishwasher position. After he thought about it, he had to agree it made sense. 'I am excited. It will be fun working in the kitchen and meeting the next Ty and Reese. Besides, we get our nights off.'

'True, but we can't leave the neighborhood.'

'Who would want to?'

* * *

The twins arrived at their extended stay motel, home for the next two weeks. They woke up at dawn and went for a run before the oppressive Nevada heat was in full effect. The ninety-degree early morning temperatures were manageable for their seven-mile run. The kitchen, even with air conditioning, was sweltering. The twins worked a double shift that included kitchen prep work and dishes. After two weeks, the next stop for the twins was a suite at the Palms.

As Zeus was opening the door to the suite, Iceman pushed him. 'Hurry up. I am dying to get inside, settle and head back downstairs. I am ready to put my money to work.'

'Spoken as the true amateur that you are.' A voice called out from the living room.

The twins entered the room to find a debonair, fifty-something-year-old sitting on an armchair with his legs elegantly crossed.

'Hello. Iceman, what is your rush to gamble your money away?'

'I don't gamble, I invest.' Iceman coolly responded.

Zeus added. 'It's true. He never loses.'

The gentleman smiled and rose from his chair. He nodded and walked past the twins to the mini-fridge. 'Zeus, can I get you something?'

Zeus nodded. 'Thanks, we'll take a couple of beers.'

The gentleman handed the beers to the twins and asked them to join him at the dining room table. 'Iceman, I assume you are quite the card player; why don't we play? Zeus, I have an appointment at 4:00. What time do you have?'

Zeus looked to find an empty wrist while Iceman reached into an empty pocket, searching for his wallet.

'Looking for these?' The gentleman held up the goodies. 'Now, let's get to work.' He handed them back the wallet and watched with a smile. 'Only too easy, but that's what we are here to correct. Call me Fingers; I am your instructor for misdirection, sleight of hand and other useful party favorites.'

'I see why they call you fingers.' Zeus observed.

'A common misperception. I am called Fingers, because of my magic fingers with the ladies, which is not included in your lesson plan. For the next four weeks, I will share my life's work with you to be proper gamblers, thieves and cheats.'

'Zeus, did you hear that; we are rolling Ocean's strong. We are Rusty and Danny with Fingers here as Ruben. Right, you are from Mars, Ocean...'

Zeus interrupted. 'I've seen Ocean's 11. George Clooney, Brad Pitt. I got it.'

'And Elliot Gould. Right, how about Frank Sinatra and Dean Martin, have you seen that?'

'No.'

'Earth calling Mars. This is a collect call; do you accept the charges?'

'You two are going to be fun. Let us get started.' Fingers added, excited to work with the twins.

Fingers, Zeus and Iceman played a variety of card games for several hours. Zeus watched the two card warriors calmly work the cards and their opponents as he struggled to be competitive.

'Iceman, Zeus was correct. You are an exceptional card player and have a keen eye for tells. Tell me, given you have posed a challenge to me, what is my tell? I am very skilled, but you managed to read me at times.'

'Your pupils. Your pupils, at times, betray you. Not your eyes, just your pupils. They dilate when you bluff. Most people's pupils dilate when they have a good hand, they get excited. Winning is a foregone conclusion to you. You get excited to bluff. The challenge to employ the skill of the game excites you.'

Zeus was confused. 'How can you see his pupils from that distance in this light?'

'Like Ted Williams, the greatest hitter in baseball history, I have 20/10 vision. What you can see at 10 feet, I can see at 20. Williams was said to be able to see the laces on a pitched baseball.'

'Very impressive, Iceman. But you also have a tell: you are always on the offensive, reading your opponent, but you forget defense. Your technique of sensory overload is effective. You blitz your opponent with a hurricane of stimulants that you use to hide in the storm. You have once constant in the chaos.'

'What's that?' Iceman was clearly disappointed.

'Your right eyebrow is slightly animated and is the window to your soul. If an opponent can block all the other stimuli you throw at them and focus on your right eyebrow, they have a peek at your intentions.'

'Impressive. Thank you. I did not know that.'

'That's why you are here.'

Zeus asked. 'What about me?' He was invited to play several hands and was anxious for Finger's evaluation.

Fingers began his evaluation, but Iceman interrupted. 'Let me have a shot.' With Finger's consent, Iceman started. 'You are an exceptionally gifted card player. The decisions you make, the cards you play, all the fundamentals are executed flawlessly. You seldom bluff. You prefer to play a clean game and play the percentages. Your first tell is the clean game: you don't make mistakes, but you never vary the script. You never lose big, but you seldom win big. The second tell is regret. When you have a good hand, you show a hint of regret. You regret winning. Very backwards.'

Fingers applauded. 'Well done, Iceman. Here ended the lesson. We'll continue to play in between other lessons. I expect that you have already surmised that I am training you in more than cards.'

Iceman responded. 'Micro-expressions.'

Fingers smiled and continued. 'Exactly, the tiniest of tells is the window into a target's soul. Their micro-expressions will detect lies, violence and fear, all precursors to intent followed by action. My work includes memory training, the ability to remember license plates, people in a diner, mission data, that sort of thing, but the two of you were exempt from that training.'

Zeus asked. 'Why?'

Iceman answered. 'We've already got it naturally. We don't need the training.'

* * *

The twins continued to wake at dawn, run, lift weights in the Palms' gym, work the first shift at Lindo Michoacan and study with Fingers well past midnight. Fingers was a night owl who arose promptly at the crack of 1100 hours. Finger's lessons included multitudinal schemes, techniques, methods and versions to cheat and steal. A couple of the twins' favorites were car thefts, break-ins and pickpockets. The series of techniques used for car theft and break-ins were similar. For older cars and basic locks, Fingers taught the twins all the simple techniques, including hotwiring, lock bumping and lock picking. Fingers explained to the twins that lock-pick guns were effective, but left a trail. Therefore, he chose to master the manual techniques. For more advanced cars and hotel rooms, Fingers had an ace in the hole.

'Give me your room key, Zeus.' Fingers asked while he removed his cell phone and attached a credit card reader to his iPhone. He walked into the hall, typed in the room number from across the hall, swiped Zeus' card, then held it to the electronic lock of the targeted room. The light immediately turned green. As the group returned to their suite, Fingers entered their room number, swiped the card, and again, the lights flashed green.

'How did you do that?' Iceman was amazed.

Zeus studied the reader for a moment. 'You have a program that hacks into the hotel's security system that clones and mimics the magnetic swipe of the desired room. How?'

'Magic is all you need to know. The same technology works with chip keys and fob keys for cars. Just use the app to take a picture of the vehicle identification number (VIN) located at the bottom of the front windshield and the doors are opened when the car is started.'

'Amazing.' Zeus loved the reader and started to reverse-engineer the process in his head. 'You use the car's technology against it.

You hack into the car's onboard computer to take ownership. Amazing. You must have backdoors…'

Finger was not interested in the technology, so he simply smiled and interrupted. 'Our employer's resources come in very handy.'

The twins really enjoyed the art of the pickpocket.

'Iceman, your height is often considered a disadvantage in pickpocketing, but your body type can work to your advantage. Height is a disadvantage, because tall pickpocketers need to bend down to retrieve a wallet from pant pockets. Your long arms and strong fingers mitigate that disadvantage. You don't need to bend down, because of your long arms. Your height requires the target to look up to make eye contact and are blind to activity below their shoulders. Your long and strong fingers provide a perfect tool for the two-finger pinch.'

Fingers used Zeus as the target as he taught Iceman the two-finger pinch for all locations. Front pockets and rear pant pockets, jacket pockets and purses. Iceman's index finger and middle finger formed a vice grip on both wallets and phones.

'Zeus, you have bulk, so the bump lift is perfect for you. In a crowd or doorway, people naturally bump into you. They won't give a second thought to the lift. The bump will be natural.'

Fingers used Iceman as the target and repeated the process for Zeus. Fingers included other sleight of hand and misdirection techniques for a proper lift in other situations, such as off a bar or table.

* * *

The final weekend of the twins' Vegas training was a big weekend in Las Vegas. While MMA was growing in popularity, nothing could compare to boxing championship fight night in Las Vegas. The casinos were packed with celebrities and high rollers, a target-rich environment for the twins.

The twins started their assault on Vegas at the blackjack table at the MGM Grand, then walked over the strip to New York, New York. Their natural card-counting skills, coupled with Finger training, treated them well. Before they left the city, they ate several slices of New York-style pizza.

'The pizza is good.' Zeus commented.

'So was my run at the MGM.' Iceman answered with a mouthful of pizza. 'The pizza is good, because they ship the water from New York. The key to pizza and bagels is the water.'

'Really, more useless information? I didn't have much luck at MGM, but I did well here.'

'That's cool. Nothing suspicious? No one notice?'

'No, you?'

'Nope.'

The twins did not stay too long at any one casino to avoid detection of their card-counting skills. They hit the run of Paris, Bally's and the Flamingo before returning to the Palms for a shower and change of clothes. They did not gamble at the Palms. Never shit where you eat. They grabbed a cab exiting the Palms and headed to the Golden Steer for dinner.

'Zeus, we are in Vegas royalty, the Golden Steer. Sinatra and Elvis ate here.' Iceman explained as he looked around in awe.

Zeus was not impressed as he looked at the old red leather booths, low lighting and Western art. 'Hasn't changed much, has it?'

'That's the whole point. This is how it looked in 1958 when they opened. Pretty cool, uh?!'

'I guess I can see it.' Zeus conceded, trying to share Iceman's enthusiasm.

The twins took their seats and were presented with their menus by a black-tied waiter, who looked to have started on opening night.

'Zeus, look, they have a seafood tower. We are definitely starting with that in tribute to Colonel Sullivan.'

They started with the seafood tower, followed by Escargots De Bourgogne and a Caesar salad.

Zeus asked. 'What does De Bourgogne mean?'

'No clue. I've never had escargots before.'

'Me, neither.'

They both enjoyed their pregame meal and the waiter explained that De Bourgogne was the region where the escargot originated. With dinner, they enjoyed the 22 oz bone-in ribeye, loaded baked potato, creamed corn, creamed spinach, mac and cheese and unlimited bread. For dessert, Iceman had a piece of cheesecake and chocolate cake and Zeus had tiramisu. After dinner, they returned to the bar. The twins scouted the bar and nodded to each other; they identified their targets. Iceman waited for Zeus to leave for the restroom, and while Zeus was gone, he stood and picked the wallet of the man next to him. The man was half turned to his friends standing behind him with his jacket slightly opened. Iceman kept his eyes forward, and his back to the friends as he pinched the wallet clean. He walked to the restroom and, on his way, snatched a cell phone from a purse hanging from a bar stool.

When Zeus approached the restroom door, he briefly paused, timing his entry to coincide with another customer's attempt to do the same. Employing a calculated maneuver, Zeus placed his left hand high on the door to distract the target's eyes, and with a swift bump, he adeptly snatched his wallet while entering the restroom.

'Excuse me, after you.' Zeus politely offered.

Zeus allowed the man to enter and reversed back to the bar. Zeus and Iceman passed each other without notice and exchanged the stolen items. Taking was easy, but returning the items was the challenge. Zeus returned to the bar, stood next to the purse, acted like he was getting the bartender's attention and returned the phone. He moved back to their seats, bumped into the neighbor as he sat down and returned the wallet. Iceman, in the meantime, entered the bathroom, passed the target and returned the wallet as the target threw his used towel away.

Iceman casually walked past Zeus, exited and hailed a cab. Zeus followed, entered the cab and they were off to the Golden Nugget in old Las Vegas for a game of 1/2 Texas Hold'em, which is a poker game and 1/2 governs the conservative betting amount, $1, $2 bets. The stop at Golden Nugget was just a friendly stop to play cards and kill time.

The twins departed the Golden Nugget at midnight to play black-jack on the north end of the strip. They hit Encore, Wynn and the Venetian. They returned to the Palms, ate breakfast and went to bed. At the crack of 1100 hours, Fingers entered the room.

'Looks like you two did well last night! Everything go smoothly? I assume there were no difficulties.' Fingers had noticed the pile of money on the dining table.

The twins took turns describing their grifts and answered a couple of questions for Fingers.

Zeus asked. 'What's the plan for today?'

'Relax, exercise, grab a steam and get a massage. Tonight, you visit Bellagio when the big game is out for fight night. The real action doesn't begin until the fight is over. Where are you eating dinner?'

Iceman responded. 'Battista's Hole in the Wall.'

'Another off the strip old school staple. Great Italian food and décor, you will love it.'

The twins relaxed by the pool after their early morning activities, took a nap, ate at Battista's and arrived at Bellagio at 2300 hours. They played at the 20/40 Texas Hold'em up from the 1/2 the prior night. The twins had won enough to bankroll the increased stakes. After three hours of Hold'em, the twins took their healthy winnings and walked over to the craps table.

The twins bet as they were instructed by Fingers. They did not bet the hard way or double numbers. For example, a hard six is two threes. They didn't bet any of the junk prop bets that only apply to one roll. The bets are tempting, but the house advantage is too high, like betting on long shots in horseracing. Fingers taught them to bet the pass line. The pass line bet automatically wins if a 7 or 11 is rolled on the come-out roll or first roll of the ice. If the come-out roll is a 2, 3, or 12, the gambler loses. If any other number is rolled, there are no winners or losers; the point is set. The gambler is a winner if the point is rolled prior to a seven being rolled.

Once the point is set, Fingers recommended betting the odds for the point. 3:1 for 4 and 10, 4:1 for 5 and 9 and 5:1 for 6 and 8. The pass line bet with odds gives virtually the same chances of winning for the house and player. Craps is the only game with this slight of an advantage to the house if bet in this fashion. With the hard way and prop bets, the house cleans up.

The twins settled themselves at either end of the craps table. For the first 90 minutes, the table was lukewarm. The twins, betting conservatively, waiting for that hot shooter to emerge, were about breakeven. That changed when Zeus picked up the dice for the fourth time and rolled the bones. Iceman doubled his pass bet from $25 to $50 in support of his friend.

'Come on shooter.' The table cheered.

'7, winner.' The crowd clapped and the cheer continued.

Zeus rolled again. '11, 11, winner.' The crowd started to gain a little energy.

'8, point easy 8.'

Zeus rolled a 6 and a 2. All combinations of eight are easy except for a pair of fours, the hard eight. Iceman bet the odds and increased his bet five times the pass bet of $50. He placed $250 behind the $50 bet already on the table. On any given roll, the odds of rolling a 7 are just under 17% and the odds for 8 are just shy of 14%. The odd bet pays 5:6, $5 pays $6, so the house has no real advantage. If Zeus could roll an eight before a seven, Iceman would win $50 for the pass bet and $300 for the odds bet, a total of $350. Zeus rolled a hard 4, then an easy 6 (4 and 2) without impacting Ice's bet. Zeus hunted for an 8 before a 7 for seven more minutes, then hit with a 5, 3 combination.

'Winner, winner, chicken dinner.' The crowd cheered.

The bets were paid, and Iceman took $250 of his winnings and increased his odds bet to the maximum 10x pass bet or $500. If Zeus rolled another 8 before 7, Iceman would win $650. Zeus rolled again for three minutes and rolled a 6,2 combination.

Zeus rolled the point, 8 twice more in the subsequent nine minutes and the table went nuclear. A mushroom cloud of high fives, cheers, hugs given to strangers to the chant of, shoot-er, shoot-er, shoot-er. Iceman took a moment while the winnings were distributed to assess his situation. Fingers instructed them to walk from a hot table and Iceman was up a nice chunk of change. He had already placed the maximum bet allowed on the pass line with his original $50 bet and $500 odds. Zeus was so worried about rolling that he neglected his gambling. Iceman thought, screw it. He had been fighting his inner voice in favor of Fingers creed. Don't ever bet the hard way. He had been struggling with his desire to bet the hard way once the point was established at 8. His inner voice was too powerful. The hard way was 4 and 4 or 44, his old jersey number, that had to be a sign especially with Zeus being the hot shooter.

Iceman dropped eleven $100 chips on the table. 'Dealer, color me up, $1,000 on the hard way and $100, dealers bet.'

The table paused except for Zeus, who was anxiously awaiting the dealer's stick that slid the magic dice.

The dealer colored or exchanged the ten $100 chips and replaced them with a single $1,000 chip. '$1,000 on the hard eight and $100 for the dealer with the gentleman, thank you, sir.'

With the gentleman, it meant the dealers bet the hard 8 with Iceman. 'Don't thank me yet.' Iceman said with a hopeful smile.

The hard eight paid 10:1. Zeus shook the dice, rolled it, and hit the 44 right out of the gates. Iceman had just won $10,000 plus the $650 for the pass bet in one roll. In all, his total for Zeus' turn was over $15,000.

He screamed. 'Motherfucker, that is some chicken dinner.'

* * *

After the twins cashed out of the Bellagio, they returned to the casino bar at the Palms. They sat at the main bar, played video poker and drank to access to come down from their high. Iceman slid an envelope over to Zeus.

'What's this?'

'Your share.'

'Fuck off, Iceman. That's yours.'

Iceman just ignored him. After the bar, they had breakfast, but were still too excited to sleep. They changed into their bathing suits, grabbed a steam and headed to the pool. The sun was up, so they laid by the pool, swam and had a couple of beers before they returned to their room for a nap.

Fingers woke them again at 1100 hours and saw their fortune had grown. The twins provided a brief account of the night.

'Don't think the hard way is a good idea, because you got lucky.' Fingers lectured.

'I don't, I get it.' Iceman acknowledged. 'But it was fun.'

'Granted. I enjoyed our time together and look forward to working with you in the coming years. You'll be happy to know that I am sending Conjar a stellar report. Your ride arrives at 1700 hours to take you to the camp for more training. What are the two of you going to do until then?'

Iceman smiled. 'As Amy Winehouse sang. *Rehab.*'

Rehab was not used in the traditional sense. Rehab was the name of the pool party at the Hard Rock Café on Sundays attended by casino industry workers. The twins ate Mexican food at Hard Rock's Pink Taco bar. For one last bit of fun, they each snatched four phones and circulated them around the pool. They waited for the patrons to notice their phones were missing. The owners asked their friends to call their phone in an effort to locate it. The pool ignited with ringing phones and confusion as the laughing twins exited.

'*Vegas, baby, Vegas.* Somewhere, Vince Vaughn, who was from Chicago and the rest of Swingers, are smiling on us, Zeus.'

CHAPTER TWENTY-NINE

The twins were picked up from the Palms and shuttled for just over three hours to the Oasis. The twins recognized the facility; they had conducted their Combat Medic Training at the Oasis; they did not know the name or nature of the facility at the time. The Oasis, the name used by the Elders team, was hidden within the Byrne Group training complex. The Byrne Group, founded in 1992, was a private military company founded by Alec Byrne. Byrne was a former SEAL Team Six officer who founded the company to provide specialized training to private military contractors. The private Military & Security (PMSC) market was estimated to reach $475 billion by 2030. The Byrne Group did not have field operators; the company was strictly a training facility located 75 miles northeast of the Nevada Test and Training Range. The facility was close to Tonopah and equidistance from Reno and Las Vegas. The Byrne Group was a small company that had a highly specialized function. The Byrne Group trained advanced predators for large private contract companies. Since its inception, Alec Byrne has worked with the Elders' team in complete secrecy. Byrne, now deceased, turned over his reign to Barry Little. Little was now the gatekeeper for the Byrne Elders's relationship. Statesmen teams conducted training for agents, senior agents and statesmen in secrecy. The Byrne trainers and clients operated independently of the Elders with the belief the agents were training for a different private military company.

Byrne operated a strategic, state-of-the-art, 10,000-acre training facility. The campus contained specific facilities, including an airfield, six tactical ranges over a variety of landscapes, ranges, simulators, armory and driving tracks with fleet and shoot houses. The shoot houses had a variety of settings designed to mimic take-down targets. Offices, hotel rooms, streets and small buildings were a part of the staging used to train assaults.

Dale Lawson and Bernie Pettibone welcomed the twins to the Oasis. Lawson, called Wyatt, was a play on words for Lawson, stood 6'1' with a wiry strong build and Pettibone, or Bone, as he was called, was 5'11' with a thick athletic build. Both were statesmen and fit the mold of assassin. They took Conjar's basic training and drilled the twins in advanced combat techniques. The statesmen provided four courses for the twins' three months of the advanced training exercise.

The first course was advanced firearms and tactics training. The statesmen provided enhancements to the shooting skills started by Conjar. The twins became experts with the HK45 and MP7 assault weapons. The twins were trained in the various shoot houses to mimic an assassination and exigency escape if necessary. The twins were proficient in dozens of other assault weapons with the use of the extensive armory and instruction. The twins became invisible, hidden in the landscape of their operating theatre. They were taught to disappear in the mountains of Nevada that mirrored the terrain of Afghanistan. The statesmen used the street sets to train the twins to find cover in their movements. Building shadows, along with other available cover objects such as dumpsters or streetlights, taught the twins to fade into the environment.

The second course was advanced martial arts training. The statesmen added Brazilian jiu-jitsu to the martial arts disciplines Conjar had already trained. Brazilian jiu-jitsu (BJJ) training focused on ground fighting and submission. The grabbing and striking style has its origin in feudal Japan. The samurai warrior could wind up bereft of his sword and needed a weaponless method of defense. BJJ supplemented the Jeet Kune Do training with the ability to fight on the ground. The statesmen also taught the Israeli fighting system, Krav Maga. The final discipline taught was the Marine Corps martial arts training. The Corp incorporated many fighting styles, including Muay Thai. Muay Thai, or Thai boxing, was a stand-up technique that implemented striking and clinching techniques. The disciple was also referred to as the art of eight limbs, because it combined the use of fists, elbows, knees and shins. Iceman's elbow strike to Conjar on their first meeting was Muay Thai; he simply didn't know it at the time. Becoming proficient in the various disciples strived to achieve Bruce Lee's ultimate philosophy, total freedom. The twins used all the lessons they received to develop, with years of training, their own fighting style. If the twins lived to see it, they would return for several years to become experts at their fighting style.

The third course was tactical and off-road driving training. Using the driving courses and the natural Nevada terrain, the twins became proficient in hazardous driving situations. The twins trained on various radius corners, hairpin turns, obstacles over varied grades and vehicles. The twins were taught how to fire a weapon and how to evade gunfire under the above conditions.

The fourth course was munitions training. The twins completed an abbreviated US Army course on explosive safety and use. The statesmen used the munitions range to conduct their training. Independent study and bookwork were critical components of munitions training. The twins became educated and proficient at disarming common improvised explosive devices (IEDs). Once the twins gained proper respect for munitions, they were trained in the plastic explosives, such as: Semtex, C4 and PE4 (the British version).

Wyatt and Bones split the 0600 to 2300 hours training schedule. The twins daily schedule, seven days a week, for the three-month advance training:

0600 hours: Enhanced protein shake, independent exercise to include running, swimming, yoga and weight training.

0800 hours: Breakfast.

0900 hours: Firearms and tactics training with Wyatt.

1200 hours: Lunch.

1300 hours: Even days, tactical and off-road driving training with Wyatt. Odd days, munitions training with Bones.

1500 hours: Snack, advanced martial arts training with Bones.

1900 hours: Dinner.

2100 hours: Independent study.

2300 hours: Snack.

2400 hours: Lights out.

Both Wyatt and Bones lived in Tonopah, NV, 20 miles from the Byrne Group campus. They both commuted; Wyatt trained in the morning session and Bones in the evening. Conjar trained with the twins the final month and spoke frequently with the statesmen.

'That Iceman is a pain in the ass.' Conjar laughed as he greeted the statesmen at the conclusion of his month of training.

'I donno. I like the arrogant fuck. Makes me laugh and the days shorter.' Bones answered as he scratched his stubble.

'I agree. Now Zeus, he is a proper gentleman. Real stand-up fellow.' Wyatt added.

Conjar agreed with both and asked. 'They the real deal or what?'

'Best I've seen.' Wyatt answered, looking at Bones for confirmation.

'I got to agree. I've seen better snipers or drivers; you know what I am saying?! Agents training better in a specific discipline, but in terms of complete package, they're unique. Having said that, never seen better in hand to hand. Those big boys can move; Iceman is especially dangerous; he anticipates like nothing I have seen. A natural.'

Wyatt added. 'The thing is with the twins, it's funny, with the same last name, even with the black and white thing, you would swear they were actually twins. They act like they came out of the same mama together. They are in complete sync with each other.'

'And they complement each other.' Bones added more detail to Wyatt's thought. 'Iceman can get going, but there is old Zeus there to keep things steady. Pretty special. We are certainly looking forward to their visits in the years to come. Conjar, you're lucky to have them to lead.'

Conjar did not pause. 'Always dangerous work, but we have the makings of a fine team.'

CHAPTER THIRTY

On the drive to McCarren's Airport, Conjar turned from the front passenger seat to face the twins. 'Your flight leaves tomorrow late morning for Logan Airport.'

Zeus nodded. 'Right, we are off to MIT for finance and Arabic language and history training.'

'Correct, but that is not what I want to discuss. I need to address the 800-pound gorilla in the room.' He turned his attention to Iceman. 'What is your plan in regard to Kathleen?'

'What do you mean?' Iceman asked, not understanding Conjar's concern.

'Don't' ever answer my questions with a question. You know exactly my concern.'

'Seriously, I don't.'

'You saw the weekly schedule for your 14 weeks of training in Boston. Your weekdays are like your weekdays at the Oasis. Independent PT to start the day, then classwork from 0800-2000 hours split between finance and Arabic.'

'Right, what's your point?'

'The weekends. The statesmen in Boston do not work weekends and you need that time for your studies. You are independent on the weekends.'

'And?'

'Iceman, please. You are in Boston with freedom. What do you think my concern is?'

'I have no idea?'

'My concern is that you will use the time in the pubs and contacting your college sweetheart rather than your studies.'

'You shouldn't have a concern. I am most definitely tackling the pubs on the weekend, no question about it, so no concern. You don't have to worry if I will; I'll save the suspense, I am. In terms of college sweetheart, she was college and not a sweetheart.'

'That doesn't work for me.' Conjar responded, intent on laying down the law.

Zeus immediately engaged. He knew if Conjar challenged Iceman and backed him into a corner, Iceman would not react well. He would go out more and blow off the classwork to spite Conjar just to prove he could. 'Before we dig in, Iceman, what is your plan? You always have a plan.'

'I am doing zero work in finance on the weekends. I'll pick up the finance crap faster than the statesman can dish it. I am fucked in Arabic and I know it. On Fridays at 2001 hours, I am going out until 2400 hours. On Saturdays and Sundays, I will work out and eat from 0600-0900 hours. I will study Arabic and eat from 0900-1400 hours. At 1401-2400 hours, I will be out. On Saturday night, depending on the night's events, I may elect to stay out later.'

Zeus, knowing Saturday night's flexible curfew was to accommodate female companionship, turned to Conjar with a look that pled acceptance. 'That seems fair.'

'What about you, Zeus? Are you going with him?'

Zeus knew Conjar was concerned for him. Conjar knew Iceman's stamina was not a pace Zeus could maintain. The less Zeus went, the better for Iceman. 'I plan on only going with Iceman on Friday and Saturday night. I'll stay in and study on Sunday, only go out for dinner.'

Conjar took a moment to evaluate his position. He was extremely relieved that Iceman committed to significant study time on Saturday and Sunday. He was right about finance, so there was room to accommodate his plan. He had to gain a little ground to maintain command. Iceman could not be allowed to change his training schedule independently. He also realized that rejecting Iceman's plan entirely would result in disaster. 'How about this? You keep your plan with one slight adjustment: on Sundays, you eat dinner with Zeus at 2001 hours and return at 2200 hours. I want you 100% for Monday's training. Fair?'

Zeus did not give Iceman the chance to respond. He played his magic card, him. 'I sure would like the company at dinner.'

Iceman stared at Zeus with a, I know what you just did, and I don't like it, look. 'Alright, that sounds fair to me.'

'What about the girls?' Conjar was forced by Colonel Sullivan to raise the subject.

Zeus cringed. 'What about them?'

'Are you planning on seeing them on the weekends?'

'Asked and answered.' Iceman dismissively responded.

'Have you spoken with her? Have you made plans to see her?'

Conjar had now insulted Iceman, who did not respond pleasantly. 'Asked and answered.'

'Are you planning on seeing her?'

Iceman returned Conjar's question with that look of his.

'You, of course, will inform me if you elect to see her.'

'No.' Iceman was now clearly angry. He had no interest in seeing Kathleen, but if Conjar did not let it go, he would contact her to spite him.

Zeus saw he needed to bridge the tension and offered. 'We will not be seeing them, so let's just move on.'

Conjar was upset with Iceman's response to his questions and order, but let the matter go. He was confident the twins had moved past their college girls and were focused on the mission. Conjar stayed focused on the critical point and let Iceman keep his stubborn no. He recognized Iceman's response was not mission critical; just spoken out of defense to his personal freedom. 'Agreed.'

CHAPTER THIRTY-ONE

The twins landed at Logan Airport and took a taxi to a bed and breakfast in Back Bay, Boston. Back Bay was an upscale neighborhood centrally located along the Charles River. The neighbor boasted several of the city's best shops and restaurants. Walking distance to Boston Commons and several other popular Boston sites, Black Bay conveniently reached other destinations with the subway. Back Bay was home for the twins for a series of three-month tours over their three years of advanced training. The six-room B&B was operated by Rebecca Kane. Mrs. Kane was a widow whose husband was killed in the line of duty as a senior agent. She was in her mid-fifties and exuded motherly warmth. Her three children were in their twenties and had moved away from home. An empty nester, Rebecca accepted the Elders' offer to run the bed and breakfast. The Elders used the bed and breakfast to house the agents trained by statesmen. An OWL corporate training center was the cover story for the bed and breakfast. The B&B had a classroom, dining room, great room and kitchen on the first floor. A gym was built out in the basement and used for hand-to-hand combat sparring and yoga. Rebecca lived in the two-bedroom coach house above the garage at the back of the property.

'Hello and welcome to Boston. I am Rebecca; nice to meet the two of you.'

Zeus answered for the twins. 'The pleasure is ours.'

After a brief tour, the twins settled into their rooms and then reported to the large dining room table for their debriefing.

Rebecca started once the twins settled in. 'Here are your training packets to include your daily schedule. Monday through Friday follows the same set of intensive routine.'

The twins examined the first page of the packet that contained their weekday schedule.

0530: Two-mile run to MIT's sports and fitness center for swimming and weight training, two-mile return run.

0830: Breakfast provided by Rebecca.

0900: Finance, Accounting and Economic studies instructed by Dwayne Washington.

1200: Lunch prepared by Zeus.

1400: Islamic and Middle East studies to include Arabic language.

1800: Dinner prepared by Iceman.

1900: Independent study.

'Any questions about the schedule?'

The twins looked at each other and both shook their heads no.

'Let us move on. I have an order form in the kitchen. Please complete the form on Tuesdays and Fridays so that I can get you what you need. Behind the daily schedule, you will find background information regarding the statesmen who are your professors. Please take a moment to read and digest the information to familiarize yourself with your professors.'

Dr. Lena Khalil: Lena was born in Beirut, Lebanon, in 1975, during the beginning of the Lebanese Civil War. Her parents were well educated and, in 1983, after living in too many years of war, were a part of the approximately one million Lebanese who immigrated during the civil war. The 1983 Beirut marine barracks bombings were the final catalyst for the Khalil family to immigrate. The Khalil family immigrated to London, finding peace and mild prosperity. Lena graduated with a double major in economics, accounting and finance. She went on to complete her masters in Middle Eastern Studies and Intensive Languages from SOAS University of London. Already fluent in Arabic, Lena studied Persian at SOAS. She is fluent in Arabic, English, French and Persian (Farsi). Lena was an agent in the analytics and investments group. She received her master's degree prior to becoming a senior agent. As a senior agent, she was charged with the Middle East analytics team. Her team did not analyze financial data for investment. Her team analyzed all data to identify potential targets for Black Ops.

Dr. Dwayne Washington: Dwayne was born and raised in Philadelphia Badlands. The Badlands was a notorious section of north Philadelphia where drug and gang violence were rampant. Dwayne, a track star in the 400-meter dash, took his gifts to the famous University of Pennsylvania program. Dwayne excelled at Penn in the classroom as well as the track, and he graduated summa cum laude with a double degree in finance and accounting. Upon graduation, he went to work for OWL. He was identified by the Elders, sent to complete his master's and doctorate in finance from Wharton, and returned to lead the investments team.

Rebecca noticed the twins had read the brief bios of the statesmen and continued. 'Any questions for me before you begin your studies?'

Again, the twins shook their heads.

'Very good. I am just at the back of the property if you need me. Otherwise, I will see you tomorrow morning at breakfast.'

* * *

The twins quickly settled into their rigorous daily routine. As expected, neither had any difficulties with the workload Dwayne provided. The preparation work during training prior to meeting Dwane built a sound foundation. The twins were prepared and excelled at the workload offered by Dwayne. Both tackled Lena's lessons in the classical and modern aspects of the Middle East with ease. Lena's lesson plan included the Islamic societies and cultures worldwide, giving the twins a working understanding and appreciation. The twins had to work diligently on learning Arabic. After a month of studies, including intensive night work, the twins spoke Arabic to each other at the B&B. In addition to their studies, the twins had little difficulty finding fun in Boston.

The twins settled into a weekend routine. On Friday nights, they started their pilgrimage in downtown Boston. They mingled with the workers, just off a week's work, fueled with released energy. On their third Friday in Boston, after a couple of stops, the twins wandered into J.J. Foley's. The bar familiar to the twins was crowded with liberated workers from all working classes assembled to roar in the weekend. The twins were no exception. While neither spoke of it in English or Arabic, both were aware they were feeling the effects of a lack of female companionship.

'I like this place. Of the places we have been to on our Friday night lights tour, I like this place the best.' Iceman started as they walked into the bar.

'Me too, let's go, two girls are leaving a spot at the bar.' Zeus had noticed.

The twins hustled to the potential opening and Iceman asked. 'Excuse me, are the two of you about to leave?'

An attractive redhead smiled at Jack. 'The bar, no. The seats, yes. Our friends just arrived and they are sitting over there.' Red pointed to two girls taking their coats off at a neighboring table. 'The seats are all yours.'

Jack smiled at Red. 'Thanks. Hi, I'm Jack and this is my friend Seamus.'

Red smiled back with a bit of caution. 'You're welcome. I'm Meg and this is my friend Linda. Nice to meet you.'

The twins took their seats and ordered a round.

Zeus asked. 'The Celtics game is about to start. Want to settle in and grab some food?'

Iceman used the bar back mirror to check out Meg when he responded. 'I could eat.'

The twins sat, talked, enjoyed their pub grub and watched the first half of the Celtics' game. With the Celtics down five, the after-work crowd began to leave. The crowd was temporarily thinned as the after-work crowd had not been replaced by the night crowd. After Meg's and Linda's friends left with the after-work migration home, they approached the twins.

Linda informed Seamus. 'We would like our seats back.'

Seamus stood and answered. 'Of course, but we did not realize you had ownership stake in these stools.'

Meg jumped in on the fun while she reclaimed her seat from Jack. 'We do, but we also have ownership of the surrounding area as well. You may stand with us for a price if you like.'

Jack mocked, looking for open stools, and asked. 'How much?'

Meg smiled. 'Rent control requires me to only charge a couple of drinks.'

'I am all for rent control.' Jack offered his knowing smile.

Seamus asked. 'Let's get it out of the way. Where are you from and what do you do?'

Linda answered. 'Providence, and Meg is from Syracuse. We are paralegals for a pretentious law firm.'

Jack replied. 'Redundant.'

Meg laughed. 'Nice, pretentious and lawyers, good one. You two?'

Seamus replied. 'Ireland and Chicago, we're in town for a couple of months for corporate training.'

Meg asked. 'Doing what and for who?'

Jack fielded the question. 'Does it really matter?'

'I suppose not.'

The Celtics lost by seven, but the group hadn't noticed. The flirtatious conversation was center stage. As the time approached midnight, Seamus became nervous.

'We have to be going.' Seamus announced as he asked for the check.

Linda, disappointed, asked. 'So soon?'

'Yes, sorry, we have to get up early for training tomorrow.'

Meg turned to Jack. 'Will we be seeing you again?'

Jack smiled. 'Of course. How about next Saturday night?'

Jack wanted to meet them tomorrow night, but did not want to come across as desperate or too forward. He chose the next Saturday night for obvious reasons: he and Zeus did not have to be back by midnight. On Saturday nights, they typically found themselves in Jamaica Plain (JP). The twins found a good fit in JP with its diverse community loaded with university folk. The twins were also known to wander into Harvard Square on a Saturday night.

'Alright, sounds good. What's the plan?' Linda asked the group.

Jack offered. 'How about we meet next Saturday at 4:00 at Galway House for a couple of pints and make dinner plans?'

Meg answered quickly. 'Perfect, we live in JP. I am surprised we haven't seen you before.'

Zeus answered. 'We haven't been in town long, just a couple of weeks.'

* * *

The twins met up with the girls as scheduled and enjoyed their company and intimate companionship for a few weeks. True to Jack's high school form, he became bored with Meg, who wanted more out of their relationship. Jack ignored her texts and calls, and the relationship fizzled. Seamus was caught in the crosshairs created by Jack. Linda, angry with Jack, ended their relationship.

Zeus shrugged off the rejection and offered to Iceman. 'We can take JP off our radar now. Pretty uncomfortable to run into them.'

'I was bored with them and JP anyways, no loss. We can just spend more time in Back Bay and head over to the Boston College bars or Harvard Square on Saturdays. JP was cool but a little too artsy for me.'

After things ended with the JP girls, Iceman was a shark on Friday and Saturday nights. He was constantly moving, always hunting for female companionship. During the euphoric highs that accompanied his manic bipolar mood, Iceman's sexual appetite was set on high. Iceman frequently abandoned Zeus, who did not share Iceman's predatorial sexual instincts, to satisfy his hunger. On Sundays, the day of Iceman, Zeus stayed around the B&B, studied, and relaxed until dinner with Iceman. The twins typically met in the North End, Boston's little Italy, for dinner. From 1400 to 2000 hours, Iceman ran free in Boston. After he gave Charlestown a couple of weeks, Iceman settled in to spend his Sundays in South Boston. The large Irish population and temperament of the Southies were a perfect fit for Iceman. Iceman enjoyed watching the end of football season and took the Patriots as his second team behind the Bears. With the football season over, Iceman headed to Old Sullivan's, his favorite Southie stop.

'What's up, Jack?' Billy, Jack's bar buddy at Old Sullivan's, asked as Jack approached the stool next to him.

Jack smiled at the Boston police officer and replied. 'As Norm Peterson of Cheers fame declared, *it's a dog-eat-dog world, Sammy and I'm wearing Milkbone underwear.*'

'Good one.' Billy smiled and drank his beer. 'You did well this week, won both games.'

Billy knew a bookie and placed bets for Jack. With his knowledge of basketball, Jack was a proficient sports gambler. 'Cool, keep it in the kitty.'

'Jack, the kitty is getting pretty big. How do you do it? I'm not complaining; I started betting with you, but what is your secret?'

'Matchups and points. The amateur sports bettor pounds the fashionable team and drives the point spread up. The great recruiting classes at Duke and Kentucky, for example, are in the news and covered by ESPN. Those teams, while popular, do not match up well with senior-led teams, especially early in the season with home-court advantage. Men against boys. The fabulous freshmen will go on to the NBA, but the seniors are better today. They may not win, but they will not lose by the point spread. Duke is great, but they were not going to beat those seniors at Florida St. by 11, especially on the road.'

'Makes sense, smart. Why don't you bet pro football?'

'I don't know enough about it. I haven't found a strategy that works.'

'Pretty disciplined approach, I like that. Speaking of gambling, we need to get out of here in a few. We are heading over to the club for a poker game. You play cards, right?'

Iceman was intrigued by the offer. 'A little. Club? As in key club?'

'Yeah, you know about key clubs?'

'Sure, we have them in Chicago. The Italians have theirs, the Irish have theirs and even the Jamaicans have one on the north side. My friend's cousin is a member of the Jamaican club. I have never been to his, as whites are not welcome. Pretty fair when you consider blacks aren't welcomed in the Italian or Irish clubs.'

'So, are you coming?'

Jack was torn. He really wanted to play cards but did not like key clubs. The clubs seemed silly to him with their secrecy, members-only signs and admittance policies. 'I don't think so.'

'Come on, you'll be my guest. I already reserved you a spot in the six-man Hold'em game. $500 buy-in.'

'I don't have $500 on me.'

'Your gambling account is more than flush to cover the buy-in. Your account is held at the club; that's where I book through. You are playing with house money. Drink up. We'll grab another round before we head over.'

Jack's desire to play cards won out. 'Alright.'

* * *

Jack walked with Billy into the key club and found a mirror image of the Chicago Irish club he had visited on a couple of occasions. A storefront with no signage greeted them, and the fire, police and union décor hung along the Patriots, Red Sox and Bruins memorabilia welcomed them. The bar, built by off-duty firemen, operated on the honor system. Each member of the club had a key to gain access, hence the name Key Club. Jack and Billy moved to the back room after greetings and introductions were made. The club was men only, with ages ranging from 21 to 81. Jack entered the back room to find the game set up and ready for the final two players' arrival.

Jack sat down and immediately evaluated the skill levels of his opponents. He quickly realized the table was not much of a challenge. He slowly played his hands and bet softly. He did not want to clean out the table quickly as he was Billy's guest. As the game played on, Jack identified the players he liked. Jack took it easy on those players and even folded winning hands. He knew they were all adults who knew the risk associated, but inviting a card shark would have gotten Billy into a jam. Jack knew the unwritten rule of poker was to play with comparable players. Coming to have a friendly game of poker, only to lose your money quickly to a top-tier player, was bullshit. Jack enjoyed the company and was just cruising along as one of the guys. His enjoyment and temperament changed when an arrogant player exposed himself. Jack hated him immediately. Frankie was also a guest of a member and was a good card player on a hot streak. Winning is a part of cards, but with the expectation of handling it with class. Frankie had no class and was an extremely vocal winner. Frankie knocked out most of the players at the table, had the largest chip count and was facing only Billy and Jack.

The hand was dealt, Jack folded and waited. Billy took Frankie on and went all in with a pair of aces and fives. His two pairs were defeated by Frankie's three nines. Jack watched Frankie; he knew by his facial expression he was more than fortunate to get his third nine on the final card.

Frankie continued his obnoxious behavior. 'Billy, the good news about losing is the embarrassment stops. I can't believe you could be so stupid to go all in with two pairs. Ridiculous.'

Tempers in the room began to boil, none more than Jack, who managed to internalize his anger and maintain a calm exterior.

'Just me and you, Jack. Chicago versus Boston. Awfully low on chips there, Jack, the pain will be over soon.'

'I don't know. I think the pain is just getting started.' Jack stared at Frankie with his acute reply. Frankie missed the threat.

Frankie suddenly felt the sting of Jack's unrestricted play. He had zero interest in being decent to Frankie and Jack was set on humiliating him. Jack went on a streak and quickly evened the chip count. The next hand was played with three spades showing with one card remaining. Both players bet aggressively and Jack knew both were going for the flush. Jack was holding the king of spades and in the event his final card completed the flush only the ace of spades could beat him. The final card was thrown, eight of hearts, no help. Jack was holding a king high hand; he did not even have a pair. He watched Frankie and knew he also missed the flush. He also knew Franky had the better hand; anything is better than a king high.

'All in.' Jack bet all his chips and bluffed Frankie.

Frankie believed Jack had the flush. 'I fold.'

Although against poker etiquette, Jack showed his winning uncalled hand. 'You just lost on a king high, man. That has to be tough.'

The group watching erupted in laughter. The former players and others had grown tired of Frankie. Jack had gotten to Frankie; he knew Frankie was going to start playing with emotion, a big mistake. The next hand was played and Frankie went all in. Jack called, their last hand, last man standing.

Frankie jumped out of his seat and slammed his cards on the table. 'Straight, you fuck, how funny is that, laughing now?'

Jack responded with his Joker laugh from Dark Knight. 'Ha… Ha… Ha… Ho… Ho… Ho…' He paused for effect. 'I found that flush you were looking for.'

Frankie was enraged. 'Fuck you. Let's play again, just you and me. $3,000 buy-in.'

'Agreed. We need to move the game up from 1/2 to 20/40. I have places to be, so I need to make quick work of you.'

With the bet moved, the stakes and tension were volcanic. Both bet aggressively on the first two hands, with each winning one. The volcano erupted on the third hand. The preflop, the first two cards dealt, delivered Jack a pair of tens. He watched Frankie's delight as he looked at his cards and bet big. Jack called him. The flop came and delivered a six, king and a ten. Frankie again bet big, and Jack called. The fourth community card, the turn, was an ace. Jack saw it immediately; Frankie had pocket aces. Looking at the four cards showing, a flush and straight were impossible. Frankie bet his three-of-a-kind with a moderate bet; he was trying to pull Jack in with a look of disappointment and the small wager. If the wager had been large, Jack would have folded. Jack called. The final card, the river, was dealt. Jack waited patiently as Frankie slowly considered his decision to lure Jack in.

'All in.'

Jack smiled. 'Ha…. Ha….Ha…. Ho….Ho…. Ho. All in.'

'Full house, aces over tens.' Frankie smiled and celebrated. 'Not so funny now, I had pocket aces and…'

'Four tens, you owe me $3,000, pal.'

Frankie was stunned; the river flowed with Jack's fourth ten. Jack saw the rage in his eyes, but Frankie walked over to shake

Jack's hand to congratulate him. Jack never let his guard down. Frankie walked around the table and removed his hand from his pant pocket; rather than shake Jack's hand, he pulled a switchblade and swung at Jack's outreached arm. Jack anticipated an attack, but was surprised by the blade. He slashed Jack's forearm, which was moving a little late and blood instantly flowed. Rather than retreat or look at his bloody wound, Jack ignored the pain and immediately threw a left hook in response. He extended his bloodied right arm, hand and fingers and windmilled Frankie in the throat. Frankie gagged, dropped the knife and reached for his injured throat with both hands. Jack drove his right foot into the side of Frankie's right knee. Jack did not use his full power, just enough to dislocate the kneecap. Jack grabbed Frankie's right arm from the floor, straightened it, was prepared to stomp and dislocate his elbow. Before Ice could administer his last act of justice, Billy tried to grab him from behind. Jack quickly reacted to the perceived attack and placed Billy in a Jiu-Jitsu hold.

'Jack, take it easy. I wasn't coming at you. Frankie had enough. He deserved the punishment you gave him, but that was enough. Any more would be a problem.'

Jack released Billy. 'Sorry about that, thanks.'

Billy, concerned about Jack's condition, offered. 'No problem, let's get out of here and get you to the hospital. That slash is pretty bad.'

'No, no hospital, no chance.' Jack thought of the Colonel; he knew Sullivan would discover the hospital visit and he would not be pleased. 'Before we go, I need a clean rag, ice, crazy glue and duct tape.'

Billy looked confused. 'Are you sure?' He looked at Jack and knew he better get the items immediately. 'Alright, no problem, we should have it in the back. One second, hang on.'

Jack trusted his combat medical training and used the clean rag to apply pressure to the large cut. The cut was a little deep for field treatment, but Jack felt it would suffice. He poured Vodka over the wound to clean it, then rubbed the ice to tighten the vessels and slow the bleeding. He applied the crazy glue to seal the wound and the duct tape to add further protection. Jack knew the crazy glue and duct tape would irritate his skin, and he would have to watch for infection, but both were a small price to pay to avoid the Colonel's wrath.

With his work completed, he turned to Billy. 'About my money…'

'Already credited to your account.'

'Thanks, Billy. Let's head back to Old Sullivan's. The first round is on me.' Jack said with a smile.

On the walk back to Old Sullivan's, Billy asked. 'Where did you learn all that shit back there? The fighting and first aid, and shit, the card playing?'

'The boy scouts.'

CHAPTER THIRTY-TWO

Approaching the end of their visit to Back Bay, the twins returned to the B&B after their run from MIT and their regular workout. During their run, the twins spoke in Arabic about their next training assignment. Neither had any clue but thought it might have something to do with SEAL training. Conjar provided basic training in several areas and the twins figured SEAL training was next as it was the only area left. They entered the B&B to find two familiar faces.

'Hello, Colonel.' Zeus greeted Sullivan and turned to Conjar, 'Long time no see.'

Iceman added. 'Miss us?'

Conjar shook his head as he shook Iceman's hand. 'More than milk and cookies.'

'Speaking of cookies, typically when kids go to camp, they get cookies in the mail. No care packages came for us Colonel. Must have been an oversight.' Iceman joked.

'I see you have not changed, Iceman. No oversight, just hustle up, grab a shower and meet us for breakfast.' The Colonel ordered and continued. 'We have much to discuss.'

The twins returned fifteen minutes later and joined Conjar and the Colonel at the dining room table. They had already finished their small breakfast and were drinking coffee as the twins took their seats.

'You eat, I'll talk. Your breakfast feast will occupy Iceman's mouth so I may have a chance to get through my material. Before I issue your briefing packets, I want to congratulate both of you on a job well done. Lena and Dwayne both sang your praises regarding your work in the classroom, well done. All your other instructors to include Conjar also hold you in high regard.'

Zeus took a moment from his eggs to respond. 'Thank you.'

'The pleasure is all mine. Iceman, I am glad to see you have recovered from your knife fight.'

'Come on, you cannot be serious. I have grown up.'

'You are telling me that new scar on your right forearm was what? An accident in the shower? I noticed you neither lied to me nor addressed my question in your initial response. I am not being vague, please refrain from being evasive. I will repeat myself…'

'No need, thank you and I understand. My fault.'

'Thank you, Iceman, for not telling me it won't happen again, but please let's try to learn and mature from the experience.'

'Yes, sir.' Iceman returned to his breakfast.

'I owe the both of you another briefing regarding your job description. Iceman, continue putting your mouth to good use and enjoy your breakfast, I am addressing the *we*.'

Iceman followed the order, continued to eat and simply nodded his consent and gratitude. While his cheesy grits were good, he was more interested in what the Colonel had to say.

'We work for a group, a group of important men that comprise the Elders. The Elders were formed after the War of 1812 with nine great minds from England and America. The founding Elders established the simple mission statement, to promote and protect British and American interest in the global theatre.'

The twins nodded their consent and continued to eat.

'We see in the dark. You already know about OWL, but allow me to detail their mission for the Elders. The work product of the Elders is passed down to OWL when the technology or investment is close to being at market. Market is defined as nearly available to the public and governments. Cutting edge technology and investments in market is stale to the Elders, but a competitive advantage for OWL. As you know, the CEO and President of OWL is Paul Stephan. Paul was an agent with the Elders in the investment division. Rather than becoming a senior agent, Paul was transferred to OWL. He is the bridge between the Elders and OWL. Paul is the only person at OWL that knows about the Elders program. OWL receives the work product passed down from the Elders group through Paul. Forensic accounting, your cover, is the investigation of companies to ensure there is no financial misconduct. The cybersecurity team offers consulting and cybersecurity software and systems.'

Iceman interrupted the Colonel and asked. 'Hang on, just wait a minute, let me get this straight. The Elders develop hacks to stay ahead of the world, use that software, code, or whatever to make sick profits and identify bad guys? When the Elders develop some next generation shit, OWL doubles down on profit by selling cybersecurity to defeat the shit the Elders created in the first place? Do I got that right?'

'I see Iceman has freed his lips; breakfast must be over.' The Colonel ignored Iceman's questions and continued his briefing. 'The cybersecurity software is developed by the Elders to defend against the previous generation of cyber-attacks implemented by the hackers. The OWL software contains backdoors to provide easier access to hack data for the Elders. Both teams sell their services to government and private institutions, the benefits of the backdoors are obvious. The forensic accounting and cybersecurity teams work together to perform deep dives into the financial, compliance and overall health of a targeted entity.'

'I'll take that as a yes.' Iceman interrupted the Colonel to answer his own question.

'This is only a summary; complete details are here in your briefing packet.' The Colonel explained to the twins as he held up two folders. 'The Elders invest their vast wealth through shell companies. Here are your briefing folders. Please take a moment to read the two group summaries highlighted.'

The twins read the summaries as instructed.

Research and Development: The research department takes data from around the world and probes for threats against and opportunities for American and British interests. The R&D group monitors the agencies that monitor foreign communications, electric systems, backdoors in commercial technology and other covert data. The R&D group is comprised of the sharpest minds in the US and England. Every agent is trained to speak a second language and is assigned to that region. Much of the celebrated defeat of the enigma machine used in World War II by the Nazis to send coded messages was done behind the scenes by R&D. The R&D group, led by Alan Turning, cracked the enigma machine. Turning used his cover as a part-time employee of the British Government's Code and Cypher school to be the front man for the team effort. The group also developed the use of Navajo speakers as wind talkers to send coded messages for the US. The R&D department touches all data using technology created by the development department. A critical team within R&D is the hackers. The brightest hackers in the world are employed by the Elders. Capitalizing on an unlimited budget, the R&D team deploy the hackers to gather data. The R&D group is years ahead of Silicon Valley, the NSA, CIA, or MI6 due to the development team. Brilliant minds free to explore without the restrictions of shareholder returns, government bureaucracy and oversight coupled with no budgetary restraints generate generational changing discoveries. The Elders enjoy a tremendous advantage and can navigate the global landscape better than any other global government or entity. The Elders do not care about privacy laws or international law, there is no oversight. The United States agreed to not spy on her allies, the Elders have no such restrictions. No data is safe from the Elders. Matt Comer is the head of R&D. Matt was identified at age 12 and after extensive study at Cal Poly, he earned his masters at age 20, he joined the Elders and worked his way up through the system.

Analytics and Investments: The information, courtesy of R&D, is interpreted by analysts and feeds investments. The revenue generated by investments fuels the operational expenses. The superior data access provides valuable insight for the investment team. Companies, institutions and commodities that clear the analytics department offer sound financial investments in the short and long term. The Elders' $900 billion portfolio also includes hundreds of thousands of acres of real estate in American and England. In addition, the Elders hold real estate in 84 countries on all continents. The land is used for training camps, staging field Ops, safe houses and real estate development. The Island, owned by the Elders, is four miles wide and eight miles long located 45 miles from Barbados, is also included in investments. The investments are made through 225 shell companies registered in the 84 countries where real estate is owned. The 225 shell companies feed into 75 parent shell companies that route through each other into 15 master shell companies. The 225 individual shell companies each take a reasonable position but not a controlling position in the selected investment so as not to draw attention. Compiling the shell companies, the master shell companies that are blind to the world, take controlling interest. The cumulative impact of all the shell companies that invest in an entity is powerful. Not all 225 invest together so as to not draw attention. Depending on the size of the investment, 50-75 shell companies will invest. The 50-75 shell companies rotate investment partners again to not draw attention. The investments generate staggering returns. The net impact of the returns on $900 billion provides a current $280 billion annual operating budget. $280 billion is never fully deployed, the excess is returned to the fund and the fund continues to grow. In addition to investment income, the development team has held thousands of patents that have generated revenue that exceeds investments. Once aged out of use to the Elders, the technology developed is sold to private and government agencies through the shell companies and offers enormous income streams. The analytics and investment team are headed by Lori Segal. After graduating from MIT in undergraduate and graduate school, she joined the Elders. She worked in R&D for five years and returned to MIT to earn her doctorate. Lori returned as a senior agent in analytics and investments. A bright and tireless worker, she was identified as a candidate to run the group. To prepare her for the position, she spent two years prior to her appointment working with the hackers.

The group leaders report to Bill Zera, the director of the Elders program. Interestingly, Zera came up through the recruitment process that identified candidates missed in the initial screening process. Zera was identified early in his college career. He attended a small college in Indiana. As an undersized star running back, major colleges overlooked Zera as well. While attending St. Joseph College in Rensselaer, IN, he quickly caught the eye of a recruitment agent. In a small world moment, a recruitment agent's nephew was Zera's roommate in college. The nephew called home and described how amazing Zera was as a football player and a person. The nephew brought Zera to a family reunion barbecue and unknowingly introduced him to the agent. The agent was immediately impressed and intrigued. The agent requested to be Zera's recruiter. After playing one year of professional football for the Rams, who moved him to defensive back, because of his sharp mind and ultra-quick reflexes, he was approached by the recruiter. After completing the training program for missed recruits, Zera's exceptional performance warranted an invitation to Black Ops. After three years in the Black Ops training program, he distinguished himself as an exceptional agent and better senior agent. Zera is a natural leader. He is a tremendous listener, patient, deliberate and brings the best out of people. After Black Ops, he was sent to Princeton where he received his master's in finance. He studied accounting at St. Joe's expecting to be a CPA. He is a CPA and CFA. He returned as a senior agent in analytics and investments. He was then promoted to group leader of R&D. He excelled as group leader and was later named director of the Elders' group. He will serve as director for ten years. At the end of his term, he will join the other living directors on the advisory board. The advisory board is comprised of former directors to assist the current director to better execute the tremendous demands of the position.

The twins looked up after completing their reading and Zeus asked. 'Is this legal?'

Iceman looked at his friend. 'Are you serious?'

Sullivan and Conjar just looked at each other. 'Next question.'

Zeus asked. 'The OWL investment example you provided us several months ago; is an example of the Elders, OWL pass down relationship?'

'Yes. The solar company we discussed began with the Elders and after a staggering return was passed down to OWL. The solar company continues to produce 30% returns for OWL, their investors are pleased.'

'What about Black Ops and recruitment and training? Where are there summaries?

'Iceman, there is nothing more to discuss about recruitment, you're already here. Conjar will continue to brief you on Black Ops. Keep the packets and turn them in before your flight tomorrow.'

Zeus asked. 'We're done here? Where are we going?'

Conjar responded. 'You're done. Sunny Barbados. A vacation of sorts.'

CHAPTER THIRTY-THREE

The twins did not arrive with Conjar at Logan Airport as expected, they arrived at a private airfield to find a Gulfstream G-700 ready for takeoff.

'You shouldn't have.' Iceman joked with Conjar.

'Trust me Iceman, this aircraft is not for you, it is for the Island's security.'

As the three entered the luxury aircraft, a lovely flight attendant greeted them. 'What beverage can I interest you once we are Airborne?'

Zeus paused and Iceman answered. 'I'm not sure about Conjar, but we would love a Bud with Jameson chaser.'

Conjar stared at Iceman. 'Enjoy your travel day, take full advantage of the free top shelf service.'

'We will.' Iceman continued. 'Anything you want to tell us about what awaits?'

'Just the usual training. We will spend the rest of the day traveling. When we arrive, we will enjoy dinner on the Island, then lights out. Training starts in the morning.'

The twins took full advantage of the five-hour flight courtesy of the Gulfstream. They enjoyed two meals, a movie and beverage service. Conjar took the time between naps to revel in the pain that awaited the twins. As the flight began to descend, Conjar called for the twins' attention.

'We are flying into a private airstrip owned by the Elders operated by two statesmen. Blank handles the amphibious helicopter and Powder, the amphibious plane. When they are not conducting Elders' business, they operate a private airfield and air charter service for tourists.'

Zeus asked. 'Powder?'

'When you see him, you'll understand. He's complexion is so fair; he got the name Powder.'

'What the hell is he doing in Barbados? Won't he melt in the sun?' Iceman asked.

'Apparently not and before you ask, Blank got his name because no one could figure out a code name for him.'

Zeus laughed. 'Everyone drew a complete blank, that's funny.'

'He's not.'

Iceman sat down his Bud. 'Roger that, a deliberate man. I have been warned.'

'When we land, we will be greeted by Blank who will escort us directly to the helicopter and on to the Island.'

'Got it.'

Conjar continued. 'In addition to Blank and Powder, two other statesmen operate on Barbados. Crocket and Tubbs, both from Miami, operate a chartered fishing company. They captain two Pursuit SC 365i, a luxury fishing boat that is a fishing yacht. The boats like the helicopter and amphibious plane can go hot if needed. When the Elders visit, the statesmen are activated, and the transports are armed. McCoy, the statesmen in charge of the Island, will give you a detailed briefing.'

'McCoy?' Zeus asked.

'Yes, McCoy. She got her code name changed to Julie McCoy when she accepted the position.'

'Julie McCoy?' Zeus asked, still confused.

'Yes, Zeus. As in your cruise director Julie McCoy from *The Love Boat*.' Conjar patiently answered.

Even Iceman did not understand the reference. 'A little help?'

'*The Love Boat*, the television show from, never mind, before your time.'

Zeus was still confused. 'Crockett and Tubbs?'

'I got this one, Conjar.' Iceman offered. 'From Miami Vice, the TV show then movie, a white and black pair of narcotics detectives. Do they have a pet alligator on the boat?'

'No. Now lock it up, don't piss Blank off.'

* * *

When the group exited the G700, they were more acknowledged rather than greeted by Blank. As they were set to take off, Iceman was relieved to watch Blank secure the doors.

'This is sure better than Air Assault School. Huge fan of closed doors on helicopters, right Zeus?'

'Don't remind me.'

Iceman turned to Zeus and whispered. 'I am pretty sure Blank got his name, because everyone was scared to piss him off. Choosing the wrong name and pissing of that black mountain of a man is not a great idea.'

After the group was well into the last leg of their journey, Conjar pointed out his window. 'You can see the Island to your port side.'

Zeus found it and asked. 'Where are all the buildings and training sites?'

'McCoy will provide a full briefing after dinner.'

'Roger that.'

* * *

Blank landed on the roof of the 45,000 sq. foot compound located in the center of the Island. The twins and Conjar exited the helicopter and without a goodbye, Blank took off and returned to Barbados. The roof had the feel of a sports stadium. The center, used as a helipad, was the field and the solar panels that surrounded the field were the stands.

Zeus looked down and asked Conjar. 'Are we standing on camouflaged solar panels?'

'Yes.'

'Developed by the solar company used to illustrate the investment strategy?' Zeus asked as a follow up question.

'Yes.'

'Cool. How does…'

Conjar walked to the elevator, hidden within the solar panels and interrupted Zeus. 'Save tour questions for your briefing packet and McCoy.'

They descended past the second floor and exited on the first. They were greeted by McCoy. 'Hello and welcome to the Island. As I am certain Conjar explained I am McCoy and I run this operation. I have been looking forward to meeting you two.

Now, come with me, we will eat and then start the introduction briefing.'

After they enjoyed the fish stew, McCoy started her briefing. The facility contains three 15,000 sq. foot levels. The upper level is reserved for the Elders and is off limits. The Elders private residence includes suites, conference room, private dining room, gym, library, parlor, and meeting rooms are for their use and eyes only. A select few have access to the second floor and obviously you are not included. The first floor contains the permanent residency, kitchen, dining hall, recreation room with a sports bar, meeting rooms, medical treatment and rehabilitation, and the gym. The basement houses 20 dorm rooms with private baths and armory. The basement is underwater with windows to view the underwater world. The basement is also a bunker that goes secure to protect the Elders in the event of an attack.'

'Like, Dr. No.' Iceman interjected himself into the conversation. 'From the James Bond movie, Dr. No's secret headquarters was miles underwater.'

McCoy ignored Iceman's interruption and continued. 'A five-mile trail surrounds the property used for daily runs and transport. After your morning training and lunch, I will highlight the exterior features of the property.'

After they walked and toured the first floor, McCoy escorted the twins to a meeting room and continued her briefing. 'We maintain a permanent staff of 10. Two statesmen to include their wives run and manage the kitchen. The couples utilize a one month on and one month off schedule. Food and supplies are delivered by air and sea by the statesmen in Barbados. You met Blank already, he is one of the statesmen I am referring. For more details on the other staff please refer to the report I am handing to you now. We currently have eight guests and with the addition of your group we are up to 11. Two of our guests are your training instructors. The other guests are either doing light continued training or recovering from a mission. We have a team that has been here a little over two weeks that will be leaving us soon. Any questions?'

The twins looked at each other and Zeus responded. 'No.'

'In terms of security, again refer to your packet, the simplest summary description is the White House. Bulletproof glass, anti-aircraft weaponry on the roof, sniper's nests and boots on the ground. The guests are our boots on the ground and in the event of emergency the statesmen stationed in Barbados as well.'

McCoy paused, took a drink of water, and continued. 'That is all I have for tonight. It is late and you begin training in a few hours, so I will let you get some rest. After reading the packet and spending a couple of days here, you will be up to speed. Conjar, do you have anything for them before I escort them to their rooms?'

'I do, but I will be brief. I just want to take a moment to give them an overview of their training for the next 12 weeks. As I am certain you have already surmised, you are here to conduct advanced SEAL training. The good news is your already completed Hell Week.'

Iceman interrupted. 'Excuse me, did you say, Hell Week? As I recall it was three weeks, not one and I speak for Zeus when I say, we would have taken one week in the Caribbean waters rather than the New York frigid waters.'

'Good thing I didn't ask. Tango and Cash, who you will meet in the morning, are the statesmen charged with your training. Please take a moment to review your daily schedule.'

0530: Independent five-mile run, three-mile ocean swim, gym workout to include yoga.

0800: Breakfast

0900: SEAL training with Tango

1200: Lunch

1300: Advanced close quarters combat training with Tango and Cash

1500: Meal break

1530: Independent study and ranger nap

1930: Dinner

2100: Night SEAL training with Cash

2400: Meal break and lights out

Conjar waited for the twins to return their attention to him and continued. 'As you can see, the schedule affords significant independent training. You know the morning routine; I am not providing a babysitter. In your room you will find our SEAL training manual. I expect you to be prepared for the daily lessons prior to meeting with the statesmen. The classroom is just as important as the field in SEAL training. Iceman, you don't pay attention to your teachers, so independent study is not foreign to you. The weaponry, tactics, historic mission assessments, and other classroom work must be executed at the highest levels. I can't stress that enough, understood?'

Iceman, feeling the comment was directed at him, answered for the twins. 'Understood.'

'The training is designed for you to study the next day's lesson plan. You execute the lesson of the day with Tango in the morning and repeat the training with Cash in the dark of night.'

Zeus nodded. 'Makes sense.'

'Much of your training to date encompassed several aspects of SEAL training. SEALS go through the 24-week Basic Underwater Demolition/SEAL school known as BUD/S. You have more than exceeded the physical conditioning, parachute jump school and land warfare challenges demanded in BUD/s. You have also already successfully completed much of the SEAL Qualification Training or SQT. You are proficient in weapons training, close-quarters combat, land navigation, demolitions, unarmed combat and medical skills. Your objective is to add combat diving, maritime operations, and Survival, Evasion, Resistance and Escape Training, or SERE Training. Under your daily schedule, you will find your master training schedule.

Combat Diving: 4 weeks

Maritime Operations: 4 weeks

SERE Training: 4 weeks

'Again, I cannot stress enough the importance of your independent study. I almost forgot, well done on your use of Arabic when conversing with each other. I took credit for the idea and passed it up the chain of command.'

'Of course, and why wouldn't you?' Iceman laughed.

'That's all I got. Tango will greet you tomorrow at breakfast. McCoy will give you a tour of the Island in daylight. Good night.' The group stood and before they exited the meeting room, Conjar remembered. 'One last thing, you have Sundays off. You earned the privilege.'

Iceman stared at Conjar with a stern look. 'Are you fucking serious. You go through all that trivial bullshit, and you reserve the most mission critical aspect of our training as an afterthought?'

The group laughed and retired for the night.

* * *

The twins awoke the next morning and exited what was, their small hotel room. Iceman laughed as he looked out the giant common room window. He wished the window were concaved, like in the movie *Dr. No*, to make the images under the sea appear larger. They found the running path with no difficulty and started their day of training. During the run, while speaking Arabic, the twins mapped out their morning PT schedule.

Morning run and swim, weight training, hand combat sparring, followed by yoga. After their first PT session, the twins showered, changed, and headed to breakfast. They were greeted by Mr. and Mrs. Zipprich who were responsible for the kitchen. Mr. Zipprich was a statesman and Mrs. Zipprich was briefed in.

'Good morning, Iceman and Zeus, help yourself to the buffet.' Mrs. Zipprich pointed to the long table that served breakfast.

'Thank you, ma'am.' The twins responded in unison.

As the twins worked on their second serving of breakfast, a short Italian looking man walked into the kitchen and grabbed a cup of coffee.

The twins stood and Iceman introduced them. 'Tango, I am Iceman, and this is Zeus, you must be…'

'Yeah, pretty obvious who you two are. How do you know who I am?'

Iceman paused and thought: *Is this guy fucking with me? A short muscle pound Italian guy, who was appropriately name Tango after the Sylvester Stallone character in Tango and Cash, is asking me how I know him?!* 'Seriously?' Iceman asked.

'No, nice to meet you two. I'll meet you on the beach at 0900.'

After breakfast, with directions from Mr. Zipprich, the twins found the path that led to the beach. Tango was there to greet them.

'Alright let's get started. Conjar informs me you are proficient in open circuit and closed-circuit SCUBA. I'll make you better. After a week of this, we'll do a week of long-distance dives and two weeks of mission focused dives. After four weeks, we move to phase two. Understood?'

'Roger that.'

The twins and Tango completed their morning training and headed for lunch. After lunch Tango slapped the twins on the back and said, 'Good first day gentlemen, McCoy, they are all yours.'

'Come with me. We will start with the west end and work our way around.' The twins followed McCoy to the west end of the building and entered a large garage that housed two fully armed JLTVs, two Jeep Wranglers and six military Zero MMX motorcycles. The twins recognized the JLTVs, the replacement to the Humvee, but Zeus had questions about the Zero MMX.

'I know the Zero MMX is electric and holds 3,500 hours on a single charge but how do they perform in this terrain?' Zeus asked. 'They were great in the Nevada desert but how about here?'

'We wouldn't have them if they were not the best. Not a great question Zeus. You will train on the motorcycles with your statemen. Please jump into the Wrangler and we will be off.'

The twins boarded as instructed, McCoy exited the garage and continued her tour. 'You have seen much of the Island on your run this morning. We are taking the same loop that you ran around to the east side of the Island. You probably noticed the worn terrain that spoke from the loop, those are used to access the ocean. Beach front encircles the Island, and the path encircles the building. The JLTVs, Wranglers and Zero MMXs created the warn path. We will use one of the paths to access the harbor.'

The twins looked around the Island as they took the path to the harbor. The foliage was dense, so visibility was limited. After a short ride the twins arrived at a massive, camouflaged warehouse. McCoy put the car in park and using her cell phone opened the large loading dock doors.

The twins walked with her and entered a massive indoor harbor that housed a yacht straight out of a movie script.

'As you can see, the harbor is indoors. Half of the harbor was a natural cove, and the other half was man made. Like the main building, the roof is covered in solar panels.'

Zeus asked. 'Why couldn't we see this from the air? Granted it was night, but there was a full moon, we didn't see anything.'

'In addition to being camouflaged, both roofs are designed to absorb all sunlight. The solar panels reflect less sunlight than dirt. If you had flown over the harbor during the day, you still would not have seen it from the air.'

Iceman asked. 'Is solar the only power supply?'

'No, it is the primary source. Solar power working with geothermal pumps is the primary source and back up source of power. We also have diesel generators for emergency use.'

'Same roof top security as the main house?' Iceman asked.

'Yes, and thank you for indulging me, you are clearly more interested in the superyacht.'

The twins smiled. Guilty as charged.

'Indulge me for a few more minutes while I describe the other seacraft. You see the five SEAL zodiacs to your back left, one is missing.'

'The one we are training with.' Zeus commented.

'Correct. The six are used for training and patrols. Docked in front of the zodiacs are two Pursuit SC 365i.'

Iceman added. 'The luxury fishing boats like Crocket and Tubs have.'

'Correct again, thank you both for paying attention. The Pursuits are 41 feet long and are motored with twin 350 hp Yamaha F350 outboard motors that generate 700 horsepower. She can giddy up and go. These Pursuits, and those operated by Crocket and Tubbs have a complete arsenal and can go hot in a moment's notice.

The Pursuits are used for fishing on Sundays, but their primary purpose is security. They are more than combat ready. They are also used in training for assaulting a yacht or good-sized ship.'

'If it is all the same to you, can we hold off on the tour of life jackets and other swell items and get to the floating village?'

'You mean the White Palace, nothing much to say.'

'Indulge us.' Zeus requested with a smile of anticipation.

'The White Palace was designed by Lockheed Martin with inspiration from a superyacht built by First Export Association of Dutch Shipbuilders or Feadship. The 212-foot mega yacht has an exterior look and feel courtesy of Feadship, the leader in superyacht design. The production and weaponry were developed and installed by Lockheed Martin, the builder of Freedom class ships for the Navy. The White Palace is equipped with a BAE Mk 49 launcher with eight surface to air missiles, two fifty-inch machine guns and a lightweight torpedo system designed by Penn State University's Applied Research Laboratory, secretly funded by the Elders.'

McCoy paused as she was caught by Iceman's blank look. 'Question, Iceman?'

'No.' Iceman reconsidered. 'White Palace? White House and Buckingham Palace?'

'Well done. That was not in your reading.'

'Pretty obvious once you know the story, my question is, what is BAE?'

'The makers of the Mk 49, BAE, a British company, is the largest defense contractor in Europe. Good question.'

'Ha Zeus, my question was good. Maybe check with me before you ask another stupid question.'

'Shut up.'

'Roger that.'

'If you two are finished, I will continue.' McCoy paused and glared at the twins, satisfied, she continued. 'The armaments are hidden from site. When activated, hydraulics are used to raise the weaponry to engage the enemy.'

Iceman noted. 'A wolf in sheep's clothing.'

'A very large angry wolf in luxurious sheep clothing.'

Without checking with Iceman, Zeus asked. 'I read two six-man teams operate the ship, could you elaborate?'

McCoy smiled at Iceman. 'Good question Zeus. The captain and a crew of five rotate every three months. The captains are retired from the Navy and are external to the Elders. After 20 years of service, dissatisfied with bureaucracy while still loving the job, the captains were identified and recruited. The crew is comprised of former special Ops personnel with the same frustrations. The two crews transition in Miami when supplies for the ship and the Island are loaded. Any major maintenance work required for the ship is done in Miami, the crew manages minor and routine work. You won't see much of the crew; they live on board. When the Elders use the White Palace, a Black Ops team joins the crew on duty.'

The twins left the harbor, completed their loop around the Island, took the occasion detour to drive the paths to the beach front and returned to base. McCoy activated her phone and the smoked windows that covered the north half of the building cleared. They walked out to a large outdoor covered kitchen and patio.

Zeus commented. 'Let me guess, solar panels above us.'

'That is correct and what you see between the patio and the path is not a lagoon.'

'It's not? We saw that from the air, sure looks like a lagoon.' Iceman responded.

'Gentlemen, that is a saltwater swimming pool designed to appear to be a lagoon.'

'What is it, like two Olympic sized pools?'

'Three with the sides contoured to give the illusion of a lagoon. The bottom and the sides are camouflaged to add to the illusion. The patio and cover are camouflaged as well.'

After meal break, independent study and dinner, the twins returned to the beach to meet with Cash. Iceman was struck again just how much Cash looked like Kurt Russell's character. Cash's long hair and wiry strong build were a dead ringer.

'You two are too much. You are Tango and Cash.' Iceman smiled as he introduced himself to Cash.

'How do you know who Tango and Cash are? We had to look it up.' Cash asked.

My older cousins turned me on to all the classics. *Point Break, Roadhouse*, you name it. Did you get the name here?'

'No, we got it from our senior agent. We have been together from the beginning.'

'If you don't mind me asking, you two appear pretty young to be statesmen?' Zeus asked uncomfortably.

'We are. We skipped being senior agents. We were on an ugly mission, lost our senior agent and got roughed up pretty bad.'

Iceman asked. 'So, you are a Ronin?'

'We both are, yes. We weren't fit to go back into the field after the mission. We were on our eighth mission and spent the final two years as an agent in medical. We trained hard to get back into the mix, but the damage was done. We train you for twelve weeks then head home for four months then return for another 12-week tour and the cycle continues.'

'Sorry for your loss and your injuries.'

'It's the job, Iceman. Tango briefed me you two are high speed, let's see how you operate in the dark.'

'Said the OWL employee.'

Iceman smirked. 'Good one, Zeus.'

* * *

The training on the Island was rigorous, but the setting made the struggle a bit less painful. The twins settled into their training routine, the highlight was most certainly their Sunday fishing trips with Tango and Cash. With one week remaining, Conjar joined the twins to complete their training. The twins had just completed their morning workout and were looking forward to breakfast when they caught up with Conjar.

'I hope you have gotten more than sun and fun over the last months. You look to me as if you have been on vacation.' Conjar skipped the formalities of hello and got straight to business.

Before one of the twins could speak, Tango responded. 'We worked them pretty hard.'

'On the fishing boat or in field exercises?' Conjar asked.

'Both.'

'Very well, hurry up and eat your breakfast, I am amending your training schedule for the final week.'

The twins ate and headed down to their rooms to shower and change. While the twins were away, Cash joined Conjar and Tango in the kitchen.

'Real story, don't hold back.'

Cash reported. 'Conjar, the reports are accurate, they are the real deal. I would take them in the field right now, they are that good.'

'Are we all set for this week?' Conjar asked after accepting Cash's report.

Cash answered. 'That was the reason I was late, I checked in with Captain Pike. His crew, the demolition equipment and targets, the zodiac, and everything else you requested are ready to launch, just waiting on us.'

Captain Pike and his crew were scheduled to depart for Miami to meet the replacement crew and restock the Island. Over the course of the six-day cruise to Miami, Pike's crew of special forces were set to assist Conjar and the statesmen with advanced training for the twins. Conjar's revised training schedule called for the twins to use a zodiac to execute several simulated assaults and demolitions. The crew acted as their target enemy. In addition to several underwater demolition missions, the twins were to be trained on various methods to assault the White Palace and crew. This level training was typically scheduled for their third year, but Tango and Cash felt the twins were ready for the challenge. Conjar and Sullivan agreed, believing the twins could stand to be humbled by the special forces crew. The six days would serve as motivation for the next two years of training. The twins were expected to quickly discover just how formidable their opposition was. Yes, they were talented and excelled, but they were far from ready for the deadly challenges that awaited them.

The twins returned to the group and all headed to the White Palace to the twins' surprise.

Iceman asked. 'Are we going out on that?'

Tango smiled. 'You betcha Iceman, you two deserve a leisurely tour with all the pampering a luxury yacht has to offer.'

Iceman looked over at the crew and back at Tango. 'I don't think those guys are interested in serving us pigs in a blanket.'

Conjar took a long deliberate look at the twins and smirked. 'We'll see just how good you are.'

* * *

Conjar and three of the crew formed alpha team; Tango and Cash with two crew members, bravo team. The twins were the kitten team. Alpha and bravo alternated running Ops to mercilessly challenge the twins. The twins operated on five hours of sleep a day. Three hours sleep at night coupled with two one-hour naps randomly staggered throughout the day was their only sleep. The twins did not keep a sleep schedule, the alpha and bravo teams executed their missions at varied times of day and night. The twins faced rested opponents as each team slept while the other team conducted training Ops. The twins slept and ate an exclusive diet of meals ready to eat (MREs) on their zodiac that was towed by the White Palace.

Alpha and bravo overwhelmed and dominated the kitten team during the first three days of training. The twins were exhausted and angry as they used their last bit of energy to complain to each other prior to catching a brief nap.

'You know they called us the kitten team, right? Because they think we are pussies.'

'Yes Iceman, you have covered that on many occasions. Shut up and go to sleep, they'll be coming for us soon.'

'I think we can beat these guys.'

Zeus rolled over and mumbled. 'You, say that all the time. You said that in basketball when you knew you couldn't win. Now go to sleep.'

'We did win several games we shouldn't have. Zeus, you there? I did beat Zapata in boxing. Zeus you asleep?'

Zeus sat up and asked. 'No, what is that stupid brain of yours up to now?'

Iceman began his mission briefing. 'We are training and not competing.'

'What the fuck does that mean?'

'We are thinking about our lessons and not using them. Like when you take a jump shot, you just take it. You don't think about the ball position in your hand, elbow location, follow through, you just shoot. The motion is second nature due to endless training. We just need to let it rip.'

'What is your masterplan?'

'I say we attack them right now. They'll never suspect it, and we can shove their laughter at us right up their asses.'

'I like it.' Zeus was surprised with his support of Iceman's plan and newfound energy.

'Then, we continue to fight and not train. We take the gloves off, fight back, and hurt these motherfuckers. We'll see who's the pussy.'

'Iceman, you do realize that is a ship full of bad asses.'

Iceman just stared at Zeus.

'What?'

Iceman held his glare.

'What?' Zeus paused. 'I get it, we are also bad ass.'

'We haven't been the last three days. We have lived up to our team's name.'

'I'm in. What's the plan?'

'Remember when we left the Island on the White Palace…'

Zeus interrupted Iceman. 'Before we were exiled to this fucking zodiac.'

'Right. There was a bowl of fruit in the kitchen. I am guessing we are about 100 yards from the White Palace. I say we swim underwater 75 yards, peek our heads up to ensure the coast is clear, swim the remaining 25 yards underwater, and board the ship is silence. We load up on fruit and attack them.'

'Throw the fruit at them?' Zeus asked, gaining excitement.

'Yes. A quick assault and hustle back to our quaint zodiac.'

'I like it.'

The twins quickly slid into the water before their better judgement allowed them to change their minds. They boarded the ship without notice and found the fruit. Iceman, a former high school pitcher, unleashed especially powerful throws that inflicted pain. The twins exited just as quickly as they had boarded, leaving several fruit inflicted bruises. The stealth assault was victorious and turned the tide of battle for the remainder of the journey. The twins lost most of the engagements over the next three days but did win some. The guerilla tactics and independent thinking implemented by the twins was a significant challenge for their battle harden foes.

On the last night prior to docking in Miami, the twins were invited to spend the evening on the White Palace. Rather than join the crew in celebration, the twins headed for their staterooms for sleep. While the twins slept, Conjar and company enjoyed the cool night with beers, music, and conversation. The center of the occasion was the twins.

Raptor, the mean and vicious leader of the special Ops crew, was the first to speak. 'They are big and fast.'

Tango added. 'And smart. Those two fuckers pick up everything the first time.'

Cash nodded. 'Iceman has a real nasty streak to him.'

Raptor returned to the conversation after serving another round of beers. 'Did I hear you say something about Iceman? He's a clever one. He has unique battle instincts for someone so young to the game. It is hard to fool or surprise him. He has that sixth sense, that we try to teach, but the great ones have naturally.'

Conjar laughed. 'Raptor, are you celebrating yourself? Are you naturally a great one?'

As the group laughed, Raptor answered. 'I am but so is Iceman. He is not as good as me mind you but good.'

Conjar grunted. 'Not yet anyways.'

Tango agreed. 'My money is on Iceman after his third year with us.'

Cash quickly jumped in. 'Don't forget Zeus. He is a hell of an operator. Conjar, you got some team in the making.'

The twins awoke to find Conjar waiting for them in the galley.

'Let's go. We're docked, and we need to get our asses to the airport.'

Zeus asked. 'Where to?'

'Back to New York.'

Iceman asked. 'For what?'

'Training.'

The twins looked at each other then went back to Conjar. 'Obviously training, back to the Barn?'

Conjar nodded consent.

'Why?' Zeus asked.

'We do it all over again. We do the exact same training in the exact same order the next two years. We will continue to build on your base. You are now proficient; in your second year you will become expert and after your third year you will be mission ready. The only difference in your training, because of your exceptional performance in Arabic, you will take Mandarin in your third year.'

CHAPTER THIRTY-FOUR

After the twins' third tour in Barbados, they returned to the Barn. With their goodbyes to the Island, they were congratulated on their successful completion of Black Ops basic training. The twins flew from Miami and drove from JFK with Conjar to the Barn. He escorted the twins to the dining room and were met by Duke.

Conjar made the introductions. 'Duke meet the twins, twins this is Duke.'

The twins looked at each other with some surprise. Duke looked more like an accountant who had traveled to explain expense reimbursement forms and 401k plans rather than the architect of missions of death. They remembered their briefing packets and the bio presented on Duke. A vicious operator who executed legendary missions as an agent and senior agent sure didn't look like much. They also remembered reports of his Napoleonic tactical skills which had to be true, because the look of him inspired invasions. Iceman thought, he must be one clever motherfucker.

Duke shook the twins' hands with surprising force. 'Nice to meet you gentlemen. Congratulations on an exceptional performance in basic, let's put that training to the test, shall we?'

The group took their seats and Iceman poured water for the group. Once settled, Duke began. 'Fredrick Byron IV is from a long line of bankers from an extraordinarily successful and influential family. His ancestors made their fortune conspiring with the British to betray the colonies during the American Revolution. He traded with both sides of the war and for his deceit as an active British spy was awarded banking rights in Boston. His grandfather, a Nazi in America, continued the tradition by assisting the Nazis in money laundering during WWII. In addition to the incredible income generated from those fees, he stole the rights and possessions of several prominent Jews in Europe. He also, along with other American sympathizers, worked with the Nazis to declare a person as a Jew even if they were not to amass an unknown fortune of art, jewelry, land, and other valuables. Parlaying the family fortune, Byron's father mysteriously made absurd returns from the events of 9/11. Because of the schemes he implemented, the true return is not known, but conservative estimates have it at 225%. Shorting the market, buying and selling stocks, and manipulating companies that directly, and indirectly were impacted both positively and negatively from the attack went unpunished. Because his investments, and those of his clients, were so vast, complex, and diverse no action was taken against him. Investigations were launched but the influential clientele backed by an army of lawyers ensured there were no repercussions. The family tree bears rotten fruit. Nothing can be done to correct the sins of the fathers but now that you know the backstory, we need to focus on the mission. The ancestors died of natural causes; Number IV will leave this earth as well but not by God but by you two.

'IV, as we will refer to him, has taken over the family business, and is a tremendously successful banker. He portrays himself as a true-blue blood of American aristocracy. He has all the education, and family lineage to support his facade. He has made vast fortunes for important US citizens by secretly laundering money, much like his grandfather, for terrorist organizations. In addition, he invests in terrorism much like his father. He cleans the terrorist's money, invests in businesses that succeed after an attack, and shorts the companies that fail. Just as his father shorted the airlines that were doomed to fail after 9/11, IV preys on the victims of terrorism. However, IV takes his inhumane investment strategy one step further. He directly funds the attacks and banks the organizations that execute terrorism. He lauders money to secretly fund the terrorists' attacks then invests other extremely wealthy and influential people's money to give the appearance of legitimacy and hide behind their protection. He knows when an attack is coming, but he is untouchable because of generations of relations built with the most powerful, and the tens of millions he has contributed to Washington. He has friends in the highest of places. He believes himself to be an American institution, hence untouchable. You will make him touchable and very much dead.'

Iceman responded simply, 'We can do that.'

Zeus just nodded.

Conjar engaged. 'Sir, if I may?'

Duke nodded his consent.

Conjar looked at Duke, and he proceeded with the briefing. 'IV maintains four residences. A penthouse in Manhattan, a villa in France, an estate in Argentina and a 75-acre mansion on the Gold Coast of Long Island. In addition, his pride and joy is his Fraser built 144-foot superyacht, Trapezites.' Duke began but was interrupted by Iceman.

'Like Jay?'

Zeus asked. 'Jay? What are you talking about?'

'Jay. Jay Gatsby, from *The Great Gatsby*. Old Egg…'

It was Duke's turn to interrupt. 'Yes, Iceman that fictious area. IV's family's compound is on the South Shore, technically not the Gold Coast but close enough. Of the four properties, the Gold Coast residence is the softest target. The other three properties, IV had built himself with the absolute best security measures. He detests the Gold Coast home, but visits because it is an important symbol of his family history. The security is vulnerable at the Gold Coast because IV spends as little time as possible at the residence. Other members of his family use it often, IV only reserves his right to the estate for the Fourth of July week. Every year he hosts, to use Ice's analogy, a Gatsby like party for 300 guests. We will execute our mission during the party. If there are no questions, Conjar you're up.'

Conjar paused and saw the twins were ready for him to proceed. 'IV always travels with two bodyguards. In addition to his bodyguards, he employs a private security team for the party. The team arrives on the third and departs on the fifth of July. A ritzy catering service handles all the needs of the party. Your cover will be as servers employed by the catering firm. Iceman, given your knowledge of bars, you are a bartender and Zeus, you will be a server. Any questions?'

Duke took over for Conjar. 'Pretty straight forward op. Iceman, three hours into the party, just as the fireworks show is to begin, you will drop an untraceable arsenic into IV's drink. Zeus, you will deliver the drink to IV. The arsenic takes 20 minutes to take effect, after delivered exit the party. The 20-minute activation period allows time to secure his computer, and a stealth retreat. Any questions?'

Zeus responded first. 'Pretty straight forward. What is this about a computer?'

Iceman was lost in thought and was silent.

Conjar asked. 'Iceman, you are strangely, and dare I say uncomfortably quiet, everything Ok?'

'What? Sorry, I was just visualizing the mission.'

Duke continued the briefing. 'We need his computer that he always carries with him. Much like the presidential football, he always has it in his possession, as his computer holds all of his secrets. He is never online with his football computer, and his encryption code is such that we need the physical computer to hack into it. He is incredibly old school; his computer is more like a rolodex than a computer. He never conducts business directly using it, he uses his football to store all his historic information, and has others execute his commands. I have a complete work up for your review tonight to include the location, and extraction plan for the football. You will find all the detailed information you will need. Your back history in the hospitality industry, the dates, times, locations you report to the catering firm, the layout and exits of the mansion, arial photographs of the property and other data you will find useful. Use tonight to study the material and mission plan, we will meet tomorrow morning to review.'

Conjar added. 'We will spend the next two days here prepping for the mission. I will challenge your backstories, exit strategy to include the computer heist and Iceman, your slight-of hand skills courtesy of Fingers. Understood?'

The twins nodded.

Duke added one last thought to the mission brief. 'We have used the staging area to build a mock, of IV's office for you to prepare. We leave for Long Island on the first to give us a couple of days of recon. If there is nothing else, we will see you tomorrow after PT.'

After the meeting ended, the twins headed to their rooms to study. 'Iceman, you good, what's up?' Zeus asked.

'Nothing.'

Zeus was not convinced. 'Ice, I know you. I know that look, and I know what your silence means. What's up? What's wrong?'

'I'm not sure. The plan just doesn't feel right.'

'Like what? Tell me.'

Iceman ignored Zeus' request. 'What did you think of Duke?'

'I don't know.' Zeus paused to consider his answer. 'He seemed pretty sharp.'

'Hmm.'

Zeus knew Iceman's simple response was trouble. 'You don't agree?'

Iceman didn't answer directly. 'Give me a minute. Let me read the briefing packet and take a walk. We can talk about it later. It's probably nothing.'

'Bullshit. I call bullshit on that. Look, I'll give you the minute, but you need to tell me everything when you are ready.'

'Roger that.'

* * *

On their run the next morning Zeus asked Iceman in Arabic. 'How did you sleep?'

Iceman responded in English. 'I didn't.'

Zeus knew, the response in English rather than Arabic coupled with no sleep, Iceman's mind was racing. 'Ready to talk to me or do you need more time?'

'I need more time.'

'Maybe think aloud to me, and we can work through it? If not just vent out some thoughts?'

Iceman was silent for five minutes, and Zeus patiently waited. He knew his friend was focusing his noisy thoughts.

'What does he like to drink? What does he drink on the Fourth of July? What does he drink on the Fourth of July during the fireworks?'

'What does that matter? You make him whatever he wants, and I bring it to him, or you hand it to him.'

'Not if it's champagne. In the packet, there is waitstaff serving the party.'

'Right.'

'They will probably serve the champagne not the bar. He has no history of a heart condition, a sudden heart attack on the Fourth is fishy.' Iceman found poking holes in the plan too easy.

'True, but it does happen.'

Iceman ignored Zeus, still lost in thought. 'And the cameras, they won't notice two monsters missing?'

'The cameras are easy to avoid given all the well-designed exit plans.'

'The exit plan is fine, and solid, but we will be missing. We will have already been on camera.'

'The packet addressed that. The hackers will wipe out the camera footage from the party.'

'People will remember us. Not a big deal but two people missing right after he dies? All the little things start to add up. The investigators have to be sold on the heart attack, the two missing monsters in the room seems off. And the cameras suddenly don't work at the same time, and this elitist fuck dies? Who is going to believe that?' Iceman was talking himself into hating the plan. He also accepted his instant dislike for Duke that he elected not to share with Zeus for the moment. Duke's arrogant tone accentuated by his British accent alienated Iceman. Simply put, Iceman did not care for Duke.

'They cover that in the packet as well. They are going to leak information to the authorities about his criminal activities so the authorities will know it's bullshit, but the public will accept it. They only care about the headlines. The authorities will know he was knocked off but will assume by a criminal organization set on retribution.'

'I know, I read the file too.'

'You clearly do not like the plan. What are you going to say at the meeting?'

'Nothing.'

'Nothing?'

'Nothing. I need to do a recon when we get to Long Island to get a better picture. All the data, and all the information is lovely but there is no human intelligence. It lacks boots on the ground information. We have a couple of days of recon, I am going to use that time to add color to the information provided. With that, I can come up with a plan.'

'What if you don't get what you are looking for? Worse or better yet, depending on how you look at it, what if you do get what you are looking for?'

'If I don't, which I doubt, we will execute the mission as ordered. If I do, we will execute my plan.'

Zeus was struggling with concern about Iceman's approach and asked. 'What if they say no to your plan?'

'They won't.'

'What if they do?'

'What if my aunt had balls?'

'She'd be your uncle.'

'Right, what if is pointless. As the Godfather said, *I'll make him an offer he can't refuse.* Got me?'

* * *

Duke started the meeting after breakfast. 'Any questions after studying the brief?'

Zeus looked to Iceman before he responded. 'No, sir.'

Conjar knew the twins well enough to know something was wrong. 'Are you sure?' He paused and studied the twins again. 'Iceman, what do you think? Anything you care to share?'

'No.'

Iceman always had something to share, and Conjar knew Ice had something on his mind. He reluctantly added. 'There is one more thing. Iceman, maintain your professionalism when I say this. IV kidnaps students from colleges, gets them addicted to drugs, and offers them as gifts to his terrorist clientele. We need his computer to locate the camps that hold the students in addition to his work history already discussed.'

Shocked, Zeus yelled. 'What?'

Duke answered. 'He has five camps that we know of, located around college campuses. One we believe is in Arizona based on missing person reports from several colleges in the area. Students from Arizona St., Arizona, other Arizona schools, and surrounding schools to include New Mexico, Utah, Nevada, and southern California do go missing. They fall off the grid from their parents and families for varies reasons. Because they prey on multiple campuses, no one school has raised concern. Our concern is that the profiles of the missing students do not match a runaway.'

Zeus asked. 'You keep saying students, not just girls?'

Conjar answered. 'Male students as well.'

342

Iceman dropped his head; it was clear to the group he was not pleased. 'Really, you let this happen? For how long?'

Zeus quickly jumped in. 'Ice, let's just fix it.' He knew his lad's blood was beyond boiling.

'Just let me off the leash, I am killing all of them. Human trafficking? This cunt motherfucker's hobby is human trafficking? I'll get your IV or whatever we call him but after that, the five are mine. He preys on girls? Little girls like my cousin? There will be no trail. Whatever you do, do not bring up jurisdiction, do not include the authorities. They are gone and trust me I will get that computer. Those are my terms, and they are nonnegotiable as am I. Got me?'

Conjar looked at Duke with a, I told you so glance and both nodded. 'Get the computer and we will handle the camps.'

Iceman was not satisfied with Conjar's response. 'You better and I am deadly serious. No turning this over to the authorities, no FBI bullshit, just a painful death.'

Conjar stared directly into Iceman's eyes, who responded, 'We understand.'

* * *

Exiting the meeting, Iceman vented to Zeus. 'Mother fuck, can you believe they knew and did nothing?'

Zeus knew Iceman was right, but had to calm him down to execute the mission. 'Dude enough, they are fixing it now, we are fixing it now. Do the job so we can end it.' Zeus snapped.

'Roger that.'

CHAPTER THIRTY-FIVE

'Don't get me wrong, this is nice and all, but do the Elders own this place?' Iceman asked as he entered the four-bedroom cottage that served as their base for the next week. The cottage, located in Oyster Bay, served the needs of the team, but not a residence Iceman expected from the Elders.

Conjar replied. 'This isn't an Elders' property, we secured this through Airbnb. Pick a room, drop your gear off, and jump back into the truck, we are off to the harbor.'

The Oyster Bay Harbor was a mile from the cottage and docked a Boston Whaler waiting for their arrival. The twins and Conjar boarded the Whaler and set off on their mission prep work. Conjar steered the boat along the coastline to find the Trapezites, the superyacht was anchored two miles from the estate.

Conjar spoke as he drove past the Trapezites. 'There you have it. You can also see his 1930 Chris Craft triple Cockpit 24' that he uses to shuttle between the estate and yacht. As we understand it, he leaves the party as soon as possible, and prefers to spend the night here. We must ensure we hit our fireworks deadline because he leaves friends and family behind shortly after the show.'

The twins nodded and Conjar continued. 'I'll take us closer to shore to look at the grounds. We won't see much; the trees block most of the view. Your packets coupled with your meeting with the catering firm will give you a better idea of the place.'

As Conjar turned towards shore, Iceman commented. 'The Trapezites and the White Palace have similar designs. The low stern of the ships is almost identical.'

Conjar nodded. 'Good catch, Ice. The Elders and IV have similar taste in superyachts.' He continued towards shore, turned to face the estate, and started back to the marina after the group took in the sights.

On the ride back, Zeus commented. 'IV's place and shit, all these places are crazy.'

Iceman laughed. 'They weren't fucking around in the Gilded Age.'

Zeus asked. 'What's with the name, Trapezites?'

Conjar and Zeus waited for Iceman who replied. 'What? How the fuck should I know?'

Zeus turned to Conjar and laughed. 'Mark this moment: Iceman officially does not have all the answers.'

Conjar added. 'Duly noted Zeus, Trapezites was an ancient currency exchange or bank, possibly the first.'

The group docked at the marina, returned to their cottage, ate, and Conjar dismissed the twins for study time. The tour made quite an impression on Iceman.

* * *

The following morning the twins went for a run, ate, showered, and were set to meet Conjar at 1000 hours for more prep work for the mission.

As Zeus entered the dining room, Conjar asked. 'Where's Iceman?'

Zeus awkwardly replied. 'About that. Here the thing, he went for a walk about. He wanted to do some independent recon.'

'He what?'

With no better explanation, Zeus offered. 'It's what he does.'

'We have a meeting scheduled; he can't elect to disappear.'

Zeus anticipated Conjar's reaction. 'You know how he is, just give him a chance.'

'When will he be back?'

'That's the thing, he'll be back when he is satisfied.'

'With what?' Conjar was beyond red in the face, he now looked crimson.

'Don't shoot the messenger. His plan.'

CHAPTER THIRTY-SIX

Iceman took an Uber to Smileys, a dive bar located in Southampton that he researched on Yelp. The Yelp review painted a dismal bar that catered to the working class that served the elite of the Gold Coast and the Hamptons. Iceman figured the workers had to drink somewhere, and Smiley's opening at 1000 hours made the choice easy. The ironic name given to the depressing bar made it irresistible to Iceman.

'I'll take a Jameson and Bud and give this guy some mouthwash too, please.' Iceman ordered his round and a shot for the only other patron at the bar.

The bartender and patron looked to each other, and then back at Iceman. 'Mouthwash?'

'First thing to hit Winston Churchill's lips every morning was a shot of whiskey, so he called it mouthwash. Good enough for Churchill, good enough for me. I'm Jack.'

The laughing patron answered. 'Nice to meet you Jack, I'm Fred, and the bartender here is Frank.'

Frank poured three shots of mouthwash and raised his glass. 'To learning something new every day.'

Jack responded. 'And to meeting new people.'

After he finished his shot and gulped his beer, Jack headed over to the juke box.

Fred approved. '*Give Me Shelter,* got to love the Stones.'

'I believe Denis Leary said it best when he described society. He told a joke that goes something like, I go into a bar and ask for a beer. After the bartender rips off a list of craft beers and IPAs, oatmeal this, summer that, cider splash, Pete's Strawberry Blond, Pete's Rally Cap, Pete's Wanderlust, Pete's Wicked Ale; Leary let's out some hate, who the fuck is Pete? Fuck you, Pete.'

The group laughed and Fred promised. 'I am going to have to remember that one.'

Jack smiled. 'I'm not finished. Leary then starts on coffee, and blows up the whole Starbucks flavors, and ordering process, and decides he'll go to 7-11 for a cup of joe. He pays for the coffee, walks out, takes a sip, and walks back in. Sorry, he says to the cashier, you spilled some cinnamon in my coffee. She replies no, I didn't, that's our flavor of the month, isn't it great? At this point Leary is beside himself and declares, that's it I am opening a bar and only serving Budweiser, black coffee, and playing the Rolling Stones.'

Fred loved it. 'That guy Leary is hilarious, totally true, people suck.'

With *Sympathy for the Devil* playing in the background, Jack got Frank's attention. 'Another round each way on me. Fred, what brings you to this stool?'

'I'm off until the fifth, meeting my guys here any minute.'

'That's cool, what do you do?'

'I work for Imperial, it's a crew management company. We do all the shit work. People outsource to us to handle all their needs for those superyachts. I clean the shit off the bottom of the ship. We finished up yesterday, and they don't need us again until the fifth.'

Jack nodded and they drank their shot. 'How does that work?'

'I am based in Miami, and we drove the ship up here for the week. Then we bring the ship back to Miami.'

'Another crew takes your place in Miami?'

'Right, another crew replaces us in Miami to take the yacht to the Caribbean.'

'That's cool, who owns the boat? Is he cool?'

'Some guy from Google, and yeah he's cool, not that I see him much.'

Just as Fred was finishing, and *You Can't Always Get What You Want* was playing, eight more patrons entered the bar. One of the patrons announced. 'Jack Collins what are you doing here? Guys do you know who this is? This is Jack Collins.'

Jack felt a little surprised and flattered, but mostly concerned about his cover. He was grateful he used his real first name when he met Fred. 'That's right, I am Jack Collins. How the fuck do you know that?'

'Guys, Jack Collins, the Army basketball player. I recognized you the second I walked in.' The other patrons recognized Jack once he was described. 'Fred, you know this guy?'

Fred answered. 'No. We just met. Jack, what are you doing here?'

'A buddy of mine parents owns a place around here. I came with him. You know me, who are you?'

'Dean, where's he at?'

'He had family obligations, so I slipped out.' Jack answered. 'Frank, I think these guys could use a round on me.'

Dean introduced Jack to the group. 'Whatever happened to you? You still play ball?'

Jack realized the scene, and the bar was perfect for his cover when he responded. 'No, don't play ball anymore. Fucked up my back, and now I am a fucking forensic auditor?'

Fred asked. 'You audit like dinosaurs?'

Jack smiled, and laughed to himself, yep this couldn't be more perfect. 'Yeah, something like that. How about you guys? You work for Imperial too? You on the same yacht as Fred?'

Dean replied. 'Those three over there are. Me and these four are on another ship.'

Jack nodded and set down his beer. 'Who do you work for?'

'Don't know his name, some asshole.'

'Right. You headed back to Miami as well?'

'Only for a couple of days, then Bermuda for a couple of weeks, and then on to Buenos Aires.'

Jack choked on his beer. 'Frank, another round on me for my new friends. Can you turn up the juke box? The Stones and us are just settling in.' Jack turned his attention back to Dean. 'What did you say the name of ship was again?'

'Trapezites.'

'That's what I thought you said.'

Jack bought drinks and sat with the crew from Imperial for a couple more hours talking basketball, Long Island, exotic locations, and a little bit about the Trapezites. Jack confirmed that IV left the party shortly after the fireworks to join the after party on his superyacht.

'Where does he get the party goers?' Jack asked Dean as he handed him a shot of Jameson.

'I am not really supposed to talk about that. We sign forms saying we will keep our mouths shut.'

Jack understood. 'I get it, cheers.' The group took their shot and Jack continued. 'I bet there is some serious talent on board, I was just wondering where they came from? I don't live the highlife like you.'

'I guess, I can talk to you about that seeing as they arrive tomorrow night. Another agency, not ours, provides the party guests. We partied with them last year on the third, wild bunch.'

Fred came over and joined the conversation. 'Jack, thanks for everything. I am pretty fucked up and hungry. We are headed over to Taco Diablo, do you want to come?'

'No, I don't think so. I think I'll just chill here for a few, and then head back. My buddy is probably looking for me.'

Fred tried again to have Jack join in the fun. 'Dean, will Alberto be there?'

'Of course, how do you think we got the invite?' Dean answered.

Jack asked. 'Who is Alberto, and why do you need an invite?'

'He's the head landscaper for the asshole that owns Trapezites. We need an invite because gringos are not welcome.'

'Why?'

'Taco Diablo, a few miles from here in Hampton Bay, caters to the undocumented workforce of the Hamptons. It's near the dilapidated motels where they sleep eight in a motel room for $1200 a month. The places are a shithole, violations of city ordinance not limited to safety, but also the definition of a motel. Motels are only supposed to lodge people for a couple of weeks, and definitely not eight to a room, but nobody gives a shit. They live like they are in a third world country. The wealthy owners, and the elected officials ignore the zoning rules because of the shortage of workforce. Taco Diablo is the place for the illegal workers that are needed for this place to function. Real Estate is so crazy expensive that they live just a couple of miles from the rich fucks but might as well be a million miles away. They are serious death traps. Diablo is just a taco shack with a picnic area, but it is their shack, so you need an invite. We have shit jobs, so we are cool and Alberto hooks us up. All we need to do is bring the beer and tequila.'

Jack responded. 'I can do that, I'm in. Let's grab one more and get out of here.'

Fred shouted. 'Jack's in, another round and I'll order the Uber.'

* * *

The group arrived at Taco Diablo with two full coolers, and several bottles of tequila courtesy of Jack. Diablo was exactly what Dean had described. A simple restaurant with a small dining room and dozen worn picnic tables resting on a pebbled patio. The atmosphere was lively with music and laughter rocking the picnic area. When the group entered, there was a momentary pause until Alberto arrived to greet them.

In heavily accented English, Alberto gave Dean a warm hello and hug. 'My brother, how's it going? Who is this guy?'

Dean smiled and reassured his buddy. 'Alberto, meet Jack, he's legit. We just met him over at Smiley's, and he's good people. Fuck, he hooked you up with all this shit.' Dean pointed to the refreshments the group had brought. 'How bad can he be?'

Over the laughter and greeting, Jack thought to himself, this is like paying homage to an Emperor or Pharaoh. From the far-way lands of liquor store, I have traveled several blocks over bumpy sidewalks to humbly honor you and your greatness. 'What's up Alberto, nice to meet you, thanks for letting me jump in with these guys.' Jack spoke in English; he thought it might be best to reserve his language skills.

The group settled in, and the beer and tequila were shared. Although invited into the picnic area, the group was only welcome to enjoy the food. The regulars sat together, and the group from Smiley's shared a picnic table in the corner. Jack left the group and headed to the restaurant. He was greeted by a lovely thirty something year old.

'Hello, I'm Jack, great place you have here. Are you the owner?'

'Hi, Jack. I'm Lorena and my family owns the restaurant. My parents own it, and my sister and I run it.' Lorena pointed to the corner and continued. 'Over there, my grandmother still makes all the tamales.'

Jack waved to the grandmother and continued. 'Great, this place is just great. Here's what I need from you. I would like to give you this.' Jack handed her five $100 bills. 'Just make whatever you think works and keep it coming. When you get low, just come find me, and we will figure out what do to next. Does that work for you?'

'Yes, yes, thank you so much.'

'I believe, from what I hear, I should be thanking you. I understand the food is a bargain at twice the price.'

That brought a giggle from Lorena as Jack returned to the group. On his walk to the designated picnic table, he shook his head in disgust. A lovely sentiment that Lorena thought her parents owned the restaurant. Jack knew from his time in Chicago that vulture lenders made predatorial loans to immigrant families to buy restaurants, convenient stores and dry cleaners. The lenders charged obscene terms, and if the family defaulted, they just found another family. Sure, if the family stood tall for thirty years, weather bad economic cycles while paying enormous monthly payments to the lenders, the business would be theirs, but they will have paid four times the market rate. Denis Leary and Fred were right, people suck. Welcome to the American Dream where the rich prey on the working class. Fuckers.

Jack placed himself on the edge of Smiley's crowd, close to the Diablo patrons. He paid close attention to the conversation in Spanish, hoping to pick up more intelligence for the mission. After an hour of eating tacos and eavesdropping, Jack decided to take the initiative.

'Alberto, thanks again for having me. This is great.'

'You are welcome, Jack but the pleasure is all mine. You are too kind to provide this magnificent feast.'

'I didn't do shit. Lorena and her family are the ones that need to be celebrated.'

Alberto laughed. 'That is true but still very kind of you.'

Jack gave Alberto a dismissive wave to convey his efforts were nothing. 'Nice of you to include Dean and company, pretty decent guys.'

'Yeah, they are alright for gringos.'

Jack laughed. 'I can't stand gringos either.'

'Dean tells me about the parties and the expense, they live in another world. I tell him he is lucky; he has the good job.'

Jack asked. 'How do you figure? He cleans shit off the bottom of a ship, picks up after the party, and from what he tells me, the owner is a real dick.'

'All the rich are dicks, but Dean gets to be with the chicas.'

'A very valid point, he told me about that.' Jack saw his opportunity to dig deeper to expose a vulnerability in IV. 'The girls are pretty wild.'

'Wild, yes wild, very. And not just the girls.'

Alberto did not sign a confidentiality agreement, so he was free to talk. Dean thought he was safe talking to his host about the ship's activities, nobody cares about the landscaper. Jack would know, he worked hard as a landscaper through high school. Dean let alcohol fuel his confidence and allowed the ship's stories to make him the life of the Diablo party. Dean told Alberto everything about IV's movements and activities. Diablo was a safe haven for the workers, this was their water cooler. Just like the bars outside the steel mill, Smiley's and Diablo's were places where the workers felt safe to swap stories and commiserate. Jack might as well be at Duggan's in Chicago listening to the union electricians, who had just left the IBEW Local 134 hall.

'Guys too, huh? Wait, you mean fags? Are you fucking kidding me? They got male prostitutes too?' Jack hated to use the term, fags, but given the machismo audience he felt it necessary

Alberto just nodded. 'Sick. They swing.'

'Swing? Like boys and girls? Bisexual shit?'

'Yes.'

'That's fucked up. I never could understand that, and how do they get these whores to the boat? Like doesn't anyone notice, or I mean, doesn't his wife get pissed?'

'They are rich, they don't care, they only care about money. They get to do whatever they want.'

'And nobody notices, and no one knows what goes on at those parties.' Jack cast his reel and teased the line. The bait was set.

'People know Jack, people know. The rich think people don't watch but they do. They think we are invisible, but we are not.'

Jack switched to Spanish to offer solidarity. 'I hear you my man, the fucking man sucks. I am grabbing another beer, you want one?'

'Sure, thanks. Jack your Spanish is excellent.'

Jack walked over to Lorena. 'Hi, can you make a fresh plate for Alberto. Load him up with whatever he likes. How are we doing on the kitty? Here is another $200.'

Jack grabbed two beers, and a half a bottle of tequila, and walked back to Alberto. He poured him a double, and one for himself. Jack had avoided tequila in an effort to remain relatively sober or at least not fall down drunk. Whiskey and tequila were not a good combination but anything for the cause. Jack needed to reel Alberto in and get the juicy details of the party. The blueprint of a plan was being drawn in Jack's mind; he just needed a little more information.

'Here you go partner.' Jack said in perfect Spanish, mimicking Alberto's rural Mexican accent. 'To the oppressed workers of the man, let us unite in a fuck you to them. Cheers.'

Alberto finished the double in one fluid drink. 'That's good.'

Jack refilled their paper cups. 'Hits the spot. Those rich fuckers don't know what they are missing, need to hire whores to have fun. Pathetic. How do they even get them to the ship?'

'They go out on a booze cruise. They depart from the harbor and party for a couple of hours then board the ship.'

Jack drank some of his beer, and Alberto joined him. 'Pregame warmups, like a tailgate. Get them fucked up and ready to party.'

'Exactly. The rich think they are so clever, he moves his boat a couple of miles further from shore so nobody can see or hear them. The booze cruise comes back, and picks them up at 4:00 in the morning, they party some more on the booze cruise, and come back at 8:00 in the morning. Maybe nobody sees or hears the party, but the workers see the results. Not hard to figure what happened when you see what washed ashore.'

Jack coughed up his beer. 'What? The whores don't spend the night?'

'No, I guess he doesn't want anyone to see them leaving the boat. He thinks he's slick. The boat pulls up like they were out all night on the booze cruise. But the workers know the deal.'

'Right. Hey look, it's Lorena. Hey Lorena.'

'Hi, Jack. Alberto, Jack had me make you something special.'

Jack smiled and gave Lorena a kiss on the cheek. 'You are just too gorgeous. Alberto, good talking to you. I leave you to eat in peace.'

Jack left Alberto, stopped at the cooler, and grabbed two beers. The tequila was gone so he only had a beer to offer Dean. 'Sorry, we killed the tequila, but I got you a beer.'

'Thanks Jack.'

'That Alberto and his crew are good guys.'

'I was gonna ask you about that. How did you talk to them? Alberto is the only one that speaks English.'

'I speak Spanish. They sure are envious of your job. They want some of that party ass.'

Dean laughed. 'Yeah, Alberto has mentioned that more than a few times.'

'Shit, I am jealous. You ever jump in on the booze cruise?'

'Shit no. I meet up with them on the third and do my thing. We got work at 10:00 on the fifth, clean that disaster zone, then ship off to Miami. I need to get my rest on the fourth. The fifth is a long ass day.'

'How do you mean?' Jack asked innocently.

'We take two boats out there, one for crew, and one for supplies for the trip to Miami. Get there at 10:00, clean the outside of the ship, then quiet as we can clean the inside, fill the two boats that brought us with the garbage. Prep the ship and get ready to pull anchor by 2:00.'

Jack saw his opportunity to validate that the hookers left the boat early and the boat was clear of civilians. 'You got plenty of beautiful babies to check out on the ride.'

'No, we don't. He gets his rocks off, does business on the boat while at sea, then has a party waiting for him in Miami. It's just his men and the crew on the boat.'

'Nine dudes? Jack asked, nailing down the final number. 'You might as well be in the Navy.'

'Nine? No 11.'

Jack thought, loose lips certainly sink ships. The alcohol induced amnesia about the NDA, coupled with the safe environment, certainly has pulled Chatty Cathy's string. 'Nine. Your crew of six, the two boat captains, and the pervert owner. Nine.'

'Pervert always travels with two bodyguards so 11.'

Jack chilled with the group until the beers joined the tequila in the recycling bin. As he finished his last beer, he approached Lorena. 'Hi there, thanks again. Amazing place and time. I am walking over to the liquor store, and ordering an Uber, can I trouble you for 30 tacos to go? Just mix them up as you see fit.' Jack reached for his pocket.

'Jack, put your money away, these are on me. Thanks for everything, I'll have them ready when you come back.' Lorena gave Jack a big hug, and a nice kiss goodbye.

CHAPTER THIRTY-SEVEN

Iceman returned to the Airbnb to find Zeus waiting for him. 'Conjar's not pleased. I'm not kidding, he is nuclear.'

'He can't be pissed. I brought tacos.'

'And beer I see. You are just making it worse.'

Iceman had the sense to at least hide the whiskey he purchased. 'I hear what you are saying but here's the thing.'

Conjar interrupted after overhearing the conversation. 'What is the thing?'

Iceman responded. 'We don't have much time, so there is no sense being gentle. Here is the plan.'

Conjar exploded. 'I am team leader, and we already have the plan.'

Iceman smirked. 'Why aren't you adorable. Come, have a taco.'

Zeus jumped in, always the gentleman in the room, and turned to Conjar 'He is more than difficult but again somehow he will be right.'

Iceman dropped his head, feeling sentimental due to the alcohol, whispered. 'You are a good man Zeus. You are my brother by another mother.'

Zeus shook his head as he accepted a taco, and a beer after Conjar nodded his consent. 'You have our attention, Iceman, the dance floor is yours.'

'I have the perfect plan. We execute the mission on his yacht.'

Conjar erupted. 'What? Absolutely not. Duke and I spent months planning this mission after countless hours of research by the analysts. We stick to plan.'

Iceman took a drink of beer, opened another taco, and waited. Zeus turned to Conjar. 'Just hear him out, what is the harm?'

'Thank you, Zeus, have another taco. We take him out on his ship at dawn after his party. I got full intel about the party from two great inside sources.' Iceman explained.

Conjar asked after he wiped his mouth after reluctantly enjoying his first taco. 'Who?'

'The workers, everybody forgets the help. He throws this Sodom and Gomorrah like party on his ship after the fireworks, and ships in whores. Like his human trafficking, that I am still homicidal about, includes young men. Here the thing, the whores leave the ship at 0400 hours. At 0530, only four guards, two posing as ship captains, and Pervert are on board.'

'Pervert?' Conjar asked.

'IV, he's called Pervert now. I gave him his new name at Diablo where the tacos are from. The workers were very specific about his routine. The whores board a booze cruise at 2000 hours, arrive at the ship at 2200 hours, party until 0400, and leave. The ship's crew does not arrive until 1000 hours with supplies for their voyage to Miami. They clean the ship, load the garbage on the two boats that brought them, and get ready to ship out.'

Conjar asked. 'How comfortable are you with the intel.'

'Very.'

'I see your point and I can understand the logic, but we don't have enough time or information to execute the mission.'

'Look, the waiter and bartender plan sucked, no offense. We have all the information we need regarding the Trapezites. Our briefing packets provided us all the intel we need. The ship's design, builder, and blueprints are all there. The Trapezites is remarkably similar to the White Palace that we trained on for months. Granted, we need equipment but everything we need is at the Barn. All we need is for the statesmen to run it out to us in the morning.'

'I have not signed off on this, but I am willing to continue listening.'

'Thanks, Conjar. Before we talk equipment, I think we should talk more about the plan. We start by sending a droid over the yacht at 0500. The droid will send thermal images to us to verify the number of guards and ensure no civilians other than Pervert are onboard.'

Zeus nodded. 'I'm with you.'

'At least one member of the security force will be asleep, probably two. I expect one to be on the bridge, and one on patrol. It might be different but a very manageable target with a stealth approach from the sea. Zeus and I scuba two miles from the Whaler, and Conjar you are our eyes. We board the ship and execute the mission just as we trained in Barbados.'

Conjar was impressed and began to buy into Iceman's plan. 'I like it so far, how about the computer, and back story? How does this look like an accident?'

'I require another Teddy Brewski, and taco to energize my genius.' Iceman opened a beer, took a bit of his taco, and continued. 'He will have the computer with him. The briefing was clear on that point. After the guards are eliminated, Pervert and I will have a nice chat. He will be relieved to have finally confessed his sins. While I fulfill my role as confessor, Zeus will set the auto pilot on a course to Argentina in international waters. Zeus and I will prepare the ship to include policing the evidence, leave the ship in party disarray, and once we are sufficiently away, throw the bodies overboard.'

Conjar was confused. 'The ship will never make it to Argentina without stopping for fuel, and how do you explain a ghost ship?'

Iceman held up one finger in a motion to request one moment. He was busy finishing his beer and taco. 'That is the beauty of the plan. The ship is not intended to ever reach shore. The ghost ship just heads off into international waters with a disabled GPS system, runs out of fuel, and just drifts. After the mission, leak the same criminal intel after we poisoned him in the first scenario.'

Zeus was the first to understand Iceman's plan. 'By the time they find the ship, if they find the ship, all the information from the computer will have already been analyzed. The ship may not be discovered for weeks at the earliest. The public will think a crooked banker made a break for it. He ditched his yacht to buy time for his escape. A helicopter or another ship picked him up, and he disappeared forever. The reality is, while he does disappear, he's not enjoying fruity drinks on some isolated island. We not only kill him, secure the computer, feed a believable back-story, but humiliate him and his ancestors in the process. We have not just killed Pervert, but his whole banking system. What prominent person would ever bank there again? Who would bank with a runner?'

Conjar added. 'We could use his disappearance with the help of his computer to seize an enormous amount of criminal assets. If we killed him as waiters per Duke's plan, the missing computer would be immediately noticed. Money would move before we could act. Your plan buys us valuable time. Even when the ship is discovered the assumption will be Pervert is fine, the computer is safe and he will resurface again. Brilliant. I have calls to make and we have work to do.'

Iceman smiled. 'Roger that.' As Conjar left, Iceman added to Zeus. 'Again, while he is a total shit bag, he is smart. He will have a counter play. I don't know what it is, but Zeus I'll give you the head nod to leave when I am set to interrogate this asshole. You want no part of what I am bringing. Per the report…' Iceman was interrupted by Conjar.

'Zera approved the plan, we are a go.' Conjar deliberately went over Duke's head. He knew Duke would go ballistic over the slightest changes to his plan let alone scraping his carefully designed mission. 'The weapons will be here tomorrow morning by 0500. We will spend tomorrow getting the weapons and equipment ready. I will test the drone and we will do another run past the yacht.'

It was Iceman's turn to interrupt. 'We should stay away from the ship; we already know all we need. Don't draw attention. Let's do a test run away from the ship on the Whaler with the drone and we will be all set. What we do need are the exact blueprints to Pervert's ship. The plans we have on Trapezites are good, but if there is any more information that would be helpful. While similar to the White Palace, the Trapezites is not exactly the same. We need to study those prints.'

Conjar agreed. 'You are right. I'll secure those and after complete study, we'll do a day and night run with the drone to get visual on the party. We'll spend the night on the Whaler and execute the mission per our agreed upon schedule.'

CHAPTER THIRTY-EIGHT

Iceman woke at 0330, and nudged Zeus as they had slept on the deck of the Whaler. Conjar was standing post and greeted them. 'Good morning, let's check the gear, do a couple of walk-throughs, and see if the drone has some good news for us.'

Zeus pointed toward the ship. 'There goes the booze cruise headed to shore as expected. If the cleaning crew is right, only the guards should remain on board.'

Conjar prepared his gear and responded. 'We'll know what we are up against in an hour. Let's get to work.'

Iceman addressed Conjar before the team broke. 'Slight adjustment to the plan. Don't be alarmed, everything is fine. I waited to tell you this part, so you couldn't say no.'

Before Conjar could react, Zeus spoke. 'Tell us.'

'Obviously, I am going IRA and kneecapping this fuck' Iceman started. 'In the movies they say put your hands up, and a struggle ensues. I am just going to shoot him in the knee to set the tone for the engagement. I'll carry him to the study, Conjar cover our six, Zeus you set the coordinates, and kill the GPS as planned.

I'll handle the safe, and Zeus wait for me, do not come in into the study.'

'You already said to stay away from the interrogation, but why?'

'Don't ask, I got it.'

Precisely at 0500, the drone reported to the team. Conjar nodded as he studied the images. 'Five enemy targets, two in staterooms, one on the bridge and two on patrol. The two on patrol are separated, each taking a side and rotating clockwise. The sleeping guard is on level two, forward stateroom. Pervert is the master suite on level three.'

Conjar handed the images to the twins, who just nodded.

'Well, no sense wasting time.' Conjar started his pep talk. 'Go get that motherfucker.'

The twins each grabbed their waterproof backpack, MP7 with silencer, HK45, duct tape and bowie knife.

'Roger that, the twins responded in unison.'

Iceman took out his secret flask, took a hit, and set it down near Conjar. 'Don't drink that, I am coming back for it.'

Conjar was shocked and asked. 'What in the hell were you thinking? We have a mission'

Iceman calmly, so very calmly responded. 'Consuming bad intentions.'

Conjar looked at Zeus who gave him the look. They knew a bad man was coming and he was brining hell with him.

The water was warm, and the tides were calm, so a minimal amount of gear was required. The twins donned the same equipment they had trained with for three years. The LAR V Draeger Rebreather, designated as MK 25, was the right choice due to its pure oxygen system that recycled air prevented expelled air bubbles. When they got to the ship, simple to say things became uncomfortable.

CHAPTER THIRTY-NINE

As they drew close to the ship, the twins removed, and stowed their MK25 scuba gear, and readied their HK MP7 silenced rifles. Conjar patiently waited for the guards to reach the 3:00 and 9:00 position on the ship to give the green light. Zeus popped out of the water first, after a brief stumble, took out the first guard on the starboard side. Iceman was right on his tail and exterminated the second guard as he approached the rear of the ship. Iceman calmly headed for the second level to find the third sleeping guard.

Conjar spoke to the twins. 'Drone has the two guards still in position, not aware of disturbance.'

Zeus headed for the bridge to eliminate the fourth guard working as the captain of the ship. He carefully walked up the stairs and approached the bridge. He reached the bridge's door, opened it quickly, and shot the guard in the back of his head. Zeus gave the guard no time to react. He pushed the guard away from the captain's position and began his work to set the ship out to sea.

While Zeus was executing the guard, Iceman moved gently down the hallway to the sleeping guard.

As he approached the door, Conjar reported. 'You have slight movement.'

Iceman accepted the report, and checked the stateroom's door, it was locked. He retrieved his picks from his web belt, and courtesy of Finger's, and worked the lock.

Conjar reported again. 'More movement, you need to get moving.'

Iceman conceded stealth for speed, abandoned the pick, and kicked open the door. The sound from the fall of Zeus' termination had stirred Iceman's target. Iceman's burst into the room triggered the guard's survival instincts. Iceman entered the room to find the guard reaching for his pistol that slept next to him like a kid's stuffed animal. The guard secured his pistol and started to aim the weapon at Iceman. Any hopes the guard felt were eliminated by Iceman flawless execution. Ice calmly faced the guard, executed him with a single shot to the guard's right eye. Iceman, walked over to the guard, and shot him a second time in the forehead. Iceman discharged his used magazine and reloaded a fresh clip. He did not bother to police the site, that was Zeus' job.

Again, Iceman sacrificed sound for speed, quickly moving to the third floor, and the master suite. He was certain Pervert was awake after the noise created executing the four guards and the sound created by Zeus firing up the engines.

Conjar reported in. 'You are clear. No movement by Pervert.'

Iceman thought. Pervert must have done some damage to himself last night to still be fucked up to sleep through that. Iceman, true to his word, entered the suite, and immediately kneecapped his prey. 'Hello and welcome to the longest 14 minutes of your life.'

Before Iceman snatched Pervert, he paused, Pervert was naked and his hair even with the night's debauchery was perfect. He looked like a George Hamilton knock off. 'Throw on those pajama bottoms, I don't want your nut sack bouncing off my ear.'

Pervert, agonizing over the pain, whimpered. 'I can't, you shot my right knee. It is impossible.'

'I can make it twice as difficult.'

Pervert eyed his left knee and elected to don the pajama bottoms.

With pajama bottoms secured with drawstring tied, Iceman escorted Pervert in a fireman carry to the study where the safe was waiting. Iceman threw him into his desk chair and paused to reflect. 'Nice room you have here, give me a moment please.' Pervert howled in pain, and yelled a constant string of profanities at Iceman, who continued. 'Excuse me, I am trying to speak with someone. You are being rude.'

'Fuck you.'

'Zeus, green light on my end. I got him from here.'

'Green light here and…' Zeus paused.

Iceman responded to the pause. 'You were told. Let me do my job and you do yours.' With that, Zeus set the coordinates, and started to police the ship.

Conjar updated the twins. 'You are all clear.'

Iceman accepted the update and continued his mission. 'Apologies are in order; I should have introduced myself. I am the man that is going to kill you. As a gentleman, I will offer you a choice. Just open the safe, I will take the computer, you will be sent to hell, and I will be on my way. Or we can do this the hard way.'

Pervert agreed, knowing he was no match for torture. He removed the picture from behind his desk howling in pain and punched in his code. The safe did not open, and he sat back down. 'I am sorry. I am in so much pain. Let me catch my breath.'

'Your valiant effort is noted but here is the thing. You really should wash your hands before operating a safe. That was the first time you ever pushed the 1 or 2. You sent out a distress signal. I do appreciate you taking the hard way. Profiting and funding terrorism wasn't enough? You had to prey on innocent students? Ok, let's get started.'

Iceman neglected to inform Pervert that his distress signal was jammed, no cavalry was coming. Instead, Iceman shot Pervert in the foot. He then threw a series of kidney punches; broke two ribs, and for the sake of sentiment to his West Point boxing days, broke Pervert's nose with a straight right. Any resemblance Pervert shared with George Hamilton were gone. Pervert expectantly cried for mercy. 'Please, I have money, what do you want? How much?'

'Anyway.' Iceman shook his head in disgust. 'The punches were just for fun. I gave you a chance, let's get the real show started. I like movies, do you like movies? Even if you do, I am quite sure you won't like this scene. I watched this movie with Denzel Washington, well it was really a remake, called *Man on Fire*. Christopher Walken was in both.'

'Please, I will give you anything.'

Iceman responded 'Again, apologies are in order for going off script, but this will only take a moment.' He proceeded to beat Pervert with furious blows again to the face and ribs. He broke Pervert's jaw and another rib.

'I am an important man with powerful friends.' Pervert struggled to respond; the broken jaw made talking difficult.

Iceman shot off an ear. 'Please do not interrupt me that is rude. Now where was I? Right, so in the movie Denzel has this knife like the one I am holding. Wait, what is that?' Iceman asked just noticing Pervert's stand-up humidor. 'Is that a self-sharping surgical steel cigar cutter I read about in Cigar Aficionado? And this just in, is that a torch lighter? I can't afford a good cigar let alone those quality products, but I read about them at the barber shop. Ok, where was I? Right, as the movie goes; never mind I'll just show you.' Iceman snapped Pervert's left wrist, breaking several bones, then proceeded to use the cigar cutter to cut off the tip of his pinky finger, and used the torch to sear the wound.'

Pervert vomited from the pain.

Iceman shrugged. 'That's a shame, that looks like an expensive rug now covered in your puke. What did you eat last night? It smells awfully bad. Anyway, I am sorry that I am no Denzel, but the scene goes pretty much like that. You know what? Let me try that again. Quite on the set, take two, and action. Iceman cut off the right pinky tip and seared. He did not break the right wrist; he needed Pervert to be able to open the safe.

Listening in, Zeus was grateful to be out of the room. At the same moment Conjar relayed. 'Still all clear.'

'No calvary be coming. Just me and you pal. Yes, take two was better but I have an improv moment for you. Just give me a minute to get into character.'

Before he could respond Conjar was on again. 'Zeus, have the bodies ready, gutted, and hustle up with the sanitation. Remember to replace the mess after the blood is cleaned. We want the ship to be staged as an after party.'

Iceman simply nodded, acknowledging Conjar's instructions to Zeus. Back to the task at hand, Iceman continued. 'My manners require me to thank you again for electing to take the hard way, much appreciated.' Iceman walked up real close and whispered gently. 'The Nazis would take a glass rod, you know Nazis like your grandad, and inserted it into a prisoner's soft penis. This is how it becomes relevant to our situation, and I do apologize for long stories. So, they would bring in a hot chick to get the prisoner aroused, once aroused, they smashed the dick, and the glass inside would shatter. Pretty rough stuff but again apologies, as I do not have a glass rod nor a hot chick; so, I'll have to rely on improvisation. I got a cigar cutter; a torch lighter, and Pervert has a dick for now. My question to you is, do you want to die with or without a dick? Your call, I am nothing if not flexible.'

Zeus, busy staging the boat, was grateful to be away from Iceman. Again, he knew the events in the study were the very reason Iceman kept him out of the room, to protect him from this moment. He was prepared only to go so far, while Iceman was prepared to go beyond the distance. Zeus wondered if Iceman was enjoying himself.

'Computer please.' Iceman whispered.

Pervert yielded and opened the safe.

Iceman simply said. 'Thank you,' and he almost executed Pervert.

Pervert screamed. 'What? I gave you everything you asked for, what more do you want?'

Iceman had zeroed in on Pervert's micro expression. A lie, deceit, subterfuge, Pervert was protecting something more valuable than life.

Conjar came over the mic. 'Iceman, what's going on? Problem?'

Iceman took a breath and freed his mind to attack the possibilities. Iceman quickly identified the second level. He turned to Pervert, returned his thoughts to the second level, and the dead guard. Due to his careful study of the blueprints, Iceman realized the room dimensions did not match.

Conjar repeated. 'Iceman, I say again, what's going on? Problem?'

Iceman did not answer. Zeus came over the mic. 'Iceman, all is secure. We are enroute to Argentina. I'll meet you at the rear of the ship. You all good?'

'Fine, always fine.' He looked the picture of death as he threw Pervert over his shoulder. 'Me and my new friend have a quick stop to make first.'

They returned to the master suite on the third level, Iceman threw him on the bed and ordered. 'Open it.'

Pervert matched Iceman's stare. 'I already opened the safe.'

'Let's save the drama, open the safe room. We both know this computer is bullshit.'

Pervert looked at Iceman with resignation. 'Help me up.'

Iceman carried Pervert to the master closet that was the size of a large bedroom and waited. Pervert entered a code on the hidden keypad, and the back wall of the closet slide open to reveal a circular staircase.

Iceman spoke into his mic. 'Zeus, come to the master bedroom, I am heading into a secret safe room, and I don't want to get trapped.'

Rather than carry Pervert down the tight staircase, Iceman threw him with words of caution. 'Watch your step.'

Iceman descended the stairs and studied the safe room. The room had a door to his dead guard's quarters, a kitchen, independent energy source, a small kitchen, living room, bed, and a desk. Because of his careful study, the size and layout did not surprise Iceman, but the décor did. The safe room was a S&M playhouse. Contraptions Iceman had no idea existed or their use were on full display. In that moment, his back was suddenly hit with a fire of pain. He had been hit. He spun quickly to find the source of his pain and shot a young Asian boy in the forehead. The boy had struck Iceman with a piece of leather spiked sex equipment that had raked Iceman's back. Hidden in the secure walls of the saferoom, the sex slave's image did not register with the drone.

'You got a fucking Gimp?' Iceman exploded in rage and disgust. He took a moment to process having to kill the boy.

'A what?'

'A sex slave, a Gimp, like in the movie *Pulp Fiction*.' Holding back the vomit that was boiling in his throat, Iceman found the real computer on the desk of the safe room. 'You took all that torture to include certain death to protect this? This must make for some interesting reading. I am guessing generations of sick fucks like you are chronicled in this thing along with all your masterplans and associates.'

Iceman double tapped Pervert in mafia fashion and returned to the office. He got busy clearing the office safe Pervert had opened. In addition to the dummy computer there was more money than he could imagine, six watches, and some kind of jewels he did not understand, nor did he have time to process. He loaded it all in his waterproof bag and hustled to meet Zeus.

While Iceman was completing his second tour of the office, Zeus retrieved Pervert and the Gimp, and policed the sex slave panic room. He had already gutted the bodies of the others to expediate their disappearance and make good chum for the sharks. The ship was policed and cruised at ten knots towards Argentina. The twins threw the bodies into the sea and took their time to distance themselves from the bodies, as the sharks soon to follow. They didn't want to be anywhere near their recipe for shark chum. They did a final inspection of the yacht. Satisfied, they threw their weapons overboard, and donned their scuba gear.

'You got it?' Zeus asked with a regretful smile on his face. He knew it was a rhetorical question.

Iceman simply responded with a smirk. 'Two computers, and some goodies, let's make like a shepherd and get the flock out of here.'

Zeus contacted Conjar. 'Mission accomplished.'

'Yes, I know. I heard you two love birds over the mic. I am 2800 yards to your northwest.'

Iceman responded, 'I missed you too, we are on the way.' With that the twins quickly jumped in the water and hustled to get far away from the ship and sharks.

The twins reached the Whaler and jumped on board. Conjar gunned the engine, and they were off. Conjar drove a mile further out to sea, cut the engine, and watched the yacht motor away.

'If this is the plan, I have a little something for you two.' Iceman chimed in. 'Turns out, Pervert had a hell of a humidor stocked with Cuban cigars, and I grifted them. The cigar cutter is not of much use for assorted reasons but the lighter works just fine. Smoke 'em if you got 'em.'

Zeus and Conjar glanced at each other knowing why the cutter, was not appropriate. As they fired up their teeth bitten cigars, the SS Minnow as Iceman had crowned the yacht, drifted away. Mission accomplished.

Iceman, unable to keep quiet, toasted. 'Keeping with the *Pulp Fiction* theme, *Zed's dead baby, Zed's dead.*'

Conjar gunned it, and the three were off to the harbor.

Zeus asked. 'Do you want ice for your hands?'

Iceman calmly responded. 'I am fine, I am always fine. How's the knee?'

'They both hurt but I'll be good.'

On the ride back, Iceman could see the pain, not related to his knees, in Zeus' eyes, so he went to make a joke.

'Hey Zeus, did I ever tell you the time?' With that he was cut off.

'Not now Iceman, not now. Too soon.'

Iceman accepted his lad's need for space. After the cigars, a couple sips of whiskey from Iceman's secret flask, the twins just fell asleep on the boat ride back. Mentally, physically, and emotionally drained; they shut down to protect themselves. After a 20-minute ranger nap the twins awoke to change into their dorky tourist clothes, threw their scuba gear into the sea before coming in to dock the boat.

In between sips of whiskey, Iceman asked. 'Wait, what do we do now?'

Conjar responded. 'I'll get to that on the ride to Logan, just let me dock the boat.'

Iceman asked to confirm. 'We are driving to Boston?'

Conjar sternly answered. 'As I said, I will tell you on the ride, now shut the fuck up and let me dock the boat.'

The twins simply answered. 'Roger that.'

CHAPTER FORTY

After the twins quietly secured the boat in their best effort not to piss off Conjar, they proceeded to his truck. The three entered the truck in silence. Conjar fired up the truck and started. 'We are going to Boston to create distance between you and the mission.'

Iceman, confused, asked. 'What? Are we just jumping a plane? Wearing what? And doing what?'

Zeus and Conjar in cadence yelled. 'Shut up.'

Then Zeus leaned over and whispered to Iceman. 'Let him finish.'

Iceman with his head dropped mumbled. 'Roger that.'

Conjar continued. 'You are heading to the mothership in Austin, TX. You will be medically examined, debriefed, and spend two months training with the R&D and analytics and investments groups.'

'Thanks for the intel.' Iceman responded and continued. 'Since we just saved the free world, I would like to buy you a quick pint at the Green Dragon Tavern where our liberty was founded. You got yourself a Paul Revere, a Sam Adams, the birth of the Boston Tea Party.'

'Sorry gents, I am not driving you to Logan.' Before the twins could ask follow up questions, the truck turned into a grassy field. 'This helicopter is your ride to Logan, not me.'

'Roger that, just one thing. If you are headed to the Green Tavern don't go to the location from the 1600's, it moved around 1890, just a helpful tip.'

Conjar replied. 'If you weren't so funny and a great assassin, I would kill you myself. Regretfully, at my age you would probably win so I will just accept the laugh.'

Iceman turned to Zeus and mumbled. 'He just called me great.' They both giggled.

Before the twins jumped into the helicopter and headed for Logan, Conjar handed each an envelope. Conjar explained the content. 'In the envelope you will find all your legitimate documentation. Your passport, driver's license, American Express Card, and debit card. Your PIN number remains the same, and you have $50k in your checking account and $200k in your savings account. Your paychecks from OWL will continue to be automatically deposited into that account. You will also find a key to a security deposit box. You each earned a $100k performance bonus. The box is in Manhattan and contains that bonus plus three additional sets of fresh, fake identities. Ok, off you go.'

'Wait, all that stuff from Pervert's safe we get to keep?' A surprised Iceman asked.

'Just the cash, the rest stays with me. We don't want you wearing a dead man's watch.'

Iceman smiled and turned to Zeus. 'I don't know how much cash is in there but it's a shitload.'

'What do the Elders need it for? Consider it spoils of victory or hardship pay. Be smart with it.' Conjar explained.

Iceman understood. This was an emergency fund in the truest sense. What do the Elder's need it for was code for no one other than the twins need know about or the location of the money. 'Thanks, Conjar.' Iceman shook his hand and Zeus followed.

The twins turned to each other with a knowing look. We did it. On to the next mission.

GUARDIAN ASSASSINS
THE COLLINS TWINS SERIES, BOOK TWO

While the Elders' leadership team is busy dissecting the twins first mission, Iceman and Zeus are transitioning from their mission back to civilian life. Waiting for their return flight, the twins meet two ladies at the airport bar. The chance encounter introduces Katie O'Brien and the beginning of her relationship with Jack. Weeks later, during an assigned retreat to Ireland, Kelly Gerrity, Seamus' love interest and Jack's cousin, is introduced. Throughout the book the couples manage to have extraordinary episodes in the face of the twins' exceedingly demanding schedule. Iceman's concerns grow regarding the status of the human trafficking operation discovered during their previous mission. The camps have not been terminated, and Iceman fears the Elders have elected to monitor the human trafficking operation for intelligence. During the year, the twins are challenged with advanced training. During advance training, Dr, Grace Monroe emerges as a guiding force for the twins and their mental health.

Assigned to the analytics department, Iceman stumbles upon the Elders' file on COVID-19. The file, later named the C-Files, is a source of intrigue that grows to obsession for Iceman. Iceman exploration triggers the need for assistance from Zeus, and two new characters important to the series, Trinity, and Atalanta. The C-Files team investigates the possibility that China manufactured the virus as a weapon of mass destruction. The team discovers the C-Files were in fact a result of an accident, however the C-Files document the creation and expected deployment of the virus was no accident. The virus was created in a laboratory and that lab was Wuhan Institute of Virology. The virus leaked from the WIV lab via infected scientists and hit the wet market and the rest is history, or so was thought. The leak was an accident, but the C-Files uncover the true purpose of the virus, a WMD. The critical point in research is identifying the original CCP attack plan. A hypothesis is formulated on the driving question, *what would China do?* After extensive digging, the answer emerges as Mexico. The investigation easily dismisses the Mexican government and moves to the cartels. The cartels are nearly dismissed as well, and the C-Files are on the verge of being closed. The critical moment for the C-Files is identifying Juan Garcia Abrego, or GA. The C-Files present evidence that the 77-year-old Garcia Abrego secretly continues to lead his fragmented Gulf Cartel from prison using maquiladoras to partner with the CCP.

As a result of the C-Files, the investigation identifies China is trailing the world economically and in virus containment because of the accident. Iceman poses a series of questions to the C-files team, starting with, *why would China stop?* The CCP is drastically behind the world, why would they stop their viral attack? Iceman believes the CCP continues to implement their guerilla war doctrine by sending infected undocumented immigrants with new variants across the border using Garcia's Gulf Cartel.